This

15/
6/8
l₅

A

John Connolly was born in Dublin in 1968. From his debut, he was swiftly launched into the front rank of thriller writers and all his subsequent novels have been *Sunday Times* bestsellers. He is the first non-American writer to win the US Shamus award.

To find out more about his novels, visit John's website at:
www.johnconnollybooks.com

THE BURNING SOUL

Randall Haight has a secret: when he was a teenager he and his friend killed a fourteen-year-old girl. Randall did his time and built a new life in the small Maine town of Pastor's Bay, but somebody has discovered the truth about Randall. He is being tormented by anonymous messages, haunting reminders of his past crime, and he wants private detective Charlie Parker to make it stop. But another fourteen-year-old girl has gone missing, this time from Pastor's Bay, and her family has its own secrets to protect. Now Parker must unravel a web of deceit involving the police, the FBI, a doomed mobster named Tommy Morris, and Randall Haight himself . . . because Randall Haight is telling lies . . .

Books by John Connolly
Published by The House of Ulverscroft:

JOHN CONNOLLY

THE
BURNING SOUL

Complete and Unabridged

CHARNWOOD
Leicester

First published in Great Britain in 2011 by
Hodder & Stoughton
London

First Charnwood Edition
published 2013
by arrangement with
Hodder & Stoughton
An Hachette UK company
London

British Library CIP Data

Connolly, John, *1968* –
  The burning soul.
  1. Parker, Charlie 'Bird' (Fictitious character)- -
Fiction. 2. Private investigators- -Fiction. 3. Missing
children- -Fiction. 4. Missing persons- -Investigation- -
Fiction. 5. Suspense fiction. 6. Large type books.
  I. Title
  823.9'2–dc23

  ISBN 978–1–4448–1442–2

Published by
F. A. Thorpe (Publishing)
Anstey, Leicestershire

Set by Words & Graphics Ltd.
Anstey, Leicestershire
Printed and bound in Great Britain by
T. J. International Ltd., Padstow, Cornwall

This book is printed on acid-free paper

For Joe Long, secret agent

I

Put the case, Pip, that here was one pretty little child out of the heap, who could be saved; . . . the legal adviser had this power: 'I know what you did, and how you did it . . . Part with the child . . . Give the child into my hands.'

from *Great Expectations* by Charles Dickens

1

Gray sea, gray sky, but fire in the woods and the trees aflame. No heat, no smoke, but still the forests burned, crowning with red and yellow and orange; a cold conflagration with the coming of fall, and the leaves resignedly descending. There was mortality in the air, borne on the first hint of winter breezes, the threatening chill of them, and the animals prepared for the coming snows. The foraging had begun, the filling of bellies for leaner times. Hunger would make the more vulnerable creatures take risks in order to feed, and the predators would be waiting. Black spiders squatted at the corners of their webs, not yet slumbering. There were still stray insects to be had, and further trophies to be added to their collections of withered husks. Winter coats grew thick and fur began to lighten, the better to blend in against the snow. Contrails of geese arrowed the skies like refugees fleeing a coming conflict, abandoning those forced to stay and face what was to come.

The ravens were motionless. Many of their far-northern brethren had headed south to escape the worst of the winter, but not these birds. They were huge yet sleek, their eyes bright with an alien intelligence. Some on this remote road had noticed them already, and if they had company on their walks, or in their automobiles, they commented on the presence of the birds.

Yes, it was agreed, they were larger than the usual ravens, and perhaps, too, they brought with them a sense of discomfort, these hunched beings, these patient, treacherous scouts. They were perched deep among the branches of an ancient oak, an organism approaching the end of its days, its leaves falling earlier each year, so that by the end of every September it was already bare, a charred thing amid the flames, as though the all-consuming fire had already had its way with it, leaving behind only the smoke smudges of long-abandoned nests. The tree stood at the edge of a small copse that jutted slightly at this place to follow the curvature of the road, with the oak as its farthest point. Once there were others like it, but the men who built the road had cut them down many years before. It was now alone of its kind, and soon it too would be gone.

But the ravens had come to it, for the ravens liked dying things.

The smaller birds fled their company, and regarded the intruders warily from the cover of evergreen foliage. They had silenced the woods behind them. They radiated threat: the stillness of them, their claws curled upon the branches, the bladelike sharpness of their beaks. They were stalkers, watchers, waiting for the hunt to begin. The ravens were so statuesque, so immobile, that they might have been mistaken for misshapen outcroppings of the tree itself, tumorous growths upon its bark. It was unusual to see so many together, for ravens are not social birds; a pair, yes, but not six, not like this, not without food in sight.

4

Walk on, walk on. Leave them behind, but not before casting one last anxious glance at them, for to see them was to be reminded of what it is to be pursued, to be tracked from above while the hunters follow remorselessly. That is what ravens do: They lead the wolves to their prey, and take a portion of the spoils as payment for their labors. You want them to move. You want them to leave. Even the common raven was capable of disturbance, but these were not common ravens. No, these were most *uncommon* birds. Darkness was approaching, and still they waited. They might almost have been slumbering were it not for the way the fading light caught the blackness of their eyes, and how they captured the early moon when the clouds broke, imprisoning its image within themselves.

A short-tailed weasel emerged from the rotted stump that was her home, and tested the air. Its brown fur was already altering, the darkness growing out of it, the mammal becoming a ghost of itself. She had been aware of the birds for some time, but she was hungry and anxious to feed. Her litter had dispersed, and she would not breed again until the new year. Her nest was lined with mouse fur for insulation, but the little pantry in which she had stored her surplus of slain rodents was now empty. The weasel had to eat forty percent of her own body weight each day in order to survive. That was about four mice a day, but the animals had been scarce on her regular routes.

The ravens seemed to ignore her appearance, but the weasel was too shrewd to risk her life on

5

the absence of movement. She turned herself so that she was facing into her nest, and used her black-tipped tail as bait to see if the birds were tempted to strike. If they did, they would miss her body in aiming for her tail and she would retreat to the safety of the stump, but the ravens did not react. The weasel's nose twitched. Suddenly there was sound, and light. Headlights bathed the ravens, and now their heads moved, following the beams. The weasel, torn between fright and hunger, allowed her belly to choose. She disappeared into the woods while the ravens were distracted, and was soon lost from sight.

The car wound its way along the road, traveling faster than was wise and taking the bends more widely than it should, for it was hard to see vehicles approaching from the opposite direction, and a traveler unfamiliar with this route might easily have found himself in a head-on collision, or tearing a path through the bushes that lined the road. He might, were this the kind of road that travelers took, but few visitors came here. The town absorbed their impact, the apparent dullness of it dissuading further investigation, then spat them back the way they came, over the bridge and toward Route 1, there to continue north to the border, or south to the highway and on to Augusta and Portland, the big cities, the places that the peninsula's residents strove so hard to avoid. So no tourists, but strangers sometimes paused here on their life's journey, and after a time, if they proved suitable, the peninsula would find a place for them, and they would become part of a community with its back to the land and its face set hard against the sea.

There were many such communities in this state; they attracted those who wished to escape, those who sought the protection of the frontier, for this was still an edge state with boundaries of wood and sea. Some chose the anonymity of the forests, where the wind in the trees made a sound like the breaking of waves upon the shore, an echo of the ocean's song to the east. But here, in this place, there were forest *and* sea; there were rocks ringing the inlet, and a narrow causeway that paralleled the bridge linking the mainland and those who had chosen to set themselves apart from it; there was a town with a single main street, and enough money to fund a small police department. The peninsula was large, with a scattered population beyond the cluster of buildings around Main Street. Also, for administrative and geographic reasons long forgotten, the township of Pastor's Bay stretched across the causeway and west to the mainland. For years the county sheriff policed Pastor's Bay until the town looked at its budget and decided that not only could it afford its own force, it might actually save money in the process, and so the Pastor's Bay Police Department was born.

But when locals spoke of Pastor's Bay it was the peninsula to which they were referring, and the police were *their* police. Outsiders often referred to it as 'the island,' even though it was not an island because of the natural connector to the mainland, although it was the bridge that received the most traffic. It was wide enough to

7

take a decent two-lane road, and high enough to avoid any risk of the community being entirely cut off in foul weather, although there were times when the waves rose and washed over the road, and a stone cross on the mainland side attested to the former presence on this earth of one Maylock Wheeler, who was washed away in 1997 while walking his dog, Kaya. The dog survived, and was adopted by a couple on the mainland, for Maylock Wheeler had been a bachelor of the most pronounced sort. But the dog kept trying to return to the island, as those who are born of such places often will, and eventually the couple gave up trying to hold on to it, and it was taken in by Grover Corneau, who was the chief of police at the time. It remained with Grover until his retirement, and a week separated the deaths of the dog and its owner. A photograph of them together remained on the wall of the Pastor's Bay Police Department. It made Kurt Allan, Grover's replacement, wonder if he also should acquire a dog, but Allan lived alone, and was not used to animals.

It was Allan's car that now passed beneath the old oak and pulled up before the house across the road. He looked to the west and shielded his eyes against the last of the setting sun, bisected by the horizon. There were more cars coming. He had told the others to follow. The woman would need them. Detectives from the Maine State Police were also on their way following the confirmation of the AMBER Alert, and the National Crime Information Center had auto-matically been notified of a missing child. A decision would be made within the coming hours on whether to seek further assistance from the FBI.

The house was a ranch-style dwelling, neatly kept and freshly painted. The fallen leaves had been raked and added to a compost pile at the sheltered side of the building. For a woman without a man to help her, a woman not of this place, she had managed well, he thought.

And the ravens watched as Allan knocked on the door, and the door opened, and words were spoken, and he stepped inside, and there was no sound or movement from within for a time. Two more cars arrived. From the first vehicle stepped an elderly man with a worn leather physician's bag. The other was driven by a woman of late middle age wearing a blue overcoat that caught in the car door as she rushed to the house. It tore, but, she did not stop to examine the damage after wrenching it free. There were more important matters to which to attend.

The two people came together and were halfway across the yard when the front door opened wide and a woman ran toward them. She was in her late thirties, carrying a little weight on her waist and her thighs, her hair flying loose behind her. The new arrivals stopped at the sight of her, and the middle-aged woman raised her arms as though expecting the other to fall into her embrace, but instead the younger woman pushed her way past them, jostling the doctor, one of her shoes falling from her foot, and the white stones on the drive tore at her skin so that she left smears of blood across them. She

9

stumbled and landed heavily, and when she rose again her jeans were ripped, and her knees were scratched, and one of her fingernails was broken. Kurt Allan appeared in the doorway, but the woman was already on the road and her hands were at her mouth and she screamed a name over and over and over . . .

'Anna! Anna! Anna!'

She was crying now, and she wanted to run, but the road curved to the right and to the left, and she did not know which way to turn. The middle-aged woman came to her and wrapped her in her arms at last, even as her charge fought against her, and the doctor and Allan were approaching as she screamed the name again. Birds took flight from the surrounding trees, and unseen creatures burst from brush and scrub as though to carry the message.

The girl is gone, the girl is gone.

Only the ravens remained. The sun was at last swallowed by the horizon, and true darkness began to fall. The ravens became part of it, absorbed by it and absorbing it in turn, for their blackness was deeper than any night.

Eventually the weasel returned. The fat corpse of a field mouse hung limply in her jaws, and she could taste its blood in her mouth. It was all that she could do not to tear it apart as soon as she had killed it, but her instincts told her to control her urges. Her self-restraint was rewarded, though, for a smaller mouse had crossed her path as she returned to her home, and she fed on that instead before hiding its remains. Perhaps she would retrieve them later, once her larger prize was safely stored away.

She did not hear the raven's approach. Her first awareness of it came with the impact of its talons upon her back, tearing through her coat and into her flesh. It pinned her to the ground, then slowly began to peck at her, its long beak carving neat holes in her body. The raven did not feed upon her. It simply tortured her to death, taking its time over her agonies. When it had reduced her to a mess of blood and fur, it left the corpse for the scavengers and rejoined its companions. They were waiting for the hunt to begin, and they were curious about the hunter who was to come.

No, the one who had sent them was curious about him, and they watched on his behalf.

For he was the greatest predator of them all.

2

There are some truths so terrible that they should not be spoken aloud, so appalling that even to acknowledge them is to risk sacrificing a crucial part of one's humanity, to exist in a colder, crueler world than before. The paradox is that, if this realm is not to be turned into a charnel house, there are those who must accept these truths while always holding fast in their hearts, in their souls, to the possibility that once, just once, the world might give them the lie, that, on this occasion, God will not have blinked.

Here is one of those truths: after three hours, the abduction of a child is routinely treated as a homicide.

$\star$ $\star$ $\star$

The first problem encountered by those investigating Anna Kore's disappearance arose out of the delay in activating the AMBER Alert. She had disappeared from a small but busy strip mall on the mainland where she had gone with a school friend, Helen Dubuque, and Helen's mother to do some Saturday shopping, and particularly to pick up a copy of *The Great Gatsby* for school. She left the Dubuques to go to the new-and-used bookstore while they went into Sears to buy school shoes for Helen. They were not excessively worried when twenty minutes went by and Anna still had not joined them; she was a bookstore child, and they felt sure that she had simply curled up in a corner with a novel and started reading, losing herself entirely in the narrative.

But she was not in the bookstore. The clerk remembered Anna and said that she had not stayed long, barely browsing the shelves before collecting her book and leaving. Helen and her mother returned to their car, but Anna was not there. They tried her cell phone, but it went straight to voice mail. They searched the mall, which did not take long, then called Anna's home, just in case she had caught a ride back with someone else and neglected to inform them, although this would have been out of character for her. Valerie Kore, Anna's mother, was not at home. Later, it would emerge that she was having her hair done by Louise Doucet, who ran a hairdressing business from the back of her home off Main Street. Valerie's phone rang while she was having her hair washed, and she could not hear it above the sound of the water.

Finally, Mrs. Dubuque called, not 911, but the Pastor's Bay Police Department itself. This was force of habit and nothing more, a consequence of living in a small town with its own police force, but it created a further delay while Chief Allan debated whether or not to alert the sheriff's department and the state police, who would in turn inform their Criminal Investigation Division. By the time the AMBER Alert was issued, more than an hour and a quarter had gone by, or more than a third of the three-hour

13

period regarded as crucial in any potential abduction of a minor, after which the child would be presumed dead for the purposes of the investigation.

But once the alarm was raised the authorities reacted quickly. The state had set procedures for such disappearances, and they were immediately activated, coordinated by IMAT, the joint organizational incident-management team. Police patrols converged on the area and began riding the routes. An evidence response team was sent to Pastor's Bay, and plans were made to forensically examine Anna Kore's computer, and to seek a signed waiver from her mother granting them access to Anna's cell phone records without subpoena. Her service provider was alerted, and efforts were made to triangulate the location of Anna's phone, but whoever had taken her had not only turned off her phone but also removed its battery, making it impossible to trace it by 'pinging' the towers.

The victim's details were passed to the National Crime Information Center, whereupon Anna Kore officially became a 'missing or endangered person.' This in turn triggered an automatic notification to the Center for Missing and Exploited Children, and to the FBI. Team Adam, the NCMEC's specialized missing children's squad, was prepped, and CART, the FBI's regional Child Abduction Response Team in Boston, was put on alert pending a formal request for assistance from the Maine State Police. The game wardens began preparations for a full search of the natural areas surrounding the scene of the presumed abduction.

When the three-hour marker was passed, and Anna Kore had still not been found, a ripple ran through the law-enforcement officials. It was a silent acknowledgment that the nature of the investigation must now inevitably change. A list was assembled of family members and close associates, the first suspects when any harm comes to a child. All agreed to be questioned, backed up by polygraph tests. Valerie Kore was questioned first.

Five minutes into her interview, an unanticipated call was made to the FBI.

* * *

Anna Kore had been missing for more than seventy-two hours, but it was a strange disappearance, if it can be said that the circumstances of the abduction of one child are stranger than those of another. It might be more correct to say that the aftermath was proving stranger, for Valerie Kore, the bereft mother, did not behave in the way that might have been expected of one in her circumstances. She seemed reluctant to appear before the cameras at first. There were no quotes from her, or from relatives speaking on her behalf, in the TV reports or the newspapers, not initially. The vanishing of her daughter only gradually became part of a public spectacle, the latest act in an ongoing performance that played upon the general fascination with rape, murder, and assorted human tragedies. It was left to the police, both state and local, to farm out information about the girl to the media, and in the first twelve hours

15

following the AMBER Alert those details were given out sparingly. Veteran reporters felt that there were mixed signals coming from the authorities, and they scented another story behind the bare facts of the girl's disappearance, but any attempts to work their police sources were rebuffed. Even the local population of Pastor's Bay seemed to have closed ranks, and the reporters had difficulty finding anyone prepared to comment on the case in even the most general of terms, although this was attributed to the characteristic oddness of the population rather than to any great conspiracy of silence.

After her daughter had been missing for three days, Valerie Kore consented to, or was permitted to give, her first public interview, in which she would appeal for anyone with information about her daughter to come forward. Such appeals had both advantages and disadvantages. They attracted more attention from the general public, and thus could lead potential witnesses to offer assistance. On the other hand, it was often the case that the more emotional the pressure applied to the culprit in these cases, the greater the walls he or she might put up, so a public appeal risked antagonizing the abductor. Nevertheless, it was decided that Valerie should face the cameras.

The press conference took place in the town hall of Pastor's Bay, a simple wood-frame building just off what was called Main Street but might just as well have been termed Only Street, since Main Street implied that there were other thoroughfares worthy of note when, in fact, the town of Pastor's Bay pretty much vanished if you

16

stepped more than a stone's throw in any direction from the bright lights of Main. There was a drugstore and a general store, both owned by the same family and situated adjacent to each other; two bars, one of which doubled as a pizzeria; a gas station; a bed-and-breakfast establishment that didn't advertise its presence, as the owners were anxious to avoid attracting the 'wrong kind' of clientele, and so relied entirely on word of mouth and, it was sometimes suggested, psychic emanations in order to secure custom; two small houses of worship, one Baptist and one Catholic, that didn't unduly advertise their presence either; and a small library that opened mornings only, and not at all if the librarian was otherwise occupied. When the media circus was given strictly controlled access to the town, it was the most significant influx of strangers that Pastor's Bay had known since the town was properly established in 1787.

Pastor's Bay took its name from a lay preacher named James Weston Harris who arrived in the area in 1755 during the war between the English and the French. One year previously, Harris had been among the small group of forty men led by William Trent who were given the responsibility of building a fortification at the confluence of the Allegheny and Monongahela Rivers in the Ohio Country. The Frenchman Contrecoeur arrived with five hundred men before the stockade could be completed, but he allowed Trent's party to depart unmolested, and even purchased their construction tools to continue building what would subsequently become Fort Duquesne.

Harris, who had believed himself to be in mortal danger, and had become resigned to death at the hands of the French, took his salvation as a sign that he should commit himself more fully to spreading the word of God, and so he led his family to the tip of a peninsula in New England with the intention of establishing a settlement. The area's natives, who had sided with the French against the English, in part because of their natural antipathy toward the English's Mohawk allies, were unimpressed by Harris's renewed sense of vocation and hacked him to pieces within a month of his arrival. His family was spared, though, and following the cessation of hostilities they returned to the site and created the community that would ultimately become known as Pastor's Bay. The family's luck did not improve, however, and the twin forces of mortality and disillusionment eventually cleansed Pastor's Bay of any lingering Harris presence. Still, they left a town behind them, although there were those who said that Pastor's Bay had been blighted by the original killing, for it never truly thrived. It survived, and that was about the best that could be said for it.

Now, after the passage of centuries, Pastor's Bay found itself the focus of serious attention for the first time since the seeds of its foundation were sown and sprinkled with James Weston Harris's blood. News vehicles were parked on Main Street, and reporters stood before cameras, the thoroughfare at their backs, and spoke of the agonies being experienced by this small Maine town. They thrust microphones into the faces of

18

those who had no desire to see themselves on television, or to speak with strangers about the misfortunes of one of their own. Valerie Kore and her daughter might have been 'from away,' but they had made their home in Pastor's Bay, and its people protectively closed ranks around them. In this they were not discouraged by their police chief, a turn of events that caused some citizens of Pastor's Bay to whisper, just like the reporters, that there might be more to the disappearance of Anna Kore than met the eye.

A table had been set up at one side of the town hall, with coffee and cookies available for the visitors. The table was staffed by Ellie and Erin Houghton, twin spinsters of uncertain vintage, one of whom, Erin, was also the town librarian, while her sister managed the mysterious, elitist bed-and-breakfast, although it was not unknown for them to swap roles when the mood struck them. Since they were identical, this made little difference to the smooth running of the community. They served coffee in the same manner in which they performed all their tasks, voluntary or otherwise: with a politeness that did not invite undue intimacy, and a sternness that brooked no disobedience. When the first reporters began jostling for space at the table, and some creamer was spilled as a consequence, the sisters made clear from the way they held the coffeepots that such nonsense would not be tolerated, and the hardened journalists accepted the rebuke like meek schoolchildren.

All questions were directed to Lieutenant

Stephen Logan, the head of the Maine State Police's Criminal Investigation Division for the southern region of the state, although he occasionally deferred to the Pastor's Bay chief of police, Kurt Allan, on local matters. If the question merited it, Allan in turn would look to the pale woman beside him to see if she had a reply, and then only if it was not possible for him to provide the answer himself. When she did not wish to respond, she would simply shake her head once. When she did respond, it was with as few words as possible. No, she had no idea why someone would want to take her daughter. No, there had been no argument between them, or nothing unfamiliar to any mother of a strong-willed fourteen-year-old girl. She appeared composed, but anyone examining her more closely would have seen that Valerie Kore was holding herself together through sheer force of will. It was like looking at a dam that was on the verge of breaking, where a keen eye could discern the cracks in the façade that threatened to unleash the forces building behind it. Only when she was asked about the girl's father did those cracks become readily apparent to all. Valerie tried to speak, but the words choked her, and for the first time tears fell. It was left to Logan to intervene and announce that law-enforcement officers were searching for the father, one Alekos 'Alex' Kore, now estranged from his wife, in the hope that he might be able to help them with their inquiries. When asked if Kore was a suspect in his daughter's disappearance, Logan would say only that the police were not ruling out any possibilities, but were anxious simply to eliminate Alekos Kore from their enquiries. Then a reporter from one of the Boston newspapers complained about the difficulties of getting information and comments from the police, and there were some murmurs of agreement. Allan fudged the answer, talking about what he termed 'familial sensitivities,' but half of Maine could have given a better answer to the question, and one that would have satisfied those with anything more than a passing knowledge of that part of the world.

It was Pastor's Bay. They were just different up there.

But that wasn't the entire truth.

It wasn't even close.

* ★ ★

I watched the press conference on the early evening news, standing in the living room of my house as my daughter, Sam, finished her milk and sandwich in the kitchen. Rachel, Sam's mother and my ex-girlfriend, sat on the edge of an armchair, her eyes fixed on the screen. She and Sam were on their way to Boston to catch a flight to LA, where Rachel was due to address a symposium on clinical advances in cognitive psychotherapy. She had tried to explain the substance of these advances to me earlier, but I could only assume that the attendees at the symposium were smarter than I was, and had longer attention spans. Rachel had friends in Orange County with whom she planned to stay, and their daughter was a few months older than

21

Sam. The symposium would take up only one day, and the rest of their time in California was to be devoted to long-promised trips to Disneyland and Universal Studios.

Sam and Rachel lived on Rachel's parents' property in Burlington, Vermont. I spent time with Sam as often as I could, but not as often as I should, a situation complicated, or so I told myself, by the fact that Rachel had been seeing someone else for more than a year now. Jeff Reid was an older man, a former executive with the capital markets division of a major bank who had retired early, thereby nicely avoiding the fallout of the various scandals and collapses to which he had probably contributed. I didn't know that for sure, but I was petty enough to envy him his place in Rachel and Sam's life. I'd bumped into him once when I was visiting Sam for her birthday, and he'd tried to overwhelm me with bonhomie. He had all the moves of one who has spent a large portion of his life and career making others trust him, justifiably or not: the wide smile, the firm handshake, the left hand on my upper arm to make me feel valued. Seconds after meeting him, I was checking to make sure that I still had my wallet and my watch.

I studied Rachel as she took in the details of the conference. She had allowed a little gray to creep into her red hair, and there were lines around her eyes and mouth that I could not recall from before, but she was still very beautiful. I felt an ache in my heart for her, and I salved it with the knowledge that all was as it should be, however much I missed them both.

'What do you think?' I said.

'Her body language is wrong,' said Rachel. 'She doesn't want to be there, and not just because she's trapped in every mother's nightmare. She looks frightened, and I don't think it's because of the reporters. I'd hazard a guess that she's hiding something. Have you heard anything about the case?'

'No, but then I haven't been asking.'

The coverage of the news conference ended, and the anchorwoman moved on to foreign wars. I heard a noise behind me, and saw that Sam had been watching the news from the hall. She was tall for her age, with a lighter version of her mother's hair, and serious brown eyes.

'What happened to the girl?' she asked as she entered the room. She had what was left of her sandwich in her right hand, and was chewing on a mouthful of it. There were crumbs on her sweater, and I brushed them off. She looked unhappy about it. Maybe she'd been planning to save them for later.

'They don't know,' I said. 'She disappeared, and now they're trying to find her.'

'Did she run away? Sometimes people run away.'

'Could be, honey.'

She handed the remains of the sandwich to me. 'I don't want any more.'

'Thanks,' I said. 'I'll have it framed.'

Sam looked at me oddly, then asked if she could go outside.

'Sure,' said Rachel. 'But stay where we can see you.'

Sam turned to go, then paused.

23

'Daddy,' she said, 'you find people, don't you?'

'Yes, I find people.'

'You should go find the girl,' she said, then trotted off. Moments later, the top of her head appeared at the window as she began exploring the flower beds. On her last visit she had helped me plant native perennials in all of the beds, for I had let the garden go a little since she and her mother left. Now there was goatsbeard and harebell, turtleheads and shooting stars, all carefully labeled so that Sam would know which was which. It was not yet dark, but the lights outside were motion-activated, and Sam enjoyed setting them off by dancing beneath them. Rachel walked to the window and waved at her. I killed the TV and joined her.

'There are times when I look at her and I see you,' said Rachel. 'Or when she talks and I hear your voice. She's more like you than me, I think. Isn't that strange, when she sees so little of you?'

I couldn't help but react, and instantly Rachel apologized. She touched my arm gently with her right hand.

'I didn't mean it to sound that way. I'm not blaming you. It's just a statement of fact.' She returned to watching our daughter. 'She likes being with you, you know. Jeff is good with her, and spoils her, but she always keeps a little distance from him.'

Go Sam, I thought. He'd probably advise you to invest your allowance in weapons and Big Tobacco.

'She's such a self-contained kid,' Rachel continued. 'She's got friends, and she's doing

24

well in pre-school — better than well: She's ahead of her class in just about every way imaginable — but there's a part of her that she keeps for, and to, herself; a secret part. That doesn't come from me. That's you in her.'

'You don't sound like you're convinced it's a good thing.'

She smiled. 'I don't know what it is, so I can't say.'

Her hand was still touching my arm. She suddenly seemed to notice, and let it fall, but it was an unhurried movement. What existed between us was different now. There was sadness there, and regret, but not pain, or not so much of it that it affected how we were together.

'Try to see a little more of her,' said Rachel. 'We can work it out.'

I didn't respond. I thought of Valerie Kore and her missing daughter. I thought of my late wife, and my first daughter, wrenched violently from this existence only to linger in another form. I had witnessed the blurring of worlds, watching as elements of what once was, and what was to come, seeped into this life like dark ink through water. I knew of the existence of a form of evil that was beyond human capacities, the well-spring from which all other evil sipped. And I knew that I was marked, although to what end I did not yet understand. So I had kept my distance from my child, for fear of what I might draw upon her.

'I'll do my best,' I lied.

Rachel lifted her hand again, but this time she touched my face, tracing the lineaments of the bones beneath, and I felt my eyes grow hot. I closed them for a moment, and in that instant I lived another life.

'I know that you're trying to protect her by staying away, but I've thought about this a lot,' said Rachel. 'At the start, I wanted you gone from our lives. You frightened me, both because of what you were capable of doing and because of the men and women who forced you to act as you did, but there has to be a balance, and that balance isn't here now. You're her father, and by keeping your distance from her you're hurting her. We're hurting her, because I was complicit in what happened. We both need to try harder, for her sake. So, are we clear?'

'We're clear,' I said. 'Thank you.'

'You won't be thanking me when she's dragging you around the American Girl store. Your wallet won't be thanking me either.'

Sam was crouching by the woods, collecting branches and twigs and twisting them into shapes.

'What brought this on?' I asked.

'Sam did,' said Rachel. 'She asked me if you were a good man, because you found bad men and put them in jail.'

'And what did you say?'

'I told her the truth: that you are a good man. But I was worried in case her knowledge of what you do meant that she connected it with its risks, and I asked her if she was frightened for you. She told me that she wasn't, and I believed her.'

'Did she say why she wasn't frightened?'

'No.' Rachel frowned. 'She just said the

strangest thing — not the words but the way she said them. She said that the bad men should be frightened of you, but she wasn't joking, and it wasn't bravado. She was very solemn, and very certain. Then she just turned over and went to sleep. That was a couple of nights back, and afterward I was the one who couldn't sleep. It was like talking to an oracle, if that makes any sense.'

'I'd keep quiet about it if she is an oracle,' I said. 'You'll have half of New England coming to her for the Powerball numbers, and Jeff would probably charge them ten bucks a head for the consultation.'

Rachel punched me on the arm and headed for the door. It was time for them to leave.

'Go date somebody,' she said. 'You're a step away from taking holy orders.'

'It's the wrong time of year,' I replied. 'You never date going into winter. Too many layers. It's hard to figure out what you're getting until it's too late.'

'Spoken like a true cynic.'

'All cynics were once romantics. Most of them still are.'

'God, it's like talking to a bargain-basement philosopher.'

I helped her put on her coat, and she kissed me on the cheek. 'Remember what we talked about.'

'I will.'

She called out to Sam, who was now sitting on the bench outside. She had something beneath her coat as she walked back, but she kept it hidden until after we had hugged, then carefully withdrew it and handed it to me.

It was a cross. She had made it from thin twigs, intertwined where she could fix them together, but otherwise held together with strands of ivy.

'For when the bad men come,' she said.

Rachel and I exchanged a glance but said nothing, and it was only when they were gone that I was struck by the oddness of Sam's words. She had not given me the cross to keep the bad men away, as a child might have been expected to do. No, in her mind the bad men could not be kept away. They were coming, and they would have to be faced.

3

Soft voices everywhere as the fall wind whispered its regrets, and brown leaves sailed in the gutters as a light rain descended, the chill of it a surprise upon the skin. There were fewer tourists on the streets of Freeport now; for the most part they came on the weekends, and on this dreary day the stores were virtually empty. The pretty boys and girls in Abercrombie & Fitch folded and refolded to pass the time, and a scattering of locals drifted through L.L. Bean to make preparations for the winter, but not before first checking in the Bean outlet, for a dollar spared is a dollar saved, and these were canny people.

South Freeport, though, was very different from its upstart, commercialized northern sister. It was quieter, its center not so easily found, its identity essentially rural despite its proximity to Portland. It was why the lawyer Aimee Price had chosen to live and work there. Now, in her office at the corner of Park and Freeport, she watched the rain trace an intricate veinery upon her window, as though the glass were an organic creation like the wing of an insect. Her mood grew heavier with each falling raindrop, with each dead leaf that drifted by, with each bare inch of branch that was newly revealed by the dying foliage. How often had she thought about leaving this state? Every fall brought the same

29

realization: This was the best of it until March, perhaps even April. As bad as this was, with sodden leaves, and cold drizzle, and darkness in the mornings and darkness in the evenings, the winter would be so much worse. Oh, there would be moments of beauty, as when the sunlight scattered the first snows with gems, and the world in those early daylight hours would seem cleansed of its ugliness, purged of its sins, but then the filth would accrue, and the snow would blacken, and there would be grit in the soles of her shoes, and on the floor of her car, and traipsed through her house, and she would wish herself to be one of the huddled sleeping creatures that find a warm, dark cave or the hollow of a tree trunk, there to wait out the winter months.

She mulled over these matters as the child killer brooded outside.

How ordinary he seemed, how quotidian. He was of average height and average build, dressed in an average-priced suit and wearing average shoes. His tie was neither understated nor overstated in its color and design, neither too cheap nor too expensive. His face was no more than moderately handsome. Were she single, and out for the evening, she might talk to him if he approached her but she would not go out of her way to do so, and if no contact passed between them there would be no sense of regret, no possibility that an opportunity might have been missed. He was, in his way, as carefully camouflaged as those species of insect and moth that mimic leaves. Now, as with such creatures,

30

he had been exposed by the stripping of branches, by fall's decay.

She craned her neck slightly. From where she sat she could see him reflected in the mirror on the wall of the reception area. He had hair like damp straw, and soft brown eyes. His lips settled naturally into a pout that was saved from effeminacy by a small scar that broke the left side of his upper lip. He was clean-shaven, with a strong chin. It lent his features an authority that they would otherwise have lacked.

There were magazines on the table before him, and the day's newspapers, but he did not read them. Instead he sat perfectly still, with his hands flat upon his thighs. He barely blinked, so lost was he in his thoughts. He must have expected himself to be forgotten; after all, he had traveled so far, and changed so much. He had a new identity, and a history that had been carefully manufactured and maintained. None of it was illegal: It was gifted to him by the court, and he had built upon it in the years that followed. The boy, barely remembered, was not father to this man, and yet he dwelled within him, frozen at the moment in which he became a killer.

Aimee wondered how often he thought back on what he had done. She suspected, from her own experience of such matters (and not only of dealing with the crimes of others, but of negotiating the wreckage of her own mistakes and regrets) that whole days might sometimes go by when he forgot his sins, or even who he truly was, for otherwise life would be intolerable and he would buckle under the strain of his deception. The only way that he could go on was by denying to himself that he was engaged in any such imposture. He was what he had become, and he had shed the remembrance of what had been just as the moth emerging from its pupal shell has left behind its caterpillar form. Yet something of that early stage must surely linger: an insect dream, a memory of a time when it could not fly, when it was other than it was now.

Your sins followed you. She knew this, and she believed that he knew it too. If he did not, if he had tried to deny the reality of them, then the one who was coming would disabuse him of such notions. The man who would soon be with them — the detective, the hunter — knew all about sin and shadow. Her only concern was that his own pain would cause him to turn his back on her, and on the man outside who had asked for her help. The detective had lost a child. He had touched his hand to the torn form of his first daughter. There was a chance that such a man would not look mercifully on one who had taken the life of a female child, no matter how old he was when he did so.

All this she would tell the detective later. For now, her attention returned to the man outside. Child killer, in both senses of the term: killer of a child, and child himself when he took her life.

She had not known the truth about him, not until today, even though she had acted on his behalf in the past: a disputed DUI, followed by a border dispute with a neighbor that had threatened to descend into active hostility. There had been no reason for him to inform her of his past, although his anxiety about the property dispute had seemed excessive to her at the time. That afternoon's revelations had clarified the situation. Here was a man who shirked attention of any kind. Even his job was guaranteed to turn any conversation about occupations in another direction. He was a tax accountant, dealing with individuals and small local businesses. He worked from home for the most part. Contact with his clients was minimal, and then limited largely to financial matters. Even when he had needed legal help, he had chosen a lawyer with a practice relatively distant from his own location. There were attorneys closer to home that he could have used, but he elected not to do so. She had thought it a little odd at the time, but not anymore. He had been afraid of word getting out, afraid of a secret shared on a pillow, or over a drink, afraid of the single indiscreet moment that might sink him.

You're always afraid, she thought. Even though you've changed so much since the crime was committed, you fear the second glance in the bar, the unfortunate crossing of paths, the moment when a guard, or a former inmate, or a prison visitor to whom you were once pointed out joins the dots and connects your face to your history. Yes, they might shake their heads and pass on, believing that they were mistaken, and you could absent yourself from their presence quickly if you felt the heat of their gaze upon you. But if they did not simply move on or, worse, if through some dreadful accident they came upon you in your new home, where nobody knew of your past, what then? Would you brazen it out? Would you accept your fate? Or would you run? Would you gather your possessions, climb into your car, and disappear? Would you try to start again?

Or would the little boy inside you, now gifted with the strength of a man, suggest another way out? After all, you've killed once. How hard would it be to kill again?

She looked at her watch. The detective had told her that he would be there within the hour, and he was rarely late.

A shape passed across the window, and a shadow briefly entered the room, moving across her body before departing. She heard the beating of its wings, and could almost feel the touch of its feathers against her. She watched as the raven settled on the branch of the birch tree that overhung the small parking lot. Ravens unsettled her. It was the darkness of them, and their intelligence, the way in which they could lead wolves and dogs to prey. They were apostate birds: It was their instinct to betray to the pack the presence of the vulnerable.

But this one was not alone: There was another perched above it. She had missed it set against the tangled branches of the tree. Now came a third. It landed on a fence post, stretched its wings momentarily, then subsided into stillness. They were all so statuesque, and they all faced the road. Strange.

And then the ravens were forgotten for now. A car appeared, an old Mustang. She had never been very interested in cars, and could not tell one vintage from another, but the sight of the automobile brought a little smile to her face for the first time that afternoon.

The detective and his toy.

He stepped from the car. As always, she watched him with a deep curiosity. He was as unsettling, in his way, as the black birds that had gathered nearby, his intelligence and instincts as strange to her as theirs. He wore a dark suit with a slim black tie. It was unusual for him, for typically he preferred a more casual wardrobe, but he looked good in it. It was single-breasted, and slim-fitting, the pants very narrow at the hem. With his pale features, and his dark hair tinged slightly with gray, he was a monochrome vision, as though he had been dropped into the autumnal landscape from an old photograph, an older time.

In the years that she had known him, she had often thought about why he was so troubling to her. In part, it was his predilection for violence. No, that was unfair; instead, it was better defined as his willingness to use violence, and his apparent comfort with it. He had killed, and she knew that he would kill again. Circumstances would dictate that he had to do so, for wicked men and women were drawn to him, and he dispatched them when there was no other option.

And sometimes, she suspected, even when there was.

Why they were called to him she did not know, but she found random phrases drifting through her consciousness when she considered the matter: stalking horse, Judas goat. Bait. There was an otherworldliness to him at times, the same feeling that might be inspired by a figure glimpsed in a churchyard at the closing of the day, slowly fading into the dusk as it walked away, so that one was uncertain whether one had merely come across another mourner in the process of departing or a presence less corporeal. Perhaps it was impossible to look at as much pain and death as this man had and not have something of the next world make an impact upon you, assuming that you believed in a world beyond this one. She did, and nothing in her encounters with the detective had made her doubt her faith. He wore aftershave that smelled of incense, and she thought that this was apt.

But he could blend in. He could not follow his chosen profession otherwise. It was not a veneer of normality that he wore. It coexisted alongside his strangeness. Even now, dressed in his smart black suit, he carried a brown paper bag in his right hand. In it, she knew, would be muffins. Muffins were her weakness. For the right muffin, at the right time, she might even betray her fiancé, and she loved him deeply.

She realized that she was toying with her engagement ring, slipping it on and off her finger, and she could not remember if it was the thought of Brennan, the man who gave the ring to her, that had caused her to touch it, or if she had begun twisting it when the detective appeared. She decided that she did not want to think about it, although this, too, she would tell the detective, at another time and in another place.

He crossed the lot and walked up the damp path that led to her building. As he did so, it seemed to her that the heads of the black birds turned to follow his progress, perhaps attracted by the blackness of his suit, seeing in him one of their own. She wished that they would leave. She adjusted the blinds at the window, altering her field of vision, but the knowledge of the birds remained. They're just birds, she thought: big black birds. This isn't a movie. You're not Tippi Hedren.

She decided to force the birds from her mind. Perhaps she had been using their presence as a distraction, a means of delaying the conversation that was about to take place. She did not want him to refuse to help her, or her client. If he did, she would understand, and she would not think less of him, but she felt it was important that he agreed to involve himself. He had told her once that coincidences bothered him. The coincidences here were off the scale.

She prepared to greet him. It was time.

⋆   ⋆   ⋆

I passed through the reception area, barely glancing at the waiting man, and entered Aimee's office. I placed the bag in front of her and opened it so that she could peer inside.

'Charlie Parker, you are the very devil,' she said, taking one of the pastries out. 'Peach? They didn't have raspberry?'

37

'They had raspberry, but he who pays the baker calls the flavor.'

'You're telling me that you don't like raspberry?'

'I'm not *telling* you anything. It's a muffin. It's got peaches. Live with it. You know, I can see why Brennan is taking so long to add a gold band to that rock you're playing with. Sometimes he probably wonders if he kept the receipt.'

I watched her shift her hand quickly from the ring. To give it something else to do she picked at the muffin, even though I could see from her face that she had little enthusiasm for it. She could usually eat one any time of the day or night, but something had killed her appetite. She swallowed the fragment in her mouth, but ate no more. It seemed to taste too dry to her. She coughed and reached for the bottle of water that she always had on her desk.

'If I find out he kept the receipt, I'll kill him,' she said, once the dryness was gone.

'A psychologist might wonder why you play with it so much.'

She reddened. 'I don't.'

'My mistake.'

'Yes, it is.'

Brennan, her fiancé, was a big lug who adored the very ground she walked on, but they had been engaged for so long that the priest earmarked to conduct the wedding ceremony had died in the interim. Somebody in the relationship was dragging heels on the way to the altar, and I wasn't sure that it was Brennan.

'You're not eating your muffin. I kind of expected it to be reduced to crumbs right about now.'

'I'll eat it later.'

'Okay. Maybe I should have bought raspberry after all.'

I said nothing more, but waited for her to speak.

'Why are you wearing a suit?' she said.

'I was testifying.'

'In church?'

'Funny. In court. The Denny Kraus thing.'

Denny Kraus had killed a man in a parking lot off Forest Avenue eighteen months earlier, in an argument over a dog. Apparently the victim, Philip Espvall, had sold Denny Kraus the animal claiming it was a thoroughbred pointer, a gun dog, but the first time Denny fired a gun near the dog it headed for the hills and was never seen again. Denny had taken this badly, and had come looking for Espvall at the Great Lost Bear, which happened to be the bar in which I worked occasionally when money was scarce, or when the mood took me, and in which I was tending bar on the night that Denny came looking for Espvall. Words had been exchanged, both men had been ejected, and then I'd called the cops as a precaution. By the time they caught up with the two men, Espvall had a hole in his chest and Denny was standing over him, waving a handgun and shouting about a retarded dog.

'I forgot you were tied up with that,' said Aimee.

'I was bar manager that night. At least we

didn't serve Denny any alcohol.'

'It sounds pretty clear-cut. His lawyer should tell him to cop a plea.'

'It's complicated. Denny wants to argue provocation, but his own lawyer is trying to have him declared mentally incompetent to stand trial. Denny doesn't believe he's crazy, and so I'm wearing a suit while Denny's lawyer tries to convince the judge of one thing and his client tries to convince him of the opposite. For what it's worth, I think Denny's crazy. The prosecution is playing hardball, but he's been in and out of the Bangor Mental Health Institute for the past decade.'

'And he still owned a gun.'

'He bought it before he found his way into the state mental health system. It wasn't like he went into the store drooling and screaming obscenities about dogs.'

Aimee was distracted by the flapping of wings behind her. A raven was trying to alight on the windowsill but couldn't get a foothold. It returned instead to the ones in the birch. Four now.

'I don't like them,' she said. 'And these are real big. Have you ever seen ravens that big before?'

I stood and stepped over to the window. I could barely see the birds through the gap in the blinds, but I didn't reach out to widen it with my fingers. On the road beyond I saw cars passing, each with at least one child inside, all coming from L'École Française de Maine just up the street. One of the birds turned its head and cawed an objection to their presence.

'How long have they been here?'

40

'Not long: since shortly before you arrived. I know they're just birds, but they're real smart, ravens. Animals have no right to be so smart, and it's as if these ones are waiting for something.'

I stared at the ravens for just a moment longer, then returned to my chair.

'Just birds,' I echoed.

She sat forward in her chair. We were moving on to the business of the moment.

'Did you see the man sitting outside?' she asked.

'Yes.'

'Anything strike you about him?'

I considered the question.

'He's nervous, but he's trying to hide it. Hardly unusual for someone in a lawyer's office who isn't a lawyer, and he doesn't give off a lawyer vibe. He's doing okay, though. No tapping of the feet, no tics, no hand gestures. Either for professional or personal reasons, he's grown good at hiding what he's feeling. But it's there: It's in his eyes.'

'Did you learn how to do that from your ex-girlfriend?'

'Some of it. She taught me how to put words to sensations.'

'Well, you both did good. That man outside has been concealing truths about himself for a very long time. He has a story that I'd like you to hear.'

'I'm always happy to listen.'

'There's a complication. I've acted on his behalf in the past — nothing serious, a DUI that we had quashed, and a minor dispute with a neighbor — and I've agreed to act for him in this matter too, insofar as I can, but I need someone with your skills to work on the ground.'

'So I hear his story, and decide if I want to take the job.'

'I want you to decide *before* you hear his story.'

'That's not how I work. Why would you want me to do that?'

'Because I want you to be bound by the same duty of confidentiality as I am.'

'You don't trust me?'

'I trust you. I'm just not sure how you're going to react to elements of his story. And if the police become involved I want you to be able to say that you're working for me, with the consequent protection of privilege.'

'But if I decline to take the case, what's the problem? How are the cops going to know?'

She took her time before answering.

'Because you might feel compelled to share with them what you learn here.'

Now it was my turn to pause.

'No, that's not my style,' I said at last.

'Do *you* trust *me*?'

'Yes.'

'You'll want to take this case. You'll have reservations about the client, perhaps, but you'll want to take the case. What he did, he did a long time ago, but it may have ramifications for an investigation that's ongoing.'

'What did he do?'

'You'll take the case?'

'What did he *do*?'

She grimaced, then sat back in her chair.

'He murdered a girl.'

4

He entered with his body slightly hunched, as though tensed to receive a blow, and there was an almost childlike aspect to his demeanor. He reminded me of an errant boy who has been called to the principal's office in order to explain his actions, and doesn't believe that he has a plausible excuse. Such men and women were a familiar sight to me, and to Aimee Price. Lawyers' offices have something of the confessional about them; in their confines, truths are revealed, justifications offered, and penances negotiated.

He was wearing dark-rimmed spectacles with the faintest of tints. The lenses did not look thick, and the magnifying effect on his eyes was barely noticeable. They struck me as a shield of sorts, an element of his armory of defenses. He called himself Randall Haight. It was the name on his business card, and the name by which he was known to his neighbors, with whom, for the most part, he maintained distant yet cordial relations, the only exception being Arthur Holden, the other party in the old boundary dispute that had left a lingering bitterness hanging like a miasma over the adjacent properties. According to Aimee, Haight had backed down before it could become a matter for the court, and therefore increasingly messy, and expensive, and public.

Public: That was the important word, for Randall Haight was a most private man.

Haight took a seat next to me, having first shaken hands in a tentative manner, his body leaning away from me even as his hand was extended, possibly fearful that I might be the one to strike that long-anticipated blow. He knew that Aimee would have told me enough to give me an adverse opinion of him, should I have chosen to form one. I tried to keep my face neutral because, in truth, I wasn't sure how I felt about Haight. I wanted to hear what he had to say before I reached any conclusions, but I could detect a mixture of curiosity and animosity in myself as I judged him despite my best efforts, and some of that must surely have communicated itself to him. I saw how he looked at me, glancing up and sideways, not quite meeting my eye. Dignity and shame fought for primacy within him, with guilt and anger bubbling beneath. I sensed it all, saw it all, and wondered what else he might have hidden away in the locked cabinet of his heart. Of the anger I was certain: I picked up on it in the same way that animals are said to be able to scent disease in humans. I was good at scenting the poisons in men, and Haight's anger was like a pollutant in his blood, infecting his system. It would always be there, waiting to well up, seeking an outlet: a complex, many-headed thing; a hydra within. It was anger at himself for what he had done, fed by his own self-pity; anger at the girl who had died, as hers was not a passive role, and dying is itself an action; anger at the authorities

44

who had punished him, blighting his future; and anger at his accomplice in the killing, for Aimee had informed me that Randall Haight had not acted alone. There was another with him on the day that the girl died, and Aimee's view was that Haight's relationship with this individual was deeply conflicted.

Anger, anger, anger. He had tried to contain it, isolating it by creating a persona and a lifestyle that allowed it no opportunity for expression. In doing so he had rendered it more dangerous, and more unpredictable, for being denied an outlet. Maybe he knew this, maybe not, but it was how he had chosen to deal with all of his emotions. He was afraid that if he allowed even a little real feeling to emerge, his entire persona would be swept away in the tide that followed.

All these things I thought as he sat next to me, smelling faintly of soap and inexpensive cologne, and prepared to expose himself before his silent judges.

'I've shared with Mr. Parker only a little of what you've told me,' said Aimee. 'I felt that it was better if he heard the rest of it directly from you.'

Haight swallowed hard. The office was warm, and there was a sheen of sweat on his face. He seemed about to remove his jacket, but as he shifted it from his shoulders he noticed the sweat patches beneath his arms and instead shrugged it back on. He did not want to feel more vulnerable than he already did, so he resisted the lapse into informality, even at the cost of his own comfort.

There was a mini-fridge beside a filing cabinet

in the office. Aimee removed two bottles of water from it and handed one to Haight. I took the second, even though I wasn't thirsty. Haight drank deeply until he noticed that neither Aimee nor I was doing the same, and I saw in his face that he was simultaneously grateful to her for seeking to alleviate his distress and embarrassed at even this small demonstration of weakness on his part. A little of the water dribbled down his chin and he wiped it away with his left hand, frowning at himself and at us as he did so. He gave me another sideways glance. He knew that I was sizing him up, taking in every small movement.

'Clumsy of me,' he said.

He removed a padded manila envelope from his leather satchel. Inside the envelope was a series of photographs, probably printed from a home photo printer. There were five in total. He spread them on the desk so that all the images were visible. In each case, the subject matter was the same, even if the specific object was different in every photo.

They were all photographs of barn doors. Two were red, one green, one black, and the other was a reproduction of a black-and-white photo from a newspaper, but the door in question looked so weathered and old that it was impossible to tell if it had ever been painted any color at all. The grain reminded me of wrinkles on skin, an effect aided by two holes in the upper portion of the barn doors, and the way that the lock bar hung lopsidedly like a half smile, so that the whole was reminiscent of an ancient face.

This photo Haight set slightly apart from the others, using the tips of his fingers. The sight of the image seemed to pain him more than the rest.

'They began arriving four days ago,' he said. 'The red one came first, then the green. There was nothing on the third day, then another red one arrived along with the black, each in separate envelopes. That one' — he pointed at the gray door — 'came this morning.'

'Mailed or hand-delivered?' I asked.

'Mailed. I kept the envelopes.'

'Postmarks?'

'Bangor and Augusta.'

'I assume these images have some significance for you?'

Haight's body tensed. He reached for his water and drank some more. He started speaking slowly, but only at first. His tale had its own momentum, and once he began telling of what he had done it moved beyond his control, almost like the killing he was describing.

'In 1982, when I was fourteen years old, Lonny Midas and I took a girl named Selina Day into a barn in Drake Creek, North Dakota. She was fourteen too, a little black girl. She wore a white blouse and a red-and-black checked skirt, and her hair was styled in cornrows. We'd spotted her around, Lonny and I, and we'd talked about her some. There was a church outside town, barely bigger than a regular house, and its congregation was all colored. Lonny and I would go by there sometimes and watch them through the window. They had services during the week, and we'd hear them talking about how Jesus was their Lord and Savior, and they'd be amening and hallelujahing. Lonny said it was funny that all those coloreds believed they were going to be saved by a white man, but I didn't think it was funny at all. My mother told me that Jesus loved everyone, and it didn't matter what color their skin was.'

At this point in his narrative he pursed his lips primly and looked to us for approval. *See? I'm not a racist, and I know the difference between right and wrong. I knew it then, and I know it now. What happened, what I did, it was an aberration. I shouldn't be judged on that alone, should I?*

But we didn't speak, because the questions were only in his eyes, and so he resumed his tale.

'I'd never even kissed a girl. Lonny had. He'd once gone into the woods with one of the Beale girls, and he told me later that she let him touch one of her breasts, except he didn't call them breasts, of course. He called them 'titties.''

And there was that prim look again. Nasty old Lonny Midas, with his crude speech and his white man's Jesus.

'But we'd never seen a girl naked, and we were curious, and everyone said that Selina Day wore nothing under her dress. So we waited for her when she was walking home from the poor kids' school, and we walked with her for a time, and then we took her to the barn. It wasn't hard. We told her there was a cat in there that had given birth to kittens and we were going to take a look at them and maybe give them some food. We just

48

asked her if she wanted to come along, like it was nothing to us if she did or not, and she thought about it, and she came. When we got to the barn she started to look worried, but we told her that it was okay, and she believed us.

'And when she found out what we wanted she fought back, and we had to lie across her to keep her from getting up and running away. We kept touching her, and she said that she'd tell the police what we'd done, and her uncles — because she didn't have a father, he was gone — and they and their friends would come for us and they'd cut our balls off. She started to scream, and Lonny covered her mouth with his hand. He pressed down real hard, so that her nostrils were blocked too. I told Lonny that we ought to let her go. I could see her eyes growing wide, and she was having trouble breathing, but Lonny wouldn't take away his hand after I told him to. I tried to pull him off her but he was bigger and stronger than I was. Eventually Selina started bucking, and Lonny sat on her chest, and then she stopped moving at all, even though her eyes were still open and I could see my reflection in them.

'I started crying, but Lonny told me to quit it, and I did. We covered her with rotten straw, and we left her there. It was an old barn on an abandoned farm. We figured it would be a while before she was found. We swore, Lonny and I, that we wouldn't tell what we'd done, not ever, not even if the cops came for us and put us in separate rooms and interrogated us, like they did on the TV shows. If we both agreed not to speak,

49

then they couldn't do anything to us. We just had to stick to our story: We never saw Selina Day and we didn't know anything about any old barn.'

All of this came out in a rush, like pus from an infected wound. It was spoken by an adult's voice, but with the words and emphases of a child's narration.

'But somebody had seen us with her. He was a farmworker from out of state, an itinerant laborer. He heard that a black girl had gone missing, and he recalled the two boys he'd seen with a little black girl that day, a black girl in a red-and-black checked skirt, just like the description that the police had passed around. He went to the cops and told them what he'd seen. He had a good eye: He remembered what we looked like, what we were wearing, everything. Drake Creek wasn't a big town, and they had us figured before he even stopped talking. They came for us, and they put us in separate rooms, just like on those shows, and a big detective told me that Lonny had put the blame on me, that it had all been my idea, that I'd tried to rape Selina Day and he'd wanted to stop me, and it was me who had suffocated her. He said that they'd have me tried as an adult, and they'd ask for the death penalty. He said I'd get the needle for what I'd done, and that I shouldn't think it would be like going to sleep, because it wouldn't be. I'd feel everything — the poison seeping into my veins, the pain as my organs shut down — and I wouldn't be able to speak or cry out because the other drugs would have paralyzed me. And there would just be me in there, all alone, without my momma or my poppa. And he said that, sometimes, they deliberately screwed around with the drugs so it would hurt more, and maybe they'd do that to me to punish me for what I'd done, for trying to rape a little girl, and for killing her when she fought back.

'But that wasn't true. It had been Lonny's idea all along, and he was the one who tried to take it too far, and he was the one who closed her nostrils and pressed his hand hard against her mouth so that she couldn't breathe. I wanted to let her go, but he was scared of what she'd say, scared that he'd have his balls cut off.'

Haight had now regressed fully. His voice was higher, and he had slipped lower in his seat so that he appeared smaller. Even his suit looked too big for him. There were tears in his eyes, and he didn't try to brush them away as they began to roll down his cheeks. He stared only inward, and I think that he had forgotten about our presence in the room, had forgotten even about the room itself and the reason he was there. Instead, he was fourteen years old, and back in a place that smelled of sweat and urine and vomit, and a big policeman with food stains on his tie was whispering to him of the pain that he was going to endure when they put the needle in.

'I was so scared of dying, I forgot that North Dakota had abolished the death penalty in 1973.' The ghost of a smile haunted his mouth, then fled back to the place where he kept all of his old specters. 'So I told him what we'd done, but I wanted him to know that it wasn't my idea. I'd

51

gone along with it at first, but I was sorry now. I should never have done it, and I wished that Selina Day was still alive. I told him of how I'd tried to make Lonny stop. I even showed him how I'd grabbed hold of Lonny's wrists in an effort to pull him off her. I remember that the detective patted me on the back when I was done, and brought me a soda. Then a lawyer came and asked if I'd been read my rights, and I couldn't remember, and he and the detective got to talking, and the subject of my rights didn't come up again after that. They let me see my momma and poppa, and my momma held me. My poppa could barely bring himself to look at me, not even when I told him that it wasn't my fault, and that I hadn't been the one who killed her. He was already sick then. He had to walk with a stick, and his skin had gone gray. He only lived for another three or four years, but I was always closer to my momma anyway.'

Haight drank the last of his water, and carefully put the cap back on. He held the empty bottle between his legs, his fingertips pressing down on the cap, as though it were a button that could cause the past to disappear, erasing all memories, all sins.

'Lonny and I were tried as adults, and we spent eighteen years each in separate facilities, from juvenile to adult. The judge ordered that all records of the trial should be sealed, both so that we could get on with our lives upon our eventual release and for our own safety because it was said that Selina Day's uncles were involved with the Black Liberation Army, although I don't know how true that was. Looking back, I think it was just thrown into the mix, a way for the prosecutor to cover himself in case anything went wrong. Whatever the reasons, there was an agreement reached that we should be given new identities in the course of our incarceration, and those identities should be known only to a handful of people, but we only found that out later. I remember the judge telling us that we'd done a terrible thing, but he believed that everyone had the possibility of redemption within them, especially children. He told us we were to be given a chance to prove that, once we'd done our time.

'After twelve years they moved us to out-of-state prisons to make the changes in identities run smoother. I was born William Lagenheimer, but I became Randall Haight between the state penitentiary in Bismarck and the Northern State Correctional Facility in Newport, Vermont. After a couple of years, they moved me to Berlin, New Hampshire, where I served out the last year of my sentence. They wouldn't tell me Lonny's new name, and I didn't want to know anyway. I never wanted to see him again, after all the trouble he got us into. Eventually, I came to Maine.'

Haight pointed to the photograph of the weathered barn door.

'This was the barn in which Selina Day died,' he said. 'They used that picture in some of the newspapers. These others I don't know, but this one is, or was, in Drake Creek. I still see it in my dreams.'

He looked at his lawyer, seeking her response to this second telling of his story. She tried to smile encouragingly at him, but it was more like a grimace. He turned to me. His mouth opened, and he spread his hands as if to add something to the narrative — an apology, or an explanation for why this was all in the past, and how he was different now — but he seemed to realize that there was nothing more that could be said, so he closed his mouth, and folded his arms, and remained silent while he waited to hear what we had to say.

'So someone has found out who you are?' I said.

'Yes. I don't know who, or how, but yes, that's it.'

'It could be a prelude to blackmail,' said Aimee.

'Has there been a blackmail threat?' I asked.

'Not yet,' said Aimee.

I shrugged. Beside me, the light of the setting sun reflected on the lenses of Haight's spectacles, and I could no longer see his eyes.

'For now, it seems that Mr. Haight here has two choices,' I said. 'He can stay where he is and deal with the consequences if this individual chooses to make public what he or she knows, or he can leave his home and go somewhere else. Maybe he can make contact with the authorities in North Dakota and see if they will provide him with another identity, although I guess he'd have to prove that he was in some form of danger as a consequence of his potential exposure, and even then new identities aren't handed out so easily.

Look, in the end, whatever the nature of his crime, he did his time. He was a child when Selina Day was killed, not an adult. Also, if one were to be cold-blooded about it, it's a crime that was committed a long time ago, and in another state. If his identity is revealed, there may be people in Maine who'll react badly, but he might also be surprised by how understanding folk can be.'

'All that is true,' said Aimee. 'But there's one detail that Mr. Haight hasn't shared with you yet. It's where he's living. Why don't you tell Mr. Parker where you've made your home?'

And I knew that this was the bait in the trap, the detail that she had deliberately held back from me, and as Haight began to speak I felt the jaws snap shut upon me, and I understood that I would not be able to turn away from this.

'I live two miles from Anna Kore's house,' said Haight. 'I live in Pastor's Bay.'

5

Randall Haight had resumed his seat in the reception area. The receptionist, shared by Aimee with the other businesses in the building, had gone home, so he was alone with his thoughts. He appeared dissatisfied as he left the room. It was there in the way that he held himself, in the pause before he closed the door behind him, the sense he gave that there was more to be said, or more that should have been said, and not by him. Our response — or possibly more correctly, my response — to his story had not satisfied him. I think that he might have been seeking some form of reassurance and consolation, not about the problem of the photographs, but about his own nature.

It was now dusk outside, and the rain continued to fall. The lights of passing cars illuminated the parking lot, casting new shadows over the office in which Aimee and I sat. Dark patches remained in the branches of the tree. The ravens had not moved, and they made no sound. I felt the urge to take a handful of stones and force them from their perch.

Traitorous birds. Apostates.

'Well?' said Aimee.

We had not exchanged a word since Haight left the office at Aimee's request so that we might discuss in private all that he had told us. The pictures of the barn doors remained on the desk. I moved them around with the index finger of my right hand, rearranging their order, as though the colors represented a code I could crack, and by doing so I would be allowed the revelation, the certainty, that I sought.

I was wondering where the lie was. It might be that I had grown more cynical as the years went by, or it might simply have been an atavistic instinct I had learned not to ignore, but a lie was hidden somewhere in Randall Haight's testimony to us. It could have been a lie of deceit or a lie of omission, but it was there. I knew, because there is always a lie. Even a man like Haight, who, in his youth, was party to a terrible crime, and who had just confessed as much to two strangers, reducing himself in their eyes, would hold back at least one crucial detail. If nothing else, it was human nature. You didn't give everything away; if you did, you would have nothing left. There were those who took the view that there was a liberation in the act of confession, but mostly they tended to be the ones who were listening and not the ones confessing. The only full confessions occur on deathbeds; all others are partial, modified. The lie in Haight's story was probably one that he had practiced, a rearrangement or omission of details that had now become crucial to his account of events, maybe to the extent that he no longer knew it as a lie at all. There had been a rehearsed element to his testimony, but I was not entirely certain that it had been solely for our benefit.

'He's lying,' I said.

'About what?'

'I don't know. I was watching him while he spoke, and there was something in the way he told his story. It was too *polished*, like he'd been preparing it for years in his head, waiting for the chance to perform it.'

'Maybe he has been. It was a turning point in his life — the worst thing that he's ever done, or ever will do. It wouldn't be surprising if he returned to it again and again, and constructed his own version of the crime and its aftermath. After all, he's probably been trying to explain it to himself for years when he hasn't been explaining it to cops or therapists.'

'A version,' I said.

'What?'

'You described it as a 'version.' That's all it is. The only people who really know what went on in that barn are Randall Haight, Lonny Midas, and Selina Day, and the only one we've heard from is Randall Haight, who says that it wasn't his fault, that he tried to stop the killing from happening, but Lonny Midas was too strong.'

'Do we accept that that's how we should think of him — as Randall Haight and not William Lagenheimer?'

'That's an interesting question. How does he see himself?'

'I notice that you didn't ask.'

'I didn't ask because I don't think that it matters, for now. For your purposes, and in the eyes of his fellow citizens, he's Randall Haight. For the most part, I imagine that's how he thinks of himself. He's had to accept the reality of his new identity, and whatever imagined history goes along with it, in order to survive.'

She made a note to herself on her legal pad, then let the subject go.

'He could be telling the truth about what happened in the barn,' she said. 'You're questioning details instead of substance. Randall Haight is not denying his partial culpability for the death of Selina Day.'

'Sure, he could be telling the truth, but if I'd been involved in the death of a young girl and could shift some of the blame onto the shoulders of another, I would.'

'No, *you* wouldn't,' said Aimee. 'Someone else, maybe, but not you.'

'Why do you say that? I don't believe I'm so honorable.'

'Honor is just part of it. Self-torment is the rest.'

She said it with a smile, but it didn't make what she had said any less sincerely meant. God preserve me, I thought, from dime-store psychologists, especially cloaked in lawyers' garb.

'He was fourteen,' I said. 'I never killed anyone when I was fourteen. If I had, I don't know for sure how I would have reacted afterward.'

'This is all beside the point.'

'Is it?'

'You know it is. Someone is taunting Randall Haight with their knowledge of what he did as a boy. At the same time, a fourteen-year-old girl has gone missing in Pastor's Bay. The similarities are troubling.'

I saw my daughter staring up at me, and heard

her asking me to find Anna Kore. I looked at my hands, and perceived the ghost of a cross made from sticks and twigs. Around my neck hung a smaller version of the same symbol: a Byzantine bronze pilgrim's cross. Sometimes we have to be reminded of our obligations to others, even at a cost to ourselves.

'Because,' I said, 'if whoever has figured out Randall Haight's identity gave a damn about Anna Kore they'd have gone to the police with what they know: The convicted killer of a fourteen-year-old girl is living in the same town from which another fourteen-year-old girl has recently gone missing. Instead, they're sending him pictures of barn doors and waiting to see how he responds.'

'Part of me still thinks it could be a prelude to a blackmail attempt.'

'Then he should go to the police.'

'If he goes to the police, they'll make him a suspect.'

'Or rule him out of the investigation, if he can answer all of their questions and if he didn't do it.'

Aimee winced at each use of the word 'if.'

'Come on,' I said. 'It's not like you haven't considered the possibility.'

'Assuming it's crossed my mind, do you really think he could have taken Anna Kore?'

'No, not unless he's playing a high-stakes game by involving us, in which case he's either ridiculously clever or he's crazy.'

'He doesn't strike me as either. He is smart, but if he's crazy he's hiding it well. What?'

I had been unable to conceal a frown of doubt.

'Crazy would be a strong word, but he's a man living with the knowledge that he once killed a child. He's been forced into a new identity, and he lives in an isolated community far from his original home. I think he's functioning under immense emotional and psychological strain. He practically hums with tension. Do you know if he's maintained any form of contact with his family?'

'He says that he hasn't. We know that his father is dead. He doesn't know where his mother is. He told me that he lived with her for a time after his release from Berlin, but felt suffocated by her presence. He also believed that, for the purposes of inhabiting his new identity, it would be better if he had no further contact with his family. That's not unusual. He'd learned to live without them for a long time, and a lot of prisoners have trouble adjusting to familial relationships once they're released. It would have been even harder for Randall, as officially he was no longer even a member of his own family.'

'That was some social experiment he and Lonny Midas found themselves involved in.'

'You disapprove?'

'No. I just don't fully understand the thinking behind it.'

'We should find out more.'

'We will.'

'And we've established that he's not crazy, but under pressure he may buckle.'

'Agreed,' I said, reluctantly.

'If he goes to the police, his old life in Pastor's

Bay will be over. He doesn't want that. He wants to stay where he is, and live out his days there. As you said, he's done his time. The law and society have no further hold on him in that respect.'

'So he'll stay quiet and hope that the girl is found?'

'That will be my advice to him, for now. Meanwhile, you'll look into who might be sending him these images, because you understand why it matters.'

She had me in a bind. Randall Haight had committed no crime in the state of Maine of which we knew. Haight was a client of Aimee's, and I had tentatively agreed to work for her on Haight's behalf. I was bound by issues of client confidentiality, to a certain extent, and it offered a degree of protection against being forced by the police to reveal details about my involvement, should it come to that. But I didn't like the situation we were in. To protect Haight, we were concealing information that might be germane to the investigation into Anna Kore's disappearance, even though there was no evidence to suggest a direct link between Haight and the crime beyond one of geographic proximity and the similarity in the ages between two of the girls involved. It was the grayest of gray areas, and I felt that Aimee was exploiting it.

'Does it bother you?' asked Aimee. 'What Randall did, does it trouble you?'

'Of course it does.'

'But more than it should? Do you feel a personal animosity toward him because of the loss of your own child? I have to ask that. You do understand?'

'I understand. No, I don't feel excessive animosity toward him. He killed a child when he was a child himself, and I get the feeling he's a bit of a creep, although I can't say why. You know that I could walk out of here, right? Nothing to which I've agreed in this office is binding.'

'I know that. I also know that you won't walk.'

'If you're right, do you want to try telling me why?'

'Because there's another child involved. Because Anna Kore is out there somewhere, and she may still be alive. As long as there's hope for her, you won't walk away. I know that you're uneasy about not going to the police. I'll work on Randall to see if I can get him to change his mind about coming forward voluntarily, but if you can find one firm connection between what's happening to our client and the disappearance of Anna Kore, I'll call the cops myself, and I'll sit on Randall until they come.'

While I wrestled with that mental image, she added, 'Because that's the other reason you'll take the case: You, like I am, are wondering if there's a possibility that the person who is taunting Randall Haight is the same person who took Anna Kore.'

★   ★   ★

I drove back to Scarborough, my eyes straining as the rain pummeled the windshield. The Mustang's lights weren't worth much in this kind of weather, but it hadn't been this bad when I left earlier, and I enjoyed taking the car out when I could. It was an indulgence, but I liked to believe that I was a man of relatively few indulgences. On the seat beside me was a printout of the names of all those involved in the prosecution of the Selina Day case that Haight could recall. He was unsure of spellings in some cases, and claimed to know nothing of where those people were now. When I asked if he hadn't been tempted to find out about them, he replied that William Lagenheimer might have been, but Randall Haight was not.

I was troubled by the Haight case, but even if there had not been the matter of Anna Kore to take into account I would still have accepted it. After all, I could do with the money, and the diversion that the job offered. Work was thin on the ground at present. Businesses and individuals didn't have cash to spend on private investigators, not unless there were large sums or considerable reputations at risk, in which case they'd approach one of the bigger agencies anyway. Even marital work, which was usually worth a trickle of income, had dried up. Spouses suspicious of their partners, believing them to be straying, would carry out their own investigations, checking cell phone records, credit card slips, hotel bookings. They'd even follow their husbands or wives themselves, or get a friend to do so, if they could find one they trusted enough, and one they were certain wasn't the third party in the possibly adulterous relationship. Many, though, would just live with their suspicions, because even if they found out that they were right, what were they going to do? Everybody was struggling. It was hard enough to keep one roof above their heads; they couldn't afford two. Sometimes economics alone were enough to keep men and women from straying, or force them to live with their doubts.

So I picked up work where I could, mostly insurance stuff, and surveillance for businesses concerned about the activities of employees. I'd even begun engaging in stolen-property recovery, but that was one step above becoming a repo man, and it was cash hard earned. At best, it involved trawling pawnshops for goods that had been sold on, and then breaking the news to the pawnbroker that he'd have to take a hit on the deal, assuming the broker was reputable in the first place and I could prove that he was selling a fenced item. At worst, it meant knocking on the doors of junkies and deadbeats and professional thieves, most of whom tended to look upon coop- eration as a last resort when lies, intimidation and — that old reliable — violence had failed to convince. In the end, you could slum it for only so long before you became part of the slums yourself.

Once it was agreed that I would take the Haight case, and Aimee had tried to stiff me on my rates as a matter of course, and I'd laughed and waited for her to get serious, she'd offered to see what she could find in the way of court documents related to the Selina Day killing. If they were sealed, as Randall Haight claimed they were, then there would be a limit to what would be available to her. In the meantime, Haight was on his way back to Pastor's Bay. There he would sit in his home office and write out a list of everyone whom he knew in the area, including all of his business contacts and all of his acquaintances, however casual, with a particular emphasis on recent arrivals in the area, and new clients. I would go up there to talk to him in a day or two, and try to establish whether there was anyone in town who had begun to act differently around him, or any new arrival who might have some connection to North Dakota, either to the juvenile facility in which Haight had served the early part of his sentence or to the state penitentiary. I'd also have to seek points of possible contact between the prisons in Newport and Berlin, although it seemed less likely that they might be the weak links, assuming the transfer under his new identity had been conducted smoothly. After that, it would be a matter of going through public and private records in an effort to establish the whereabouts of such individuals, in case one of them had made his or her way to eastern Maine and there had crossed paths with Randall Haight.

As I drove, I thought about the purpose of taunting Haight. Blackmail was the obvious answer, but that would presume the individual involved was not responsible for the disappearance of Anna Kore. Why potentially draw attention to yourself if you've already committed a serious crime involving the abduction of a young girl?

The second possibility was sadism: Someone

66

was enjoying watching Haight squirm, either for purely vindictive reasons or because he or she might have lost a child in similar circumstances, and tormenting a man guilty of a crime against a child is the next best thing to tormenting the person responsible for the crime against *your* child.

The third option was the one that interested me most, although I tried not to favor it too heavily in case I prejudiced myself, thereby risking missing crucial evidence to the contrary. That option, as Aimee had stated, was that Randall Haight was being targeted by the person who had taken Anna Kore, probably as a prelude to making Haight the scapegoat for the crime. If that was the case, then it would require Haight to panic and run, and the information about his past to be anonymously revealed to the police and the press, diverting the course of the investigation away from the person responsible for Anna's disappearance and toward Haight. Then again, if Haight didn't run, the information could still be leaked, and the investigation would take a new direction anyway.

Or Haight might find himself unable to handle the pressure and, advised by his lawyer, he could approach the police and confess the truth about his past, thereby theoretically removing the only weapon that his tormentor had to use against him: the secret nature of his past crime.

But Haight didn't have an alibi for the day that Anna Kore had disappeared, and that was a serious problem. He had told us that he was at home, going through the books of a furniture company based in Northport. The physical books and receipts were a mess, and he had intended to spend the entire day just trying to get them into some kind of order. Unfortunately, he was struck by a twenty-four-hour bug, and spent most of the time vomiting, or dozing in a nauseated state on his couch. Therefore he had not logged on to his computer, and he had not used the telephone or the Internet. Neither did he have any visitors, and what little he had eaten he had taken from his fridge at home. There was no food delivery to confirm his presence in the house. So Randall Haight, upon approaching the police, would then become a suspect, and even if he was entirely innocent his life would be altered by what followed, and Haight wanted to hold on to his current life if at all possible. He understood that nobody was likely to give him another new identity, and the power of the Internet meant that, once his past became known, the truth would follow him forever, or so he believed.

Randall Haight was a soul in torment. Aimee had tried to reassure him that she and I would do everything in our power to protect him, but I saw in his eyes that he knew better. His carefully constructed life was disintegrating, and the mask that he wore was peeling away from his skin, flaking and falling, to reveal once more the face of the killer William Lagenheimer.

6

The rain falling, the light gone, and the warmth of bars siren-calling to the men and women passing on the slick streets, although those who answered would probably have found their way to such places anyway, or at least to places like this particular dive in Woburn. The men and women who congregated there had little desire for their homes, and those who shared those homes with another knew that there was no great anticipation for their return.

It was called the Wanderer, and could best be described as having evolved, in its way, although its evolution was comparable to that of a primitive creature that had exchanged gills for lungs, clambered from sea to shore, and then progressed no farther, dispensing entirely with any further notion of advancement in favor of a barely refined primitivism. Its particular evolutionary path had proceeded as follows: A drunk passes another drunk a bottle; the two drunks find a bench upon which to rest the bottle; a third drunk, but one less drunk than the others, arrives and helps them pour their drinks; someone puts a wall around them so they have something to lean against as they poison themselves with alcohol; a roof is added so that the rain doesn't fall into their booze; a sign is hung up outside, notifying all and sundry that the Wanderer is now open for business. The end.

It had a floor of cheap green tile reminiscent of a hospital canteen, blackened by the cigarette butts that had been crushed into it over the years. There was a jukebox in the far corner, but nobody could ever recall its having been in use. It remained lit, and ostensibly available for business, but only drunks and non-regulars ever tried to make it play a song, and then it simply swallowed their money and remained silent. Complaints about the recalcitrant nature of the jukebox were always met with a shrug by the bartender, who would inform the complainant that the jukebox was rented, and it was all to do with the rental company, and only the company's staff was permitted to mess around with its innards, all of which were lies so barefaced it was a wonder the bartender's tongue didn't turn to ash and fall from his mouth before the last one could even be spoken. But if the complainant really cared that much about his fifty cents, the bartender would continue, he could write a letter, assuming the name of the company could be unearthed to begin with, which would be difficult because the company didn't exist. The jukebox was the bar's own, and had been ever since the original company behind its presence went out of business. It didn't make the bartenders much from its gradual accumulation of fools' quarters, but it garnered them a degree of amusement. Occasionally a patron might try to hit the jukebox to make it play, or at least return his money, at which point he would receive a warning, if he was lucky, or be ejected, if he was unluckier. If he was very unlucky, and had been

70

acting the asshole prior to taking on the jukebox, he would be ejected via the back door, and he might stumble along the way, and thus bang his head and hurt himself, which would occasion no great sense of regret on the part of anyone except himself.

Rarely were such actions necessary, though. For the most part, locals understood the nature of the bar, and non-locals rarely frequented it. Its name was not inapt, as it had no fixed identity of its own and attracted those with no particular national, sporting, or racial allegiances about which to get excited. It was owned by a Pole, managed by an Italian, and its bartenders were all mongrels, their only common denominator being their whiteness, for Woburn, Massachusetts, was ninety percent white, five percent Asian, and five percent whatever was left, and the non-white ten percent tended to give the Wanderer a wide berth. That was just the way things were, and nobody bothered to comment on it.

The Wanderer's décor was neutral, mainly because it didn't really have any décor, unless you counted a single cracked Budweiser mirror. Its chairs were mismatched and rested unevenly on the floor. Its tables were black and red, with faux-marble surfaces. The stools along the bar were dull steel with black vinyl seats that were last upholstered when John McNamara was still managing the Red Sox and they were bumbling along at .500, right before Joe Morgan replaced him and the team went on to win nineteen of twenty to take the AL East title, an achievement that went relatively unnoticed in the Wanderer,

71

as it didn't have a television at the time, and still didn't have one now. The Wanderer took no more interest in sports than it did in politics, art, culture, movies, or any other facet of existence unrelated to the act of pouring booze and receiving money for it in return. It had regulars, but beyond greeting them by name when they were so inclined none of the bartenders cared to investigate further the circumstances of their lives. For the most part, those who frequented the Wanderer came to be left alone. They didn't care much for other people, but then they didn't care much for themselves either, so at least they were consistent.

But it was still in business after more than forty years, because it knew its market. That market was drunks and wife-beaters. It was women a step above whoredom who'd been selling themselves for so long in return for drinks, company, and a different bed that they'd somehow managed to convince themselves that such short-term arrangements qualified as actual relationships. It was new arrivals with a one-name contact who were looking for work, and weren't particular about the work in question, or whether a Social Security number was required, or whether or not it was entirely legal. It was workers in worn boots and checked shirts who left messages behind the bar for other men, and businessmen in cheap suits and tieless shirts who stopped by on their way to Someplace Else, or To Meet A Guy, or for some similarly vague reason that justified a temporary halt at the Wanderer.

And it was individuals like the two men who sat at the bar close to the jukebox, their jackets zipped even though it was warm inside and they were on their second beers, their backs to the barred window that looked out on Winn Street. There was a *Boston Herald* folded in front of one of them, but it appeared to be unread. Neither of them was a large man, and a decade separated the younger from the older, although there was a similar hardness and weariness to their features. The younger of the two had light curly hair, and wore no jewelry: no rings, no watch, no chains. His brown leather blouson jacket was of the kind that was fashionable in the eighties but had been bought long after. His jeans were a faded blue, and speckled with fake paint marks. His sneakers bore the Nike swoosh, although they had never been near a Nike factory. A bottle of Bud stood before him, but he had barely sipped from it.

His companion was stockier, with long black hair greased back from his forehead but cut short at the sides and back, giving him a vaguely tribal aspect. He sported a two-day growth of beard, and his right hand repetitively twisted a pack of Camels: top, side, base, side, top, side, base, side. There were two gold rings on his right hand, and one on the little finger of his left. A thick gold chain looped around his right wrist, and another around his neck, a gold cross dangling from it. There were tattoos on both of his arms, mostly hidden by the sleeves of his black leather jacket, but the dark edges of the artwork on his back were visible at the base of his neck. He wore Timberland boots, heavily scuffed, and dark blue Levis. There was scarring around the thumb and forefinger of his right hand. It looked like an old burn.

His second beer was almost gone, and he was debating whether it was worth his while to order another. His name was Martin Dempsey, and his accent betrayed a life of wandering. In Irish bars, surrounded by immigrants, his many years on that side of the Atlantic found expression in his voice. Here it was less obvious, though still present in the rhythms of his speech. The other man was named Francis Ryan, and his accent was Boston Irish, with only the faintest hint of something else beneath it.

They were not regulars at the Wanderer, and nobody of their acquaintance frequented it. All Dempsey knew was that the Irish were not among its ethnic regulars, which was enough for him. It was out of town, off the beaten track. It was Elsewhere. That was precisely why they had chosen it, for there were now few places where it was truly safe for them to show their faces. The tiredness around their eyes, the strain lines around their mouths, were recent additions. These were hunted men.

'You want another?' said Dempsey.

'Nah, I don't think I'll be able to finish this one.'

'Why did you order it, then?'

'Politeness. I didn't want to see you drinking alone.'

'But I am drinking alone, 'cause you're not drinking at all. What's wrong with you?'

'I don't like drinking too much before a job.'

'From what I can see, you don't like drinking after a job either. You don't like drinking, period.'

'I can't handle it the way you can. Never could. The hangovers kill me.'

'You can't get a hangover on two beers. A child couldn't get a hangover on two beers.'

'Still, we have a job.'

'A job? We don't have a job. We're errand boys delivering a message. A job is different. A job has purpose, and a quantifiable outcome. A job has a reward at the end of it. This is a waste of my talents.' He corrected himself. 'Sorry, 'our' talents.'

'Go have a smoke. It'll kill some time.'

'I'm trying to quit.'

'Then why are you carrying around a pack of Camels?'

'I said I was trying to quit. I didn't say that I had. Anyway, do you see me smoking? No. I'm not smoking. I'm just toying with a box.'

'It's a thing, a, you know, a displacement activity.'

'Where the fuck did you learn words like 'displacement activity'?'

'I'm trying to improve myself.'

'The only way is up.'

'Just have one, will you? Stop playing with them.'

'Sorry,' said Dempsey, and he meant it, but still he kept moving the pack.

Ryan looked at the clock above the bar.

'You think that clock is right?'

'If it is, it's the only thing in here that's right. Even the jukebox is crooked, and there isn't a straight edge in the place. Fucking disgrace, is what it is.'

'It's old.'

'It's not old. Castles are old. France is old. This place isn't old. It's just badly built. It's a hole. It's worse than a hole. A hole is just empty. This is a hole with junk piled up inside it and deadbeats propping up the walls.'

'It's old for around here,' said Ryan.

'You have shares in it?'

'No.'

'Does your old man own it?'

'No.'

'Your mom turn tricks in the men's room?'

'No. She couldn't make enough here to cover the cab fare.'

'Then what's it to you if I criticize it, especially if it's true?'

'It's nothing to me.'

A couple in their late twenties at the table behind them laughed loudly and made a joke about Harvard and MIT. They looked too well dressed for the Wanderer, and even without the joke it was clear that they were slumming it for a night. The woman wasn't bad-looking, but her face was a little too long, and her mouth had too many white teeth for its size. The man wore a striped Ralph Lauren polo shirt, and khakis. His hair was excessively neat, and was held in place by a product that Ryan suspected was not meant to be worn by men. As far as Ryan was concerned, the guy looked like a dick, but although he was younger than Dempsey by six years, Ryan's attitude toward the world was less combative, and he had learned that if he allowed himself to be riled by every dick he encountered in his daily life he'd be dead of an aneurysm before he reached thirty.

Dempsey scowled at the couple's reflection in the mirror behind the bar, and Ryan felt his stomach tighten. Sometimes there was no telling how Dempsey might react to even the most innocuous of situations. For now, though, he contented himself with giving them the hard eye.

'You said it: nothing,' said Dempsey. 'That's what they are to us. This isn't our neighborhood. These aren't our people. We can say what we like about them.'

'I know that,' said Ryan. 'You think the clock is right?'

'Don't change the subject. You were born where?'

'Champaign, Illinois.'

'You ever been back there?'

'No. My old man was working out there when I was born. Didn't spend more than a month there before we moved to Southie. I've never been back.'

'Right. Don't get sentimental about a place that you left when you were a child. Remember what Oscar Wilde said.'

'Who's Oscar Wilde?'

'Jesus. He was a writer.'

'I never heard of him. That clock must be right. It feels right.'

'He said that 'sentimentality is the bank-holiday of cynicism.''

'I don't know what that means.'

'It means that if you're sentimental you're

really a cynic deep down. You don't want to be a cynic. I should know.'

'I'm not sentimental. I just think there are worse places than this.'

'There are worse places than just about anywhere. That doesn't mean anything, unless you're living in the worst place in the world, in which case it can only get better.'

'Africa.'

'What?'

'I figure the worst place is in Africa somewhere, one of those countries where they're starving and fighting and cutting off limbs. I've seen pictures: women with no arms, little children. Animals, they are.'

'Whatever. We have our share of them here as well. You don't have to go to Africa to find them.'

'Can I take a look at your watch? I want to check if that clock is right.'

'Leave the watch alone. What are you so worried about?'

'I don't want us to miss him.'

'We won't miss him. In fact, the longer we wait, the less likely we are to miss him.'

'Hey.' Ryan beckoned the bartender to him. 'Is that clock right?'

The bartender sidled over, wiping his hands on a dishcloth that hung by his belt over his crotch. He was skinny and bald, with bad teeth, and had tended bar at the Wanderer for almost two decades. Some said that he could even remember a time when the jukebox worked. He wore a green T-shirt with the bar's name on the left breast. The T-shirts were not for sale. Then again, nobody had ever tried to buy one.

'Yeah, I make sure it is. I don't want to spend a minute longer in here than I have to.'

'That's the spirit,' said Dempsey. 'Make the customers feel wanted.'

'If I make them feel wanted, they'll stay,' said the bartender. 'They'll try to talk to me. I don't want the customers talking to me.'

'Not even me?'

'Not even you.'

'Anyone would think that you didn't want to make any money,' said Dempsey.

'Yeah, I was saving up to buy a yacht with my tips, but that dream died.'

'The clock is right,' said Ryan. 'We should go.'

'Yeah, yeah, all right. Jesus, you're like an old woman.'

There was more laughter from the couple behind them, louder this time. Dempsey looked back at them over his shoulder. The laughter was silenced, but it was followed by a soft giggle from the woman as the man said something to her. Dempsey took one of the cigarettes from the pack and stuck it between his lips but didn't light it.

'You know them?' he asked the bartender.

'No,' said the bartender. 'But then I don't know you either.'

'You need to be more selective with your clientele.'

'It's all natural selection here.'

'Yeah? Well, you're about to see Darwinism in action.'

Dempsey was on the guy before Ryan could

even react. By the time Ryan reached the table, Dempsey had his forearm jammed under the preppie's chin, and his knee in the guy's balls, the whole weight of Dempsey trying to force him through the wall.

'Did you say something about me?' said Dempsey. 'Well, did you?'

Some of his spittle landed on the man's face, which was rapidly turning a deep red. The guy tried to shake his head, but he could barely move it. A choking noise forced itself from his lips. The woman beside him reached out as if to pull Dempsey's arm away. He turned his head toward her and said, 'Don't.'

'Please,' said the woman.

'Please what?' said Dempsey.

'Please leave him alone.'

'You're not laughing now, are you, you horse-faced bitch?' said Dempsey. 'Answer me. *Answer me!*'

'No, I'm not laughing.'

As if to confirm the fact, she began to cry. Carefully, Ryan touched Dempsey on the shoulder.

'Come on, let it go. We're done here.'

Slowly, Dempsey released his hold on the man.

'Go back to fucking Cambridge where you belong,' he said. 'If I ever see you again, I'll rape her and make you watch.'

Dempsey rose and backed away. He was breathing hard. His victim was so shaken that he hadn't moved. That was the way with the weak ones: If you were on them fast, and shocked them enough, you didn't need to cause them any real harm.

The bartender watched Dempsey carefully. He hadn't made any effort to stop what was taking place, but that was because he'd seen it all before, and was prepared to let events take something of their course before intervening. Still, he didn't look impressed. They wouldn't be welcome here again, not that they had any plans to return.

Dempsey tossed a twenty on the bar.

'Toward your yacht,' he told the bartender.

'I'll name it after you,' said the bartender. 'Do you spell 'Asshole' with one s or two?'

'You can spell it with one s. That way, we'll know it's yours when we set fire to it.'

He picked up his pack of cigarettes and dropped them in his jacket pocket.

'Come on then,' he said to Ryan. 'Let's get it over with.'

7

The house was unexceptional in every way, just one more anodyne suburban box in a street composed of identical suburban boxes outside Bedford, each with its car in the drive, and the flicker of TV screens in front rooms. There were Halloween decorations in place: tombstones, and scarecrows, and pumpkins that had begun to rot, drawing the last of the night insects. Ryan felt the weight of beer pressing on his bladder. He could have gone to the men's room at the Wanderer if it hadn't been for Dempsey and his actions. Now here Dempsey was again, cursing the existences of people he didn't even know, as though the quality of his own life was worth more than the change from a nickel.

'Look at all this shit on the lawns,' said Dempsey, as he parked the car. 'How many of these people really have children of their own, you think?'

'What do you mean?'

'You don't think there's something wrong with lonely old men putting out Halloween crap to attract children?'

'No, I don't think there's anything wrong — ' Ryan began to say, then caught himself before he went any further. It didn't seem wise to suggest that there was anything okay about using Halloween decorations to attract children, because that raised the specter of why one might be trying to attract them to begin with. He tried again. 'You're making it sound bad when it isn't. It's not like that. It's just people getting into the spirit of the season, like at Christmas.'

'Don't get me started on Christmas either,' said Dempsey.

'You know, you're a miserable bastard.'

'And you're too trusting. It'll be the death of you.'

Dempsey checked his gun, which prevented him from seeing the look that Ryan sent his way. Had he glimpsed it, he might have reappraised his relationship with the younger man. Instead, it was lost to him. When he surfaced, Ryan's forehead was furrowed only by the slightest of lines.

'We're just supposed to talk to him,' he said.

'We *are* going to talk to him. We just want to make sure we have his full attention when we do. And when did you get so sensitive?'

'He's not a tough guy. I've met him.'

'You want to try an experiment? Here's an experiment. Close your eyes.'

Ryan didn't close his eyes. He didn't want to. He didn't like being around Dempsey with his eyes closed. He was coming to the conclusion that he didn't like being around Dempsey even with his eyes wide open.

'Why should I close my eyes?'

'It's just a thing. Come on, do it.'

Ryan closed his eyes, and waited. Five seconds went by before Dempsey said, 'Okay, open them again.'

When Ryan did so, the muzzle of the gun was

an inch away from his face, and although a part of him had been expecting something of the kind, the shock was still enough to cause his sphincter to loosen in response, and he had to tense it to bring it under control before he shamed himself.

'You see?' said Dempsey. 'Tough guy or not, that hole commands attention.'

Ryan swallowed. He didn't speak until he was sure there was enough moisture in his mouth and throat.

'Are you finished?' he said.

'I'm just kidding with you,' said Dempsey as he lowered the gun. 'You really are too sensitive.'

Ryan shook his head. He wanted to take deep breaths. He wanted to put his head against the cool window and wait for the waves of dread to stop pulsing through him. He wanted to stop running and hiding. He had started to believe that the fear of what might come was worse than the thing itself.

'Don't shake your head at me,' said Dempsey. 'What?'

'Nothing.'

'Hey, I'm sorry, all right?'

'Yeah.'

'Come on, don't be like that.'

'You almost made me piss myself.'

Dempsey smothered a grin. 'My bad.'

'It was all that beer you made me drink.'

'All that one bottle?'

'Beer just goes through me. I don't know what it is about it. Maybe I got an allergy.'

Dempsey stepped from the car, the gun now

hidden in the folds of his coat, and Ryan followed. There was nobody around, and no cars moved along the street. Ryan was a little happier being this far from Boston. The last job like this had been in Everett, which had originally been part of Charlestown way back, and even its historical connections to their old stomping ground had made him sweat. If they showed their faces in Charlestown proper, they'd be dead before the nearest lights changed.

They walked up the short drive to the front door, Dempsey taking in the untended lawn and the weeds in the flower beds as they went.

'That's a disgrace,' he said.

'It'll be winter soon,' said Ryan. 'Weeds will die. Lawn won't grow. What does it matter?'

'It's an indication of a state of mind. You take care of all of your affairs or you take care of none of them. That's how he's in this trouble to begin with.'

'Because he didn't mow his lawn?'

'Yeah, because he didn't mow his lawn. What is it with you tonight?' Dempsey rang the doorbell, but his attention was fixed on his partner.

'There's a game on. I'd prefer to be watching it.'

'Yeah, well there's a game on here too. This is what pays your bills. You need to step up to the plate here. You don't pay attention, you make mistakes.'

'He drives a gypsy cab. What's he gonna do, overcharge us?'

A shadow appeared behind the frosted glass,

giving Dempsey just enough time to raise a finger in warning before the door opened a crack and a woman's face appeared. Ryan could see that she had the security chain in place, but it looked loose to him; that, and the fact she had answered the door after dark, meant that her husband probably wasn't home yet. Now Dempsey would have something else to complain about, since it was Ryan who had hustled them from the bar to begin with.

'Mrs. Napier?' said Dempsey.

The woman nodded. She looked tired and badly worn, just like her clothes, although Ryan thought that she might clean up well. The little that he could see of her body seemed trim.

'We're looking for your husband,' said Dempsey.

'He's at work,' she said.

Ryan watched her trying to gauge the situation. It was after eight, there were two strangers at the door, and they now knew that the man of the house wasn't around. She had two choices: number one, to claim that there was someone else there with her, or —

She went for number two.

'I'm expecting him back soon, though. I can give him a message, if you like.'

'We'd prefer to wait and give it to him ourselves, if it's all the same to you,' said Dempsey.

Mrs. Napier's mouth opened and closed. Ryan could see her getting worried. Maybe she knew about her husband's work on the side, or perhaps she'd just guessed when the cash began

86

to flow more freely. He wondered if she was the kind to ask questions. If she was, then her husband wasn't the kind to answer them. He'd always struck Ryan as sullen and taciturn, and his wife didn't have the face of a woman who was being smothered in spousal affection. Whatever she knew or suspected, it was enough to connect their arrival on her doorstep with any doubts she might have about the state of her husband's affairs. Ryan liked to think that he could blend in with a crowd and look like a regular guy, but Dempsey carried the smell of the streets with him. At best, they could expect her to call and warn him. At best.

'Well, I'm not sure when he'll be home.'

'Soon,' said Dempsey. 'You told us he'd be back soon.'

'That changes. I never know. He drives a cab. If he's having a good night, then sometimes he stays out late.'

'It's quiet all over tonight,' said Dempsey. 'I don't figure this for a late one.'

'Obviously you're free to wait in your car,' said Mrs. Napier. 'It's cold. I'm going to close the door now.'

She tried to follow through, but Dempsey's foot was in the gap. Ryan watched the pallor seep into her face.

'Please take your foot away,' she said.

'We'd like to wait inside,' said Dempsey. 'Like you say, it's cold out.'

'If you don't remove your foot, I'll call the police.'

'That settles it, then,' said Dempsey. His hand

shot through the gap and grabbed Mrs. Napier by the hair, pulling her face toward him until it was sandwiched by the door and the frame. He let her see the gun.

'Take the chain off.'

'Please — '

Now he pressed the muzzle hard against her forehead. 'I won't ask again.'

'I can't take it off without closing the door.'

'You don't have to close it all the way.'

'I have to close it a little.'

'That's okay. Give me your left hand.'

She hesitated. Dempsey pressed the gun harder against skull. She yelped in pain.

'Easy,' said Ryan instinctively, and Dempsey bared his teeth at him in warning.

'Give me your hand,' he repeated.

She did as she was told. Her wrist was very thin, and as brittle as the skeleton of a bird. Dempsey turned her hand so that her fingers were flat against the frame of the door. He handed the gun to Ryan, then slipped a knife from his pocket. He flicked the sharp blade and pressed it hard beneath the top knuckles of Mrs. Napier's fingers. Seconds later, blood began to flow.

'If you screw around, I'll cut off the tips of your fingers,' said Dempsey. 'Close the door against your hand and lose the chain.'

Slowly, she closed the door. They heard her fumbling with the chain.

'It still won't open,' she said. She had started to sob.

'Try harder.'

She pushed against the door, trying to close the gap a little more. The pressure on her fingers made the blood flow faster.

'It hurts,' she said.

'And you can make it stop,' said Dempsey. He was getting anxious. The street had been empty until now, but Ryan could see the figure of a man approaching from the east, walking his dog before bedtime.

The chain came free. The door opened.

They stepped inside.

* * *

'Nice. Your husband buy this?'

Dempsey was standing by a flat-screen TV, the kind that was so large you had to pivot your head to take in the whole picture. It looked as if it had only recently come out of its packaging. Beneath it was a Blu-ray player, a cable box, and an amplifier for the home theater system. It was a neat set-up, spoiled only by the clothes drying on a rack by the radiator behind the TV.

Mrs. Napier nodded. She was still pale, and shaking with shock. Ryan had found a clean cloth in the kitchen and had given it to her so that she could bind her wounded hand. The blade hadn't required much pressure on it to break the skin, and there was a lot of blood soaking through the material.

'New? It looks new.'

Mrs. Napier found her voice. 'It's pretty new.'

'Driving a cab must be more lucrative than I thought,' said Dempsey. 'If I'd known just how

89

much money could be made on it, I'd be driving one myself. How about it: You think we should go into the cab business?'

Ryan didn't reply. He thought Mrs. Napier might be about to vomit. The first floor of the house was an open plan, with only a decorative arch separating the kitchen from the living area. Ryan moved toward the sink.

'Where are you going?'

'She's in shock. I'm going to get some water for her.'

Dempsey looked at Mrs. Napier.

'Are you in shock?'

She didn't reply for a moment, then said, 'I don't know. I feel nauseous.'

'Shock it is, then,' said Dempsey.

There were cups on the draining board. Ryan filled one with water and brought it back to Mrs. Napier. She took the cup, but didn't say thank you. Ryan wasn't exactly waiting for her to do so, but still, it would have been polite.

'Why are you shocked, though?' asked Dempsey. 'Are you shocked because you're hurt? Are you shocked because we're here? Or are you shocked because your cab driver husband seems to be able to afford Donald Trump's own home theater?'

Mrs. Napier sipped her water and kept her eyes down.

'What's your name?' said Dempsey.

'Helen.'

'So, Helen, your husband been buying anything else that we should know about? You had a new dress lately? Maybe you're eating out in nicer places? You can tell us. We'd like to know.'

'Just the TV.'

'*Just* the TV?' Dempsey laughed. He moved to the bookshelves, which were sparsely populated with books — a couple of paperback novels, a book on home finance, and a set of encyclopedias so old that they probably still contained pictures of airplanes with propellers — but had a whole shelf devoted to new Blu-ray discs, most of them still in their plastic wrapping. He checked out the titles, running his fingers along the spines, then stepped into the kitchen, examining the white goods, opening drawers. When he was done, he told Ryan to keep an eye on the woman while he went upstairs. Soon they heard closet doors slamming, and the tinkling of glass as something small and delicate broke. Helen Napier tried to get up, but Ryan put his hand on her shoulder, forcing her back into the chair.

'Why are you doing this?' she asked.

'I'm sorry.'

'No you're not.'

She was trying not to cry, and she succeeded. The sight reminded Ryan uncomfortably of the woman back at the Wanderer. It didn't make him feel good about himself.

When Dempsey came back downstairs, he had a shoebox in his hand. He squatted before Mrs. Napier and showed her the contents. The bills were neatly stacked and bound: twenties only. Ryan guessed there were probably two or three grand in the box.

'You don't trust the banks?' said Dempsey.

'I don't know what that is,' said Mrs. Napier, and Ryan believed her.

'It's money, that's what it is.'

'I didn't know it was up there.'

'Husband keeping secrets from you? That's bad. Once the lies start, it's the death of a marriage.' He leaned in so that his face was close to Mrs. Napier's. 'You want to know how it got there? I'll tell you. Your husband doesn't just drop passengers at their destinations. He picks up and drops off packages too. He's a regular courier service for protection money, cocaine, marijuana, maybe a little heroin. He's not a dealer, but he works for the dealer. Our problem is that your husband now maybe fancies himself as a little bit of a dealer after all, an independent operator. Just a little bit.' Dempsey placed a thumb and forefinger close together. 'Teeny-tiny. With that in mind, he's been skimming from the product: enough to earn himself some extra cash, and irritate the people who were paying for the full weight, not most of the weight, because if they'd wanted cornstarch and talcum powder they'd have gone to Walmart. So that means we have to talk to him and find out how much he's taken, and how much he's made, and reach an agreement about restitution. See?'

'My husband doesn't use drugs,' said Mrs. Napier.

'What?' Dempsey appeared genuinely confused.

'I said, 'My husband doesn't use drugs.''

'Who said anything about 'using' drugs? Your

husband is *transporting* drugs. *Doing* don't enter into it. If he was skimming and then consuming he'd be even dumber than he is already, and you'd be watching *American Idol* on an RCA with a coat-hanger aerial. You know, you don't seem so smart. That's really unfortunate, because in my experience dumb bitches are the ones who drag their husbands down, and not the other way around. Is it your fault that all this has happened? Maybe you were the one who wanted the nice TV, and better clothes, and trips to Florida to work on your tan. Is that it?'

'No,' she said. 'I don't want any of those things.'

'So what do you want?'

She swallowed hard. 'For this to be made right.'

Dempsey patted her bare leg, then let his hand linger there a couple of seconds too long. 'Maybe you aren't so dumb after all.'

He looked at his watch.

'Phone your husband. Find out where he is.'

Mrs. Napier shook her head. 'You're going to hurt him.'

'No, we're not. We're just here to slap his wrist.'

'Then why do you have a gun?'

'Jesus, you as well. You married the wrong guy.' Dempsey jerked a thumb at Ryan. 'You and him should get together. I have a gun because often people are excitable, and it's my experience that seeing a gun helps to calm them down. On the other hand, sometimes people don't recognize the gravity of a situation, in which case the gun tends to focus their minds wonderfully.

93

Do as I tell you: Call your husband, and soon all of this will be over.'

Mrs. Napier stood, wiping at her tears. Dempsey stayed close behind her as she went to her purse and retrieved her cell phone from it.

'What are you going to say?' he asked.

'I don't know. What do you want me to say?'

Dempsey smiled. 'Now you have the right idea. You ask him when he's coming home. Tell him — ' Dempsey's smile widened. 'Tell him his new TV is on the fritz. You turned it on and smoke started coming out of the back, so you turned it off again, and now you're worried. You got that?'

'Yes, I understand.'

Just to make sure that she did understand, Dempsey showed her the knife again, letting her see her reflection in it. She already knew what the knife could do, and what he was prepared to do to her with it. In her case, it was more effective than the threat of a gun. A gun was a weapon of last resort, but a blade had the capacity to be incremental in the damage that it could inflict.

Mrs. Napier pressed the Redial button and her husband's name came up on the screen. Dempsey held his head close to hers so that he could hear both ends of the conversation, but the phone went straight to voice mail. He nudged Mrs. Napier and, somewhat haltingly, she passed on the lie about the TV and asked her husband to call her and let her know when she could expect him home. After that, she returned to her chair.

Ryan went back to the kitchen and made a pot of coffee, and the three of them sat in uncompanionable silence waiting for the arrival of the elusive Harry Napier. After half an hour had gone by, Dempsey began to get fidgety. He walked around the room, looking at framed photographs, leafing through papers in drawers and in closets, and all the time Mrs. Napier's eyes followed him, furious and humiliated. Dempsey found a photo album and began turning the pages. He stopped when he came to a photograph of Mrs. Napier in a bathing suit. It had probably been taken four or five years earlier, and it showed off her figure to good effect.

'You don't have children, right?' said Dempsey.

Something gaped darkly in Mrs. Napier's eyes before she answered, like a wound briefly exposed, but Ryan saw it.

'No, we don't have children.'

Dempsey removed the photo from its page and held it up for Mrs. Napier to see. 'Means you still look like this, then, doesn't it?'

'Jesus,' said Ryan. 'Do you — ?'

'Shut up,' said Dempsey, not even glancing at Ryan. His eyes held Mrs. Napier's. 'I asked you a question. You still look like this?'

'I don't know. That was taken so long ago.'

'How long?'

'A decade?'

'That a question, or a statement?'

'A statement.'

'You're lying. This picture isn't ten years old. Five maybe, but not ten.'

'I don't remember. I don't look at old pictures very often.'

Dempsey laid the album on a chair but kept the photo. Once more, he squatted before Mrs. Napier, looking from the photo to her, and then back again.

'Do you recall why we came here, Mrs. Napier. Or Helen? Can I call you Helen?'

Mrs. Napier didn't answer the second question, only the first.

'You said you were here to give my husband a slap on the wrist.' Ryan saw her scratching anxiously at her left leg, just above the knee. There was a deep redness there, and he wondered if she had some skin condition, or if the scratching was a nervous tic.

'That's right,' said Dempsey. 'We're here to give him a message about how bad it is to steal, to make him understand the consequences of his actions. I know you think we want to kill him, but we don't. Killing is bad for business. It attracts attention. If we kill him, then we also have to kill you, and suddenly we're looking for sheets and sacks, and we're taking night drives to marshes and woods, and, frankly, we don't have that kind of time on our hands. Similarly, I'm getting bored waiting around your lovely but dull home. We do have to get that message to your husband, but maybe you can pass it on to him for us. Or, more precisely, for me.'

Dempsey looked at Ryan. Ryan shook his head. 'No.'

'I wasn't asking your permission. I'm indicating that you should leave and wait for me outside.'

'Come on, man, this isn't right. She's frightened enough. Napier will make amends. He's got no choice.'

'Wait in the car, Frankie,' and Ryan heard the warning in his voice, and knew that if he pushed it further Dempsey would be on him, and a confrontation would occur that might require serious action, and it wasn't time for that, not yet.

Mrs. Napier's mouth folded down, and she began to tremble.

'Please,' she said. 'I've done all that you've asked.'

She looked to Ryan for help, but Ryan wasn't going to help her. He wanted to, he really did, but he couldn't.

'I'm sorry,' he said again.

'No,' said Mrs. Napier. 'No, no, no . . . '

Dempsey stood. He reached down and stroked Mrs. Napier's hair.

'Close the door behind you, Frankie,' he said, and the last thing that Ryan saw was Dempsey taking Mrs. Napier by the hand and leading her to the couch, her feet dragging behind her as she tried to resist, her face turned away from him, her eyes still pleading with Ryan for help that would never come.

Ryan closed the door and walked to the car, his hands in his pockets and his head low.

It couldn't last. Everything was falling apart.

Soon, he believed that he might have to kill Martin Dempsey.

8

It was not yet nine. I sat in my office at home, listening to the rain fall on the roof, a strangely comforting sound. The clouds had smothered the moon, and from my window I saw no artificial light break the darkness. There were only variations of shadow: trees against grass, land bordering black water, and the sea waiting beyond. Beside me I had a cup of coffee, and the list of names connected with his trial that Randall Haight had provided. I found myself thinking about Selina Day. I wanted to see a picture of her, because in this she had been all but forgotten. For Haight, she was a ghost from his past inconveniently summoned to the present by the taunts of another. The story of her life had been written, and given its conclusion. If she mattered at all it was simply because she shared an age with Anna Kore, and it could only be hoped that they did not already share a similar fate.

So I began trawling the Internet for details about the killing of Selina Day. There was less information than I might have wished, mainly because her death occurred in the glorious days before anything and everything ended up on the Internet, either as fact or speculation. Eventually I had amassed a small pile of printed pages, most of them from the archives of the local *Beacon & Explainer*, detailing the discovery of Selina Day's body, the beginning of the investigation, and the eventual questioning, indictment, and sentencing of two unnamed juveniles in connection with the crime. The reports never failed to mention the race of the murdered girl, and the story gravitated toward the front of the paper only when the ages of the boys involved became an issue.

But I found that for which I had been searching: a picture of the murdered girl. In it, she was younger than she was when she died, probably by three or four years. Her hair was worn in pigtails, and she had a pronounced gap between her upper front teeth that might eventually have been corrected by braces. She was wearing a checked dress with a lace collar. The photograph had been taken side-on, so that Selina had turned her head slightly to face the camera. It was not a formal pose, and she appeared happy and relaxed. She looked like what she was: a pretty little girl on her way to becoming a young woman. I wondered why a more recent photo had not been used, then figured that this was the picture her mother had chosen to represent her. This was how she had wanted her daughter to be remembered, as her little girl but with a whole life ahead of her. One could not look at such an image and not feel grief for those left behind, and anger at the end Selina had met.

The accompanying articles did not include the kind of hand-wringing features usually inspired by such cases, typically represented by the twin poles of 'What Is Happening to Our Children and What Can We Do to Make Them Better People Less Inclined to Kill Teenage Girls?' and 'What Is Happening to Our Children and Can We Make Them Better People by Locking Them Up Forever, or Trying Them As Adults and Sentencing Them to Death?' Instead, the reports remained studiedly factual, even after a minimum eighteen-year sentence had been passed on each of the boys. As soon as the case had concluded, it appeared to fall entirely from view.

That was, I supposed, hardly surprising. A small community would not wish to have that particular wound repeatedly reopened: a murder committed by two of their own, a pair of apparently normal young boys, against a black girl, who was not one of their own by virtue of her race but was still only a girl. The situation was further complicated by the fact that the black and white communities in that part of North Dakota shared a common bond through baseball. North Dakota, along with Minnesota, was one of the few states in the Union where blacks and whites had always played together with little trouble. Freddie Sims and Chappie Gray had been the first black athletes to play semipro baseball in North Dakota, soon followed by Art Hancock, the 'black Babe Ruth,' and his brother Charlie. Eventually the Bismarck town team attracted the great Satchel Paige, and it was in North Dakota that Paige played alongside white men for the first time. Upon retiring from the game, a number of the black players decided to spend the rest of their lives in Drake Creek, and there was still a small museum in the town devoted to their achievements. In other words, the sex-related killing of a black girl by two white boys would have threatened the delicate racial balance that this part of North Dakota had managed to maintain for so long. Better to deal with it, then set aside all that had happened as extraordinary and move on. And perhaps those who felt that way were right: The killing of children by children is a terrible exception, or it was until gangbangers and ignorant men began glorifying the code of living and dying by the gun in projects and ghettos. Each instance deserved to be examined, if only so that some understanding of the individual circumstances might be reached, but whether or not there was a general lesson for society in a case like the Selina Day killing seemed unlikely.

Still, by the end of my search I had confirmed a number of the names on Haight's list: the two public defenders appointed to the boys, the prosecuting attorney (who was the same in both cases), and the judge. The witness statements were minimal, as the boys had confessed to the crime before trial, so the issue at hand became purely a matter of sentencing. No mention was made of the deal that Randall Haight had claimed was struck, the social experiment that would ultimately allow him and Lonny Midas to escape the shadow of their crime, publicly at least. Again, that wasn't particularly unusual; to some degree, it would have been dependent on the progress made by the boys while in custody, and no sane prosecutor, defender, or judge hoping for a degree of advancement in the judiciary would willingly have become a public party to such an agreement in the immediate aftermath of the trial.

I started working on the four names. One of the public defenders, Larraine Walker, was dead; she had died in a motorcycle accident in 1996. The second public defender, Cory Felder, had dropped off the radar, and I could find no record of him after 1998. The prosecuting attorney was a man named R. Dean Bailey. That name rang a bell. A couple of keystrokes later, R. Dean Bailey was revealed as a repeatedly unsuccessful challenger for a Republican nomination to Congress. Bailey's views on immigration, welfare, and, indeed, government in general were colorful to say the least, even by the standards of some of the vitriol that regularly emerged from the extreme conservative wing of the Republican Party. In fact, like most of his kind, his views on federal government could best be summarized as 'keep it as small as possible unless it's convenient for me and my friends to have it otherwise, and as long as I can still be a part of it and stick my nose in the federal trough'; or, to put it another way, it's all waste except for the part that benefits me.

Meanwhile, his views on race, any religion that didn't involve Christ, anyone whose first language wasn't English, and the poor in general would have earned him sidelong glances at a Nazi Party convention. Thankfully, somewhere on the Republican National Committee common sense continued to prevail against giving Bailey a national forum for outpourings that bordered on hate speech and sedition. I couldn't begin to imagine what journey he had taken from being a prosecutor prepared to allow two boys convicted of second-degree murder a chance at a normal life to someone who was now advocating letting the poor starve and proposing limits on the right to religious freedom, but it didn't seem likely that he would be overjoyed at being reminded of the Selina Day case. Bailey was now a partner in the law firm of Young Grantham Bailey. A quick search produced a list of cases that routinely pitted YGB's exclusively wealthy and influential business clients against communities and individuals whose quality of life had allegedly been damaged, sometimes to the point of mortality, by the actions of those for whom Bailey and his partners acted as mouthpieces, firefighters, and bully boys. They seemed particularly adept at employing delaying tactics that caused cases to drag on for years, draining their opponents of funds and energy or, as in some particularly odious cases, until the plaintiffs simply died and their cases died with them. I made a note to call Young Grantham Bailey in the morning, if only to see how Bailey might respond, then put a line through it. Randall Haight had enough problems without drawing the attention of a man like R. Dean Bailey to him, especially an R. Dean Bailey who had undergone some form of reverse Damascene conversion.

That left the judge, Maurice P. Bowens. According to Haight, Bowens had been the prime instigator of the proposal to offer the boys new identities prior to their release. I found a short online biography of Bowens, prepared upon his retirement from the bench. He had begun practicing law in Pennsylvania, but had subsequently moved to North Dakota, eventually becoming a federal-court judge there. He had retired in 2005, indicating his desire to live permanently in his home just outside Bismarck, there to watch the 'mighty Missouri flow by his doors,' as he put it.

There was only one Maurice P. Bowens listed in the Bismarck directory. Having nothing better to do, I called the number, and a woman answered on the third ring. I gave her my name and occupation, and asked if this was the residence of the former judge. She told me that it was.

'I'm his daughter, Anita,' she said.

'Would it be possible to speak to your father? It's in connection with one of his old cases.'

'I'm sorry. My father has suffered a series of strokes over the past eighteen months. They've left him very frail, and he speaks only with great difficulty. I take care of his affairs for him now.'

'I'm sorry to hear about his illness. I'd be grateful if you could mention to your father that I called. It's about Randall Haight, or William Lagenheimer, depending upon how your father chooses to remember him. I'm acting on Mr. Haight's behalf. Please tell your father that, as far as I'm aware, Mr. Haight hasn't done anything wrong, but he's in a difficult situation and any information that your father might be in a position to pass on to me would help.'

'What kind of information were you looking for?' she asked.

I mentioned the Selina Day case, and the

agreement that had been struck with R. Dean Bailey. I asked for any background to the agreement that her father might be able to give, along with any further details that he felt might be pertinent. I was stumbling in the dark, to be honest, but at this point any light that he could shed on the case would be better than none.

If the names I had given Anita meant anything to her, she didn't say. She agreed to take my numbers, both fax and phone, and my e-mail address. I also gave her Aimee Price's details, and said that I was employed by her on Haight's behalf, and was therefore bound by rules of client confidentiality. She said that her father was sleeping, but as soon as he woke she would mention my call to him. I thanked her, hung up, then called Aimee Price to let her know that I had established some form of contact with Bowens. After that, with nothing more to be done for now, I made myself a simple meal of penne with pesto and ate it while watching the news on the portable TV in my kitchen. Anna Kore's disappearance was the second story after a big crash north of Augusta, but it was clear to me that the networks were already losing interest. After all, there were only so many ways to say that no progress had been made. Anna Kore would make it back to the top of the news only if she was found, alive or dead.

When the news had concluded, I took a Willy Vlautin novel into my office and lay back on my battered old couch to read, but that picture of Selina Day kept intruding on my concentration.

105

Eventually I think I must have dozed for a time as I was going over the details of Randall Haight's story in my mind. Reality blurred in the way that it does when one drops unexpectedly into sleep, and I thought I saw Haight outside my window peering in at me. His skin was very pale, and there were wrinkles on his scalp and cheeks that I had not noticed before, as though his skull had begun to shrink. He raised his right hand and plunged it into his flesh, and his face came away. What was exposed was bloody and waxen, but still recognizably him. He repeated the action over and over, alternating hands and discarding the remains at his feet like a spider shedding its external skin in order to grow, until only a blank visage remained where once his features had been, the eye sockets empty and yet, somehow, still weeping.

A pinging sound from my computer brought me back to consciousness. There was an e-mail in my in-box from Anita Bowens, consisting of a short message and an attachment. The message read:

> My father hopes that Randall, as he now thinks of him (and, as he hopes, Randall now thinks of himself) is doing well, that he has grasped the chance to leave his past behind while still regretting his actions, and sends him his kindest regards. Nevertheless, he requests that there should be no further contact with him from either Randall or yourself regarding this matter. Anything of relevance to your inquiries can be found in the accompanying documents.

106

Yours,
Anita Bowens

P.S. I know a little of the history behind this case, for my father has referred in the past to the 'imperfect agreement' reached with the prosecutor, Mr. Bailey. The documents included here should indicate the reasons for my father's dissatisfaction. For now, it's enough to recognize that he wanted the boys to be tried as juveniles, not as adults. Both the attorney general and the district attorney disagreed, as did Mr. Bailey, and prosecutorial discretion won out. Rather than abandon the boys entirely to the dubious mercies of the system, the price of my father's acquiescence was a new start for them once their sentences were served. I suspect that my father still believes he sold his principles too cheaply.
A.B.

I opened the attachment. It consisted of a scanned copy of Maurice Bowens's letter to the Supreme Court of Pennsylvania indicating his decision to cease practicing in the state in protest at its continued insistence on trying children as adults and allowing them to be sentenced to life without parole; and an article published in a law journal expanding on the theme.

According to the article, which contained more recent footnotes updating some of its points and statistics, Pennsylvania was one of twenty-two states, along with the District of Columbia, that allowed children as young as seven to be tried as adults, and one of forty-two that allowed children to be sentenced to life without parole for a first criminal conviction. Pennsylvania alone accounted for more than twenty percent of the children in the United States who faced the prospect of dying behind bars if convicted. Bowens's piece argued that, by 'enthusiastically' sentencing thirteen- and fourteen-year-old children, and younger, to die in prison, both for homicide and non-homicide offenses, the state was guilty of 'cruel and unusual' punishment and was therefore in violation of the Eighth Amendment of the Constitution, of international law, and, theoretically, of the Convention on the Rights of the Child, which, as Bowens pointed out, the United States had signally failed to ratify, making it and Somalia the only countries to refuse to do so. He said that such a law took no account of the vulnerability of children, of the developmental and legal distinctions between children and adults, and of children's capacity for growth, change, and redemption.

'By allowing the incarceration of children without hope of parole, we have shown ourselves to be unworthy of the trust and responsibility placed in us as lawmakers,' Bowens concluded. 'We have confused punishment with retribution, and sacrificed justice to injustice. But, worst of all, we have allowed cruelty and expediency to govern us, permitting our humanity to fall away. No country that treats the most vulnerable of its young people in this way deserves to call itself civilized. We have failed in our duty as lawmakers, as parents, as protectors of children, and as human beings.'

I forwarded the email to Aimee, then printed

108

out the letter and the article and added them to the file on the case. I hadn't known about the Convention on the Rights of the Child, but being in bed with Somalia didn't strike me as anything about which to be proud. It wasn't hard to figure out why the Somalis hadn't signed — any country that swells the ranks of its armies with child soldiers wasn't in much of a position to sign anything other than a receipt for more guns — but last time I looked, the United States military wasn't so depleted that it was forced to recruit in grade schools. Still, it was clear that somebody somewhere in the US government had come up with an argument against signing an agreement to protect children. Whoever it was, I'm sure that his kids were proud of him, and the Somalis sent him a card at Christmas.

So Bowens had left Pennsylvania, worked his way up the ranks of the North Dakota judiciary, and eventually had found himself judging a case that tested his principles once again. But instead of resigning again in the face of prosecutorial intransigence he had struck a deal guaranteeing the boys a fresh start, even if it meant compromising his principles, because better a small victory than no victory at all. If his daughter was to be believed, the nature of that compromise had tormented him ever since.

I looked again at Bowens's letter. I regretted that I hadn't been able to talk to him in person, and that any further communication between us now appeared to be unwelcome. Given the opportunity, I would have asked him about the third person involved in that killing decades ago, the

109

final apex of the triangle connecting three lives: Lonny Midas. Haight had presented Midas as the instigator of what had occurred, but, as I'd pointed out to Aimee, that might simply have been the complexion that Haight chose to place on events. Again, I was reminded of how he had reverted at times to an unnerving juvenility during his description of the killing and its aftermath. It was the response of a cornered child, facing punishment for doing something bad, to blame someone else for the worst of it. I wanted to learn more about Lonny Midas, but unless I could find him and ask him face-to-face about the death of Selina Day it seemed that I would have to rely on the testimony of Randall Haight alone. But Haight was self-serving at best in his depiction of his role, and at worst a potential liar.

I had begun doodling while I thought, and stopped when I saw that I had drawn a crude outline of a girl's head, framed by beribboned pigtails. Liar: I kept coming back to that word. Why was I so convinced that Haight's account of the murder was not simply revisionist but contained moments of active concealment? After all, what could be worth hiding? He had admitted his involvement in a terrible crime. The fact that he claimed it was Lonny Midas who had smothered Selina was important only in that it represented the culmination of a sequence of events to which he had been a party, and for which he and Midas were both equally culpable. Perhaps he had fought against Midas at the end, but would he have tried to pull him off when Midas began raping Selina? Would he have joined in himself? What was the point at which he realized that it had all gone too far — if, in fact, he ever gained that realization?

I knew then that my problem with Randall Haight was that not only did I not believe his story in its entirety; I didn't like him. I couldn't say for sure if that was because of what he had done, and the death of my own child, in which case I needed to put it from my mind if I was to continue working on his behalf, or because of some more deep-rooted revulsion, a sense of him as a contaminated soul hiding itself behind a veneer of normality.

And I went to sleep dreaming of faceless men.

9

Ryan didn't like sitting in the car alone. This was the kind of neighborhood where somebody might just take it into his head to call the cops because a lone man was waiting in a strange car on a quiet street where unfamiliar cars stood out; that, or this same somebody might decide that the cops didn't need to be involved, and a tap on the window to inquire whether there was a problem might serve just as well to clear matters up, maybe with a couple of buddies hanging in the background to make sure nobody got the wrong idea.

He tried to remember the last time he'd eaten: not a grabbed slice of pizza on the run, or some greasy fries in a bar whose name he couldn't remember an hour later, but a proper meal, either eaten alone or among friends. It was a week at least. He wasn't even sure that he had friends anymore. The best of them wouldn't want to see him, because if he stayed out of their way they couldn't talk about what they didn't know if curious souls came calling, while the rest of them would drop a dime on him without a second thought. He could walk away, of course. There was always that option. But he had a role to play in what was happening, and he wanted to see it out to the end. In a strange way, Dempsey was now the closest thing he had to a friend. They weren't particularly close, and they didn't even like each other much, but they were dependent on each other. Need bound them together, but for how long? Sands were spilling through the hourglass, and Ryan didn't know how many grains were left.

He looked toward the Napier house. The drapes were drawn and he could see no sign of movement inside. He slammed the palm of his hand against the dashboard, then repeated the action over and over until the car started to rock and his hand smarted. He shouldn't have left the woman alone. He knew what Dempsey was going to do, but he'd turned his back on it and closed the door behind him, letting Dempsey make him his bitch as assuredly as Dempsey was making Mrs. Napier his bitch over in the house. He leaned down and lifted his trouser leg. The little revolver sat snugly in its holster. He slipped it out and stared at it, letting it rest on his thigh. He'd begun carrying it recently, even though he already had another gun tucked into the waistband of his pants. Nobody knew about the revolver, and certainly not Dempsey. In fact, Dempsey was the reason Ryan had begun carrying the revolver in the first place. Dempsey's behavior was becoming increasingly erratic. Ryan had previously only ever encountered junkies and alcoholics who behaved in that way, veering from friendly to threatening in an instant, the only thing predictable about them being their unpredictability, but Dempsey was neither an addict nor a drunk. He stuck to a couple of beers when he hit a bar, and Ryan had never seen him take so much as a single hit on a doobie. Maybe he needed to be medicated, but Ryan wasn't about to suggest that he see a shrink. Ryan shut his eyes, then opened them quickly as the vision of a muzzle filled his consciousness. In the instant he'd looked into that black, unblinking eye, he had felt the limits of his own existence, and the fact of his mortality was impressed upon him. He wondered if he would see the bullet that killed him, if, in that final split second, the eye would turn from black to silver-gray, filling then emptying, entering and then exiting, taking his life with it.

'*I'm just kidding with you.*' That's what Dempsey had said, but he hadn't been, not really. It was as though Dempsey had looked deep into Ryan's heart and seen his potential for treachery. The gun was a warning.

See, Frankie, I'm older than you — older, and harder, and wiser. I know how you think because I was like you, once upon a time. That's the difference between us: I was like you once, but you were never like me. It's the small advantage that age bestows, the consolation prize for the loss of speed, the diminished reaction time. You know how the young think, but they don't know how you think. For men like us that's important. You stay a couple of steps ahead of the young all the time, so that when they turn on you, when they go for that gun, you already have yours in your hand because you've been expecting what's coming.

I know you, Frankie.

I know you.

Ryan shivered. The voice had sounded so clear

114

to him, as if Dempsey were sitting there next to him, the gun in his hand. But Dempsey wasn't as smart as he thought he was, and Ryan wasn't as young and callow as Dempsey had adjudged him to be. If Dempsey kept pulling shit like that gun trick earlier in the evening, Ryan would be forced to provide his own solution to whatever psychological difficulties Dempsey was enduring. He thought about going back into the house, pressing the revolver against the back of Dempsey's neck while he was buried in the Napier woman, and pulling the trigger. The image was so inviting that he felt his finger slipping over the guard and fastening on the trigger, instinctively applying the pressure required.

When the cell phone rang, he almost pulled the trigger in shock.

He didn't need to look at the caller ID. Just like Dempsey, Ryan carried two cell phones: one for personal use, along with a little general business that was always conducted discreetly, and another that was changed weekly. Calls to the second phone only came from one destination. Ryan answered on the second ring.

'Where are you?'

That voice with its distinctive rasp, the voice of the man who had brought them to this pass, who had lowered them to the status of prey. Their fates were linked to his, and they were still waiting for him to find a way to make it all good again. Neither Ryan nor Dempsey had spoken the thought aloud, but they had both begun to suspect that they might die waiting for that to happen.

'The cab thing. He still hasn't shown. We found cash, though.'

'Cash? Good.' That was what they'd been reduced to: foraging for enough cash to enable them to keep moving and stay alive. 'Forget about the guy. We'll deal with him another time. You know the Brattle Street Theater?'

'The movie place? Sure.'

'Find somewhere to park, close as you can get to it.'

'Now?'

'No, next month. Put Dempsey on.'

'He's not here. I'm in the car. He's inside.'

'Why?'

'In case, you know, the guy comes back.'

'Who's in there with him.'

'A woman. The guy's wife.'

There was silence on the other end of the line, and Ryan knew that the man was connecting the dots. He had always been good at figuring people out, or so it had seemed. He'd just lost that gift when it came to his enemies.

'Get him out of there. This is important.'

He hung up. Ryan now had the gun in one hand and the cell phone in the other. He slipped the gun back in its ankle holster, the cell phone into his pocket, then made his way quickly across the street. A man passed, a newspaper under his arm and a beer can in one hand, concealed in a brown paper bag. The man nodded at him, and Ryan nodded back. He kept his eye on the guy all the way to the Napier house, but the man didn't look back. Ryan had left the front door unlocked when he stepped outside. It banged against the wall when he opened it too quickly, and he called out from the hallway just in case Dempsey panicked and came out waving a gun or a knife.

'It's me! We have to go.'

He knocked on the living-room door before entering. He saw Dempsey buckling his jeans. Helen Napier was kneeling on the couch. Stockings and panties were lying coiled together on the floor. She was adjusting her dress, pulling it down to cover her thighs while keeping her back to the door. Her shoulders were shaking. She did not turn to look at him.

'Is she okay?' asked Ryan.

'What do you think? If it's any consolation to you, I was gentle with her. Your timing is good, though, I'll give you that. A few minutes earlier, and I might have been annoyed at the intrusion.'

Dempsey checked the room to make sure he hadn't dropped anything, then spoke to Mrs. Napier.

'Helen,' he said.

She stiffened but still did not turn her head.

'You have a choice,' he continued. 'You can tell your husband what happened tonight. From what I hear, he's the kind who could get all hot under the collar about a thing like this, and it might lead him to come looking for me. If he does, I'll kill him. He brought this on you by his own actions, but he won't see it that way. And, you know, it won't help you anyway. I knew a man once whose girlfriend was raped. He could never look at her the same way again. Could be he thought that she was soiled goods. Whatever the reason, they broke up. End of story. Think about that before you go shooting your mouth off to your husband. I was you, I'd just tell him that we called, that we put the fear of God into you, and he should sort out his affairs before we come calling again.' Dempsey picked up the shoebox of cash. 'In the meantime, I'll take the money as an interim payment on what was lost. We'll be on our way now. Go fix yourself up. You don't want him seeing you like that when he gets home.'

He brushed past Ryan on his way out the door.

'You coming?'

Ryan was still staring at Mrs. Napier.

'You want to apologize to her again?' asked Dempsey. 'You can, if you think it will help.'

But Ryan just shook his head. There was something wrong about what he was seeing: not just the act that had been committed, but the aftermath. He tried to put his finger on it but couldn't, and then Dempsey was pulling him away, and they were walking to the car, and the assault was forced from his mind for a time as he told Dempsey about the call.

'Regular nine-one-one,' said Dempsey. He was counting the money in the shoebox, flipping his finger through the bound bills. Dempsey separated four hundred in twenties, split the stack evenly in two, then stuffed two hundred into his wallet and two hundred into Ryan's coat pocket.

'Walking-around money. If he gives you more, just take it and keep your mouth shut.'

'How much was in there?' asked Ryan.

'Two-five now, plus change.'

Ryan laughed. It was that or pull over by the side of the road and beat his fists against the sidewalk in frustration.

'All that for a lousy three grand?'

'Hey, I had a good time.'

Now Ryan did pull over, causing the driver behind them to honk his disapproval. He turned in his seat, ready to release his belt and tear Dempsey's throat out, but Dempsey already had his hand on the butt of the gun. His left hand was raised, one finger extended in warning.

'What? You going to kill me?' asked Ryan. 'You going to pull the trigger this time?'

'No, but I'll break your nose with it, and I'll go further if you make me. You want to make me do that to you?'

'You raped a woman, just for three grand.'

'No, I didn't. I had the three grand anyway.'

Ryan almost lost it again, but the sight of the gun revealing itself to him brought him back to his senses. His shoulders collapsed, and he laid his forehead against the steering wheel. He felt ill. His face was bathed in warm, clammy sweat.

'Three grand,' he whispered. 'Three grand and change.'

'Maybe you haven't been keeping up with developments, Frankie, but Mr. Morris is hurting. Two grand here, a grand there, a couple of hundred from the junkies — it all adds up. It keeps him in business, and keeps us in a job. More to the point, it's keeping us alive. Our credit isn't so good right now, and the bank of

119

goodwill has closed its doors.'

'He's drowning,' said Ryan. 'He's going down.'

'That's not what I said, and if I was you I wouldn't be saying things like that out loud either. It might get taken as disloyalty. It's swings and roundabouts. Everybody's hurting in this economy. He'll come good again. He just needs time.'

Ryan raised his head. Dempsey's face was expressionless. It gave no clue to whether he believed a word that he was saying.

'You're going to start driving now, Frankie, okay?'

'Okay.'

'We good?'

Ryan nodded.

'Let me hear you say it.'

'We're good.'

'Right. Now let's go see what he wants.'

They drove in silence toward Cambridge. Eventually Dempsey let his head rest against the window, his eyes fixed on distant lights. Ryan smoked a cigarette, and thought about a boy he once knew, Josh Tyler, who died in a lake at some summer camp in New Hampshire when his canoe capsized. Josh could swim, but the kid in the canoe with him couldn't, or not well enough. He panicked, and dragged Josh under the water. The kid was kicking, and one of the kicks caught Josh in the side of the head and knocked him unconscious. Somehow the kid made it to the canoe and managed to hold on to it, but by then Josh Tyler was dead. Drowning men will drag you down if you let them, thought

Ryan. Sometimes, to survive, you have to let them sink.

They found a spot not far from the entrance to the Brattle Street Theater, and sat back to wait.

'What's on there?' asked Ryan.

'*The Friends of Eddie Coyle*,' said Dempsey. 'I read about it in the paper.'

'I don't know it.'

'What do you mean, you don't know it?'

'I said I don't know it. I've never seen it, never even heard of it. It must be new.'

'No, it's not new. It's old. Nineteen seventy-three. Robert Mitchum and that guy, the one from *Everybody Loves Raymond*. Boyle, Peter Boyle. He's dead now. Real good in that movie. I can't believe you never heard of it, you growing up in Boston and all.'

'I didn't go to movies much as a kid.'

'Still, you should know it.'

'What's it about?'

'A snitch.'

Dempsey didn't say anything else. Ryan felt him looking at him, but didn't say anything, just waited for him to continue. Eventually, Dempsey did.

'Eddie — that's Mitchum — decides to rat out his buddies to avoid doing time. He's old. He doesn't want to go back in the can.'

'And?'

'And what?'

'How does it end?'

'I'm not going to tell you how it ends. Go rent it sometime.'

'I'm not going to rent it.'

'Well, I'm not going to tell you how it ends.'

'Fine.'

'Yeah, fine. You're some asshole, you know that?'

'You're the asshole, not telling me how it ends.'

'You want to know how it ends?'

'No, I don't care now.'

'You want to know?'

'No.'

'You want to know. I know you want to know.'

'Right, tell me.'

'It ends with a guy being tied to a chair while another guy forces him to watch the fucking movie, that's how it ends.'

Ryan let a beat go by.

'I don't think that's how it ends.'

For the first time that evening, Dempsey smiled at something that didn't involve another person's misery.

'Asshole.'

'Yeah,' said Ryan, and he was reminded of why sometimes he didn't mind being in Dempsey's company. It wouldn't stop him from killing him if the time came, but he might make it quick. 'All of this is so important, what's he doing at a movie?'

'He likes movies. He says they help him think more clearly. He always goes to a movie when he's struggling with a problem. Then it ends and he has a solution. I guess it's something to do with sitting in the dark and letting the pictures wash over you. And even if he doesn't come up with an answer he's got to spend some time hiding in the dark. It's easier than hiding in the daylight.'

'Amen to that.'

'Yeah. Some good-looking women around here.'

'College girls.'

'They got no time for men like us, not unless you catch 'em drunk.'

His words brought back to Ryan the look of fear on the girl's face, and the way Dempsey had set out to humiliate the man with her, leaving him with a choice that was no choice: He could throw a punch, and Dempsey would beat him, and beat him bad, or he could suck up Dempsey's poison and walk away with his body intact but his pride in tatters. His girlfriend had been forced to beg Dempsey to leave them in peace. Ryan had seen that happen before, and had often watched something die in the eyes of the woman involved when it did. Her boyfriend was weak, and his weakness had been publicly exposed. Somewhere deep inside, the woman always wanted the guy to fight back, to win or to take his beating. There was a strength in winning a fight like that, but there was a strength, too, in being unwilling to become another man's bitch, win or lose, in not allowing him to break you down or paw your girlfriend without consequences.

And what Dempsey had done in the bar had set him up for what he'd done later to Helen Napier. His blood had been up, and she'd suffered for it.

'He's coming out,' said Dempsey, and Ryan followed his gaze to where Tommy Morris was slinking out of the movie theater, his head low, his hair hidden by a wool cap. Tommy Morris, carrying the stink of failure on him, the stink of death.

Tommy Morris, the drowning man.

★　★　★

Tommy Morris's family had always been two-toilet Boston Irish. They had aspired to better things, which led them to leave behind the West Broadway projects of D Street in Southie for what they considered to be the more salubrious surroundings of a Somerville three-decker, even as their neighbors sneered at their aspirations. In Boston the working-class Irish distrusted success, political success aside, as that was just criminality by another name as practiced by the Boston School. General success, though, only made others feel bad about their own situation, their ambitions for betterment that stretched no further than winning the nigger-pool lottery.

So it was that the Morris family was spoken of in disparaging terms just for not wanting to stay mired in the mud at the bottom of the pond. When Tommy's father, who owned a florist's, bought a new delivery van, black paint was poured over it before it was even a week old. Tommy never forgot that, and years later he would visit his own kind of vengeance on South Boston, helping Whitey Bulger flood it and the rest of the city with cocaine. It was said of Tommy that he hated his own, which is always the sign of a man who secretly hates himself. It made him vulnerable, although he chose not to recognize that vulnerability, believing instead that by consolidating his position and acting cleverly he could somehow overcome the fault line that ran beneath the foundations of his life.

Tommy had started out with stealing, and hijacking truck-loads, the way most of his peers did, then briefly graduated to bank jobs before realizing that shakedowns were easier to plan, harder to trace, and carried less chance of serious jail time or having his head blown off. Tommy Morris, they used to say, was always smart like that. He wasn't like the other project rats. The real wolves, the ones like Whitey and his sidekick Stevie Flemmi, used to scoff at Tommy. They called him 'Two-Bit' Tommy, and sometimes 'Mary' Morris because of his preference for avoiding violence. It made him appear less of a threat to them, and so he survived Whitey's relentless purging of his rivals, the bullets to the head and the slow strangulations that left Whitey as top dog, aided by a nickel stretch in Cedar Junction that spanned the worst of the killing, during which he kept his head down and his mouth closed.

When Tommy came out, Whitey's cocaine operation had been brought to its knees by the DEA, decades of collusion between rogue FBI agents and Whitey were being revealed, and so many guys were turning federal witness that there weren't enough tape recorders to go around. Meanwhile, the Italians were a shadow of their former selves, ruined by internal squabbles and by Whitey's willingness to sell them out to the feds. Tommy Caci and Al Z, the now-departed linchpins of the Boston Mafia, were trying to rebuild, but there was a gap in the market, a vacuum to be filled, that Tommy and his peers were able to exploit, particularly once Whitey, facing indictment, fled the jurisdiction. Tommy — solid, careful, reliable — prospered.

But he was growing old, and there were hungry young men who felt that their time had come, led by Oweny Farrell, the most ruthless of them all. Quickly, so fast that Tommy barely had time to register the threat before it was upon him, his operation began to fall apart. That old fault line, whose existence he had denied for so long, widened, and his world crumbled into it. He was isolated, and the whispering started. Tommy Morris was no longer solid. Tommy Morris wasn't sound. Tommy Morris was a threat, because Tommy Morris knew too much. Men whom he had trusted began to keep their distance from him, so that they would not catch a stray bullet when the end came. Money disappeared, and with it his allies. Tommy knew his history. He remembered Donald Killeen, who had been top dog in Southie until, in 1972, Whitey decided that Killeen's reign was over and had him shot to death on the evening of his son's fourth birthday party. As if to emphasize the ease of the transition, and a sense of continuity, Whitey had subsequently taken over Killeen's former headquarters, the Transit Cafe, as his own base, renaming it the Triple O's.

Tommy had no intention of going out like Killeen.

But still they kept chipping away at him — the cops, the feds, his own kind. He had been forced to seek a sit-down, and one had been agreed for a bar in Chelsea after hours. On the day of the proposed meet, Tommy had received an anonymous call advising him not to attend.

And that was when Tommy Morris had gone to ground.

★ ★ ★

Tommy slipped into the back of the car.

'Drive,' he said.

'Drive where?' said Ryan.

'Doesn't matter. Just drive.'

Ryan pulled out and headed away from the city. Dempsey handed over the shoebox filled with money. Tommy counted it and passed them another two hundred dollars each from the stash.

'You can add it to what you took already,' he said.

'I'm hurt, Tommy,' said Dempsey.

'You will be if I catch you with your hand in the register again,' said Tommy. Dempsey said nothing, but he cocked an eyebrow at Ryan.

'You got news?' asked Dempsey.

'Yeah, I have news.'

'About Oweny?'

'No,' said Tommy. He seemed distant, confused. 'Maybe. I don't know.'

Dempsey looked at the older man in the rearview mirror. 'What is it, Tommy?' he asked, and there was genuine solicitude in his voice.

'It's personal,' said Tommy at last. 'It's blood.'

II

Don't ask us what it's like
In that moment when the body
skitters away
from that stupid
sheepy shape of breath.

Down here, no one asks.

We all died

boot to throat.

We all went out
Shrieking some bloody name.

from *The Dead Girls Speak in Unison*
by Danielle Pafunda

10

There are places along the Maine coast that are stunningly beautiful, often in a picture-postcard way that attracts tourists and snowbirds. Those stretches of the shoreline are dotted with expensive houses masquerading as summer cottages, and the towns that service them offer gourmet delicacies in the grocery stores, and chichi restaurants with waitstaff who make their efforts at service feel like hard-won favors for the undeserving.

But there are other places that speak of the ferocity of the sea, of communities sheltering behind buttresses of black rock and shingle beaches against which the waves throw themselves like besieging armies, gradually eroding the defenses over centuries, millennia, certain in the knowledge that eventually the ocean will triumph and smother the land. In those places the trees are bent, testament to the force of the wind, and the houses are weathered and functional, as sullen and resigned as the dogs that prowl their yards. Such towns do not welcome tourists, for they have nothing to offer them and the tourists have nothing to give, except to serve as a mirror for the natives' own disappointments. Theirs is a hardscrabble existence. Those with youth and ambition leave, while those with youth but without ambition stay, or drift away for a time before returning, for small

131

towns have their lures and a way of sinking deep hooks into skin and flesh and spirit.

Yet there is a balance to be maintained in such locales, and there is strength in unity. New blood will be welcomed as long as it plays its part in the great extended scheme of daily life, finding its level, its part in the complex machinery that powers the town's existence: giving enough at the start to show willing, but not so much as to appear ingratiating; listening more than speaking, and not disagreeing, for here to disagree may be construed as being disagreeable, and one has to earn the right to be disagreeable, and then only after long years of cautious, mundane, and well-chosen arguments; and understanding that the town is both a fixed entity and a fluid concept, a thing that must be open to small changes of birth and marriage, of mood and mortality, if it is ultimately to stay the same.

And so there were communities like Pastor's Bay along the Maine seaboard, each different, each similar. If Pastor's Bay was distinctive, it was only in its comparative lack of beauty, elemental or otherwise. There was no beach, merely a pebbled shore. A tangle of jagged rocks ringed the peninsula at its eastern extreme and made any approach by boat hazardous if one didn't know the tides. From there, a road led through a mix of old- and new-growth forest, past houses old and houses new, houses abandoned and houses reclaimed (including the one in which Anna Kore's mother sat, red-eyed and hauntingly, terrifyingly still, her head filled with the thousand deaths of her child and a

132

thousand visions of her safe return, each conclusion to the tale fighting for supremacy) until it found the town, its buildings almost leaning inward over the main street, the shades on the windows lowered slightly in pain, the skies above cloud-heavy and lowering, all life now tainted by the absence of one girl. Finally, leaving the town behind, the road undulated over uneven, rocky ground before arriving at the bridge to the mainland at a point almost half a mile to the south of the causeway of rock and dirt and scrub grass that, before the building of the first bridge, offered the sole path for those who wished to leave, either permanently or temporarily, and preferred to do so without paying the ferry toll.

The first bridge, the old wooden construct erected by the Heardings in 1885 with the proceeds of a tax levied on the residents, seemed set to put paid to the ferry forever, but the Heardings sank their pilings incorrectly, and a big storm in 1886 set the bridge to swaying, and people heard it moaning in its torments and went back to using the old path for foot traffic and the ferry for the transport of goods and livestock. The Heardings were forced to look again at the bridge, and the ferry continued its service while the repairs were made. By the time they had resunk the pilings, and reassured the natives of the bridge's solidity, their business had gone belly-up because they had lost the trust of their neighbors. The Heardings closed their lumberyard and departed for Bangor, where they opened up for business under a new name, and denied any knowledge of bridges, or unsound pilings, or Pastor's Bay. Still, the Heardings' bridge stood for eighty years, until the passage of trucks and cars began to tell upon it, and its moans and cries resumed, and a new bridge began to take shape alongside it. Now all that was left of the Heardings' bridge were the old pilings, for say this about the Heardings, if nothing else: They might have botched the job the first time, but they got it right the second. It was simply their misfortune to find themselves in a town where folk preferred things to be done right from the get-go, especially where their personal safety was concerned, and most particularly when it came to bridges and water, for they had the fear of drowning that comes from living close to the sea.

Randall Haight lived southeast of town. He'd given me clear directions, and I remembered his car from his visit to Aimee's office. He came to the door as I pulled into the yard. His pale-pink shirt was open at the neck, and he wore suspenders instead of a belt. His pants were high on his waist, and tapered at the leg, offering a glimpse of sensible tan socks. There was an element of the old-fashioned about his appearance, but not studiedly so. It was not an affectation; Randall Haight was simply a man who took comfort in older things. He did not step down into the yard, but waited for me to reach the door. Only then did he remove his hands from his pockets to shake my hand. He was chewing at the inside of his lower lip, and he snatched his hand back after only the merest contact. His reluctance to have me in his house was palpable, but so was his greater unhappiness at what was happening to him.

'Is something wrong, Mr. Haight?'

'I got another package,' he said. 'I found it in my box this morning.'

'A photograph?'

'No, different. Worse.'

I waited for him to invite me into the house, but he did not, and his body continued to block the door.

'Are you going to show me?' I asked.

He struggled to find the right words.

'I don't have many visitors,' he said. 'I'm a very private man.'

'I understand.'

He seemed about to say more. Instead, he stepped aside and extended his left hand in a robotic gesture of admittance.

'Then, please, come in.'

But he said it with resignation, and with no hint of welcome.

* * *

If Haight was, as he said, a private man, then it appeared that he had little about which to be private. His home had all the personal touches of a show house: tasteful, if anonymous, furniture; timber floors covered with rugs that might have been Persian but probably weren't; dark-wood shelves that hadn't come from Home Depot but from one of the better mid-price outlets, in all likelihood the same place that had supplied the

135

couch and chairs, and the cabinet in which sat the TV, a big gray Sony monster with a matching DVD player beneath, and a cable box. The only individual touch came from a pair of paintings on the wall. They were abstract, and original, and looked like a slaughterhouse yard, all reds and black and grays. There was one above the couch, and another above the fireplace, so it was hard to see where someone might sit without looking at one or the other. Haight spotted the direction of my gaze and picked up on my involuntary spasm of revulsion.

'They're not to everyone's taste,' he said.

'They certainly make a statement,' I replied, the statement being 'I killed him, Officer, and spread his guts on a canvas.'

'They're the only things in and of this house that have increased in value over the last couple of years. Everything else has tanked.'

'And you an accountant. I thought you'd be better prepared for the recession.'

'I suppose it's like doctors trying to diagnose their own ailments. It's easier to find the flaws in others than to figure out what's wrong with yourself. Can I offer you a drink, or coffee?'

'Nothing, thanks.'

I took in the books on the shelf. They were mostly nonfiction, with an emphasis on European history.

'Are you a frustrated historian?' I asked.

'It's an escape from what I do for a living. I'm curious about strategy and leadership. To be honest, I don't see many effective examples of either in the business world. Please, sit.'

136

I headed for the couch that faced the TV, but he looked flustered and suggested that I take one of the armchairs instead, then waited until I was seated before lowering himself into his own chair. It was the only item of furniture that showed any real sign of use. I could see the indentations of cups and glasses on the right arm, and a slight darkening of the fabric where Haight's head had rested over the years.

For a couple of moments, neither of us spoke. I had the uncomfortable sense of being in the presence of someone who had recently been bereaved. The house spoke of absence, but I couldn't tell whether I was just picking up on its relative lack of character or something deeper. Because, of course, nobody really lived here; Randall Haight owned it and put bad art on its walls, but Randall Haight was an artificial creation. Perhaps, at times, William Lagenheimer moved through its rooms, but William Lagenheimer didn't exist either. He had disappeared from the world, and was now just a memory.

And all the time I was aware of Haight's nervousness, although he tried to conceal it. His hands shook, and when he clasped his fingers to stop their movement the tension merely passed on to his right foot, which began to tap on the rug. I supposed that if I had once killed a child, and now felt that I was being targeted in the aftermath of another child's disappearance, I would be nervous too.

Haight passed me a typed list of names detailing those individuals for whom he had recently begun to act as an accountant, and any new arrivals to Pastor's Bay. I glanced at it, then put it aside. The names meant nothing to me for now.

'What is it that you've been sent, Mr. Haight?' I asked.

He swallowed hard, and shifted a battered art volume from the coffee table between us. Beneath it lay another brown cushioned mailer with a printed address label.

'There was a disc. I've left it in my laptop so that you can see it, although it's not the worst of what I found.'

He pushed the envelope toward me with his fingertips. I pried it open with the point of my pen so as not to contaminate it any further should it be required as evidence at some point. Inside I could see pieces of paper of various sizes, most of them glossy. They looked like more photographic prints.

'I'll be back in a moment,' I said.

I went to my car and removed a box of disposable plastic gloves from the trunk. Haight hadn't moved while I was gone. The light in the room changed slightly as the clouds moved outside, and I realized how ashen he was. He also appeared to be on the verge of tears.

I reached into the envelope and removed the images. They were all of a similar nature, and all featured young girls, none of them older than fourteen or fifteen, and some much younger than that. They had been photographed naked on beds, and on carpets, and on bare floors. Some of them were trying to smile. Most of them weren't. The photographic paper was standard

Kodak. It was possible that a computer expert might be able to tell the type of printer from which the images came, but that would be useful only in the event of a prosecution, assuming the individual responsible for creating the photos was found with the printer in his possession.

'I don't like that kind of thing,' said Haight. 'I'm straight, but they're just children. I don't want to look at naked children.'

There it was once again: that primness, that need to reassure the listener that the killing of a young girl had been a temporary deviation. He had not carried teenage desires for young girls into adult life. He was a normal man, with normal sexual inclinations.

'And the disc?' I said.

'It arrived in the same envelope, wrapped in tissue.'

His laptop was on the floor beside his chair, already powered up and on sleep. Seconds later, I was looking at an image of an old barn door, but not the same one as last time. This door was painted a bright red. As the camera drew nearer, a gloved hand reached out and pulled open the door. The interior was dark until the camera light clicked on. There was straw on the stone floor, and I caught glimpses of empty cattle pens on either side.

The camera stopped midway down the barn's central aisle and turned to the operator's right. On the floor of one of the pens a set of girl's clothing was laid out: a white blouse, a red-and-black checked skirt, white stockings, and black shoes. Their positions roughly corresponded to the dimensions of a girl's body, the way a parent might lay out a day's outfit for a young child, but they also gave the uncomfortable impression that the wearer had somehow disappeared, vanishing in an instant, drawn into the void as she was lying in place in the barn, staring up at wood, and cobwebs, and pigeons or doves, for I could now hear the birds cooing softly in the background.

The screen went dark. That was all.

'What was Selina Day wearing when she died, Mr. Haight?'

He took a moment to answer.

'A white blouse, a red-and-black checked skirt, white stockings, black shoes.'

The details of her attire would probably have been included in the newspaper reports of the case. Even if they weren't, they would have been known in the area, given that she had died in her uniform. Either way, it wouldn't have been difficult for someone to put together a facsimile of what she had been wearing simply by doing a little research. Specialist local knowledge would not have been required.

'You know, I think I will have a cup of coffee after all,' I said.

He asked me how I took it, and I asked for milk, no sugar. While he was in the kitchen, I watched the video again, trying to find any clue to the location of the barn that I might have missed: a feed bag from a local supplier, a scrap of paper with an address that could be enlarged, anything at all, but there was nothing. The barn was a stage set with an absent player.

140

Haight returned with my coffee, and what smelled like a mint tea for himself.

'Tell me about Lonny Midas, Mr. Haight,' I said.

Haight sipped his tea. He did so carefully, even daintily.

His movements were studiedly effeminate. In everything that I had seen him do so far, he seemed to be trying to communicate the impression that he was weak, inconsequential, and posed no threat. He was a man who was doing his best to fade into the background so as not to attract the attention of others, yet not so much that his desire to blend in would become overpowering, and thus mark him out. He was a youthful predator turned old prey.

Because in all that followed, in all that he told me that afternoon, the fact remained that he and Lonny Midas had acted together in stalking, and then killing, Selina Day. Midas might have been the instigator, but Haight had been beside him right until the end.

'Lonny wasn't a bad kid,' said Haight. 'People said that he was, but he wasn't, not really. His mom and dad were old when they had him. Well, I say 'old,' but I mean that his mom was in her late thirties and his father in his late forties. His brother, Jerry, was a decade older than him, but I don't recall much about him. He'd left home by the time — well, by the time all the bad stuff happened. Lonny's mom and dad weren't just old, though; they were old-fashioned. His dad had wanted to be a preacher, but I don't think he was smart enough. Not that you have to be smart to be a preacher, not really, but you need to be able to bring folk along with you, to convince them that you're worth following and listening to, and Lonny's father didn't have that touch with ordinary people. Instead, he worked in a warehouse, and read his Bible in the evenings. Lonny's mom was always in the background cooking or cleaning or sewing. She doted on Lonny, though. I guess with her older boy gone, and her husband lost in the Good Book, Lonny was all she had left, and she gave him the kind of love and affection that I think she craved for herself. In that way, she was a lot like my mother, though she took what we did a lot harder and was less forgiving. Had she lived, I don't know how welcoming she would have been once he was released. I think it was better for him that they both died while he was inside.

'But she was always so grateful when I came over to play with Lonny, or when she saw us together on the street. Her face would light up, because it seemed as if there was someone else who liked Lonny almost as much as she did.'

'Are you implying that there were those who didn't care much for Lonny?' I asked.

'Well, when you're young there will always be some kids that you get along with, and others that you don't. With Lonny, you could say there were more of the latter than the former. Lonny had a temper on him, but he was intelligent with it. That's a bad combination. He was curious, and adventurous, but if you got in his way, or tried to stop him from getting what he wanted, then he'd lash out. He used to tell me that his

142

father would beat on him for the slightest infraction, but that just made Lonny want to spite him more. He couldn't control Lonny. Neither of them could. In the end, I guess Lonny couldn't even control himself.

'I wasn't like that. I wanted to toe the line. No, that's not true: My instinct was to toe the line, but like a lot of quiet, shy kids I secretly envied the Lonny Midases of this world. I still do. I think we became friends because I was so unlike him in action, yet I believed that I was a little like him in spirit. He would draw me out of myself, and sometimes I managed to keep him in check, to talk him down when it seemed like his tongue and his fists were going to get him into trouble. Man, but he got me in hot water I don't know how many times, and my parents weren't like his. They weren't much younger than his mom and dad, but compared to them they were kind of laid-back. Lonny's dad beat him when he did wrong, but my dad was always in my mom's shadow, and she just went back to reading parenting books after I started getting in trouble, as if they were at fault and not me. They thought Lonny was a bad influence on me, but it wasn't that simple. It never is.'

'How long had you known each other before you killed Selina Day?'

For the first time, he didn't wince at the mention of her name. He was partially adrift in a reverie of the past. I could see it in his eyes, and on his face. He had even begun to relax into his chair a little. He was back in a time before he was a murderer, when he and Lonny Midas were just kids getting into scrapes that would have been familiar to generations of kids before them.

'We were friends from grade school. We were inseparable. We were brothers.'

He smiled, and there was a dampness to his eyes. William and Lonny, the little killers.

'What about girls?' I asked. 'Were either of you seeing anyone?'

'I was fourteen. I could only dream of girls.'

'And Lonny?'

He thought about the question. 'Girls liked him more than they liked me. I don't think it was so much that he was better looking than I was, but he just had that way about him. I think I told you back in Ms. Price's office that he'd kissed a couple of girls, and maybe copped a feel or two, but nothing more serious than that.'

'And before Selina Day, had you or Lonny ever suggested finding a girl and taking her off somewhere?'

'No, never.'

'So why Selina Day?'

He sipped his tea again, delaying his response. Somewhere upstairs, a clock struck the half hour. Outside, the light began to change, and the room grew darker. The alteration was so sudden that, for a second or two, Randall Haight was lost to me, or so it seemed, just as the camera had struggled to adjust to the darkness of the barn, and I knew with a cold certainty that a game was being played here, but a different game than the one I had earlier assumed. No truth was absolute, especially when it came to a man who, in his youth, had killed a child, and

144

Haight was consciously constructing a narrative that he believed would satisfy me. But it was a narrative that was always open to change and adaptation, just as he had held on to facets of his youth that he could expand into his performance as an adult, allowing him to fade into the background and become Randall Haight.

'Because she was different,' he said at last, and there was a flash of the grit that must have drawn Lonny Midas to him as a boy, the possibility that, deep down, they shared a common soul. 'She was black. There were no black girls at our school, and there were boys who said that black girls were easy, and Selina Day was easier still. Lonny said that his brother knew a boy who raped a black girl and got clean away with it. Maybe those were different times, but not so different. The law had one ear for the blacks and one ear for us, and the hearing wasn't the same in each ear.

'Lonny was the one who suggested it, but I went along with it. Oh, I tried to talk him out of it in the beginning. I was frightened, but I was excited too, and when we started touching her it was like my mind filled up with blood, and all I wanted to do was tear at her clothes and rub myself against her and find her dark place. Is that what you wanted to hear, Mr. Parker? That I liked it? Well, it's the truth: I did like it, right up until the time Lonny covered up her nose and mouth to stop her from screaming. He didn't quite manage it, though. I heard her through his hand, like a kitten mewling, and that was when the blood started to flow backward, and

145

everything went from red to white. I tried to pull Lonny from her, but he pushed me back and I tripped and hit my head, and I lay there and kept my eyes closed because it was easier to lie there than to fight him, easier to lie there than to watch her buck and scratch with her eyes bulging and her legs kicking, easier to lie there until she stopped moving, and I could smell what he'd done, what he'd made her do.

'In a way, I was glad when they came for me. I'd have told in the end anyway. I'd have walked into the station house on my way home from school someday, and they'd have given me a soda, and I'd have told them what we did. There would have been no need to threaten me. I'd just have wanted them to listen, and not to shout at me. I couldn't have held it in. I think Lonny understood that. Even as we covered her up in the corner of the barn, and he made me promise not to tell, he knew that I'd let him down. If he'd been older, I think he might have killed me too, and taken his chances by running, but he was only fourteen, and where would be have run to? That was the last time we talked. Even at the trial, we didn't talk. After all, what could we have said to each other?'

'Do you think Lonny blamed you for confessing?'

'He wouldn't have told, not ever. He only confessed after I gave us both up.'

'But there would have been evidence at the scene even if someone hadn't seen you. Eventually they'd have found out it was you.'

'Maybe. I don't know. Lonny thought they'd

blame a black man. He said black men were always killing black women. His daddy said so. They lived rougher lives than we did. He was certain that if we kept our heads down and stayed quiet, we'd get away with it. We were fourteen-year-old boys. Fourteen-year-old boys don't kill little girls. Big men kill little girls. That's who they'd have been looking for: a big man with a thing for little girls. Like the one who sent those pictures.'

My coffee was going cold. I hadn't wanted it anyway. I'd just been trying to find a way to make Haight relax and open up. It had worked, in a sense, although now I wanted to walk away and leave him to his troubles. I could see Selina Day dying on a dirty barn floor, and I didn't need any more images of dying children in my head.

'And you've never seen Lonny since then?'

'I told you: The records were sealed. His name was changed. I'm not sure that I'd even recognize him anymore.'

'What about your parents? I know your father died while you were incarcerated, but your mother?'

'My momma stayed in touch with me for a time after I came out of prison, and gave me a place to live, but I couldn't stand to see the way she looked at me. I turned my back on her. For all I know, she's dead now. I'm alone. There's just me.'

'And how do you think of yourself, Mr. Haight?' I said.

'I don't understand. Do you mean morally, as

147

a consequence of what we did?'

'No, I mean by what name do you know yourself? Are you William Lagenheimer or Randall Haight?'

Again, he took some time to answer.

'I'm — I don't know. Many years ago, I put William Lagenheimer from my mind. I suppose it made life easier. William did that awful thing, not Randall Haight. Randall Haight is just an accountant living in a small town. He's never done anything wrong. That's an easier personality to inhabit, I think.'

'And William?'

'He doesn't exist anymore. There's only Randall.'

'And even Randall Haight doesn't really exist, if you think about it.'

He looked at me, and I could feel him reassessing me, recognizing that, if I were still not fully aware of the rules, then I had at least come to understand the nature of the game.

'No, he doesn't. Sometimes I'm not sure who I am, or if I'm even anyone at all. I don't want to be William because William killed a little girl. I don't want to be Randall Haight because Randall jumps at his own shadow, and Randall doesn't sleep so good at night, and Randall spends his entire life waiting for someone to put two and two together and force him to run. When I look in the mirror I expect it to be dark, or empty. I'm always surprised at the sight of my own face, because it's not one that I recognize. What's inside and what's outside don't match up, and they never will.'

He frowned. It might have been that he had

said more than he wanted to, or that he was simply so unused to talking about his former life and identity that it confused him and caused him distress.

'Mr. Haight, what do you want me to do for you?'

He gestured at his laptop, at the photographs. 'I want you to make all of this stop. I want you to find out who's doing this and make him stop.'

''Him'?'

'Him, her: It doesn't matter. I just want this to end.'

'And how do you propose I should do that?'

He looked surprised, then angry.

'What do you mean? I'm hiring you to make this go away.'

'And I'm telling you that it's not going to go away. If I find the person who is doing this, then how should I respond? Threaten him? Kill him? Is that what you want?'

'If it allows me to continue living in peace, then yes.'

'That's not what I do, Mr. Haight.'

He leaned forward in his seat, jabbing at me with a finger.

'On the contrary, Mr. Parker, that's very much what you do. Just as you now know a lot about me, I read up on you. You've killed. I've read the names.'

'I'm trying not to add to that list. Do you want to be serious, Mr. Haight, or should I just leave you to your elaborate fantasies?'

He stood up. 'You can't talk to me like that.'

'Sit down.'

'This is my house and — '

'*Sit down.*'

He gave it a couple of seconds for the sake of dignity, then sat.

'I need you to think carefully about what I'm going to tell you,' I said. 'You're either being tormented by someone who thinks it's amusing to see you sweat, or you're about to be blackmailed. The person targeting you has only one card to play, one weapon to use against you, and that's the fact that you've kept your past secret for so long. The most effective way to neutralize the threat is to go to the police — '

'No.'

' — is to go to the police, tell them everything that's been happening to you, and let them take it from there.'

'But it's not just about the police,' said Haight. 'Suppose this person chooses to send details to the newspapers? Suppose he decides to post notices all over Pastor's Bay, telling everyone about the child killer living in their midst? And even if he doesn't, do you think the police here will be able to keep it quiet, assuming they'd even want to? This is a small town. You get ticketed in the morning here and by lunchtime they're joking about it at the post office. My life will be ruined, and it won't be enough just to leave Pastor's Bay, or Maine. My name and picture will be all over the Internet. I won't be able to work, or even live in peace. You're asking me to commit professional suicide, and I may as well follow through with the real thing immediately after.'

He put his face in his hands, and kept it there.

'You're forgetting something,' I said.

'What's that?'

'The timing of all this.'

He lowered his hands to the bridge of his nose, his eyes peering over the pyramid they formed.

'Meaning Anna Kore,' he said.

'Yes. If this comes out against your will, you'll be a suspect. Let's go through that day again. What do you remember of it?'

'Why?'

'Because I want to know. Start at the beginning.'

'I was out of town that morning. I left shortly after nine.'

'You had appointments?'

'Only one. It was in Northport. You know this.'

'What did you do after that?'

'I had lunch, came home. I felt ill. I told you that the first time we met.'

'Did you meet anyone, have any visitors, make any calls?'

'No. Again, I told you: I lay on the couch. I fell asleep.'

'When did you wake?'

'I don't remember.'

'Did you spend the night on the couch?'

'No, I went to bed.'

'Was it dark then?'

'I think so. I don't know. Please stop!'

'These are the questions the police will ask you, Mr. Haight, if your past comes out. You'd better have good answers for them too, especially

151

if someone has anonymously informed them that the local accountant is a convicted child killer.'

'God. Jesus God.'

He lay back in his chair, his eyes closed.

'You're talking about preempting something that may not occur,' he said.

'You're being goaded by someone who knows about Selina Day. Already that person has begun to step up the campaign against you by sending you pornographic images of children, the possession of which is a crime. I don't believe it's going to stop there. The next step is to start hinting at your past to the wider community.'

'I need to think about it,' he said at last.

'You do that, but I wouldn't think for too long. There is one other thing.'

'What?' He sounded weary.

'You should consider that you're neither being blackmailed nor tormented simply over a past crime.'

'Then what?'

'It could be that you're being set up for the disappearance of Anna Kore,' I said.

With that I left him to consider his future, or what little of it remained to him.

11

The Pastor's Bay Police Department occupied one part of the municipal building, along with, according to a sign outside the door and a brief glimpse of the interior through its windows as I passed by, the town clerk's office, the fire department, local sanitation, and assorted meeting rooms, cubbyholes, unoccupied desks piled high with paper, and probably the Pastor's Bay collection of Halloween costumes, Santa Claus hats and beards, and stuffed-animal heads. The disappearance of Anna Kore meant that the demands on the building had increased significantly, and there were now various state police vehicles, dark unmarked SUVs, and a mobile crime-scene unit parked in its lot alongside a single, slightly battered Pastor's Bay Police Department Explorer. There was also the Winnebago that CID sometimes used as a mobile command post, but I could see no signs of activity around it.

I had wanted to see Randall Haight in his own environment, as though by doing so I might come to a better understanding of him, but the only conclusion I had drawn from our encounter was that Haight remained a lost soul, a deeply confused and conflicted man. Increasingly, Judge Bowens's social experiment, well-intentioned though it might have been, appeared to have resulted in profound existential consequences for the young man whom he had tried to help. That, in turn, raised the question of whether or not Lonny Midas had endured a similar crisis of identity.

There wasn't much in Pastor's Bay to occupy those with time on their hands: a few stores, the local bars, a bank, and a post office. The town's pharmacy wasn't part of a chain, and occupied an old redbrick building at the western end of Main Street. A hand-lettered sign on its door warned: WE DO NOT STOCK OXYCONTIN. There had been a rash of robberies at drugstores in the state, most of them carried out by sweaty, twitchy young men looking for little more than a way to feed their own addictions using Oxycodone, Vicodin, and Xanax. For the most part they favored blades over guns, and they were desperate enough to lash out at customers and pharmacists who didn't cooperate. They'd have to be pretty dumb to come all the way out to Pastor's Bay to score, though. Even if they managed to get away from the town itself there were five miles of narrow two-lane road before they reached another major route, which meant it would be easy to pick them up once the alarm had been raised.

I walked back toward the municipal building. The Explorer was gone. I hadn't noticed it leave. Some detective I was. I still had no sense of Pastor's Bay as a place, and no real idea of how I was going to set about tackling Randall Haight's problem. Maybe if I hung around long enough somebody would feel the urge to confess. There was a coffee shop called Hallowed Grounds across the street, so, with no better option to hand, I went in and ordered a Turkey Nudo sandwich and a bottle of water.

'You have trouble with drugstore robberies around here?' I asked the guy behind the counter who took my order.

'Not yet,' he said. 'You planning a heist?'

'I just noticed the sign on the pharmacy door that says it doesn't stock OxyContin.'

'Pre-emptive tactics,' he said. 'Guess you'll have to shop elsewhere for your opioid needs.'

'Funny,' I said. 'You're so dry you could be used as kindling.'

I took a seat at the window to watch the town's comings and goings while the kid put my order together. He was in his early twenties and already had enough piercings and tattoos to suggest that he viewed his body merely as a work in progress, a canvas for a largely uninspired collection of ideas revolving around Maori culture, Buddhism, Celtic mythology, and Scandinavian death metal, judging by his T-shirt which depicted a Kiss reject who, if I remembered correctly, had been jailed for murdering another Kiss reject, and maybe burning a church or two along the way. Say what you like about Gene Simmons, but the worst he could do would be to date your daughter. Very loud music was playing very softly on the store's sound system, to which the barista was shaking his greasy hair over the coffee and baked goods. The Turkey Nudo had been premade and shrink-wrapped, so I was okay, unless it was laughing boy who had made it in the first place.

I wondered if he'd taken into account the effect gravity would have on his skin and muscle tone as the years went by. By the time he was fifty, some of those tattoos would be around his knees.

Hell, I thought, pretty soon I'll be fifty, and I was already sounding like an old man. Let the kid have his fun. Had Jennifer lived, she'd have been within sight of her teens by now, and I'd be worrying about piercings, and boys, and beginning sentences with 'No daughter of mine is going out dressed like . . . '

But she hadn't lived, and it would be a few years before I had to worry about Sam in that way. Maybe she'd keep me young, but taking cheap shots in my head at a kid from a small town like Pastor's Bay who was just trying not to get dragged down by the place wouldn't help any. I'd end up like Lonny Midas's father, not understanding, and not wanting to understand.

He brought me my sandwich and water, and threw in a packet of chips free.

'All part of the service,' he said. 'I'm not happy until you're not happy.'

His kindness made me feel even more guilty. Just to rub it in, the music changed. Guitars were replaced by a piano, and a woman's voice with a foreign accent began to sing a cover version of a song that sounded vaguely familiar, although it took me a moment to place it. I looked back at the counter, where the kid was bopping along in a more restrained manner to this one as well.

'Hey, is that . . . *Abba*?' I asked.

'I don't think so.' He trotted to the stereo and

picked up a CD case. 'Susanna, uh, I think it's pronounced 'Wallumrød,' with a weird line through the ø. It's my girlfriend's, but I can only play it at certain times of the day, usually when the place is quiet. It's a management thing. Some people find it kind of depressing.'

It wasn't depressing. It was soft, and sad, and haunting, but not depressing.

'It's a cover of an Abba song,' I said. 'Lay All Your Love on Me.' And please don't ask me how I know that.'

'Yeah, Abba? Don't think I'm familiar with them.'

'Swedish. Same neck of the woods as that Norwegian Count Whatever on your T-shirt, more or less. Not as big on church-burning, though, or not that I can recall.'

'Yeah, the Count is one mean bastard. I just like the music, though. Music's music, you know. Quiet or loud, it's either good or bad.' He changed the grounds in the coffee maker, and started filling a pot. 'You a cop?' he asked.

'Nope.'

'Fed?'

'Nope.'

'Reporter?'

'Nope.'

'Rumpelstiltskin?'

'Maybe.'

He laughed.

'I'm a private investigator,' I said.

'No shit? You here about the Kore girl?'

'No, just some boring client stuff. Why, you know her?'

'Knew her to see around.' He corrected himself. 'I *know* her to see around. She seems okay. Runs with a younger crowd, but it's not like there are so many kids around here that you don't know everyone by name.'

'Any idea what might have happened to her?'

'Nuh-uh. If she was a little older, I'd have said that she might have lit out for the city. Boston or New York, maybe, not Bangor or Portland. They're no better than here, not really; they're just bigger. If you're gonna run, run far, or else this place is going to haul you right back again.'

'You're still here.'

'I'm trying to change the system from within, fighting the good fight, all that kind of bullshit.'

'If not you, then who?'

'Exactly.'

'So you don't think Anna Kore ran away?'

'Nope. Not that girls her age don't run away, but she doesn't seem like the sort. Everyone says she was okay.'

'That doesn't sound good for her.'

'No, I guess not.'

He went silent. Susanna Wallumrød was singing about her few little love affairs. She sounded weary of them all.

'Did she have a boyfriend?'

'I thought you said that you weren't here about her.'

'I'm not. I'm just professionally curious.'

He folded his arms and sized me up.

'Chief Allan said I was to tell him if anyone came asking about her.'

'I'm sure he did. I figure I'll be talking to him

158

soon enough. So: Did she have a boyfriend?'

'No. Her mom was — is — pretty protective of her, or that's what I heard. Anna was kept on a tight chain, you know, having a single mom and all. She probably would have eased up on her eventually.'

'Yeah. Well, with luck she'll still get that chance.'

'Amen to that.'

He turned his back and started rearranging the last of the pastries. I continued eating, and watched the folk of Pastor's Bay go about their business. Although school was done for the day, I saw no young people on the streets.

'Thanks for the sandwich,' I said. 'I'll see you around.'

'Sure. You have a good day now.'

I drove toward the bridge, the sun now long past its zenith. I thought about Selina Day, and Lonny Midas. I wondered where Lonny was now. Haight had told me that Lonny's parents died while he was locked up, but there was still his older brother, Jerry, to consider. Maybe Lonny had been in touch with him since his release, but if so, then what of it? What could Lonny Midas tell me that Haight couldn't? Then again, I was assuming that Haight was the only one whose secret had been discovered. If the information had come from someone involved with the two men during the period of their preparation for release, then Midas might have been targeted too.

But I was also aware of something else that Haight had revealed: his belief that, had he been

159

older, Lonny Midas might have been willing to kill him to ensure that he remained silent about what they had done. Could Lonny Midas have borne a grudge against Haight throughout the period of their incarceration and, upon his release, set out to find him and undermine his new existence? Could Lonny Midas even have abducted Anna Kore to further that aim? They were big jumps to make: too big. They were symptoms of my frustration, and part of me wanted to walk away and let Randall Haight sink or swim depending on how the situation developed. What kept me from dropping the case back into Aimee Price's lap was the slim possibility that Anna Kore's disappearance was somehow linked to Haight's past, but so far I could discern no direct connection between them.

The bridge came into view, the slowly rotting pilings of its predecessor beside it like a shadow given substance. I was halfway across when the black-and-white Explorer emerged from a copse of trees on the far side of the water, lights flashing, and blocked the road. I had been expecting to see it ever since the kid at the coffee shop mentioned the chief of police's edict. It was my own fault for overstepping the line.

I kept going until I cleared the bridge, then pulled over and placed my hands on the steering wheel. A man in his late thirties, shorter than I was but with the build of a swimmer or a rower, climbed out of the driver's side of the Explorer, his hand on his weapon and the body of the vehicle between us. His hair was black, and he

160

wore a mustache. Chief Allan looked older in person than he did on TV, and the mustache didn't do him any favors. He approached me slowly. I waited until he was close enough to see my entire body, then carefully shifted my left hand to roll down the window.

'License and registration, please,' he said.

His hand hadn't shifted from the butt of his gun. He didn't seem nervous, but you never could tell with small-town cops.

I handed over the documents. He glanced at them, but didn't call them in.

'What's your business here, Mr. Parker?'

'I'm a private investigator,' I said.

I caught the flash of recognition in his eyes. Maine is a big state geographically but a small one socially, and I'd made enough noise to be on the radar of most of the law enforcement community, even peripherally.

'Who's your client?'

'I'm working on behalf of a lawyer, Aimee Price. Any questions will have to be directed to her.'

'How long have you been in town?'

'A few hours.'

'You should have reported in to us.'

'I didn't realize I had that obligation.'

'You might have considered it a courtesy call under the circumstances. You know where the police department is?'

'Yeah, it's where everything else is. Left at sanitation, right at the clerk's office, then straight on till morning.'

'It's right at sanitation, but close enough. I

161

want you to haul on back there and wait for me.'

'Can I ask why?'

'You can ask, but the only answer you'll get is that I'm telling you to go. The next step is for me to put you in the back of my vehicle and drive you there myself.'

'I'll bet your cuffs bite.'

'Rusty too. Could take a while to get them off.'

'In that case, I'll be heading back to town in my car.'

'I'll be right behind you.'

'That's very reassuring.'

He waited for me to make a turnaround, and it was only when I was safely back on the bridge that he got into the Explorer. He stayed close behind me all the way, although he was kind enough to kill his lights. The kid with the tattoos was standing at the door of the coffee shop when I pulled into the municipal lot. I gave him a wave and he shrugged. No hard feelings, I thought. You did the right thing.

The chief pulled in beside me. I got out and waited for him to join me. He indicated that I should head inside. There was a sprightly looking woman in her early sixties behind a desk just inside the door, surrounded by neatly piled files, a pair of computers, and a dispatcher's radio. She smiled politely as I entered, and offered me a cookie from a plate on the desk. It seemed rude to refuse, so I took one.

'You carrying?' asked Allan.

'Left-hand side,' I said.

'Take it off, and leave it with Mrs. Shaye.'

I kept the cookie between my teeth, removed

my jacket, and handed over the shoulder rig.

'Thank you,' said Mrs. Shaye. She wrapped the straps around the holster and placed it in a cardboard box, to which she appended a playing card: the nine of clubs. She handed another nine of clubs to me.

'Don't lose it, now,' she said.

'Likewise,' I said.

'Take another cookie,' she said. 'Just in case.'

'In case of what?' I said, but she didn't get a chance to answer. Instead, Allan pointed to the left, although his office was to the right. He walked me to one of the town meeting rooms, one so small that I made it look crowded all by myself.

'Make yourself comfortable,' he said. 'I'll get Mrs. Shaye to bring you coffee.'

He closed the door behind him, then locked it as well. I took a seat, finished my first cookie, and put the other one on the table. There was a window that faced onto the rear lot, and I watched a man in overalls working on a second police-department vehicle, a Crown Vic that had clearly been purchased used from another department, with marks on its door where the decal had been removed. Hard times in the city, hard times by the sea.

Mrs. Shaye arrived with coffee and sugar and another cookie, even though I had yet to eat the second one. A long hour went by.

And the sun set on Pastor's Bay.

* * *

163

Randall Haight sat at his kitchen table, his hands palm down on the cheap wood, staring at his reflection in the window. He did not know the man before him. He did not know Randall Haight, for there was nothing about him to be known. He did not know William Lagenheimer, for William had been erased from existence. The face in the glass represented an Other, a pale thing marooned in darkness, and an Otherness, a realm of existence occupied by unbound souls. The setting sun burned fires in the sky around his visage. His diary lay before him, the pages filled with tiny, almost indecipherable handwriting. He had begun writing down his thoughts shortly after his release. He had found that it was the only way to keep himself sane, to hold his selves separate. He kept the diary hidden in a panel at the base of his bedroom closet. He had learned in prison the importance of hiding places.

There were locks on the windows and locks on the doors. He would usually have started cooking his evening meal by now, but he had no appetite. All of his pleasures had dissipated since the images started to arrive, and the latest batch had turned his stomach. What kind of person would do that to a child? He was grateful to the detective for taking them away with him. He did not want them in his house. The girl might get the wrong idea about him, and he did not want that to happen. The balance between them was precarious enough as things stood.

Randall now understood why the detective had reacted so strongly to him back at the lawyer's office. Randall hadn't liked the sense of revulsion that came off the detective at that first meeting, the way he didn't seem particularly sympathetic to the threat that the messages posed to Randall's peace of mind, to his life in Pastor's Bay. It had led him to search for more information about the detective, and what was revealed was both interesting and, Randall supposed, moving. The detective had lost a child to a killer, but here he was working on behalf of another man who had killed a child. Randall struggled to put himself in the detective's position. Why would he take on such a task? Duty? But he had no duty to Randall, not even to the lawyer. Curiosity? A desire to right wrongs? Justice?

It came to Randall: Anna Kore.

A chicken breast sat defrosting on a plate by the sink. Regardless of his absence of appetite, he had to eat. He would get weak and sick otherwise, and he needed his strength. More than that, he had to be able to keep a clear head. His very existence was under threat. His secrets were at risk of being discovered.

All of his secrets.

The TV was playing in the living room behind him. Cartoons, always cartoons. They were the only programs that seemed to keep her calm. He heard a sound behind him, but he did not turn.

'Go away,' he said. 'Go back to your shows.'

And the girl did as she was told.

12

Sometimes good things happen to those who wait.

This wasn't one of those times.

Shortly before eight p.m., after I'd been cooling my heels for so long that my feet had gone to sleep, I heard the door unlock and a massive figure entered the room. His name was Gordon Walsh, and he was primarily a homicide specialist with CID. Our paths had crossed in the past and I still hadn't managed to alienate him entirely, which counted as a miracle on a level with the dead rising up and walking. He had previously worked out of Bangor, one of what was, until recently, three CID units in the state, but a reorganization of the division had reduced this to two, Gray and Bangor. I had heard that Walsh had transferred to Gray, and was working out of the Androscoggin DA's office. It wasn't too much of a burden for him to bear. He lived in Oakland, virtually equidistant from both Gray and Bangor. Pastor's Bay fell under the authority of CID in Gray as it lay in the northern part of Knox County, although in a case like this, such territorial definitions tended to be fluid, and Gray's complement of sixteen detectives could be supplemented by some of their peers in Bangor if necessary.

Now here was Walsh, looking like a man who has just been roused from a deep sleep in order to rescue an unloved cat from a tree. He took in my black suit, and my dark tie, and said, 'The undertaker called. He wants his clothes back.'

'Detective Walsh,' I said. 'Still field-testing the tensile strength of polyester?'

'I'm an honest public servant. I wear what I can afford.' He rubbed the hem of his jacket between his fingers and winced slightly.

'Static?'

'Uh-huh.'

'It's the air.'

He was still leaning against the wall, and his mood didn't seem to be improving. If anything, he was growing more and more unhappy as the seconds ticked by. Walsh wasn't one for hiding his feelings. He probably wept at calendars with pictures of puppies, and howled at the moon when the Red Sox lost a game.

'They send you in to soften me up?' I said.

'Yeah. We're hoping you'll respond to a mellow tone.'

'You want a cookie? They're good.'

'Had one. They are good. I have to watch my weight, though. My wife wants me to live long enough to collect my pension. Not any longer than that. Just until the check has cleared.'

He detached himself from the wall before it started to crumble under the pressure and dropped into a chair at the opposite end of the small table. Outside, the man in overalls had finished working on the Crown Vic. He'd kept going even after the light faded, turning on the garage illumination so that he could finish the job. He was packing away his tools and his lights when Allan

167

came out to talk to him. The mechanic took a pack of cigarettes from the pocket of his overalls, and he and Allan had a smoke while they circled the car, the mechanic presumably pointing out its flaws as they went. Pretty soon, I'd know how the car felt.

'What do you think of him?' said Walsh.

'Allan? I don't know anything about him.'

'He should be someplace else instead of out here in the williwigs. He's smart, and he's committed. He's been good on this Anna Kore thing so far.'

He left her name hanging like a hook. I didn't bite, or not so hard that the hook stuck.

'Are you the primary?' I asked.

'That's right. If you dressed for a funeral, you're too early.'

'Who's the DS?'

Each investigation had a primary detective who, in turn, reported to a detective sergeant who acted as supervisor.

'Matt Prager.'

I knew Prager. He was good, even if he did have an inexplicable fondness for show tunes and musical theater. It made sense to have him and Walsh working together on the Kore case. They were two of the most senior detectives in the Maine State Police, and they generally played well with others.

'So,' he continued, 'while I'm sure you're royally aggrieved at being forced to sit here and watch the world grow dark when you could be off dispensing your own brand of justice someplace else — that, or cleaning up behind the bar you work in when times are tough and the world has temporarily tired of heroes — you should recognize that this is the center of an ongoing investigation into the disappearance of a young girl, and Allan did right to haul you in and let you steam for a while.'

'I don't have a problem with what he did.'

'Good. So, back to the suit. Your client suit, I take it?'

'On occasion.'

'We need to know.'

'You'll have to call Aimee Price and put your request to her. I'm working on her behalf. I can't tell you anything unless she clears it first.'

'We did talk to her. She makes you seem reasonable.'

'She's a lawyer. They're only reasonable on their own terms.'

'Well, then you have that much in common. I know you: If there's trouble, and you show up, then you're involved. Coincidences go out the window where you're concerned. I've no idea why that is, and if I were you I'd worry about it, but for now what it tells me is that your reason for being here probably intersects with the Anna Kore case at some point, and I want you to tell me exactly where that point lies.'

'This is a circular conversation. I'm employed by Aimee Price, which means that any client information is privileged.'

'There's a girl's life at stake.'

'I understand that but — '

'There is no 'but.' It's a *child*.'

His voice was raised. I heard scuffling outside

the door, but nobody else entered.

'Listen, Walsh, I want Anna Kore brought home safely just as much as you do. All I can tell you is that, as of now, I don't believe my client had anything to do with her disappearance, and I've found no evidence of a connection between my inquiries on the client's behalf and your investigation.'

'That's not good enough. You don't get to make that call.'

'My hands are tied here. Aimee's solid, and I like and trust her, but I know that if I breach the rules of client confidentiality she'll have me hauled over hot coals, and that's aside from any further action her client may take. I'll tell you again: As far as I'm aware, the client's case is unrelated to the disappearance of Anna Kore, but I have advised the client to contact the police about the matter with which we're dealing, just so there's no confusion.'

'And how did your client respond to this magnanimous gesture on your part?'

'The client is thinking about it.'

Walsh threw up his hands.

'Well, that's just great. That's set my mind right at rest. Your client is going to *think* about a duty to share information that may be pertinent to an ongoing investigation. Meanwhile, there's a fourteen-year-old girl missing and, in my experience, the people who abduct fourteen-year-old girls don't tend to have their best interests at heart. And you, you spineless son of a bitch, are shifting your moral responsibilities on to a *lawyer*. You're right down at the bottom of the swamp

170

now, Parker, mired with the weeds and the parasites. You, of all people, should know better. Have you seen the news? Have you watched Valerie Kore crying for her child? You know what she's going through, and there'll be worse to come if we don't find her daughter in time. You want that on your head, a man who lost his own child, who understands — '

It was the mention of Jennifer that did it — that, and the fact that I knew Walsh was right. Immediately I was on my feet, and Walsh was on his. I heard myself shouting at him, losing control, and I wasn't even aware of the words that I was saying. Walsh was shouting back at me, spittle flying from his mouth, his finger jabbing at my face. The door behind us opened, and Allan entered along with another older patrolman I hadn't seen before, and in the background were faces staring at us: Mrs. Shaye; the mechanic; Walsh's partner, Soames; two state troopers; and a pair of men in suits.

Even in my anger and self-pity, in the self-righteousness that I was using to mask my shame, I recognized one of them, and I knew that the game had taken another turn. I stepped back from Walsh, and from my own worst instincts.

'I want a phone call,' I said. 'I want to call my lawyer.'

★   ★   ★

The door was locked again, and once more I was alone. I wasn't under arrest, and I hadn't been charged with any crime. Neither had a telephone yet materialized. It was possible that they could hold me for obstructing the course of justice, but Aimee would swat that one out of the sky with a flick of her wrist. The problem, as I simmered in the chair, was that I felt the truth of Walsh's statement. I knew better than to behave the way that I was behaving. I knew because I carried the memory of a dead child with me wherever I went. The weight of her loss was heavy on my heart, and I would not and could not wish that pain on another person. Legally, I was within my rights to withhold what I knew about Randall Haight; morally, I was beneath contempt, for Haight's right to privacy was subordinate to a child's right to life.

Yet while I felt that Haight was engaged in an act of misrepresentation, a manipulation of the truth for his own ends, I still did not believe he was involved in whatever had befallen Anna Kore. At the same time, despite my assurances to Walsh, I could not be certain that his troubles and the girl's disappearance were not connected simply because I had not yet found any evidence to link them. But if they were linked, then I could not believe that the person who was sending photographs and discs to Haight would be careless enough to leave evidence on the contents of the envelopes, or even on the envelopes themselves. Still, that was not my call to make. I didn't have a forensics lab in my basement, and who knew what trace evidence or DNA evidence might be found if the envelopes and their contents were submitted for examination?

But I was also troubled by the man I had seen staring back at me from the doorway of Chief Allan's office. We had never met, but I knew his face: I had watched him hovering around the outskirts of a RICO trial in Augusta earlier in the year, and while I was being interviewed in the aftermath of a smuggling operation that had made the newspapers during the summer. His name was Robert Engel, and he had the nebulous title of Deputy Supervisor of Operations in the Organized-Crime Squad of the FBI's Boston Division. In effect, he had a roving brief, and acted as a conduit for information and resources between the New England divisions and the three units of the Organized-Crime Section at FBI headquarters in Washington — La Cosa Nostra and racketeering; Eurasian/Middle Eastern crime; and Asian and African criminal enterprises — as well as working with the Joint Terrorism Task Forces to uncover potential sources of terrorist funding through the medium of organized criminal activity. Engel was an accomplished diplomat, carefully navigating his way through the FBI's own cutthroat world of internecine warfare as well as its ongoing feuds with sister agencies — in particular the Bureau of Alcohol, Tobacco, Firearms, and Explosives. In addition, he had worked to rebuild the Bureau's reputation in Boston following revelations of collusion between some of its agents and leading organized-crime figures in the city.

There was no apparent reason for Engel to be in a boondocks police department during the investigation into the disappearance of a young girl. Nevertheless he was here, and his presence explained some of the odd features of the case, including the length of time it had taken for Anna Kore's mother to make a public appeal. It suggested a conflict of views, and Engel's presence meant that there were at least two arms of the FBI involved in the Kore investigation. Plus, if Engel was involved, then the feds either knew about organized criminal activity in Pastor's Bay or were watching for someone at the periphery, someone with connections that extended beyond the town's limits.

I needed to talk to Aimee, for both our sakes. It was now more important than ever that we convinced Randall Haight of the necessity of coming forward and revealing the nature of the messages that were being sent to him and the reason for them, even at the risk of disrupting his carefully safeguarded existence. It was one thing to rile the Maine State Police, and I had sound reasons for wanting to do that as little as possible. My PI's license had been rescinded in the past for angering the MSP, and any future action taken against me might well result in its permanent forfeiture. Screwing around with the FBI was another matter entirely. The cops would have to charge me or let me go, but the feds could put me behind bars for as long as they wanted. Aimee would probably be okay, as even the FBI tended to dislike jailing lawyers without good cause. I, on the other hand, was only a PI, and while I was aware that there were those in the Bureau who were interested in me and, for reasons of their own, were prepared to give me a degree of protection, they did so out of a sense of duty rather than any great personal fondness, and they might well view a spell in a lockup, either county or one more shadowy, as a useful way of reminding me of the limits of their tolerance.

Eventually, after almost another hour had gone by, the door was unlocked. This time it was Allan who entered, and the door stayed open. Behind him, the building was relatively quiet. Engel and his acolytes, Walsh and the staties, all were elsewhere. Apart from Engel I could see only the older cop with his cap under his arm, and a pretty young woman wearing sweatpants and an old Blackbears T-shirt who seemed to have taken over from Mrs. Shaye for a time but was now putting on her coat in preparation for departure.

'You're free to go,' said Allan. He didn't look pleased about it.

'That's it?'

'That's it. It's not my call. I had my way, you'd have told us everything you know by now.'

'You won't believe this, but I wouldn't have blamed you if you'd taken the hard road.'

'Save it. We'll find out who you were speaking with, one way or another. We've already started asking about your car. This is a small community, and it's on its guard. Someone will have seen you parked, and we'll take it from there. You be sure to let your 'client' know that. You can collect your gun and your phone from Becky.'

I handed my playing card over to Becky. She wasn't as friendly as Mrs. Shaye, and she didn't look as if she ate many cookies, but I thanked her anyway. When I got to my car, I turned on my cell phone and called Aimee. She answered on the first ring.

'Thanks for rushing to my aid,' I said.

'I thought you might feel I was threatening your masculinity. Have they let you go?'

'Reluctantly. I don't want to do this over the phone, and I'm too tired to talk face-to-face now. Can you make time for me in the morning?'

'First thing. I'll be there at eight. In the meantime, I've spoken to our client.'

'And?'

'I think he may be starting to see the light after your earlier conversation with him, but he's still reluctant to come forward.'

'Twist his arm,' I told her. 'He comes forward soon, or I'm giving him up.'

I killed the connection. I was tired, and I almost considered trying to find a bed for the night in Pastor's Bay, but a quick look along the deserted main street convinced me otherwise. Eventually I might have to stay nearer to the town, but I had no desire to stay *in* it. It might have been my weariness after hours spent in that small room, and the pall that the disappearance of Anna Kore had cast over the place, but I felt that, even without the trauma of her vanishing, I would still have been anxious to leave Pastor's Bay behind. Seeing it now, empty of souls, I felt the wrongness of it: There was not meant to be a town here, or not this town. The very first stone

176

had been laid incorrectly, the first house built in a bad location and with an inhospitable aspect, and all that had followed was rendered skewed and unbalanced by those initial mistakes. James Weston Harris's death at the hands of the natives should have served as a warning of what was to come, but it was too late to undo the damage, too late to start again, and so all who lived here had to resign themselves to these deep imperfections or deny them entirely while wondering why they, and the town, never truly prospered.

My cell phone beeped. I had an incoming message, but it came from a blocked number. I opened it anyway. It read:

CHIEF ALLAN IS TELLING LIES.

I closed the message and looked again at the dark, ugly street, as though waiting for the sender to be revealed as a shadow among deeper shadows, but nothing moved. Tiredness be damned. My desire to leave Pastor's Bay was now overpowering. I turned the key in the ignition and heard only a death rattle. I tried again, and this time even the rattle was absent. My battery was dead. Before I could start cursing the god who had ever brought me to this place, there was a tap on my window. The mechanic was standing beside me, another cigarette fixed between his lips. I rolled down the window.

'Need a boost?' he asked.

'In every way,' I replied.

His truck was parked nearby, and he returned

with a booster pack for the battery. He opened the hood, attached the clamps, and told me to give her a try. The car started instantly. I kept my foot on the gas while I reached into my wallet for a twenty. He saw what I was doing and shook his head.

'Don't worry about it,' he said. 'Maybe between this and my mother's cookies you won't think so badly of us when you leave.'

'Mrs. Shaye is your mother?'

'Yep, and she doesn't hand over those cookies to just anyone. I'm Patrick Shaye, but everybody around here calls me Pat. And I know who you are; by now, the whole town probably knows.'

We shook hands, and he removed the booster pack from the Mustang's battery.

'Nice machine,' he said. 'You tend it yourself?'

'Some.'

'I like these old cars. Anything goes wrong with them, it can be fixed easily. You don't need computers, just grease and knowhow.'

'I saw you working on that Crown Vic out back. I take it you have the contract to service the town's vehicles?'

'Yep, and with luck I'll still have it tomorrow after the chief hears I helped you out. He's not the forgiving kind, the chief. Pays not to cross him.'

He said it lightly, but there was an undercurrent of something harsher. I didn't press him on it. He said good-bye, then added, 'I figure we'll be seeing you again, right?'

'Why do you say that?'

'Because you look like the kind of fella who

doesn't run because a dog barks at him, even a dog with teeth like the chief's.'

'He strikes me as being good at what he does.'

'He is, but that's being good at policing a small town with small-town problems.' He opened the door of his truck. 'Thing is, we have a bigger problem now.'

'Anna Kore.'

'That's right.'

'You don't think he's up to finding her?'

'That's not for me to say.'

'Is that why the FBI is here?'

He shook his head and grinned. 'Nice try, Mr. Parker. I just fix cars.'

I stayed behind him for a mile or two, and he flashed his hazards at me when he turned off the main road. I drove on and thought about the message on my cell phone. Allan had barely spoken to me, and I couldn't find anything in the few words we had exchanged that might be open to doubt or suspicion, which meant that the person who had sent the anonymous text message, probably using a proxy website, was referring to something outside my sphere of knowledge. Then again, it might simply have been an attempt to muddy the waters, just as the packages sent to Randall Haight might be, in which case it was possible that one person, or group of persons, was responsible for both.

I was starting to wish that I'd never heard from Aimee Price, or met Randall Haight, even without the further complications suggested by the presence of the FBI agent, Engel. Engel was a heavy hitter. If he had left his Boston lair for

Pastor's Bay, it was because there was something in the circumstances surrounding the girl's disappearance that interested him. But all that really interested Engel was organized crime and terrorism, and I had no desire to face mobsters or terrorists unaided.

I stopped at a gas station and made another call, this time from a pay phone, because the gentlemen I was calling in New York didn't like calls from cell phones.

Then again, the gentlemen in New York weren't really gentlemen at all.

13

The apartment was on the second floor of a grim building on Fourth Avenue in Brooklyn. It wasn't the ugliest block on the avenue, but it was close. Fourth had been rezoned in 2003 in the hope of creating Brooklyn's Park Avenue, with tony upscale living environments replacing body shops. Unfortunately, corners had been cut by City Planning early in the process, and the first condos to be built following the rezoning eschewed retail units and storefronts on the first floor in favor of vents and parking garages. The planners had eventually realized their mistake, but it was too late to undo the initial damage, so Fourth was now an uneasy mix of boutiques, restaurants, and urban brutalist façades.

To the man checking the numbers on the building's intercom, it seemed that the only thing Fourth had in common with his beloved Park Avenue was the traffic, every lane of it. Given the choice, he'd take somewhere on Fifth or Seventh farther up the Slope in a heartbeat. Then again, that assumed he actually had some interest in living in Brooklyn, which he hadn't. People could talk all they wanted about how it was the new Bohemia, but he wasn't buying, he hadn't cared much for the old Bohemia, and everything that he needed could be found on the island of Manhattan. As far as he was concerned, the other four boroughs could be cut with a big blade and towed out up to Greenland, apart from the strip of Queens containing JFK, and they could run ferries to that. As for Jersey, that was why there was water separating it from Manhattan. In his darker moments, his proposals for renegotiating Manhattan's relationship with New Jersey included filling in the tunnels and blowing up the George Washington Bridge before pointing big guns west, just in case those left on the other side got any ideas. Admittedly, somewhere else to dump bodies would have to be found, but into every life a little rain had to fall.

There was no camera embedded in the intercom panel beside the main door to the building, and no names beside the buzzers. He pressed the number that he'd been given, a woman's voice asked his name, and he gave it, or he gave a name. In this business, nobody really expected anybody to use their real names — not the middlemen, not the johns, and certainly not the girls. His personal experience of such matters was limited, but through choice and orientation rather than any naïveté about the ways of the world.

He was buzzed in and took the stairs to the apartment, avoiding the elevator. Lights came on as he walked, a vague concession to eco-consciousness in a building so poorly constructed that he could almost see the signals changing outside through the joins in the walls. Most of the apartments he passed were silent. An earlier check of the building's records had revealed an occupancy rate of about sixty percent, and there were already signs of wear and neglect on the carpets and fittings.

The apartment he sought was at the end of the

corridor. He knocked at the door, watched the spy hole darken, and was admitted. The woman wore a red sweater dress over a pair of dark-blue jeans. Her feet were bare, and she smelled of cigarettes. Her hair was platinum with red streaks, as though she'd recently suffered a head injury and hadn't got herself together enough to wash out the blood. He figured her for mid-thirties, aged by a hard life. That was the way of her business. It had worn her out, and now she had either moved up the ranks to active pimping or had taken the maid's role for a cut of the money.

'Hi, honey,' she said. 'Just through here.'

To the left was a bathroom and a closed door, but she showed him into a living area to the right. There were two more doors off the living room — one open, one closed. The first one led into a narrow kitchen. There was a pack of tortilla chips on the counter, and a half-eaten sandwich alongside a glass stained with milk. The other door was closed, but he thought that he could hear another television playing faintly behind it.

'Are you a member of the law-enforcement community?' she said.

'No, I am not.'

'I have to ask,' she said.

'I know how it works.'

It was a myth that an undercover cop had to identify himself as such if asked, especially as anyone with half a brain could see that such a requirement might deliver a fatal blow to the whole concept of undercover operations, but he was surprised by how many in the woman's line of work still considered it a myth worth believing. Technically, a lawyer might argue entrapment, but equally the definition of 'entrapment' was somewhat nebulous, particularly in a situation like this, where the intention to commit a crime was obvious from the start. It was all moot in the end. Most criminals were dumb, and he took the view that the whole science of criminology was essentially flawed, since much of its theory was based on the study of criminals who had been caught, and were therefore either stupid or unlucky, as opposed to the study of those who had not been caught, and were therefore smart and had a little luck on their side, but just a little. Luck ran out, but smart was for life.

He produced an envelope from his coat pocket and laid it on the table, just as he had been instructed to do when he made the original call. The woman glanced inside, gave the bills a quick flick with her fingers, then placed the money in a drawer below the TV.

'You mind if I frisk you?'

He raised an eyebrow. 'Why would you want to do that?'

'There's been trouble in the past — not for us, I assure you, but for others in the same business. They've had guys produce knives, ropes. We're concerned about safety, yours as much as ours.'

He wasn't quite sure that was the case, but he allowed her to pat him down inexpertly.

'Thanks for being so understanding,' she said. 'You're going to have a good time.'

'Can I see the girl now?'

'Sure. She's right through here. You'll like her. She's just what you ordered.'

He followed the woman down the hall and past the bathroom to the closed door. She knocked and opened at the same time, revealing a pleasantly furnished bedroom with low lighting. There was another TV here, with a DVD symbol bouncing around the screen. The room was heavily scented, but not enough to fully mask the stale odor of sex.

The girl on the bed was wearing a baby-doll nightdress. Even her makeup couldn't hide the fact that she wasn't long past owning a baby doll as well. Twelve or thirteen, he thought. Dark roots showed in her blond hair.

'This is Anya,' said the woman. 'Anya, say hello to Frederick.'

'Hi,' said Anya, and even in that one word he could hear her foreignness. One side of her mouth lifted, but nobody would have termed it a smile.

'Hi,' said the visitor, but he sounded doubtful.

'Is there a problem?' said the woman.

'She's not what I ordered after all,' he said.

Immediately, the woman's tone changed, but she tried to stay on the right side of polite. 'We spoke on the phone,' she said. 'I took down the details myself. You asked for a blonde.'

'She's not blonde. She dyes her hair. I can see her roots.'

Anya's eyes moved from face to face, trying to follow the conversation. She could tell that the visitor was unhappy, but no more. She didn't like it when they started out unhappy. It usually made what followed that much harder. She pulled her legs closer to her body and wrapped her arms around them. She rested her chin on her knees, which made her look younger still. There were rubbers on the nightstand beside her, and a box of tissues.

'I'm sorry,' said the woman, 'but the agreement was made. Look, once the lights go down you won't hardly notice the difference, and not where it matters.' She grinned lasciviously. 'Now, if you'd like to take a shower — '

'I don't want a shower,' he said. 'I want my money back.'

All pretense of courtesy disappeared from the woman. Her upper lip involuntarily curled into a feral snarl, like a dog giving a final warning before it bites.

'That's not going to happen. You paid for the hour. You can play Parcheesi with her if you like, or talk about how your day has been, or you can just take a walk right back out the door and go someplace else. The choice is yours, but the money stays here.' She made one last effort at being conciliatory. 'Look, honey, why argue and spoil a beautiful encounter? You're going to have a good time.'

'You told me that already.'

'She's a nice girl. You'll like her.'

'I don't care if she's Miss American Pie. She's not what I ordered.' He took out his cell phone. 'Maybe I should call the police.'

The woman backed away from him. 'Rudy!' she shouted. 'We have a problem.'

The closed door at the end of the hall opened, and he heard the TV more clearly. There was a hockey game on. He didn't know who was playing. He took no interest in the sport. Only white people truly appreciated hockey, and that was because they didn't know any better.

The man who emerged was wearing track pants, sneakers, and an oversized Yankees shirt. He was in his late twenties, and gym-toned. His dark hair was neatly cut. He looked like a college student on spring break, except for the Llama tucked into the front of his pants. It had pearl grips, and a chrome finish that caught the light.

Rudy sidled up the hall, pausing at the bathroom door. He hooked his right thumb into the band of his sweatpants, close to the butt of the gun, and leaned against the doorjamb. He looked bored. The visitor figured Rudy wasn't very bright. A bright man would have been alert for danger. Rudy was too used to hustling underage girls and overweight johns. The visitor was neither.

'What seems to be the trouble?' said Rudy. His eyes swiveled lazily to the woman.

'He says the girl isn't what he ordered. He wants his money back.'

Rudy spat out a laugh and gave the visitor his full attention. 'What do you think we are, man, Sears? We don't do returns, and we don't do refunds. Now, you can stay and have a good time with Anya or you can take a cab over to Hunts Point and see if they might have what you're looking for. The cash stays here, though.'

'I want my money.'

Rudy changed tack. 'What money? I don't see no money here. This money, did it have your name on it? The Federal Reserve, they make it out to you personally? I mean, I got money, but I don't think it's yours. You didn't bring no money in here. You just came to visit, have a little fun. I don't recall no money changing hands. Bro, money changing hands for pussy — that's illegal. You ought to be careful what you say. Now, your time is ticking away. I was you, I'd go colorblind for the rest of the hour and just enjoy myself. So, what do you say?'

The visitor seemed to consider for a moment. 'I still think I should call someone,' he said. 'This really isn't very satisfactory at all.' His finger hovered over the keys on the bulky black cell phone.

The woman moved farther away from him and stood behind Rudy.

'Prick,' she said. 'You're a jerk, you know that? Coming in here and wasting our time. You deserve to get your ass kicked.'

'I'm warning you,' said Rudy. 'You need to put your phone away and get out of here right now.'

Rudy's hand moved closer to the butt of the gun, but he still didn't draw it. Maybe he wasn't so inept after all, the visitor thought. The old axiom about never pulling a gun that you didn't intend to use sprang to mind. Either Rudy was prepared to kill him, in which case his hesitancy was linked to his understanding of the finality of the act, or he wasn't prepared to fire, in which case he was hesitating because he was afraid. The visitor believed that the latter was probably the case, although if it turned out to be the former then, well, he could deal with that as well.

'You know what General Patton said about pearl-handled grips?' said the visitor. 'He said that only a New Orleans pimp would carry a pearl-handled gun. Guess he was wrong. Looks like shitty New York pimps carry them too.'

Now Rudy did reach for the gun, and the visitor shifted the cell phone in his hand. Two barbed darts shot from the tip, penetrating Rudy's shirt and attaching themselves loosely to the skin on his chest as fifty thousand volts coursed through his body. Rudy fell to the floor, convulsing madly. The woman ran for the living room, screaming for help, while the visitor appropriated Rudy's pimp gun for himself.

A second man appeared in the doorway of the bedroom, bigger than Rudy but dressed the same way. His hair was shaved tight, and he had blunt, Slavic features. Unlike Rudy, he was sufficiently alert to have a gun in his hand already, but not prepared enough to make himself a smaller target. The two shots from Rudy's gun hit him in the chest. He held on to the frame of the door, then collapsed to his knees. He raised the gun again, and the third shot flung him back, his knees trapped beneath him, his body convulsing just as Rudy's had, but this time to a different end.

The visitor kicked the dead man's gun away and kept moving. The living room was empty, but he could hear the woman in the kitchen. He followed the sounds and found her searching in the silverware drawer. He kicked at the drawer,

189

trying to slam it closed on her hand, but she was too fast. She came at him with the carving knife, but her arm was high, the blade raised to the level of her head, the tip arcing down. He stepped inside her reach and used his left forearm to force her hand against the wall while his right brought the gun down on the side of her head. He hit her twice and she slid to the floor, moaning. After checking that there was no one else in the apartment, he went back to the hallway and saw that Rudy had crawled into the bathroom. Carefully, the visitor approached the open door. Rudy had already removed the second .38 from under the sink when the visitor appeared in the doorway.

'Don't,' said the visitor.

Rudy fired, but he was still shaky from the electric shock. The bullet took a chunk out of the plaster a foot to the right of the visitor's body, and in response he emptied two shots from the Llama into Rudy, then tossed it aside. He entered the bedroom. The girl named Anya had crawled into a corner by the window, her hands on her ears.

'*Odensia*,' he said. '*Bystro*.'

The girl didn't move. She was trembling hard and stared at him without blinking, as though fearful that, in the instant her eyes closed, he would put an end to her. The visitor tried to remember the word for 'friend,' and managed to dredge something from his memory.

'*Drug*,' he said, then corrected himself: '*Druz'ja*.'

It seemed to have the desired effect. The girl stopped trembling, although she still looked

190

frightened. He repeated his injunction to her to put some clothes on. The girl nodded and went to the closet, retrieving a pair of jeans and a sweatshirt decorated with a spangled cat. He watched her as she dressed, but she didn't seem to mind. He figured that, after all that she'd been through, being semi-naked in front of a stranger was a minor inconvenience. She slipped on a pair of laceless sneakers. He indicated that she should go ahead of him, then followed her into the living room.

He thought that he heard a sound from the hall outside, a door opening and then quickly closing again. The gunfire had been unfortunate but not unexpected, and the visitor did not panic. He searched the apartment, finding two iPhones and a BlackBerry, as well as $4,000 in cash, not including his own $1,000. The woman had stopped moaning and had lapsed into unconsciousness. Her breathing was shallow, there was a blue tinge to her skin, and blood was flowing from one of her ears. He wasn't sure that she'd live, which suited him just fine.

He took the girl's hand and pulled her into the bathroom, forcing her to step over Rudy's body. He could hear sirens approaching as he opened the window, revealing the fire escape. He made the girl go ahead of him, and stepped down after her. A Lexus pulled in at the curb, and he put the girl in the back before climbing into the passenger seat.

'So how'd it go?' said the driver. He was short and dark-haired, wearing old jeans and a worn leather jacket. He didn't look like the kind of man who should be driving a Lexus, not unless he'd stolen it. His name was Angel.

'Noisy. Messy,' said his partner, both professionally and personally. His name was Louis, and he was dressed like an executive with one of those shadowy, discreet firms that handle other people's money, and handle it well. His hair was cut close to his ebony skull, his skin almost entirely unlined. It would have been difficult to tell his age were it not for the gray beard that he had begun to cultivate, an unconnected goatee and mustache arrangement known in the trade as a 'balbo' but known to his partner as 'that fucking growth on your face.'

'Bad?' said Angel.

'Two down, one pending.'

'You get hurt?'

'No.'

Louis took out the phones and the BlackBerry, and checked the numbers and contacts.

'Lot of good stuff here,' he said. 'Lot of names.' He took a netbook from under the seat, powered it up, and began transferring the contact details from the devices to the computer.

'You know,' said Angel, 'I gotta ask: Are we on a crusade?'

'Unless you got a better word for it,' said Louis. 'Sometimes I wish you'd never introduced me to Charlie Parker. I suspect that he may have contaminated me with idealism.'

'You think you've come a long way. I used to just steal stuff.' Angel looked in the rearview mirror. The girl stared back at him. Her eyes were those of a shell-shocked soldier.

192

'You okay, honey?' he asked.

'I don't think she speaks much English,' said Louis. He dredged up the remains of the little Russian that he knew. '*Kharasho?*'

The girl nodded.

'*Ty v bezopasnosta. Druz'ja.*'

'What did you say?' asked Angel.

'I told her she's safe, and we're friends. That's all I got. Anything more, we'll have to stop in Brighton Beach and get a waiter to translate.'

He felt pressure on his arm. The girl's pale hand rested on his forearm.

'Dina,' she said. 'No Anya. Dina.'

'Dina,' repeated Louis. He took her hand in his, and held it as they drove.

★　★　★

The shelter was in Canarsie, almost within sight of Jamaica Bay. When they were a block away, Angel made a call from one of the stolen cells. He told the woman who answered that they had a young girl with them who was the victim of sex traffickers, along with the phones used by those responsible. They killed the lights in the car, and pointed out the shelter to the girl. He handed her the phones, and the cash.

'We'll watch you, Dina,' said Louis. He touched two fingers to his eyes, then turned them to the girl, and toward the shelter. '*Ja tvoj dryg.*'

Angel opened the passenger door for her. The girl put one foot out of the car, then paused.

'*Ya nichevo ne videla,*' she said.

Louis raised his palms in frustration and

shook his head. 'I'm sorry, I don't understand.'

The girl frowned, then spoke again, this time in English. 'I see nothing,' she said carefully, then left them. They marked her progress, watching for strangers on the street. A door opened as she approached the shelter, and a woman appeared. Gently, she laid a hand on Dina's shoulder, and ushered her to safety.

Dina did not look back, and the gentlemen from New York drove away.

14

Dempsey and Ryan were sitting in a chain coffee joint at Boston's Scollay Square. If there was a more sterile part of Boston than Scollay, then Dempsey hadn't found it yet. Oh, there were places that were skankier and rougher, projects and wastelands and dumping grounds, but Scollay Square was in the heart of downtown, a series of unforgiving slabs that formed Government Center, dominated by City Hall and the JFK Federal Building. Scollay had once been the home of Boston's elite way back in the eighteenth century. Bowfront houses and grand row houses followed in the nineteenth century, and then the immigrants arrived and the elite left, and Scollay became the center of commercial activity and entertainment in the city, the latter centered on the grand Howard Athenaeum, later known as the Old Howard. In the 1960s it was decided that old was bad, and ugly was good, and Scollay was earmarked for destruction. The existence of the Old Howard presented the only real obstacle to the plan, and a group of concerned citizens pressed for its renovation, a campaign rendered null and void when the Howard burned to the ground in 1961 for no cause that anyone could establish, although there were plenty of people prepared to take a guess. As Dempsey well knew, there was no shortage of guys in Boston who knew how to light a match. The

195

destruction of old Scollay had subsequently given birth to the strip joints and porno theaters of Lower Washington, although the excesses of the Combat Zone were now largely the stuff of memory.

For now, though, Scollay Square was safe territory, so far as any such place could be found in their current situation, on the grounds that someone would have to be crazy to try to whack anyone within sight of City Hall and a building that was crammed with feds the way a newly filled salt cellar was crammed with salt. Dempsey didn't know for sure if there was a price on all their heads, not yet, which was why the meeting had been arranged. His belief, which he had not expressed to Ryan but which he suspected the younger man shared, was that it was only a matter of time before final sentence was passed, if it had not been agreed already in their absence. The hit would have to be sanctioned; unsanctioned hits brought an immediate death sentence for those involved, or that was the theory. In reality, except in exceptional circumstances, the sentence tended to be passed solely on the man who had pulled the trigger, and not on the man who had told him where to point the gun. But if a decision had been made to put Tommy Morris in the ground, then the additional expense of a couple of bullets for the men who had remained loyal to him was unlikely to trouble those behind the hit. Like any good gambler, Dempsey just needed to clarify the extent of their exposure before he played his hand.

They lounged at the table with their coffees, watching the tourists and businesspeople pass by. One of the restaurants had dumped a pile of stale doughnuts and bagels outside for the birds to eat, and the seagulls fought the pigeons for a share of the spoils. Dempsey had ordered coffee for Ryan, who was now looking at his cup suspiciously.

'What is this?' he asked.

'A latte.'

'What's in it?'

'Coffee. It's coffee. You asked for a coffee.'

'Yeah, but a regular coffee.'

'That is a regular coffee. They just add milk to it.'

'I like to add my own milk.'

'Just drink it. You need to broaden your horizons.'

Ryan sipped warily at the cup. 'It tastes milky.'

'I swear, I don't care how many cops are around, I'll leave you bleeding on the floor if you don't shut up and drink your coffee.'

Ryan sulked. A fine rain was descending, so fine that you knew it was falling only because of the sheen on the ground, and the way everyone was wearing what Ryan called the 'Boston rain face,' a kind of grimace that spoke of deep dissatisfaction with God and the elements. Dempsey drank his coffee. At times like this he wished that he still smoked instead of just carrying around a pack of Camels as a reminder to himself of what he had to avoid, which he acknowledged was perverse. A cigarette took some of the tension away but left the edge.

On his lap was a copy of the *Boston Phoenix*. The gun lay inside, and he kept his right hand closed on it. Only when Joey Tuna appeared, his hands buried deep in the pockets of his overcoat, did Dempsey even begin to relax. Joey owned a fish market in Dorchester, which paid good; and he did a little business on the side involving drugs, guns, protection, whores, and loan sharking, which paid better; and he had connections up and down the Northeast. Joey's uncle, who was younger than he was, which Dempsey could never quite figure out, and even better connected, which he could, was doing a dime stretch in Cedar Junction, except everyone of Joey's generation still called it Walpole. For a meet like this, one involving a situation where trust was at a premium, Joey was the go-to guy, since it was understood that the only person who pulled out guns around Joey Tuna was Joey Tuna. Joey was a guarantee of safe conduct, but Dempsey was still wary, and didn't like the idea of someone waiting until Joey was gone to try his hand at some other form of conduct. Better, then, to meet here, in a place that was safe, and public, and cop-heavy, as long as those self same law-enforcement officials didn't look too hard through the tinted windows.

Joey's real name was Joey Toomey, but most people who knew him called him Joey Tuna. He had another name, though, among the lowlifes, one that was never spoken aloud in his presence, and only whispered at other times.

They called him Joey Tombs.

Joey entered the coffee shop and pulled up a chair. He must have been closing in on seventy by now, but he looked good for it. His hair had gone white when he was in his thirties — behind his back, people joked that it happened when a customer asked for credit — giving him a prematurely distinguished air that had done nothing to harm his rise to his present position of authority. He had the natural bulk of one who had spent most of his life doing hard physical labor, and was still regarded by women of a certain age as a good-looking man, at least until he opened his mouth: Joey Tuna had never bothered having his teeth fixed, so his smile resembled a busted picket fence. Dempsey knew that he had a wife, although nobody had ever met her. Like her husband, she wasn't one for unnecessary socializing.

'Terrible weather,' said Joey. All those years in Boston had barely left a mark on his accent, as though he had just got off the boat with a sack on his back. Dempsey was not the only one who sometimes struggled to understand what Joey was saying. 'I can't even see the rain and I'm soaked to the skin.'

Dempsey and Joey shook hands. Ryan received a nod for his troubles.

'What can I get you, Mr. Toomey?' said Ryan. He was always polite around the older men, Dempsey noted. Ryan was clever like that. Respectful. Had things worked out differently, he might have gone a long way.

'You think they got tea here?' said Joey. 'I never come into these places. You could buy a share in a plantation for what they charge for a cup of coffee.'

'They got tea, but you won't like it,' said

Dempsey. 'They use the water from the boiler. It won't taste right. It's never the right temperature for tea.'

Joey raised his eyes to heaven. He was out of his comfort zone here, which was just as Dempsey had intended. Joey Tuna liked restaurants where his name was known and the laminated menu hadn't changed since V-J Day. Joey Tuna didn't drink, he didn't do drugs, and he didn't frequent bars. He ate sandwiches six days a week at an untidy desk in an office that smelled of fish, and drank stewed tea from a battered metal pot warmed by a single electric ring. Joey Tuna was a traditionalist, a paid-up member of the old school, a patter of backs and a shaker of hands. Joey Tuna was a smiler of broken smiles, an honest broker for dishonest men, a recorder of old, dusty debts and unwise promises made in haste. Joey Tuna was a cold, merciless vacuum; there were fish on his slabs that held more warmth.

'Coffee, then, coffee,' said Joey. 'Black with a bit of milk. None of that mocha shite, or whatever it is.'

Ryan got up to place in the order.

'How you doin', Joey?' said Dempsey. His back was to the wall, and his right hand remained hidden beneath the paper.

'I'm good. Arthritis is acting up, though. It's the weather, and the time of year. I'll be crucified like Christ on the cross from now until April.'

He took a handkerchief from his pocket and blew his nose. 'Something wrong with your hand, Martin?' he said.

'Nothing at all, I'm pleased to say. It responds quickly to stimulus.'

'We'd better hope that nobody breaks a cup.'

'These are troubled times, Joey.'

'Is there ever any other kind?' Joey put his handkerchief away, but slowly, and he made sure that only the tips of his fingers entered his pocket. 'You couldn't have picked somewhere with more heat, could you? The feds won't have far to take us if they come for us. They could just lock the door and leave us here.'

'There's a lot of bad blood. I figured it couldn't hurt to have the law on my side.'

'You don't trust me?'

'You I trust,' said Dempsey, and he was careful not to let the taste of the lie show on his face. 'It's the others I'm less sure of, and I can't hide under your coat for the rest of the day.'

Joey looked away. 'It's longer than that you'd need to be under there, the way things are going.'

'Which is why we're here. Tommy is concerned.'

'And so he should be. So are we all.'

'So what's to be done?'

'He should just walk away. I've told him that.'

'He can't afford to walk away. He wants to rebuild.'

'It's all gone, or as good as. They'll bury him under the ruins of what's left.'

'Well, you see, Joey, he's trying to figure out where it all went wrong. If he can do that, he thinks he can put things right.'

'Poor investments. Bad luck. Could happen to

anyone. Once it starts to go south, it goes fast. It's like a boulder tumbling down a hill. When it's big enough, and it builds enough momentum, it can't be stopped. It rolls, and it crushes anyone caught in its path. I tried to tell him that, but he wouldn't listen.'

'Well, it seems to Tommy that people might actively have conspired to send that boulder his way. He thinks that he's been set up for a fall.'

'A bad workman blames his tools, Martin. You know that. He's made mistakes, and now he's looking for someone else to shoulder the responsibility. It's understandable, but that doesn't make it right. There are debts that have to be settled. Unless he wins the Mega Millions, he's going to have to offload his business interests in order to meet his obligations.'

'They're all he has, Joey. If he walks, he's left with nothing.'

'He has his life.'

'For how long?'

'What's that supposed to mean?'

'You know what it means.'

'No, I don't.'

'Come on, Joey, you're too old to play the virgin.'

Ryan arrived with the coffee.

'Is there milk?' said Joey.

'You said you wanted it black.'

'Black, then milk. I didn't want them fucking around with it behind the counter, sprinkling shite on it.'

'I'll get you the jug,' said Ryan.

'Nah, you do it. Not too much. Just add a bit

of color to its cheeks.'

Ryan looked at Dempsey. He had no idea what that meant.

'Brown it,' said Dempsey. 'Like an Asian girl.'

Ryan moved off, even more bewildered than before.

'Too old to play the virgin, eh?' said Joey. 'You have some mouth on you. You should have more respect.' But he was grinning.

Ryan came back with the coffee. Joey looked at it, tried it, and nodded.

'Good lad. Now go outside for a minute, will you? Take some air.'

'It's raining,' said Ryan.

'It's good for the skin. Off you go.'

Ryan sighed and went outside with his coffee. He stood with his back to them, one hand holding his coffee, the other on the gun in the pocket of his black leather jacket. He had cut away the lining especially for that purpose, a trick Dempsey had taught him.

'He's all right,' said Dempsey. 'You could have let him stay.'

'He's young, and I'm not sure how much he knows or doesn't know. He's a listener too, and I don't like people to listen unless I tell them to. It's not for me to betray confidences. As for Tommy and his troubles, that's where we stand on the matter. You don't want to go overcomplicating it.'

'Tommy is worried that it has already been complicated.'

'You're talking about the girl.'

'That's right. It's out of order.'

'The girl has nothing to do with this.'

'We're here because of the girl. Tommy wants to be sure that Oweny doesn't have her.'

'He doesn't. I asked him. He doesn't have her. He said so.'

'With all due respect, that's what he'd tell you.'

'Careful now, Martin.' Joey wagged a calloused finger at him. 'I've always been very tolerant of you. You're brighter than ten of the rest of them put together, but don't think you can belittle me. I'm telling you now, Oweny doesn't have the girl. If he did, you'd have known about it long before this. What would be the point in taking her and then not using her as leverage? Jesus, I don't think he even knew about the girl until you mentioned her to me.' Joey sipped his coffee. 'That's not a bad cup of coffee,' he said. 'I'm glad I'm not paying for it, but it's not bad.'

The coffee seemed to make him relent somewhat or, as Dempsey suspected, it gave him an excuse to alter his approach, to adopt a different persona. Had the stakes not been so high, Dempsey might even have enjoyed watching the performance.

'It's terrible,' said Joey. 'A young girl being taken like that. What's the world coming to, Martin?'

And then Joey switched masks again, and Dempsey felt any lingering respect that he had for the old operator fall away like so many scales from his eyes.

'Who knows what's being done to her, you know what I mean? There are deviants out there who'd think nothing of forcing themselves on a child, raping her and then leaving her to die in a ditch. If she was blood to me, I don't know what I'd do. I suppose I'd do anything, anything at all, to try and help her.'

He placed his hands together, his thumbs meeting to form the sign of the cross, just as they did every Sunday when he knelt down to pray at eleven o'clock Mass at St. Francis de Sales, his head bowed and his eyes closed, as though God cared to hear the prayers of one such as he.

'We know people up there, Martin. We have connections. If Tommy does the right thing, we can act on his behalf. We'll have men out combing the bushes. We'll put the screws on every pervert between here and Canada. We can help him, Martin, but only if he wants to help himself.'

And Dempsey wondered if they did, in fact, have the girl, and if this was all part of the game: Lure Tommy in when he's weak, and then finish him off before letting the girl go. For they would let the girl go; even a blackened husk of a man like Joey Tuna wouldn't want the death of a child on his soul.

'I'll be sure to let him know that,' said Dempsey.

'You do whatever you want. I'm here to help if I'm needed.'

'Even if Oweny doesn't have her,' Dempsey continued, 'Tommy wants him to back off. Oweny's acting like Tommy's already in the grave and left everything to him in his will.'

'Tommy's dying, Martin. He just doesn't want to admit it. When you're dying, the vultures start to circle.'

205

'Oweny's not circling, Joey. He's pulling the meat from Tommy's bones while he's still alive. Tommy's not just dying; Oweny's killing him.'

'There are other concerns here, Martin. You've said so yourself. You're no virgin either. If Tommy's desperate, then he's vulnerable. He's been around a long time. He can name a lot of names. He could hurt a lot of people. We had enough of that in the past.'

'Tommy's not like that, Joey. You know it. He's sound.'

'You ever been to federal prison, Martin?'

'No.'

'Well, if you had you'd know that half the guys in there are locked up because they trusted someone who they thought was sound. Everybody's sound until it comes to the moment when they're not, when their survival is at stake and they have to cut a deal to go on living. If I were Tommy, I'd be looking for a way out now. One way out is a stone's throw from here.' And he jerked a thumb at the nest of law enforcement behind his back.

'I'd know, Joey. If he was thinking along those lines, I'd know.'

'Don't be a fool. You wouldn't know until they came knocking on your door with a federal arrest warrant. Then you'd know, and it'd be too late to do anything about it. There are men in this town who have no intention of dying in prison, and I'm one of them. Don't be thinking that you're safe either. He'll rat you out along with the rest of us. That's how they work, those bastards. They want everything, every name that you can vomit up, every man and woman who ever did you a favor in your life. It's all or nothing with them, all or nothing.'

'Tommy's not trying to cut a deal. I'm telling you that.'

'Ah, you're telling, you're telling.' Joey waved at him in dismissal. 'You listen to me — the only telling you need to do is tell Tommy that he has to come in. We'll arrange a sit-down. We'll work things out. If he's sound, like you say he's sound, then he has nothing to worry about.'

Joey put a meaty paw on Dempsey's wrist, holding it so tight that the tips of Dempsey's fingers began to tingle. There were beads of spittle on Joey's lips, and Dempsey could smell the lingering stench of fish that always hung around the man.

'Do you understand me, Martin?' said Joey, the stink of him all over Dempsey now, his skin burning as though he were allergic to this foul man. 'You tell him to come in, or maybe you give me a call and let me know where we might be able to find him. That's all you have to do. You'll be looked after, and so will he. I promise you that. It will all be done the right way.'

They both knew what was being spoken of here. It was an act of betrayal, after which there would only be two choices left: Walk off to exile, or pretend that a life in Boston might still be possible, taking whatever work they put your way until they eventually decided to put a bullet in you, because you couldn't trust a man who'd sell out his boss.

Dempsey pulled his hand away. He looked at

his watch. Oweny's representative was now fifteen minutes late. The arrangement was that Joey would come in first, and his presence during the meet would ensure that all exchanges remained civil, except Oweny's man hadn't shown yet. Outside, Ryan had finished his coffee and was dancing anxiously from foot to foot.

'Oweny's boy should be here,' said Dempsey, but Joey had stood up and was now buttoning his coat.

'Where are you going?' asked Dempsey. 'The sit-down hasn't happened yet.'

'Yes, it has,' said Joey, and Dempsey felt the air leave his body as surely as if he'd been punched in the stomach. Oweny's boy wasn't coming. He had never been coming. Instead, Joey spoke for Oweny. Joey spoke for them all, every one of them, every man who wasn't Tommy Morris and wasn't linked to Tommy Morris, every man who wanted Tommy silenced with a bullet through the back of the head, the smell of the lime that would be used on his body burning his eyes, and a hammer close by to knock his teeth out when it was done. Sentence had been passed. All that remained was its execution.

'The girl?' said Dempsey. 'Tell me the truth. He wants to know. You said Oweny didn't have her. But do you have her? Is she leverage in this?'

But Joey was already somewhere else in his mind. His body just hadn't arrived there yet.

'You tell him to come in, Martin. Don't make us go looking for him. I like you. I like the boy outside. I wouldn't want anything to happen to either of you. So talk to Tommy. Make him see sense. You're a smart man. You'll find the right words. Take care, now.'

He left the coffee shop, patting Ryan on the back as he went. Ryan watched him go, then turned to stare at Dempsey, his mouth agape, one hand raised in a 'WTF?' gesture, the other still holding on to the gun in his pocket.

Good lad, thought Dempsey. Keep a hold on that gun. He was thankful now that he had arranged the aborted meet for here and not for somewhere in Dorchester or Charlestown, as Joey had first suggested. If he'd agreed to that, he'd be on a warehouse floor by now and someone would be hammering nails into his hands and his feet to make him talk.

He walked to the door, the newspaper held awkwardly over the gun. There was a woman coming in and he slipped by her, jostling her as he went. She said something, but he didn't hear her. He was concentrating on the world outside, on the plaza that suddenly seemed more empty than before, on the faces that suddenly seemed more knowing, more threatening. In the time since he had stepped into the coffee shop, his realm of existence had become a desolate, merciless place.

He told Ryan to get moving, and together they floated out into this hostile universe.

15

Aimee was forced to cancel our morning meeting owing to an incident of domestic violence that left a fifty-year-old man with a broken arm, a fractured skull, and a collection of busted ribs. His assailant was his forty-three-year-old wife, who weighed barely ninety pounds fully clothed and soaking wet, and was so soft-spoken that only bats could hear her. Apparently her husband had been beating on her for the first nineteen years of their marriage, and so she had decided to mark the start of their twentieth year together by encouraging him to turn over a new leaf through the judicious application of a lump hammer while he was sleeping off a drunk. A women's refuge for which Aimee provided pro bono services called her in to speak to the woman, so Aimee had postponed our discussion until the afternoon.

There was only a scattering of worshippers at the eight a.m. Mass at St. Maximillian Kolbe in Scarborough when I arrived. I slipped into a pew at the back, and kept my head down throughout. I didn't go to church so much anymore; I went when I needed consolation, or just a space in which to breathe for a time. I found a peace there, the peace that comes from distancing oneself from the mundane, if only for a little while, and embracing the possibility of a peace beyond this world. I could never tell when the urge to seek out that space would strike me, but it came to me that morning after Aimee postponed our meeting, and I did not fight it.

Louis had once asked me if I believed in God after all that I had seen and all I had gone through, most particularly the loss of Susan and Jennifer. I gave him three answers, which was probably at least two more than he had been expecting. I told him that I found it easier to believe in God than not to believe, for if I believed in nothing then the deaths of Susan and Jennifer were pointless and without reason, and I preferred to hope that their loss was part of a pattern I did not yet understand. I told him that the God in whom I believed sometimes looked away. He was a distractible God, a God overwhelmed by our demands, and we were so very, very small, and there were so very, very many of us. I told him that I understood how that could be the case. My God was like a parent always trying to watch out for His children, but you couldn't always be there for your children, no matter how hard you tried. I had not been there for Jennifer when she most needed me, and I refused to blame my God for that.

And I told him that I believed in God because I had seen His opposite. I had seen all that He was not, and been touched by it, and so I could no more deny the possibility of an ultimate goodness to set against such depravity than I could deny that daylight followed darkness, and night the day.

All this I told him, and he was silent afterward.

When Mass was over, I drove out to the Palace Diner in Biddeford and ate breakfast. Some

211

might have felt that it was a ways to go for breakfast, but those people hadn't eaten in the Palace. I lingered over coffee, and read the newspaper, and just as I was relaxed and ready to face the day my phone beeped to indicate that I had a new message. I read it, saved it, and felt my good humor vanish.

I returned home and began working my way through Randall Haight's list of names, using distinguishing information to trace their movements over the years in case any had been employed in a capacity that might have brought them into contact with prisons, and cross-referencing names and addresses against prison records in an effort to establish if anyone in Pastor's Bay had either served time in North Dakota, Vermont, or New Hampshire, or had close relatives who had served time in those states. I drew a blank on them all, but it was only the first stage in what might prove to be a long, drawn-out process of picking apart the weave of dozens of potentially interconnected lives.

I drove to South Freeport shortly after one, and parked in the lot beside Aimee's building. There were no ravens in the trees today. They were elsewhere, and that was fine with me. In the past, I had seen great black ravens squatting on the walls of the old prison at Thomaston, and they had seemed at once both monstrous birds and more, entities that mutated as I watched them, emissaries from a world more tainted than this one. That image had never left me, and now when I saw such birds I wondered at their true nature, and their true purpose.

I smelled coffee brewing when I stepped into the office, and Aimee's voice called a greeting from the little kitchen beside reception. Seconds later, she appeared carrying a pot on a tray, along with a pair of chicken wraps and two purple asters in a vase.

'Very domesticated,' I said. 'He might marry you after all.'

'Your fascination with my marital arrangements never ceases to amaze me,' she said. 'If I didn't know better, I'd suspect you were jealous and wanted to take his place.'

'I'm just thinking about the free legal aid.'

'Thanks. If you keep getting picked up for asking awkward questions, you'll need to drive around with permanent counsel in the passenger seat of that man toy you drive.'

'It's just a car.'

'A Camry is just a car. That's a midlife crisis on wheels.'

I took a seat at her desk. She poured the coffee, I took a wrap, and we began.

'So, where are we?' she said.

'We're nowhere.'

I told her about my conversation with Randall Haight, my encounter with Allan, and my subsequent dealings with Gordon Walsh. I didn't tell her that he had used my daughter's murder to prick my conscience, or about the blowup that followed. I told myself that it wasn't relevant, which was only partly true. Then I showed her the latest envelope that had been sent to Haight. Her face betrayed no feelings as she examined the photographs. Neither did she comment on the short film of the clothes laid out in the barn, but merely watched it in silence. When it was over, she said only, 'It's escalating.'

'Yes.'

'You had those pictures with you when the cops took you in?'

'They were in the trunk.'

'You're lucky they didn't search your car. You could have been in a whole lot of trouble. I'll keep them here for now, and mark them as case evidence.' She put the envelope in a plastic bag, sealed it, and placed it in her safe.

'What else?' she said.

'I've begun trawling the list of names Haight gave me in the hope of establishing a connection, but there's nothing so far. Unless I can come up with a smoking gun pretty quickly, we're looking at a fingertip search through personal lives that could take weeks or months. But if it turns out that Haight's problem is linked to the abduction of Anna Kore — '

'Assuming it is an abduction,' Aimee interrupted. 'Kids that age do run away, you know.'

'I don't get the impression that she was the kind,' I replied. 'I didn't get that vibe from Walsh either. They're worried. Let's accept that she's been taken against her will.'

'Agreed. Reluctantly.'

'Then our problem remains this: We still have no way of knowing, as yet, if Haight's difficulties are connected to her disappearance.'

'And that's a big leap anyway.'

'Look, I'll be straight with you. My conversation with Walsh pricked my conscience. It wasn't pleasant, and we exchanged some harsh words, but he was right and I was wrong. I'm not sure that we're entitled to make the call on whether Haight's problem is material to the investigation into Anna Kore. Personally, I still don't like the aspect of coincidence here. One girl disappears, and a man jailed for the killing of another girl of roughly the same age finds himself the target of threats from an unknown source. Because these are threats: threats of revelation, threats of blackmail, maybe even threats of physical harm at some point in the future.

'Leaving that aside, we have a duty to tell the police what we know. We're withholding evidence that may be linked to the commission of a crime. Now, I accept that legally it's a gray area, and it's unlikely that either of us would end up behind bars for it, but I don't want a murdered girl on my conscience, and neither do you.'

Aimee finished one half of her wrap and started on the other. I had taken only a bite or two of mine, but then I was careful about speaking with my mouth full. Aimee had no such concerns. She had once told me that one of the problems with being a lawyer was that there was either too much to say and too little time in which to say it, or too little to say and too much time to fill.

'I spoke to Haight again an hour ago,' she said, still chewing.

'And?'

'He has suggested a compromise.'

'Which is?'

'Through me, he hands over all the material

215

that he's been sent so far to the police for examination, but I don't reveal the source.'

I thought about it. 'They won't go for it. For one thing, you'll have to explain the relevance of the photographs and the disc. Once you do that, they'll want to interview him, and he'll be on their suspect list, and as we know, he doesn't have an alibi for the period during which Anna went missing. Even if, by some miracle, it was agreed that he wasn't a suspect, he'd still have to come forward to be fingerprinted and give DNA samples in order to exclude him from any evidence found on the envelopes or the photographs.'

'I didn't think it would work either,' she said. 'He knows that his options are growing more and more limited, but I don't believe he'll break until he's trapped in a corner. You're serious about going to the cops if he doesn't come around?'

'I don't want to ruin a man's life, but part of me feels that the consequences of approaching the cops might not be as terrible as he thinks.'

'No?' She sounded skeptical.

'They'll be bad, but people have survived worse.'

'He'll need protection,' she said.

'I've thought about that. We can put the Fulcis on the house.'

Some of the blood ran from Aimee's face.

'You're not serious. They're — ' She tried to find the right word, but the choices were over-whelming. In the end, she settled for 'insane.'

'They're not insane,' I said. 'They're medicated. The medication keeps them borderline sane. Now,

216

if they weren't taking their medication then I might accept your diagnosis, but, with respect, you're not a member of the medical profession. I'm not sure you should be tossing words like 'insane' around, especially where the Fulcis are concerned. They're very sensitive men. They're also very big, sensitive men.'

'Is it true that one of them attacked a judge with his gavel?'

'No.'

'Thank God.'

'It was an attorney. *Their* attorney. But that was a long time ago, when they were young and foolish. And he wasn't a very good attorney anyway, otherwise he wouldn't have been hit with a gavel. Look, they may not be smart, but they'll dissuade any morons with a couple of drinks under their belts who might have decided that Haight needs some harsh justice. He can probably do a lot of his work from home if we have to keep him contained. He may even decide that he wants to leave town for a while. If so, we can find a place for him to stay. It doesn't have to be a motel room. We can put him somewhere pretty nice. I don't think Mr. Haight would want to be without a degree of comfort.'

'We seem to have decided that he's coming forward, though he continues to maintain that he won't.'

'It's just a matter of time. Even if Anna Kore turns up safe and well, it won't solve Haight's problem. I tried to explain some of this to him yesterday, but he's a strange man, and a selfish one too.'

'What do you mean?'

'His only concern is the continuation of his existence as Randall Haight. The fact that a young girl may be in danger doesn't seem to cross his mind.'

'Not everyone is as self-sacrificing as you.'

'Spare me the sarcasm.'

'I wasn't being sarcastic,' she said. She gave it a couple of seconds, then continued. 'Are you having problems dealing with our client? You don't have to like him, but you do have to be able to handle him without letting your dislike for him show.'

'I can handle him, and I can conceal any negative feelings I may have about him,' I said. 'But you need to be clear on the extent of his self-interest, and the only way we can get him to act as we want him to is by making it appear that his actions serve his own ends. If we're to make him come forward, then perhaps he needs to understand that if something bad happens to the girl, and it turns into a murder investigation, there's a good chance the cops will find out who he is and what he did, and the rest of it will come out as well. If there is a connection between the two cases, the best — the very best — that he can hope for is to be known as the man who let a girl die when he might have been able to provide evidence that could have saved her. He could also end up in prison, and I don't think that would suit him. He'll do hard time as a convicted child killer linked to another child killing. He won't survive a year.'

She nodded. 'I told him we were meeting, and

that I'd call him when we were done. The threat of being returned to jail, unlikely as it might be, could be enough to persuade him to talk to the police. It's probably the only thing he fears more than the revelation of his past. Is there anything else I should know?'

'Kind of. You should know, but I don't think it'll make you any happier. The situation is more difficult than it first seemed.'

'I find that hard to believe.'

'Two things: The first is that while I was languishing in a broom closet in Pastor's Bay I saw a fed named Robert Engel lurking in the background.'

'So? The state police have asked for FBI assistance. It's not unusual in cases like this.'

'Child abductions are not Engel's bag. He deals with organized crime: Italians, Russians, Irish. That's not to say that any of them are above kidnapping, but what would criminals be doing taking a girl from Pastor's Bay, Maine?'

'What do we know about Anna Kore's family?'

'Not much, but I intend to find out more.'

'And the second thing?'

I showed her my cell phone with the anonymous text message about Chief Allan.

'Shit,' said Aimee. 'Pastor's Bay is a regular nest of vipers. Hasn't anybody told them that gossiping is bad for the soul? So what's Chief Allan lying about, if anything at all?'

'For that you need to see the second message. It came through while I was finishing my breakfast.'

I handed her the phone. There were ten words to the message:

**CHIEF ALLAN IS A PEDOFILE.
HE PRAYS ON YOUNG GIRLS.**

'God,' said Aimee. She pushed the phone away as if it were infected. I could see her running the numbers in her head, sizing up the angles. I had done the same earlier, and none of the results had pleased me.

'It could just be a local with a grudge,' I said. 'He's a small-town police chief, so you can be sure that he's managed to cross a couple of people in his time. He tickets the wrong guy, makes someone put down a dog that bit when it shouldn't have, didn't let a possession bust slide. It doesn't take much.'

'But if it's true? My God, a fourteen-year-old girl has gone missing from his jurisdiction. If he's involved, he's manipulating an investigation of which he may be the focus.'

'We're getting ahead of ourselves,' I told her. 'But I want help, and not Fulci help. I need to be able to track Allan, but he knows me, and when Haight presents himself to the police I'm going to be as popular with the cops as blackflies at a wedding, at least for a little while. I'm also worried about Engel. He deals with some seriously unpleasant people, and if there's a mob angle to this we'll have to move carefully, for our sakes and Haight's.'

'What are you suggesting?'

'It's already under way. I've asked some

friends to come up from New York. They'll be here tomorrow.'

Aimee knew to whom I was referring. She had heard the stories.

'You know,' she said, 'I'll be very curious to meet these friends.'

★ ★ ★

I spoke to Haight shortly after Aimee concluded her second conversation of the day with him. He sounded dazed, and less certain of the wisdom of keeping silent about what was happening to him, and I knew that soon we'd be facing the police in an interview room. Haight might not have realized it yet, but it was probably the best move he could make under the circumstances. The only part of our exchange that seemed to throw him was my final question.

'Mr. Haight, in the course of your work have you ever had dealings with criminal enterprises?'

'What do you mean by that?' he said. 'What are you implying?'

'I'm not implying anything. All I'm asking is if, either knowingly or unknowingly, you might have come into contact with businesses that could have organized-crime connections? I'm talking about strip joints, gambling clubs, loan sharks, or even seemingly legitimate operations that weren't quite so legitimate when their books were examined?'

'No,' he said, and he sounded definite about it. 'I deal with small businesses for the most part, and none of them have ever given me any real

221

cause to be concerned. They also know better than to ask me to collude in any illegal activities.'

'That's fine, Mr. Haight,' I told him. 'I just wanted to be sure.'

'I like my work,' he said. 'Some people might find it dull, but I don't. I like its sense of order. I don't want to lose my job, Mr. Parker. I don't want to lose my clients, and my friends. I don't want to lose this life.'

'I understand.'

'No,' he replied. 'You think you do, but you don't understand at all.'

And he hung up the phone.

16

Joseph Anthony Toomey, or Joey Tuna as he was known to his customers at the Dorchester Central Fish Market, a name that implied Dorchester was coming down with fish markets as if they were going out of fashion, sat in his office calculating the day's takings and planning his orders for the week to come. Around him, the market was quiet. The day's work was done by seven p.m., and in reality there was little cause for Joey to be there after hours, but he enjoyed the silence of the old building, broken only by the low hum of the refrigerators and the dripping of water. Each part of the day had its own rhythm, its own cadence, and after so many years of working the market Joey's own body was now attuned to the cycles of his business. It was why he knew that he would never be able to retire: He was connected to this place as surely as if an umbilical cord joined him to it. Without it, he would fade away and die. He loved the market, loved the feel of it, the sound of it, the smell of it. He carried it with him in his heart, his thoughts, and on his clothes and his skin. His wife, his beloved Eileen, liked to joke that there were creatures living in the sea who smelled less strongly of salt and fish than her Joey. And what of it if he did? It was where we had all come from to begin with, and we could still taste it in our sweat. The sea had given life to Joey, and continued to support him. He tried never to be far from it, and had always lived within earshot of the sound of breaking waves.

Still, he was always on site with the first of the workers, the processing crew that came in at six a.m. to commence the cutting of the fish, mostly haddock, tuna and swordfish. Throughout the day Joey's was generally an unobtrusive presence, for he trusted his employees to do whatever was necessary to ensure the smooth running of the operation; after all, most of them had been with him for many years, and by now he was convinced that even the gentlest involvement by their employer was largely an inconvenience to them. They each had their own areas of responsibility, they worked well together, and when Joey stuck his nose in he only managed to confuse everyone. It was better if he simply ensured that they had fish to sell every morning, a safe in which to put the money every evening, and enough cash left at the end of the week to pay everybody's wages.

So he would make a cursory check at 7:45 a.m. before walking the floor with a mug of tea in his hand, shooting the breeze with his customers, checking that they were happy, enquiring after the well-being of their businesses and the health of their families, offering help where it might be needed, and carefully recording each acceptance of such favors in his mental ledger of debtors and creditors, for not every debt could be counted in dollars and cents. Joey knew the name of every significant man and woman who crossed the threshold of the

Dorchester Central Fish Market, and the names of many of the less significant ones as well. He could judge minute changes in the state of a restaurant's finances by the pattern of its orders, and he was careful to monitor any signs of fragility, both to guarantee that, in the worst event of a closure, his bills would not be among those left unpaid, and because troubles for some represented good fortune for others. Loans could be advanced, agreements signed, portions of businesses acquired for next to nothing, and once Joey or his associates had a seat at the table they would feed and feed and feed. To those who were vulnerable, or who knew no better, Joey Tuna's offers of a helping hand were potentially cancerous in their malignity.

After the delivery trucks went out to the restaurants, Joey would often disappear for a few hours to take care of matters unrelated to the purchase and sale of seafood, then come back in the late afternoon to balance the books, count the cash, and deal with any minor problems that might have arisen during the day. Recently, these were increasingly related to extensions of credit, and bills that were past due but were different in nature from those that might lead to Joey and his kind taking an interest in the business. They were, for now, temporary setbacks being endured by those who had been on Joey's books for decades, men who were wise to Joey's ways but knew him also as a fair trader, a man who kept his word and didn't gouge honest men. True, there was a side to Joey that should be avoided, but he was by no means unique in this, and some of his customers were at least as hard as he was. Joey didn't cheat. He didn't mix frozen lobster meat in with the fresh. He didn't soak his scallops overnight, knowing that they would absorb their own weight in water, transforming one pound into two; and you could do the same with haddock too, although they didn't absorb as much. If he was forced to freeze fish, he froze only the oilier kinds — tuna, sword, salmon — but he would tell the buyer that it had been frozen, and therefore wouldn't taste as good, even as he priced it lighter. With Joey Tuna, you knew what you were getting.

The recession was bad for everyone, and Joey sympathized, but if he let his sympathies get in the way of common sense he'd be on the United Way list, he and the men and women who worked for him. It was all a question of balance. Joey had his competitors, just like anyone else, and they'd be happy to take disgruntled customers off his hands. In this city, the jungle drums beat all the time; an hour after someone mentioned that he was unhappy about the price per pound, you could be damn sure there would be a phone call, and the offer of a better rate. Joey himself wasn't above hustling, so why should anyone else be? He didn't like losing customers, though, and three times since the summer he'd been forced to offer gentle discouragement to a couple of restaurateurs who'd been tempted to take their business elsewhere, the threat made more palatable by some temporary sweeteners.

Hard times for honest men, and some dishonest ones too.

That evening, only the desk light burned in Joey's office. The pot of tea on the electric ring had brewed to a rich yellow-brown, and tasted as strong as sucking on the leaves themselves, but Joey didn't care. A mug of it sat at his right hand, and it was warming his bones. Joey didn't touch alcohol. He wasn't a prude about it, and he didn't mind others doing it, but he'd seen the damage it had inflicted on friends and family, and had decided that it wasn't for him. He had learned from the mistakes of the Winter Hill Gang, whose members he had watched succumb to some of the very vices they had encouraged in others. He also understood his own nature: He suspected that he had an addictive personality, and was afraid that if he started boozing, or gambling, or whoring he might never stop. So he drank tea, and ignored the horses, and remained faithful to his wife, and anyone who judged him by appearances only, and heard him joke about his fear of addiction, might wonder whether such a man, so self-aware, so mindful of his flaws, really had any reason to be concerned that, once he began to engage in a certain act, he might doubt his inability to pull back from it.

But such an individual would not have seen Joey's fists at work, because Joey Tuna liked to work with his hands. Once Joey started pounding on someone he didn't stop, couldn't stop, because his world would go black and there would be only the rhythm of flesh on flesh, over and over, methodical yet unreasoning, expelling the life from the body punch by punch. And when at last the light began to pierce the murk — a red beam,

227

like a shepherd's warning dawn — and he saw the work that his hands had wrought, his body aching, the muscles in his stomach and back on the verge of tearing, the meat that was left behind gave him no more pause for thought than a gutted fish or a headless shrimp.

That was why Joey Tuna now left the beatings to others, although he tried to ensure that they were doled out only when absolutely necessary. Punishments of a more final kind were also strictly controlled; more than ever before, probably, now that Whitey had gone to ground. The necessity for them was less frequent, of course, and such acts less advisable even as a last resort. Oh, there were still young hotheads who thought nothing of waving a piece in someone's face, who liked the feel of a gun in their waistband; the big men on the block who wanted to 'make their bones,' as the greasers would say, by putting one behind some poor bastard's ear. But most young men like that didn't live to be old, and a lot of those who survived would grow old with their permanent, limited view interrupted by the vertical lines of prison bars. Joey himself had done time when he was a young hothead and didn't know any better, but the years inside had cooled him down some, and when he came out he was a different man. He was that rare breed: a man who learned from his mistakes, and didn't repeat them. Rarer still, he was a criminal who thought that way. He had that in common with Tommy Morris, his protégé, along with the fact that they were both full Irish, a heritage that had marked them as outsiders for so long. In the Boston criminal circles through which they had moved, mongrels were the norm.

Usually Joey enjoyed these moments in the silence of his office. He took pleasure in making the accounts balance, in knowing that his business was running efficiently and profitably. He craved order. He always had, even as a boy. He was neat, and he never lost anything. Everything in its place, and a place for everything. Tonight, though, he was distracted. This Tommy Morris thing was giving him a hernia, but he should have expected that Tommy wouldn't just lie down and die.

He still struggled to pinpoint exactly when Tommy had begun to lose control of his operations, and why, but once the rot set in there were too many who were prepared to exploit his weakness, and Joey had tacitly, and then actively, encouraged them to do so. There was no room for sentimentality in business, but Joey wished that his relationship with Tommy hadn't come to such an end. He had a soft spot for Tommy, always had, but Joey had backed his horse now, and the race was running. Oweny Farrell would win it in the end, for it had been rigged from the off, but Tommy needed to be removed quickly at the risk of leaving the track littered with dead riders. They might even have had Tommy by now if it wasn't for Martin Dempsey. He was a cool one, make no mistake. Joey would almost be sorry to see him dead too.

But Tommy Morris. What to do about Tommy Morris?

And, as if he had summoned him from the darkness, Tommy answered.

'How are you, Joey?'

Joey looked up from his papers. There was a storage room to his left. He kept his records in there, along with reams of computer paper, and fresh stationery, and anything else that he didn't want tainted by damp or the smell of the floor below. The door was always open, because his employees knew better than to be in there without his permission, and it was only the door to the office itself that he locked. Now Tommy Morris emerged from the storage room, what little hair he had left cut short, his face unshaved, his paunch lapping at his belt like a pale tongue, peeping out from beneath the fabric of his golf shirt, hairy and somehow obscene. He was wearing a pair of blue overalls from the fish market, open to his crotch. He must have been in there for the best part of an hour, waiting patiently until the market was quiet, until just the two of them were left.

'Tommy,' said Joey. 'You scared the life out of me. What are you doing hanging around in closets. You turning queer on me, Tommy? You a Mary?'

He smiled at his own joke, and Tommy smiled back. He seemed to have more wrinkles than before, and the beard that was coming in was entirely gray. Failure will do that to a man, thought Joey: failure, and the knowledge of the imminence of his own mortality.

Except Tommy wasn't alone in feeling the Reaper's breath. In his right hand he held a

230

pistol. The suppressor made it appear both sleeker and uglier than it already was. Not that he'd need it, not really. There was nobody to hear the gun, and the glass and walls were thick. But it was like Tommy to take care of the little details and fail to take account of the bigger picture. It was why he was broke, and running, and why he had only Ryan and Dempsey left at his side.

'You know me better than that, Joey. I always had an eye for the girls.'

That was true. Tommy was never without a couple of women on the go at the same time. Joey had had the devil of a time finding the girls in his current stable in the hope that he might catch Tommy with his pants around his ankles.

'You should have settled down like me,' said Joey. 'If you do it right, it removes the need for all that kind of nonsense, or most of it. Why don't you pull up a chair and take the weight off your soles?'

Tommy stayed where he was. The gun hadn't moved. It was still pointed at Joey, who was unarmed. There was no gun in his desk drawer. He had no call to have one. He was Joey Tuna, the go-between. When he had to be, he was Joey Tombs, the dispenser of justice, but it was justice that had been agreed upon beforehand, settled upon by wise heads. It was always the right thing to do.

'This place hasn't changed,' said Tommy. 'I think those may even be the same papers on your desk.'

'There's no cause to change what has always

231

worked, Tommy. I make money. Until the downturn, we were even growing a little every year. We do things right here. We dot the i's and cross the t's. We're so clean, the IRS is sure that we're dirty. It was like that when I took over the business from my uncle, and God willing it will stay like that when I'm gone.'

He didn't flinch as he spoke those words. He wasn't going to give Tommy the satisfaction. Anyway, it wasn't over yet. He might still talk the younger man around.

'You remember when I gave you your first job here?' he said.

'I remember,' said Tommy. 'Cleaning up guts and scales and slime. I hated the smell of it. I could never get it off my hands.'

'Clean work always smells dirty,' said Joey. 'Honest work.'

'Sometimes dirty work smells dirty too. It smells of blood and shit. It smells like this place. I think you've been here so long that you've become confused. You can't tell the difference anymore.'

Joey looked affronted. 'You know, you were always a lazy bastard. You didn't like hard work.'

'I had no problem with hard work, Joey. My old man worked the piers, and my mother cleaned office floors. They taught me the value of honest labor. It was you who dangled the soft option in front of me, the promise of easier money.'

'So you're blaming me for what you've become? There's a coward talking, if ever I heard one.'

'No, I'm not blaming you. It wouldn't have mattered who suggested it to me first, I'd still have turned. I was a kid. Stealing from trucks, breaking into warehouses — that was all second nature to me. Still, you opened the door. You showed me the way. I was always going to fall, but you were the one who gave me the push.'

Joey reddened. He licked at his lips, and the fighter in him was revealed. Under other circumstances, he would have been rolling up his shirt sleeves by now and balling his meaty fists.

'I looked out for you too,' he said. 'Don't you forget that. When you overstepped the line, when you got above yourself, I stopped them from hurting you. There were men who wanted to break a hand, a leg. That bastard Brogan wanted to blind you for dealing on the side, but I spoke up for you. I told them you were ambitious, that you could make something of yourself with the right guidance. You got off lightly: a bit of a beating, when it could have been much worse. And when they were done, I gave you the space to work. It was the making of you. *I* was the making of you. When Whitey thought you were a threat, I talked him down. You'd be rotting under Tenean Beach or in a shallow grave by the Neponset River if it wasn't for me. I told him you were sound. I told them all that you were sound. I gave them my word on it, and no more could a man ask for than the word of Joey Tuna. It was always sound. You judge a man by his soundness, Tommy. You know that.'

'And are you looking out for me now, Joey? Do you have my best interests at heart.'

233

'You're in trouble. You're vulnerable. It's when a man is vulnerable that temptation comes knocking. There are people who want to know that you're sound, that's all. A sound man has nothing to fear. So they came to me. They always come to Joey Tuna. I bear no grudge and no man bears a grudge against me. Both sides can always sit down in safety when Joey Tuna is involved. It's been that way for forty years.'

'Like you said, why change what's always worked, right?'

'That's right. Never a truer word spoken.'

'So why change now? I don't see a neutral man here.'

'I have everyone's best interests at heart, Tommy. All we wanted to do was talk with you, clear the air.'

'Is that why Oweny's boys have been looking for me, to clear the air? I never took them for the conversational kind. Most of them can't put two words together without stumbling or swearing.'

'You've been keeping your head down, Tommy. People were worried. They didn't know where you were. You could have been lying dead in a ditch by the side of the road.'

'I could have been sitting in the Federal Building, you mean, spilling my guts like a fish on one of your blocks.'

'People were concerned. They just wanted to be sure.'

'That I was sound.'

'Exactly, that you were sound. I knew you were, Tommy. I told them so. I said to them, 'Tommy Morris is sound. I'll prove it to you. I'll bring him in, and we'll talk, and you'll see the kind of man he is: a sound man.' I came looking for you, Tommy, but I couldn't find you. When that happens, well, you can't blame someone for being concerned.'

'So you enlisted Oweny's boys to help you.'

'Oweny has his own questions for you. He wants to buy you out. He wants to do it right.'

'Is that so?'

'You know it. Oweny's sound too. Always has been. Just like you. Two sound men.'

'Oweny, sound? If Oweny was a fish you wouldn't feed him to birds. He was always a traitorous little shit. You know that Oweny's boys kicked down the door of a friend of mine? Two nights ago. They roughed her up. She lost teeth. They wanted to know where I was, but she couldn't tell them. I hadn't been to see her in weeks. I was keeping my distance from her to protect her, and look what happened.'

'I'm sorry to hear that,' said Joey. 'A man should only raise a hand to a woman as a last resort.'

'Funny thing is, I didn't think that Oweny knew about her. I'd been very careful. I'll bet you knew about her, though. You know everyone's affairs. That's why you're the man to turn to, because you have your finger on the pulse.'

Joey laid an index finger on his desk, the pulse finger itself, and tapped it hard on the wood to emphasize each word as he spoke: 'People. Were. *Concerned!* You weren't going to come in of your own volition. You had to be made to come in.'

'Is that why they took my niece?'

'I don't know what you're talking about. I told your boy Martin the same.'

'She's my sister's girl. She lives in a quiet little town, far away from any of this. Did you find her? Did Oweny find her?'

There was something in Tommy's tone, a kind of madness, as he spoke about his niece, that sent a deep ache of fear through Joey's belly, as though Tommy, knowing that he himself was doomed, had fixed upon the girl as his salvation. Joey had seen it before in men who were about to die. They began obsessing upon a friend, a parent, a picture in a wallet, a Miraculous Medal, anything to keep out the reality of what was coming.

'We don't kidnap little girls, Tommy. That's not our style.'

'Yeah? Since when?'

'Jesus, Tommy, what do you think we are, pedophiles? Deviants? Oweny doesn't have her. People don't do that, not to their own, not sound people. They just wanted to talk. If they had the girl, they'd have let you know. A message would have been sent, and then the girl would have been allowed to go home once you'd come in. Our people wouldn't behave any other way. We're not like the Russians. We're not animals.'

Tommy nodded. The gun wavered in his hand. Joey saw his advantage, and pressed it.

'Come on, now, Tommy. Put the gun away and we'll forget about this. I'll make some calls. I'll let everyone know they can relax. I'll tell them that Tommy Morris is as sound as he ever was.

Sound as a bell, eh, Tommy? Sound as a bell.'

Tommy began to button the overalls. They were too small for him, and he struggled with the buttons, but he didn't look down.

'And the meet? The sit-down where Oweny didn't show but you did? Martin seemed to think that a message was being sent.'

'A message? Sure, Tommy, there's always a message. The message was that you should come in and clear all this up, put people's minds at rest. Now you've had it from the horse's mouth.'

'No,' said Tommy. 'That wasn't the message Martin picked up at all.'

'Well, he was wrong, Tommy. My mind is at rest.'

'Good,' said Tommy. 'Then your body can join it.'

He kept the gun low and against his belly as he fired, so that the overalls took the blowback. The first shot took Joey in the belly. Joey said, 'Ah.' He sounded disappointed, as though he'd caught Tommy doing something shameful. He supported himself against the desk and Tommy shot him again. Joey tumbled to the floor, taking a handful of invoices with him. His mug fell to the floor and broke. He lay beside the shards of broken crockery, the tea dripping through the gaps in the boards. His breath came in short gasps, and there was blood in his mouth. His hands hovered above his wounds, for he could not quite bring himself to touch them. He kept blinking, like a man fearful of facing a bright light.

'Ah,' he said again. 'Ah, no.'

Tommy stood over him. 'I never liked you anyway,' he said. 'You were never sound.'

And he left Joey Tuna to die in that place, with his face against the cool boards and the taste of it infusing his final breaths, his last gift to the old thug who had created him.

17

A cold night in Boston, and the rain now beating down. It had fallen continuously throughout the day, varying only in its intensity, as though the heavens were determined to sluice the world clean. The lights of the taller buildings, always out of place in Beantown, seemed to brush the clouds above, piercing them and letting the rain pour through the holes. Tonight it was a city of sodden clothing, of suspect shoes that welcomed the damp, of plastered hair that curled and frizzed, and raindrops cold-kissing necks and breasts, of fuzzed neon reflected in puddles like swirls of paint, of slow-moving traffic and impatient pedestrians skipping dangerously past wheels and fenders, ignoring warning beeps and flashing lights. Even the girls heading for the clubs and bars had been forced to swathe their legs and arms for fear of goose bumps, and their frustration was writ large on their faces. Later, the ones who hadn't found a partner for the night would give up the fight and let the rain ruin their coiffure and smear their mascara, and they'd swear and giggle as they struggled to find a cab, for the cabdrivers would make a killing that night.

But the cold: God, that was the worst of it. It bit and gnawed, its white teeth working on fingertips and toes, noses and ears, like a carrion feeder picking at a corpse in the snow. Winter was one thing: winter, with snow on the ground and clear blue skies. You knew where you stood with winter. But this, this bastard weather, no accommodation could be reached with it. Better not to have come out at all, but that would be to give in to it, to allow it to have its sway over the city, to sacrifice a night out because the elements were conspiring against you, especially when you were young, and nubile, and had money in your pocket. Maybe when you were older, and had less to seek and to prove, the weather might give you pause, but not now. No, such nights were precious, and hard-earned. Let the rain fall; let the cold bite. The warmth and the company will be more welcome for the struggle that it took to find it, and there is little that is more lovely than to watch rain fall in the darkness from the comfort of a chair, a glass in your hand and a voice softly whispering smiling words in your ear.

Seated in their car on East Broadway in Southie, waiting for their moment, Dempsey and Ryan watched the local kids go by. The two men were thankful for the rain, for it kept heads down and obscured the view through the windshield. Both wore headgear: Dempsey a black wool hat, Ryan a Celtics cap, making him look like any one of a dozen mooks gorilla-walking their way along the main drag at this time. They came out of central casting, those guys, with their tats and their oversized T-shirts, with their misplaced sentiment for an island that meant nothing to them in actual terms, a place they could identify on a map only because of its shape. Dempsey and Ryan knew their kind well. They held ancestral grievances passed on by their parents, and their parents' parents. Their racism was ingrained but inconsistent. They hated blacks but cheered on the Celtics, who had barely a white face among them. They had older brothers who could still recall the busing program of the mid to late seventies, when Garrity and his so-called experts ignored the warnings from both inside and outside South Boston and paired poor white Southie with poor black Roxbury, two sections of Boston's immigrant community that had suffered more than most because of the consequences of bad urban planning; the intransigence of the all-white Boston School Committee that played upon fears of integration, and effective ghettoization, including the deeply flawed B-BURG experiment which walled the blacks inside the former Jewish neighborhoods of North Dorchester, Roxbury, and Mattapan. Sure, there were racists and bigots in Southie and the Town, because there were racists and bigots everywhere, but busing played into the hands of the worst of them, and even succeeded in uniting the previously warring Irish and Italian communities against a single common foe with a different skin. Hell, Ryan's old man, who was smarter than most of his neighbors put together and was a member of the Boston branch of the International Socialist Organization, had found himself on the receiving end of threats from the assholes on the Tactical Patrol Force because he'd formed a council to help ensure the safety of black pupils at his son's high school. Ryan hadn't thanked him for his liberal

241

views since he was the one who had taken the beatings for his father being a 'nigger-lover,' but he respected his old man more now for what he'd done.

The years had changed Ryan, but he kept many of those changes hidden.

Now he sat behind the wheel and wondered at what they were about to do. By Dempsey's feet lay the shoebox they had taken from the Napier house, but it was no longer filled with money. The device that it contained was crude but effective: little more than a lead-azide detonator and two pounds of pentaerythritol tetranitrate, or PETN. The explosive's lethality had been compounded by the carpet tacks that Dempsey sprinkled liberally through the mix. Ryan had watched, appalled, as Dempsey put it together in the motel room earlier.

'What are they for?' he asked

'They're for added value.'

'But they'll . . . '

He trailed off. His mouth felt too dry. This was wrong. It should be stopped.

'They'll what? Hurt people? Scar them? What do you think the point of this is, Francis?'

Ryan found some saliva. 'To take out Oweny Farrell.'

'No, it's to take out Oweny Farrell and everyone around him. It's to leave nobody from his inner circle standing. It's to send a message that Tommy Morris isn't down and he isn't out, and his meal tickets aren't up for grabs.'

'They won't let it slide. They can't.'

'They will if he gives them no other choice.

They sat back and waited to see what Oweny would do, and how Tommy would respond. This is Tommy's response. This is his way back.'

Ryan turned away. His fingers shook. He lit a cigarette to calm himself.

'This is not right, Martin. This is not what we are. There'll be people in there who have nothing to do with it.'

He tried to visualize the damage that a hail of tacks would do in an enclosed space, and felt vomit well up in his throat. Had Tommy told Dempsey to do this, or had Dempsey come up with the idea himself? Dempsey was the one to whom Tommy relayed his orders, unless, as with Helen Napier, Dempsey was otherwise occupied. Ryan had to take it on trust that what he heard from Dempsey was the true substance of their conversations. If Tommy had really endorsed this course of action, then all was lost and there was no longer any rightness to his cause.

'Look,' said Dempsey, 'it's this or Tommy rolls over and dies.'

Seconds ticked by.

'That might be for the best,' said Ryan. He said it so slowly, and so softly, that Dempsey had to lean forward to be sure he was hearing him right. Ryan's face was still turned away from him. The cigarette was in his left hand, but his right hand was no longer visible. From the angle of his arm, it was somewhere close to his belt. Dempsey grew still. On the table beside him was his gun. Casually, he rested his hand inches from it.

'I thought we'd had this conversation already,

Francis,' he said. He was surprised at how relaxed he sounded. His fingertips brushed the grips.

Ryan's shoulders trembled. Dempsey thought that he might be on the verge of tears. There was a tremor in his voice when he spoke again.

'I mean, look at us. We're making a bomb. We're going to slaughter and maim. I'm not like you, Martin. Maybe I'm not as tough as you. I've delivered beatings with the best of them, but I've never killed. I don't want to kill anyone, not even Oweny Farrell.'

'How did you think this was going to end?'

'I don't know: with a sit-down, maybe, with everybody compromising. I thought Joey Tuna would see us right. I thought — '

'You thought what: that you were dealing with reasonable men?' There was no mockery to Dempsey's tone. He merely sounded tired, and there was a horror in his voice at what he had allowed himself to become.

'No,' said Ryan. 'Just men. Just ordinary men.'

'They were never ordinary, Francis. Ordinary men lead ordinary lives, but not them. They all had blood on their hands and on their souls. We're tainted by it too, just by being around them.'

'Have you killed, Martin?'

Now he turned to look at the older man. Ryan had heard stories: Dempsey worked alone, and the people he took care of didn't surface again. Wherever they were, they were buried deep. Now Ryan wanted to hear confirmation from Dempsey's own mouth.

'Yes,' said Dempsey. His eyes were empty.

'For Tommy?'

'And before Tommy.'

'Who did you kill, Martin? Who did you kill before?'

'It doesn't matter.'

But it did. It mattered to Ryan. Dempsey was born in Belmont, but he'd come to them from abroad. The whispers were that he'd been a bomb-maker, that he'd planted devices in Northern Ireland for the Provisionals, and in Madrid for the ETA Basques. Now he couldn't return to Europe because, even with some form of peace established in both conflicts, there were those with long memories and scores to settle. Tommy had given him a home and a role to play, and Dempsey's reputation had gone before him when there were problems that needed to be handled.

Before Ryan could question him further, Dempsey spoke again.

'You say you've never killed, Francis. You say that you can't. But before all this is over you may be put in a position where you have to pull the trigger on someone to save yourself. Have you thought about that?'

'Yes,' said Ryan. 'I've thought about it. I even dream about it.'

'And in the dreams, do you pull the trigger?'

Dempsey waited for the answer, the only light coming from the lamp on the table, its glow catching the sharp, glittering spikes of the tacks.

'Yes,' said Ryan at last. 'I pull the trigger.'

'Then maybe you can kill after all. Who do you

kill in your dreams?'

'Faceless men. I don't know who they are.'

'But you kill them anyway?'

'Yes.'

'What about me?' said Dempsey. 'Would you kill me in your dreams? Do you kill me in your dreams?'

Ryan had come this far. There was no point in turning back now.

'I've thought about it.'

'Not dreamed it, but thought it?'

'Yes.'

And Dempsey saw that Ryan's hand was within striking distance of whatever was lodged in his waistband, and the reality of all that Ryan had said hung in the air between them like a white handkerchief waiting to be dropped on a dueling field.

'It's all right, Francis,' said Dempsey. 'I know you have. I've seen it in your eyes.' He moved the shoebox slightly with his left hand, shielding his right from view. 'But I'm not the enemy here. Whatever you might think of me, I'm not the one you have to fear. If we turn against each other now, we'll do their work for them. We have to trust each other, because we have nobody else.'

Ryan took in his words, still uncertain. 'You frighten me sometimes, Martin. You take it too far. That woman the other night, she didn't deserve what you did to her. No woman deserves that.'

'But you didn't try to stop it.'

'I should have. I was weak.'

'No, you're not weak. It's not weakness to avoid the battle that you can't win. That's just common sense. And what was she to you? Nothing. Nobody. You look out for your own, and let the others swim or die.'

Ryan's right hand was still hidden.

'So where does that leave us, Francis?' said Dempsey. 'Where do we stand?'

The cigarette bounced in Ryan's fingers. A clump of ash fell to the carpet. It distracted Ryan from his thoughts. Instinctively, he moved, extending one foot to stamp on it. Dempsey glimpsed his right hand. There was no gun. Dempsey's eyes flicked to the side and glimpsed Ryan's gun by the sink, left there when he went to clean the glasses that they'd used earlier.

Now Ryan glanced his way. He saw the gun, and Dempsey's fingers brushing its burnished steel, and the cold light in Dempsey's eyes.

'Jesus,' he said.

'It was nothing personal, Francis. You were just sounding a bit strange.'

Ryan let out a long, straggly breath. 'I was only talking.'

'I couldn't see your hand.'

'You were going to kill me.'

'If I was going to, then I would have. I don't want to kill you, Francis. I like you. And I told you, we have to stick together, for our sakes and for Tommy's. If we don't do this, they'll pounce. Don't think you'll be able to cut a deal with them, because you won't. We've stayed with Tommy too long. They'd never be able to rest or turn their backs on us. They'd always be wondering, doubting, and in time they'd put an end to their concerns because it would be easier that way. It's all or nothing now. If we send out a strong enough message, we can make them reconsider. We take out Oweny, take out his crew, and suddenly the tables are turned.'

'They'll want revenge,' said Ryan.

'No, not if it's just Oweny and his people who suffer. They'll understand that they made a mistake, that they should have backed Tommy and not him. It's about a show of strength. It has to be brutal, and it has to be final.'

Ryan walked to the table and looked down at the device. He picked up a carpet tack and held it to the light, examining it the way an entomologist might examine an unfamiliar yet clearly dangerous insect.

'Joey Tuna offered me a way out,' said Martin. 'This morning, when we were talking, he asked me to rat on Tommy. He told me I could walk away if I made the call and let them know where Tommy could be found.'

'And me?'

'He didn't mention you, Francis.'

Ryan nodded. He understood. They would have killed him just to be sure.

'What did you say to him?'

'Nothing. I'm here, aren't I? I'm with Tommy, and I'm with you. We're different, you and I, but we need to stick together on this. And remember, you're not killing anyone. I made this, and I'll put it in position. The blood will be on my hands, the mark on my soul.'

Ryan twisted the tack one last time, then

dropped it in the shoebox.

'No,' he said. 'It'll be on my soul too.'

And now here they were, the rain pattering on the roof of the car, no lights within to expose them, the device on the floor at Dempsey's feet. Ryan couldn't help but think of it as a living creature, a monster in the box waiting to be unleashed. They should have bored air holes in it so it could breathe. He could almost hear the beating of its heart.

In an ideal situation Dempsey would have planted the device earlier, but the bar was Oweny's place, and there was no way that he could gain access to it in advance. The bar was small, and it would contain the blast. In the confined space, the device's effects would be catastrophic. The problem was getting it in there. He'd told Ryan that he planned to take the simple approach. In one hand was a brick, in the other the device. The brick would take out the window, and the device would follow.

'What's the delay on it?' Ryan had asked, causing Dempsey to pause.

'Where did you learn about delays?'

'Same place I learned about everything else — from television.'

'Five or six seconds.'

'It's not much. You'd better not trip or wait for the light once it's set.'

'I wasn't planning on helping anyone across the road.'

Even through the rain-spattered windshield, Ryan could see Oweny Farrell's big head from where they sat. He recognized some of the others as well. There were a couple of women too. He hoped they would leave to go to the bathroom before Dempsey started walking. It might make what was to come easier to live with.

'You just start the engine as soon as I get out,' said Dempsey. 'Be prepared for the blast, let it come, then move. Don't look at it, and don't stare once it's happened. You won't want to see the aftermath, and I don't want you freezing.'

'I understand, Martin.'

'Okay.'

Dempsey picked up the box and the brick, resting them in the crook of his arm. He was wearing a hooded sweatshirt under his coat, and he raised the hood to hide his face as he left the car. Ryan was about to wish him good luck, then didn't. One of the girls in the bar was laughing, her mouth wide and her head thrown back. She was pretty, and not in the hard way of most of the women who hung around with Oweny and his boys. There was a pale fragility to her features. Her hair was very dark. She couldn't have been more than nineteen or twenty. In most bars in Boston, they'd have asked for ID and given her the bum's rush, but not there, not in Oweny's place.

He saw Dempsey lift the edge of the shoebox to arm the device as he stepped into the cold night air. Most of the box was wrapped in tape, but Dempsey had left one corner torn and unsealed so that he could easily access the fuse that would ignite the detonating agent. Dempsey started toward the bar, his fingers poised over the gap in the box, and then there were lights in

Ryan's rearview mirror, and he heard sirens, and Dempsey was walking quickly back to the car, the device still in his arms, the brick discarded on the street. Ryan started the engine, and they pulled out behind a beverage truck just as the first of the patrol cars screeched to a halt outside the bar, more coming behind it, and the big black van of the SWAT team in the middle of them all like the queen bug among its subjects.

'Man,' said Ryan. 'This is bad. This is so bad.'

'Just drive. They're not looking for us. They couldn't have known.'

Ryan just kept going straight until they hit the rotary by the water. There he turned left, past the statue of Farragut, past the Francis Murphy ice skating rink. It was only when they reached the empty Castle Island parking lot that Ryan realized he had brought them to a dead end. He swore and began to reverse awkwardly, but Dempsey calmed him down.

'Easy,' he said. 'Take a breath. We're okay.'

Ryan did as he was told. He breathed deeply once, twice. He felt the monster twitch in the box at Dempsey's feet. Perhaps Dempsey felt it too, because he opened the car door and walked to the edge of the lot, then tossed the box into the water. They drove back to the rotary and took First Street out of Southie.

'Why were they there?' asked Ryan. 'Why did they come?'

But they didn't get the answer until later, when Dempsey took the call from Tommy and learned that Joey Tuna was dead.

III

When we creak your step,
when we crack your glass,
when we tap, tap, tap,

that is a bone

that is all we have

though we are very shiny,
and filled with beetles.

We are made entirely of bone.

from *The Dead Girls Speak in Unison*
by Danielle Pafunda

18

Randall Haight felt the difference in the house as soon as he returned from the store, as though a charge of static electricity held by the carpets and fabrics had been voided. He stood in the hallway, a paper bag cradled in his left arm, the coldness of the ice cream inside making itself felt through the fabric of his sweater. He had chocolate as well, and soda, and cinnamon candies. She liked the smell of all of them, and they had a calming effect on her; quite the opposite of most children, he thought, but then she was so very different from other children.

The trip into town had already provided him with one unsettling experience. He had seen Valerie Kore on the street, accompanied by a man whom he didn't recognize but who, by his size and stance, he believed to be a policeman of some kind. Mrs. Kendall, who worked part-time at the drugstore, was talking to her, her right hand resting on Valerie's shoulder, her face close to the younger woman's as she offered what Randall assumed were words of hope and consolation. Then Danny, the weird but decent kid who ran the Hallowed Grounds coffee shop, came out and gave Valerie a white paper bag loaded up with pastries and muffins, and something inside her broke at this small, unexpected gesture and she had to walk away, the cop trailing in her wake. Randall watched her go, and tried to pin down his feelings at the sight of her. Sadness. Empathy.

Guilt?

The cop had caught him looking at her. Randall hadn't overreacted, though. He'd just smiled sadly, because that was what he believed a regular person would have done, a *normal* person. He was an actor inhabiting a role, and he inhabited it well, but as soon as she was gone from his sight he pushed her from his mind. Instead, he found himself looking at the faces of those whom he passed even as he exchanged friendly greetings with them, and peered in the windows of the businesses on Main Street, waiting to see if someone might look back, their eyes lingering a little too long on his, betraying themselves to him.

Which one of you is it? Which one of you knows, or thinks you know?

But there were no answers to be found, no suspicions to be confirmed, and he had driven back to his house in silence, wondering if the mailman had come yet, fearing what he might find in his box. To his relief, there were only bills, and his subscriber's copy of *National Geographic*. No photographs, no films, no images of naked children, and he tried to make himself believe that it might be over even as he acknowledged this as just a brief respite.

Now, safe once again inside his home, Randall sensed an unaccustomed emptiness, an absence. He moved from bedroom to bedroom, checking closets and under beds. He looked in the master bathroom and the guest bathroom, the latter of which had never been used. Finally, he went to the basement and stood in front of the door. She liked the basement; it was dark, and cool. Sometimes he heard her singing to herself down there. When he was angry or working he'd tell her to be quiet, but she never listened. She sang jingles from the TV, and old pop songs that he'd almost forgotten existed, and ditties that she'd make up herself, tuneless rhymes that got inside his head and worried at him with their sheer randomness. But the basement was her hide-away, her refuge, and he was content to leave it to her. He tried not to disturb her when she was there because there was no way to tell how she might react. Once she'd flown at him in a rage, her nails headed straight for his eyes, but mostly she just tended to scream and scream, the sound of it bouncing back at him from the stone walls.

He needed to know where she was. He kept all the windows and the outer doors locked, although that was more to keep people out than to keep her inside, for he lived in fear of intrusion into his life. By now the girl showed no signs of wanting to leave him. He wondered if her hatred of him had become a kind of love, her need a channel that connected the two opposing emotions. She was almost like a daughter to him, a recalcitrant, difficult, demanding child, and he was the father because he had made her what she was.

He hadn't seen much of her for the past two days. She'd hidden herself away when the detective came, as she always did when a stranger appeared. Earlier that same day, he'd caught a glimpse of her passing through the kitchen while he worked at his computer. He didn't like the TV on when he was trying to concentrate. She'd learned that lesson quickly, and now she just stayed away from the living room until after five. The last time he had actually spoken to her was to tell her to go back to her TV shows on the evening following the detective's visit.

He knocked on the basement door. There was no reply.

'Hey,' he said. 'You down there?'

He opened the door and spoke to the darkness. She disliked sudden intrusions and unexpected noises.

'You can watch anything you like now. I've finished my work for the day. I'll sit with you, if you want me to.'

He could see the night light burning against the far wall. There was a small pile of books in the corner, still unread, and a stuffed animal that he'd bought for her at Treehouse Toys when he'd been doing some work down in Portland.

He advanced to the first step, still reluctant to trespass. Early on, before he'd come to understand her ways, and she his, she had tried to knock his feet out from under him when he entered the basement, and he had barely managed to hold on to the rail and prevent himself from breaking his neck. A huge splinter had pierced his palm, and even though he'd managed to get the bulk of it out, some shards had penetrated deep into his flesh and had begun to fester, so that he'd been forced to see a

258

doctor and have them removed under local anesthetic. After that he'd locked the basement door, and taken away the lead for the TV. Depriving her of TV was the worst punishment that he could inflict upon her, and always led to a battle of wills between them. He had learned to lock the lead in his safe because she would find it otherwise, but those periods when the TV was no longer hers to control were the worst between them. In retaliation, she would do her best to irritate him, tapping on the wall at night while he tried to sleep, or rearranging his papers so that he lost track of his accounts, or spilling milk in the fridge while he was out and then turning the power off so that he had to empty the contents and wash it out to remove the sour stink. Finally, a compromise would be reached, and TV rights would be restored, but the conflict always took its toll on both of them and they had each learned that it was better to avoid such confrontations to begin with.

But relations between them were not always so hostile. Sometimes, especially on cold nights when the old house creaked and moaned, and the wind found the gaps in the boards and under the doors, and branches cracked beneath the weight of snow and ice, she would climb into his bed unbidden, and press herself against him, stealing his warmth, like a dream made real.

He descended farther, crouching so that the entire basement was visible to him, and felt panic, and fear, and loss.

But, most of all, he felt a kind of relief.

She was gone.

259

19

It was a cold, damp night at the end of a long, dismal day. I had been called back by the defense in the Denny Kraus case, and then had to wait around for hours close to the courthouse on Federal Street as Denny's attorney tried to maintain his composure while dealing with a prosecutor who was determined to prove that Denny was mentally competent to face trial, and with whom Denny repeatedly agreed. The attorney was young, and court-appointed, and he should have put pressure on Denny to keep his mouth shut, although it wasn't entirely his fault. The state wanted Denny to go down for murder, for reasons that I couldn't grasp but were probably linked to politics, and ambition, and someone seeking to make the figures look good at the end of the year. A more battle-hardened attorney than Denny's would have found a way to negotiate a compromise deal that satisfied everyone, except possibly Denny, but then what Denny wanted didn't really matter. He probably should have thought harder about his plans for the future before he killed a man over a dog.

While I was kicking my heels waiting for my moment of glory in the witness box, I continued delving into the personal details of those on Randall Haight's list of new clients and recent arrivals in Pastor's Bay, but I was starting to believe that it was a dead end. I had to proceed on the basis that it wasn't, but I couldn't shake my gut feeling that there was nothing hidden behind those names, nothing useful to be found. It raised the possibility that the person who was tormenting Randall Haight might have been lying dormant for a long time, waiting for the right opportunity to use Haight's past against him. If that was the case, I was faced with the almost impossible task of investigating every adult who had crossed Randall Haight's path. Equally, though, someone from Randall's past might have spotted him on the streets of Belfast, or Portland, or Augusta, or while passing through Pastor's Bay itself, then discovered his address and proceeded to target him without ever having exchanged even a word with him.

But I had reached one conclusion at least: If by the following morning I hadn't heard confirmation from Aimee that Haight was prepared to be interviewed by the police, I was going to call Gordon Walsh myself and suggest that he talk to Haight, even at the risk of poisoning my relationship with Aimee and potentially leaving myself open to charges and imprisonment for breach of client confidentiality. The final push had been provided by a realization that should have come to me the moment Haight showed me the photographs of naked children. Someone who was in possession of sexually suggestive photos of underage kids might well be capable of taking a child to satisfy his urges. It was the connection I needed to silence my conscience about any betrayal of

Aimee or Haight that I might have to commit.

My name was called shortly after three p.m., but my period under cross-examination could have been measured in nanoseconds. Even the judge seemed to be losing the will to live after a day of questioning that had merely confirmed what everybody already knew: Denny Kraus was crazy, because in his situation only a lunatic would deny that he was crazy.

After I was done in court, I headed up to Nosh on Congress and shot the breeze for a while with Matt, one of the partners in the place. If someone had told me a couple of years ago that Portland needed another bar selling burgers, I'd have laughed in his face, and you wouldn't have heard me above all the other people who were laughing too. Then Nosh opened and folk started tasting the burgers, and a general agreement was reached that, yes, maybe we had needed just one more bar selling burgers, as long as the food was this good. And because I felt that I owed it to myself after the day I'd had, I ate some bacon-dusted fries too, and pushed the boat out by sipping a Clown Shoes brown ale, and gradually the day began not to seem so bad after all.

The channels through the Scarborough salt marshes appeared only as swaths of a deeper blackness against the tall grass as I drove home, like lengths of dark ribbon dropped from the sky. I turned into my driveway, the headlamps reflecting on the windows of the empty house. I entered through the back door leading into the kitchen, and turned on the light.

The moisture had beaded on the main window that faced north, and someone had written on the glass with a finger, cutting long careful lines through the water. The words were written in a child's hand, a hand with which I was familiar, for it had communicated with me once before in attic dust. It had been so long. I thought that they were gone, but how could they ever truly be gone? Now one of them had returned, the echo of my dead daughter, and where she went so too walked her mother, a stranger, more nebulous figure. If my daughter was a small, cold star, then her mother was the night sky against which she lay.

The words on the glass read:

THE GIRL IS ANGRY

I approached the window. The letters had only recently been written; there were still rivulets of moisture running from them, as though the words were wounds cut in flesh, bleeding their message. Through the gaps in the condensation that they had created, I saw the woods.

I went back outside and stood in my yard, staring at the trees, willing them to emerge, but they did not. Perhaps they were no longer there, but there was a stillness to the night that spoke of watchfulness, and even the marsh grass had ceased its whispering. Then the wind returned from the sea, and it tossed the grass and the trees, and it blew some of the shadows away. I erased the words with my fingertips, touching the places that she had touched as I did so, and I wondered at how a man could be haunted and both love and fear the entities that walked in his footsteps.

I stayed at the window, watching the night deepen, imagining my lost daughter's voice speaking those words to me, imagining her small, pale form passing beneath the trees, traces of moonlight causing the bare branches to crisscross her body, binding her with lengths of darkness. I thought of that old ghost story about the monkey's paw, and the couple who wish upon it that their dead son might be returned to them, and their horror when they realize the literal nature of their wish's fulfillment.

And I wondered, not for the first time, if my grief had willed them back into the world.

★   ★   ★

I went to bed at midnight, after thinking for a time about the meaning of the words on the glass. They seemed like a warning, but of what I could not be sure. To what girl did they refer? Somehow I slept deeply until three a.m.. Had I tried to explain to a psychiatrist how that might be possible after a dead child had written on my window, I might have begun by arguing that when one encounters enough strangeness, then what is strange ultimately becomes familiar. The mind can accommodate itself to almost anything, given time: pain, grief, loss, even the possibility that the dead talk to the living. And I understood, too, that this was all part of a larger pattern, a signpost on a journey whose ultimate

264

destination I could not know. I had resigned myself to what was to come, whatever it might be, and that resignation brought with it a kind of peace. So I slept, and I was grateful for sleep. When I could no longer sleep, then I would know that I was going mad.

At one minute after three, I woke. There were sounds coming from below my bedroom: bangs and crashes and barrages of strings. It took me a moment to realize that the TV was on.

But I hadn't watched television before going to bed, and I would never have left it on if I had.

Making as little noise as I could, I reached for my gun and slipped from the bed. The room was cold. I was naked from the waist up, and my skin seemed to tighten in the chill air. The bedroom door was open, and the hall was dark, but as I reached the stairs I could see the light from the reflected images on the TV screen dancing on the wall. I tried to control my breathing as the blood thudded in my ears. The banister railings were wide, and I would be exposed as soon as I descended to the third step from the top. If it was a trap, then moving slowly and carefully would do me no good. I would simply be an easier target.

There was another series of loud explosions from the TV, and I used the sound to mask my descent. I went down fast, staying against the wall, the gun held close to my body in my right hand while I used my left for balance, but nobody sprang at me from the shadows, and there were no shots. The security chain was still in place on the front door. To the left of the stairs was my office, but the door was closed, just as it had been when I went up to bed. Ahead of me was the living room, the door standing open, the television visible through the gap. It was showing a Road Runner cartoon. There was only one door into the room. I had no choice.

The living room was empty. The couch and the easy chairs that faced the television were unoccupied. The TV remote was lying on the left side of the couch, close to the arm.

I left the TV on and returned to the main hallway. I checked the kitchen first, but it too was empty and the back door was locked. Finally, I went to my office. I gripped the handle, flung the door open, and waited, but there was no reaction from within. I checked through the crack at the hinges but could see nothing. Eventually, with no other option, I stepped in with my gun raised, but my office was as I had left it the day before, even down to the sweatshirt I had thrown across my desk after coming back from an errand at the grocery store a few days earlier.

Despite the cool of the night, I was now bathed in sweat. I made a cursory check of the upstairs rooms, just in case, but the house was empty. I returned to the living room and stared at the TV. The Road Runner was gone, and a Bugs Bunny cartoon had replaced it. Yosemite Sam was hunting with his big gun. It could have been a power surge, I supposed. I turned it off at the top of the set, and killed the power at the socket, just in case.

I was halfway up the stairs when the TV blared into life again.

I kept the gun by my side as I entered the room. It was still empty, and the remote lay where it had been, but the switch at the wall had been turned back on.

A droplet of perspiration slid down my back. There was a smell that hadn't been there before, or if it had, then I hadn't noticed it with the fear and adrenaline. It was a hint of perfume, though a cheap and sickly sweet one, the kind that no grown woman would wear —

the girl is angry

The words were not said aloud, and yet I could hear them in my head, a repetition of the message on the window.

you have to be careful daddy you have to be careful

'Daddy.' My god, my god, my god.

But there was nothing there, or nothing that I could see. I placed my hand on the television and pressed the On/Off button gently. The screen went black, and the indicator light went from green to red. I stepped back and waited. I got as far as five in my head when it came back on again, just in time for Bugs to burst through the drum, munching a carrot, to say 'And Dat's De End!'

Except it wasn't, because the station's indent flashed and instantly Bugs was back again. I even knew the cartoon: 'Hare Brush.' I remembered it from my childhood. Bugs and Elmer switch personalities, so that in the end Elmer wins, but he has to become Bugs to do so. I had laughed and laughed. Even in my teenage years, after my father died, I'd laugh when I caught the cartoon again. It was an escape from a world of black and gray and bright, bright red, an escape from hurt and grief, from the memory of pain: the pain of my father's loss, the pain of my mother's sorrow . . .

The pain of a boy holding one hand over your mouth while the other fumbles beneath your skirt, the second boy pulling away as he realizes what he has done, and what is about to be done, yet too weak to prevent it from happening. Pain in your mouth and your lungs, pain in your back and behind your eyes, pain growing and growing until it seems that your body is too small to contain it all, that it must explode from you like the air from a bursting balloon, like the death of a red star, because when the end comes it comes redly: red behind your eyes, red spraying from your mouth and nose.

And dat's de end, except it isn't, not for you, because you never went away, because you're an angry girl, and people have to be careful around angry girls. Angry girls break things, and hurt things, and they wait for their chance.

And angry girls watch cartoons to escape for a time from their rage.

I stepped closer to the couch and reached for the remote. The sickly scent grew stronger, and I smelled what lay beneath it: not decay but blood and human waste, because whatever was in the room had stayed as it was at the moment of its passing. It was both a girl and not a girl. The best of it was elsewhere, sleeping, unknowing. What was here was all that had been left behind.

careful daddy careful careful

She was on the couch; almost a palpable

268

presence. I couldn't see her, couldn't hear her, but she was there. I waited for her hand to close upon me as I took the remote, but it did not. The device was moist to the touch. There was condensation on it, although there should not have been. I stepped back from the couch, the remote in my hand, and the smell came with me. Tentatively, I lifted my hand, and caught the odor of her on the plastic.

I glanced at the TV. The image flickered, the action changing, and behind it I thought that I glimpsed a face reflected in the screen. I walked around the side of the couch, keeping my distance from it. When I was behind it, I raised the remote and killed the picture.

no daddy no she wont like it

And in that instant I saw her suspended in the darkness of the screen like a soul trapped in the void: a black girl in a torn white blouse seated on the couch, her hands by her sides, palms up, her knees scraped raw; blood on her chin, and on her lips, and blood dried in lines that ran from the corners of her eyes like red tear stains. She opened her mouth and screamed silently, her whole body shaking with the force of her anger: a child frustrated, a child deprived of her desire, a child dragged from a world of brightness back into a world of pain. Then she was gone, and there was only my own reflection in the otherwise empty room.

I turned off the TV for the final time, and I did not sleep again that night.

Not even with the TV cable safely hidden away in my bedside locker.

20

It was November, and hunting season was about to begin. I couldn't say from where precisely my objections to much of what passed for hunting came. Perhaps it was the fact that I was a townie through and through. My father, who had spent his days walking city beats in New York, occasionally made forays into the great outdoors on weekends to clear his lungs and replace vistas of tall buildings with vistas of tall trees, but I think he viewed it as an obligation rather than a pleasure. He felt that he should occasionally feel grass beneath his feet, and not be forced to step around trash and needles and used rubbers to do so, because that was what regular people did. In truth, though, he was happier in the city. He tended to come back from those walks with the slightly relieved air of a man returning from a successful and relatively painless visit to the dentist.

My grandfather, who was a policeman in Maine, had not hunted. He argued that he did not need the meat, and the act of stalking an animal gave him no joy. He dutifully enforced the state's hunting laws but was not above turning a blind eye to those citizens who broke the ban on Sunday hunting, especially those who were already working long hours to make ends meet, and for whom Sundays provided the only opportunity to supplement their family's diet. In the poorer parts of Maine, bringing down a mature deer and freezing and curing the meat could save a family four or five hundred dollars on food, and those who hunted for this reason were part of an older ethos. They took pleasure in the act of hunting, but it was combined with a functionality and practicality that was admirable. They wasted nothing of what they killed, and if they were particularly fortunate in their endeavors they shared with those who had not been so lucky.

But the hunting of moose for trophy antlers left me cold, and I had yet to meet someone who enjoyed the taste of bear meat. I disliked the attitude of those who came up from the cities to hunt: their braggadocio, their faux machismo, the unpleasant transformative effect of guns and camouflage on otherwise unremarkable men, for in my experience it was generally men who hunted in this way. They brought money into the state, and guiding them was a welcome source of income for those who lived hardscrabble existences in the County, and in the shadow of the Great North Woods. Still, the guides viewed a certain number of them as fools, and fools with guns, which are the worst kind, and regarded most of the rest with little more than benign tolerance. Their money was welcome, their actual presence less so.

And how did I square this with the fact that I declined to hunt an animal but had hunted men; that I would not turn my gun on a deer, or a bear, but I had seen men fall by my hand? To be honest, I didn't think about it too much. Life was simpler that way.

Life was simpler, too, if one did not think too hard about the images of dead girls reflected on dark television screens. I might almost have believed that I had dreamed the events of the night before had not some faint trace of the girl's perfume still lingered in the living room, and had the marks of my hand not still been visible on the kitchen window, where I had erased my daughter's message. I walked outside with a cup of coffee in my hand and sat on the back step, staring at the woods and the marshes beyond. They preferred the night, my shadow wife and my drifting child, taken from this life by one who bore the name of a traveling man. I still did not know what to call them: traces, perhaps, or echoes.

The thought of my daughter moving through moonlit woods, sometimes watching her father from the darkness, and leaving messages for him on windowpanes (for that was what she did when she was alive, drawing hearts and faces and dogs on my car windshield when I wasn't around, so I would know that she was thinking of me) brought with it both comfort and a deep, unmanning sadness. I did not fear for her, though, as she followed those paths between worlds. She did not walk them alone. Her mother walked beside her, and her mother wore a different mask, for whatever had brought her back to me was not love alone.

If my daughter was a spirit, then my dead wife was a shade.

*   *   *

I went to work on the Kore family, seeking some hint to why Engel and the FBI might have an interest in them beyond any concern about Anna Kore's presumed abduction. Anna's mother, Valerie, was born Valerie Mary Morris in Dorchester, Massachusetts. She was twenty-nine when she married Alekos Kore in a ceremony in the St. George Greek Orthodox Cathedral in Philadelphia on June 8, 2007. Since Anna Kore was born on November 28, 1995, her mother had either waited a long time before marrying Anna's father or Alekos Kore was not related by blood to Anna. So where was Alekos now, and if he was not Anna's father, who was? According to the official police statements, they were still trying to contact Alekos, although they had not yet gone so far as to brand him a suspect in Anna's disappearance.

More digging: a CN-2 change-of-name application for Anna Mary Morris, a minor, had been filed with the Knox County probate court on August 1, 2007. In addition, an affidavit of diligent search had been filed confirming that all reasonable efforts had been made to trace the child's other biological parent, one Ronald Doheny. Oddly, the judge had not requested a special publication notice, or a search of the five branches of military service, as was often the case in such circumstances. Clearly the judge in question had been content to accept that attempts to find Doheny had proved fruitless in the past. That was interesting. It suggested that

273

somebody had spoken quietly to the judge about Doheny. Reading between the lines, I was willing to bet good money that Ronald Doheny was believed dead. If that was the case, and there was no formal evidence of his demise, then the judge would have required more than the word of Valerie Kore or her legal representatives, assuming she had even sought legal assistance, as technically none was required for a change of name. So if you didn't have a body, and nobody had sought a legal declaration of death, assuming seven years had gone by since Ronald Doheny had stopped accepting calls, then what would it take to persuade a judge to let sleeping dogs, and sleeping corpses, lie?

It would take the word of a cop, and a senior cop too.

Dig again: Anna Mary Morris was born in Dorchester, Mass. Search for Ronald Doheny, and Massachusetts. Dismiss the eighty-year-old man who had died of cancer after a long and happy life with his wife of fifty-eight years. Dismiss the high-school football star who had wrapped his car around a tree two years before Anna was born. Dismiss a chronically obese used-car salesman ('Ronnie's the Real Deal!'), and a prodigiously gifted eight-year-old child violinist.

Leave Ronald Doheny of Somerville, Mass.: twenty-one years old when he skipped bail in December 1997 on charges of possession of a Class A substance for sale or distribution, which in Massachusetts in the late 1990s probably meant heroin. Dig, dig, dig: Ronald Doheny, one of three men found in an apartment in Winter Hill, Somerville, along with three kilos of heroin. That meant Doheny was looking at a mandatory fifteen years, which was tough for anyone, but particularly for someone who had barely attained his majority.

Winter Hill meant the Winter Hill Gang, as the newspapers dubbed it: a loose affiliation of mainly Irish-American hoodlums, with some Italians thrown in to improve the quality of the food. Buddy McClean and Howie Winter were the big names at the start, until McClean was shot dead in 1965, leaving Winter in principal control until the end of the 1970s, when a series of federal indictments for fixing horse races shook up the leadership and landed him and most of his associates in jail. That allowed one James 'Whitey' Bulger to make his move, and he remained in charge until 1994, when he fled a federal indictment. His lieutenant, Kevin Weeks, subsequently turned cooperating witness in 2000, but the Winter Hill Gang had weathered the storm, and remained a functioning part of Boston's underworld.

Search for Morris and Winter Hill, and come up with Tommy 'Ash' Morris: a couple of arrests, and a stretch in Old Colony in the mid-eighties, when it was still known as Bridgewater, for possession of a pair of loaded and unlicensed firearms and a quantity of cocaine, but otherwise clean for decades, which meant that Tommy Morris had either turned over a new leaf, which seemed unlikely, or had simply become much better at being a criminal. A further search provided no direct link between Valerie Mary Morris and Tommy 'Ash' Morris, but Tommy was older than Valerie by eighteen years. Cousins, or something closer? I was betting closer, based on Special Agent Engel's presence in Pastor's Bay.

Dig, dig, dig: names and histories, places and trial reports. Dig, dig, dig: calls to Boston, messages left, favors called in and favors promised. Dig, dig, dig, then wait. At noon, an e-mail came in from an ex-BPD cop turned private investigator in Fitchburg, sent from a Hotmail address that would never be used again after this message.

Tommy Morris was Valerie Kore's older brother. There were links to any number of articles, the most recent from this week concerning the killing of one Joey 'Joey Tuna' Toomey, an Irish-American businessman and a beloved scion of the Boston fish trade. There was a further link from that report to a Sunday magazine feature entitled 'Meet the Old Boss, Same as the New Boss,' a consideration of the current state of organized crime in the city that included various mentions of power struggles in the Boston underworld, and particularly among Irish-American elements still working to fill the void left by Whitey Bulger's enforced absence. The e-mail concluded with a single line from my source: 'Tommy Morris is going down.'

Suddenly the stakes had been raised, and I was glad of the impending arrival of Angel and Louis. In the meantime I called Aimee and told her of what I had found. More than ever, we

276

needed to protect Randall Haight, if and when he came forward, because I had the feeling that the rule of blood was about to be invoked. Engel was in Pastor's Bay because he believed that Anna Kore's disappearance might be a consequence of her uncle's criminality. Even if it wasn't, he would expect her uncle to try to involve himself regardless. That was the rule of blood: Blood came before everything. I also repeated to Aimee my earlier ultimatum, based on the pedophiliac nature of the photos received by Haight and on Anna Kore's age: Haight needed to confirm that he was willing to talk to the police, and he needed to do so quickly. Aimee was angry at having a gun put to her head. She asked me to give her a couple of hours, and I agreed.

'And what about those text messages?' said Aimee.

'There have been no more,' I said.

'Are you going to tell the police about them? They contain serious allegations about one of the principals in the investigation.'

I noticed that she was careful not to use names.

'Not yet,' I said.

'One rule for our client, and one rule for you, right?' she said, and hung up.

* * *

Tommy Morris had taken a bus from Logan after killing Joey Tuna, and stayed the night at an inn in Newburyport, eating in his room, watching television, thinking of what he had done to Joey, of what he had ordered done to Oweny Farrell and how it had not come to pass. He couldn't figure out how the cops had got to Oweny so fast, but it didn't matter. Joey Tuna was dead, and it was only in the quiet of the inn that Tommy felt the impact of the enormity of what he had done. There would be no forgiveness, no possibility of a rapprochement. He was a doomed man now, and they would unite to hunt him down. Joey's uncle would demand it. Honor would demand it. Sound practice would demand it.

But his niece was still missing. In a way, this had begun with her. Not only was he a man whose business had collapsed, and who now faced a hostile takeover from a competitor; he could not even protect his own family. His sister had fled from him. He had driven her away. He loved her, but he had forced her from his sight. She and his niece were the only surviving blood that meant anything to him. He would not leave it to the cops or the hated feds to search for the lost girl. He knew now that Joey and Oweny had not been responsible for her disappearance. She had not been a pawn in the game that they were playing.

Tommy liked chess, so the analogy pleased him. He had only three pieces left on the board but he refused to concede, even as all potential for movement was being limited by the forces arrayed against him. He had his knight, Dempsey; his rook, Ryan; and himself, the trapped king. He played with combinations of moves on the little travel set that he carried with him everywhere, deliberately allowing his own forces to be routed until he was reduced to these three — king, knight, rook — and he took his inability to secure victory not as a rebuke but as a challenge. He stayed awake all night, moving and thinking, and only when dawn came did he allow himself to sleep.

He had a throwaway cell phone, and with it he stayed in touch with Dempsey. He didn't tell him where he was, just advised him to take Ryan and get out of town. He needed more time to think, to play, to test the moves.

Later that evening he summoned Dempsey and Ryan to him, and the three men headed north.

★   ★   ★

At the same time, two other men were also drawing nearer to their northern destination. Music played in the car, a subdued yet intricate classical piece that at first hearing appeared to consist only of the same extended phrase repeated, but on closer listening gradually revealed tiny yet significant differences and developments. It was a song of humility and wonder, a wordless ode to the Divine.

'How much longer?' asked the passenger. Angel's dark curly hair had less gray than his years merited, and his face had fewer lines than his sufferings might have earned. He wore a *Big-Bam-Boom* era Hall & Oates T-shirt, boot-cut jeans that were a size too big for him, and a pair of designer yellow-and-turquoise sneakers that he had bought for almost nothing in an outlet. The sneakers had a certain rarity value, mainly because the company responsible for their design had realized its terrible mistake in creating them almost as soon as they saw the light of day, and quickly discontinued them when it became clear that their likely customer base consisted solely of the mentally ill, blind people with cruel friends, and, had they been able to put a name on him, this man, who was neither mentally ill nor blind but merely unusual in a great many ways.

Beside him, driving with his eyes barely open, was Louis, who had long been shaving tight his own graying locks, but not in any effort to hide the aging process, not if his beard was taken into account. His suit was gray, his shirt white, his knitted wool tie black. His shoes gleamed.

'How much longer?' said Angel again.

Louis checked the dashboard. 'Another hour.'

'Of this? You have to be kidding me. The tune hasn't changed since it started. It's like a really quiet car alarm for nervous people.'

'No, another hour to Boston.'

'Great. In the meantime, can we play something else?'

'No.'

'I'm bored.'

'What are you, nine years old? Shut the fuck up. Go to sleep.'

'I did sleep. This put me to sleep. Then I woke up, and it was still playing. I thought I'd died and gone to hell's waiting room.'

'It's not the same piece.'

'It sounds like the same piece. This guy Arthur Pärt is running a scam.'

'That's Arvo Pärt. You are a philistine, man.'

'Yeah, the Hungarian.'

'Estonian.'

'Just turn it off. I swear, the hillbilly shit was better than this.'

'You complained that that all sounded the same too.'

'It did, but at least it had words, and it was too annoying to be dull. I hear any more of this and we'll have to get an elevator put in the car.'

'Maybe some of those inspirational pictures as well, like they have in the offices of companies that are about to go under,' said Louis. 'You know, 'Let Your Imagination Soar,' with a photograph of an eagle, or 'Teamwork,' with those meerkat rat things.'

'A dung beetle,' said Angel. 'A picture of a dung beetle, and 'Eat Shit: You've Been Retrenched.' I hate that word 'retrenched.' At least 'redundant' is honest. 'Let go' is honest. 'Fired' is honest. 'Retrenched' is just a way to sugar the pill, like undertakers refusing to use the word 'death' and talking about 'passing on' instead, or doctors telling you that you have a 'condition' when what they really mean is you're riddled with cancer.'

'It's from the French,' said Louis. 'Retrenching is digging a second line of defense. It means that you've been cut off again.'

'What does that have to do with being fired?'

'Literally? Nothing, I guess.'

'See?'

'No. Why, you worried about your future?'

'Yeah, it gets shorter every day. That fucking music makes it seem longer, though.'

'It's nearly done.' The piece concluded. 'There, see? You want to spoil anything else?'

'Why, you got something else worth spoiling?'

'I put a load of discs in the player before we left.'

'What's up next?'

'Brian Eno, *Music for Airports*.'

'I don't know it. Is it loud?'

'Louder than Arvo Pärt.'

'Silence is louder than Arvo Pärt.'

They drove on. The music commenced. It was not loud. It was not loud at all.

'You're killing me,' moaned Angel. 'You're killing me softly . . . '

★ ★ ★

The hunters were gathering.

Boston's war was moving north.

Hunting season was about to begin.

21

Louis and Angel came to the Bear shortly before closing. I hadn't worked there for a while, and Dave Evans, the owner, seemed to be getting on fine without me, a fact that I tried not to take personally. Also, Aimee was paying me well, and like a good squirrel, I'd been carefully storing away enough nuts to see me through winter and beyond. But I liked the buzz of the place, and I'd never felt that working behind a bar was a dishonorable profession, particularly somewhere like the Bear where there was little tolerance for jackasses, and enough cops and repo men dotted around to ensure that any misbehavior would be frowned upon, if not actively discouraged if it persisted. Even without the presence of the law, the Bear was well able to handle the rare difficulties that arose. This was a neighborhood bar, an escape for a couple of hours, and the rules, though unwritten, were understood by nearly all.

'How's the Denny Kraus thing working out?' Dave asked me, as I juggled separate checks from a bunch of genial New Yorkers who had left their capacity for simple division at the state line.

'He's still denying that he's crazy.'

'They have met him, right? Denny Kraus came out of the womb with an extra hole in his head. When he stands in a draft, you can hear it whistle.'

283

'The judge knows he's crazy. The prosecution knows he's crazy. Even his own lawyer knows he's crazy.'

'What did you tell them?'

'That he was crazy.'

'It's unanimous, then.'

'Except for Denny.'

'What does he know? He's crazy. Thank God he didn't shoot anyone in here.'

'Why, you want to be the first one who does?'

'Absolutely. On the day I retire, I'm taking some of the chefs down. The wait staff I'll spare. I always liked them.' He looked over my shoulder as I sorted the checks. 'Split check?'

'Yep. Five of them.'

'It's a hundred bucks. It divides evenly.'

'I know.'

Dave scowled at the New Yorkers. 'We need a stricter door policy,' he said, and trotted off to see if any of the kitchen crew needed to be reminded of how Dave hoped to celebrate his retirement.

Aimee had left a message on my cell phone informing me that Randall Haight had finally decided to come clean about his past and its unwelcome intrusion into his new life. He would present himself at Aimee's office the next day, and she planned to inform the state police of her client's availability before she left the office, although she had decided not to give them his name in advance. I agreed that we should meet up to discuss our plans for the interview after the Bear closed for business.

Haight's decision to talk to the police was still

the right one, in my view, even leaving aside any concerns about Anna Kore. As a sole operator, I didn't have the resources to do what he wanted me to do, not under the circumstances. The furor surrounding Anna meant that I couldn't do what I would usually have done, which was to talk to people, including, as discreetly as possible, Haight's clients, local folk, even the cops. It could have been done without letting them know the specific nature of the harassment, and in time I was confident that I could have closed in on the person or persons responsible.

But, as the coffee shop incident had revealed, Anna's disappearance meant that anyone nosing around Pastor's Bay would immediately attract the attention of the police, and no independent investigation would be permitted. In a way, it was possible that by speaking to the police Haight would free me up to work more effectively on his behalf, assuming I could cut a deal with law enforcement that would allow me to nose around as long as I fed back any relevant information to them.

Angel and Louis appeared shortly after we called last orders. I had warned Dave that some friends might be arriving late in the evening, and he'd promised to make sure they were looked after, but even he seemed a little taken aback when they arrived. Maybe it was Angel's sneakers, or Louis's beard, or a combination thereof, but Dave froze for an instant, as though he had somehow been assigned the role of greeting the first extraterrestrial visitors to Earth and had just realized the possible personal consequences involved. Angel raised a hand in greeting, and I was about to acknowledge it when a figure appeared at the bar. I allowed my raised hand to rest just below my neck, two fingers pointing to my shoulder. It was a sign that Angel, Louis, and I had agreed upon shortly after they first began helping me out: Keep your distance. They disappeared into one of the back rooms, but not before Angel had a quiet word in Dave's ear, presumably to say that he was not to remind me of their arrival, and to bring some beer.

Three stools had freed up at the bar, and the center one was now occupied by Special Agent Robert Engel. He wore a jacket and jeans, and a crisp white shirt open at the neck.

'Dress-down day at Center Plaza, Agent Engel?' I said.

'I'm trying to blend in with the locals.'

'I could find you a Portland Pirates shirt, or a moose-antler hat.'

'Or you could just get me a drink: Dewar's, on the rocks.'

I poured him a generous measure, and he put a twenty on the bar.

'It's on me,' I said. 'Take it as a reminder of what common hospitality looks like.'

'Still sore about your time in the Pastor's Bay visitors' suite?'

'Psychologically and physically. Those chairs weren't made for comfort.'

'It could have been worse, although I hear the county jail is nice.'

'Maybe we could arrange a tour.'

'Even without one, I guarantee that it's nicer than a federal holding cell.'

'Is that a threat, Agent Engel?'

'I prefer Special Agent Engel, although I admit that it's a mouthful. And, no, it's not a threat. I don't believe you respond very well to threats. With you, I reckon it's carrots all the way, not sticks. Is there a place where we can talk?'

I nodded to Dave to let him know that I was done. Already, the bar's clientele was starting to drift home. I gestured toward one of the booths in the corner, as far away from Angel and Louis as possible, then poured myself a cup of coffee from the pot and joined Engel.

He was probably my age but his face was unlined, and if there were gray strands in his blond hair, they were well hidden. His mouth was very thin, his lips a horizontal cut in his face, his eyes a washed out gray-blue. In an adversarial situation, he would cut a forbidding figure. My guess was that he didn't have many friends.

Boo-hoo.

'So,' he said, 'it appears that despite your driving a flash muscle car around a small Maine town Chief Allan has yet to discover the identity of your client. He is dogged, though. Pretty soon he'll be down on his hands and knees examining tire tracks.'

I could have told him there and then that Randall Haight was about to make himself known to the police, but there would have been no percentage in it for me. It was better to listen, and wait, and see what I could get him to reveal

287

for little or no cost.

'I had no reason then to believe that my client's difficulties were linked to the Anna Kore case. I explained that during my conversation with Detective Walsh, the details of which I'm sure he passed on to you.'

'Most of them. He was distinctly rattled when he left. I got the impression he might have said something to you that he subsequently regretted. You do have a way of getting under people's skin, I'll give you that. I imagine it makes you good at what you do, although at some risk to your own personal safety. I bet you've picked up some cuts and bruises along the way.'

'I'm a fast healer.'

'Lucky for you. Some of those who crossed you have been less fortunate. Do you know that you're flagged on our system?'

'Yes, I do. And you knew that I was aware of it, otherwise you wouldn't have asked the question.'

'It's very interesting. You've led a charmed life.'

'Really? You know, sometimes it doesn't seem that way to me, and the FBI is not blameless in that regard.'

Engel made a minute adjustment to his features in an approximation of sorrow. 'That was an unfortunate choice of words. I apologize. What I do recognize is that, your occasionally lawless nature and periodic poor judgment apart, your actions have generally contributed to the removal of certain unwanted elements from our society. We have that in common, even down to the sometimes lawless nature and errors of judgment. I have some questions for you. They're general, and they shouldn't impinge upon any requirements of client confidentiality, but they'll enable us to move forward in our conversation and, indeed, in our relationship.'

'Do you talk like that to all of your dates?'

'Yes.'

'How's that working out for you?'

'Not so well.'

'Hard to believe.'

'Isn't it?'

He took a sip of his whisky and bared his teeth at the taste, like a rat testing the air.

'Is your investigation ongoing?' he asked.

'It is.'

'Are you likely to be a continuing presence in Pastor's Bay as a consequence?'

'Probably.'

'How convinced are you that your client's interests are not connected to the Anna Kore case?'

I paused. The bargaining was about to begin.

'Uncertain.'

'That's not what you told Detective Walsh.' He practically wagged his finger at me and added 'tut-tut.'

'I've modified it since then. That's why I used the past tense when you brought the subject up earlier. I *had* no reason to believe there was a connection. I've become more open-minded since then.'

'On what basis?'

'Pastor's Bay is a small town. My client's difficulties are, well, personal rather than professional in nature. They pertain to an incident in his youth. I'm starting to think that it might be wise for him to approach the police about them. By doing so, he may at least rule out one avenue of investigation for you, and perhaps even point you in a useful direction. But I base that only on a dislike of coincidence, and nothing more.'

'Have you made this opinion known to the client and, indeed, to his lawyer?'

'My change in position is relatively recent, but I feel that both would be inclined to listen to me, and to act on my advice, if I made it known.' I'd been hanging out too much with Aimee Price. I sounded like an attorney. 'There is also the matter of ensuring that the client's right to confidentiality is respected, and his safety is assured.'

'Why would his safety be in question?'

'A young girl is missing. There are newspaper reporters around, and TV cameras. Sometimes people jump to conclusions.'

'We're talking to a lot of people. Their faces haven't appeared on TV, or in the papers. No harm has come to them. Local residents have been interviewed, and no suspicion has fallen on them among their neighbors.'

'Well, maybe it's not the locals that concern me.'

Engel bared his teeth again, but this time there was no whisky involved.

'What do you know?' he said.

'I know that there's a connection between Anna Kore and Tommy Morris, late of

Somerville, and possibly an associate of 'the Hill.''

'Well, well. You have been busy.'

'You gave it away by your presence in Pastor's Bay. You should have worn a mask.'

'Noted,' said Engel. 'Anna's his niece, as you may or may not be aware by now. Valerie Kore, nee Morris, is Tommy Morris's significantly younger sister and only sibling. He took care of her after their parents died in a car accident when she was four, assisted by assorted aunts and relatives, but they've been estranged for a long time.'

'Ever since someone put Ronald Doheny in the ground, and then forgot where he was buried?'

Engel shrugged. 'Doheny was a runner for Morris, who was trying to carve out his own patch after Whitey went on the run. Doheny screwed up. He was a loudmouth, he crossed a customer, and the aggrieved customer sold him out to the cops. He was facing a long stretch inside, and pressure was put on him to cut a deal and turn informant. He made bail, then vanished. Missing, presumed crab food.'

'Did Morris know that Doheny was seeing his sister?'

'Not at first, but it didn't take him long to find out who had impregnated her. At that point, he probably wanted to kill Doheny, but would have settled for him doing the right thing.'

'And then Doheny gets pinched, and someone decides that he's unreliable and needs to be silenced.'

'Tommy Morris killed him, or had him killed. That's what we heard, although the killing would have been sanctioned from higher up. Soon after, his sister left Boston. She drifted around, but she kept straight. She is, by all accounts, a good citizen. No drugs, no booze, no contact with her brother and his people. She worked in Philly for a while, met a guy there, married him on the quiet. Her brother didn't know.'

'Alekos Kore.'

'Right again. They're now separated, but she hasn't sought a divorce.'

'She wanted to hold on to his name,' I said. 'If her brother comes looking for her, she'd be Valerie Kore, not Valerie Morris. It wouldn't keep her safe if he started digging, but it would be enough to evade casual inquiries.'

'Even if he did find her, and we think he's been keeping tabs on her, psychologically she'd left the Morris name behind.'

'And you knew who she was because *you'd* been keeping tabs on her all this time.'

'That's right.'

'Does her brother know that his niece is missing?'

'Her brother is in trouble. He's made some bad business decisions, and we've been fortunate in some of our efforts against him. His days are numbered.'

'You haven't answered the question. Does Tommy Morris know?'

I could feel that Engel wanted to look away, but he managed not to break his gaze. Still, he was a mass of 'tells.' Engel was concealing truths.

'We've tried to keep the girl's relationship to Morris quiet, and her mother says that she hasn't been in contact with him.'

'Do you believe her?'

'We did at the start. Now we're not so sure. She's desperate, perhaps desperate enough to turn to her brother for help.'

'So he knows?'

'He knows. Do you read the papers? A man named Joseph Toomey, known to his friends as Joey Tuna, was found shot to death in a fish market in Dorchester yesterday. One of his employees left his car keys at work, went back to retrieve them, and saw the office light burning. There was a lot of blood. Two shots, fatal but not immediately so — he'd been left to die. Joey was the ambassador for the Irish mob in Boston. He was the go-between, the kingmaker, the problem solver. He was untouchable. On the surface, he was neutral. In reality, he sided with the status quo; all that mattered was the efficient running of business, which was good for everybody. As Tommy Morris became more of a liability, he threatened that stability. A decision was made that it might be best if he were to keep Ronald Doheny company, except Tommy went to ground. Most of his men have abandoned him, but he still has a couple of loyal followers. They met with Joey on the day of his killing. Apparently, they wanted to know if he had sanctioned the kidnapping of Anna Kore in order to draw her uncle out. Joey denied it. Then he was killed.'

'You know who pulled the trigger?'

'Officially, no. Unofficially, we believe it was Tommy Morris himself.'

'Unusual. You'd think he'd palm off a job like that to his people.'

This time, a response flickered. It was like the briefest ripple on the surface of an otherwise smooth pond where an unseen creature had flicked a fin. There was something there, something interesting.

'I told you, he doesn't have many people left,' said Engel. 'It could be that it was personal for him. The ones who've been around for a while, they learn to bury their feelings deep. They hold on to the grudges, then wait for a time when they're justified in making a move.'

'You seem very well informed. You have a wire somewhere?'

'We have lots of wires. That's why we're the Federal Bureau of Investigation, not the Local Bureau of Supposition.' He was settled again. That brief flash of uncertainty was gone. 'It's also why, if you're concerned for the safety of your client, we can guarantee that he'll be looked after. We can put men on him, or move him out of town for a while. It is a 'he,' right?'

I did a little cheek-puffing and imitation weighing up of potentially grave consequences, then allowed that the client was indeed male.

'He doesn't want to leave town,' I said. 'In fact, that's something of a deal breaker for him. He has a nice life in Pastor's Bay. He wants to hold on to it. And I don't want federal agents on him. Half the people in here probably smelled you as law the minute you arrived, and the other

294

half didn't have to because they were lawmen themselves. If someone like Tommy Morris is going to be sniffing around this, then I want as little attention as possible drawn to our client. If it comes down to that, I'll look after his protection myself.'

'You sure about that?'

The straight line became a jagged scar: a smile, assuming you didn't look for warmth or reassurance in a smile, or anything resembling a decent human emotion.

'Go on. I'm listening.'

'Tommy Morris has left the reservation, and we believe he's heading this way.'

'All the more reason to keep my own client safely off the board.'

'It's your call. When can we expect to talk with this elusive gentleman?'

'I want more.'

'Really?'

'I want freedom to investigate on his behalf. In return, I'll share any information of relevance with Walsh.'

'He won't like you being on his turf. Neither will Allan.'

'They'll just have to hold their noses.'

'I'll talk with them and see what I can do.'

'I'm sure you can convince them, you silver-tongued devil, you.'

'And in return we get access to your client?'

'I'll get in touch with his lawyer.'

'That shouldn't be hard, since she just walked through the door.'

I turned and spotted Aimee. She hesitated

when she saw that I was with someone. I beckoned her forward, and introduced her.

'Aimee, this is Special Agent Robert Engel of the FBI's Boston field office. Special Agent Engel, Aimee Price. Special Agent Engel likes to be called 'Special Agent Engel,' Aimee. It's a matter of some pride.'

Aimee looked confused but said nothing. Special Agent Engel smiled in the way an executioner might smile at the condemned man's last good gag just before he dropped the ax.

'Special Agent Engel and I were just discussing client safety, but we're all done now,' I said.

Engel rose, and thanked me for his drink. 'I'll let discussions commence,' he said. 'I look forward to hearing from you both very soon.'

He left more than half of his whisky on the bar and headed for the door.

'He didn't finish his drink,' said Aimee.

'I think he only asked for it so as to seem more human.'

'He certainly needs something.'

'Agreed. When he looks in the mirror, his reflection probably wants to punch him in the face.'

'What did you discuss?'

'I let him wear me down to the point where I felt that perhaps our client should present himself for interview, and in return he told me more than I knew before, and maybe a little more than he wanted me to know, because he believed that he was getting the better part of the deal. It may be that he'll also persuade Walsh and Allan to let me operate on Haight's behalf, or just to give me enough room to breathe.'

'So you didn't feel obliged to let him know that Haight had already made his decision? That's almost, but not quite, dishonest. Are you sure you didn't train to be a lawyer?'

'I'd have flunked insincerity.'

The Bear was now almost empty, and the stragglers were being encouraged to make their way home, or at least somewhere else that wasn't the Bear. I poured Aimee a glass of white wine, put it on my tab, and said, 'I have a treat for you. What are we missing here?'

'Good company.'

'Good company. Exactly!' I placed my hand on the small of her back and steered her toward the back of the bar. 'But in the absence of it, I have some people I'd like you to meet instead.'

It had been months since I had seen them. Louis's new beard was certainly striking, I had to give him that. They both stood as we approached.

'Aimee Price, I'd like you to meet Angel. And this is his close friend, Old Father Time . . . '

22

They checked into a suicide motel just out of Belfast, the kind of place that Dempsey always associated with estranged fathers, commission-only salesmen, and hookers who kept the lights down low so the johns couldn't get a good look at their faces. It had probably been built in the fifties, but it was too ugly and dilapidated to merit the description 'retro,' and the only restoration job worth doing on it would have involved restoring the lot on which it stood to a condition of vacancy. It struck Dempsey that he was growing disturbingly used to staying in such places, to eating without looking at his food, his eyes constantly scouting for familiar faces in unfamiliar places, for the car that disgorged a passenger while the driver kept the motor running, for the gaze that lingered just a moment too long, for the approaching figure and the moving hand, for the sight of the gun that would, in time, surely take his life.

No wonder he was plagued with stomach pains and constipated to hell and back. He could now hardly recall a time when he was not fearful, not wary. He had to force himself to remember beery afternoons in Murphy's Law at First and Summer, in the shadow of the big generating station, and Philly-steak spring rolls in the Warren Tavern in Charlestown, or just sitting with a coffee and a newspaper in Buddy's on

Washington Street in Somerville, the old diner's elevated position giving him a sense of inviolability, of safety. All gone now, all gone, and he would never be able to return to them. Instead, there were just anonymous rooms in dumps like this one, rooms that always smelled of smoke despite the No Smoking signs, and food eaten out of paper and plastic, and the constant grinding ache in his guts.

Half of the cars and trucks in the motel's parking lot were keeping Bondo in business, and the other half had problems that even Bondo couldn't fix. He tried to figure out what these people were even doing here. Were they, like him, rootless persons, drifting men? The old woman in the office wore her glasses on a gold chain, and the fats in her body made liquid noises as she walked. She had tiny feet. Dempsey couldn't understand how she managed to remain upright. She confirmed that she was happy to take cash for two rooms, on the grounds that 'there weren't never nothing worth stealing in them anyway,' and therefore guarantees of credit were largely unnecessary. There was coffee available in the mornings from seven until nine, she told them, but Dempsey took one look at the stained pot, the dusty foam cups, the sachets of powdered creamer, and decided that he could wait until they found somewhere more appealing for a kick-start. Tommy paid for two nights, and told the woman that they might stay longer, 'depending on how good the hunting is.'

'We ain't never full,' she said. 'We always got room.'

Dempsey took another look at the peeling paint in the reception area, at the snow-screened portable TV playing an inexplicably popular sitcom aimed at people who thought that a grown man living with his mother was the height of humor, at the sign warning that checkout time was ten a.m. ('AND NO EXSEPTIONS!'), at the woman's painted expression and barrel-like form, as though she were a living matryoshka doll capable of containing infinitely smaller but no less unwelcoming versions of herself, and decided not to comment on the motel's apparently infinite capacity to absorb new guests.

There was music coming from a bar next door to the motel, and Dempsey asked if there was any chance of getting food there. The woman snorted.

'They got pickles,' she said, 'but I wouldn't go eatin' 'em.'

Dempsey said that he'd pass. There was a sheaf of fast-food menus at the desk, so he grabbed a couple and brought them with him to the room that he and Ryan would share on the first floor, while Tommy took the adjoining room for himself.

'I talk to you for a minute, Tommy?' said Dempsey, as he allowed Ryan to enter the room ahead of him. Tommy nodded. He lit a cigarette and Dempsey indicated that they should walk a little farther into the lot, away from the main building. There were no stars in the sky, and Dempsey could feel the weight of the clouds, the sky itself pressing down on them. He had never felt more constricted, more hemmed in by forces

300

both human and elemental.

Tommy had not informed them of what he planned to do before they picked him up in Newburyport, but Dempsey had guessed as soon as he told them to head north. They had passed most of the trip in silence, with not even the radio to distract them from their thoughts, Ryan in the passenger seat, Tommy stretched out in the back, sometimes dozing but mostly just staring into space. Now they were here, within striking distance of Pastor's Bay.

'You didn't want to talk in front of Francis?' said Tommy. Dempsey could smell stale sweat on Tommy, and there were stains on his pants. Tommy had always been an elegant man. Even at the worst of times, he kept himself neat and clean. The stale odor of him, his wrinkled clothes and unshaved face, troubled Dempsey more than what Tommy had done to Joey, and the aborted action he had ordered against Oweny's crew.

'No,' said Dempsey. 'I thought it should just be us two.'

'You let him sit in on the meet with Joey Tuna?'

'No.'

'Anyone would think you didn't trust him. Is there something you'd like to share with me?'

Again, Dempsey wished that he still smoked. It was becoming a kind of mantra. He felt that he had nothing to do with his hands, nothing to occupy them. He pushed them hard into his pockets for fear they would betray him, their movements revealing his barely restrained fear.

'I got a lot of things on my mind,' said

301

Dempsey. 'I don't know where to start.'

'Take your time. We got all night. I haven't been sleeping so good, and I'm afraid to start popping pills.'

Tommy took a long drag on the cigarette and examined the glowing tip. It seemed to hypnotize him. He stared at it, unblinking, the other man forgotten, his face gray with stress and exhaustion. Dempsey wondered just how long it had been since Tommy Morris enjoyed an undisturbed night's sleep. Uneasy lies the head, and all that. The only head that rested less easily was the one that would soon be detached from its body.

'How did it come to this, Tommy?' he said.

'Huh?' Tommy emerged from his daze. 'Come to what?'

'Us, here, living out of money taken from a shoebox. You ever thought about how it all fell apart so fast?'

'Yeah, I thought about it.'

'You come up with any answers?'

'More questions. No answers. You?'

Dempsey chose his words carefully.

'After the meet with Joey, I started thinking that maybe all of them had it in for you from the start, and not just Oweny. I mean, how long had Joey been stringing us along, claiming to be the middleman when he was secretly on Oweny's side? And if Joey was whispering in Oweny's ear he was doing it because it had been sanctioned from above, and he hadn't just started last week, or last month. People had agreed on it. We started figuring we were unlucky, but the more I look at it the more I think that someone was talking out of turn.'

'To the cops? The feds?'

'Doesn't have to be them. All this person needed to do was pass the word to Joey. We trusted him. We thought he was neutral. But he wasn't. He never had been, not really. Joey could have used the information as he saw fit: an anonymous tip-off to the cops, a word to Oweny. Look at it: horses that were supposed to fall didn't fall like they should have, and Joey laughed it off and told us that these things happen, that everybody took a hit on that one. Our couriers and dealers get picked up, and Joey tells us that the feds had a snitch in Florida, and he was looking to figure out who it was, and we weren't the only ones who were concerned. We get a tip on a bond warehouse, and when we hit it there's only a tenth of what we were told was there, and the cops are crawling all over us before we even get the truck out the gate. Joey told us that it was lousy information, that the Contadinos nearly lost a crew the same way, but I ask around and there's no talk about the Contadinos pulling a warehouse job that went south. And we get cut out of deals that should have been shared: pads on construction, on concessions. Jobs are pulled, and we only find out about them after the fact. I look back on it now and it was an accumulation of small details, like we were being picked at, like we were slowly being eaten alive. Everyone else was making money, but not us.'

Tommy listened to all that he had to say,

punctuating it with pulls on the cigarette. His right middle and index fingers were the burnt orange of a polluted sunset.

'So who was the snitch?'

Dempsey shrugged. 'I'm just saying. I could be wrong.'

'You think it was Francis?'

Dempsey shook his head forcefully. 'No, he's a good kid. He's just young, that's all. And, you know, so many guys have drifted away. It could have been any of them or, you know, it could have been Joey himself, working to undermine you so that Oweny could take your place.'

'If there even was a snitch.'

'If there was,' agreed Dempsey.

'So, what else?'

'Joey. I have to tell you, Tommy, I wasn't expecting it. I never thought you'd go after him.'

'It had to be done.'

'Did it?'

'I had to know for sure. I had to know that they didn't have her.'

But that wasn't why you killed him, thought Dempsey. That was why you went to see him, but not why you put him down. I always suspected that you hated him. I just never knew how much. Tommy had told him once that it was Joey who wanted Ronald Doheny dead. Tommy had argued for sparing him, because even if he was a braggart and a fool and a promiscuous little bastard who should have kept his hands to himself, he was still the father of his sister's child. Joey wouldn't hear of it, though. He wanted Doheny gone, and he wasn't the only

304

one. If Tommy wasn't prepared to do it, then someone else would, but it would look bad for Tommy, and maybe people, important people, would start doubting his commitment to the cause. They might even wonder if Tommy, like Whitey before him, was snitching to the feds, selling out his associates to secure his own position. They might decide that Tommy wasn't sound. Joey had put all of this to Tommy at the fish market after hours. He had shown Tommy the new backlit table in the butchering room, the sharp knives hanging clean in preparation for the next morning's work. Fillets of fish could be placed on the backlight, Joey explained, revealing the presence of parasites in the flesh that could then be removed.

'That's what we're doing now,' said Joey. 'We're picking out the parasites. We're taking the blade to them, and afterward the flesh, *our* flesh, will be clean. If in doubt, Tommy, you take it out. That's the new rule. Don't give anyone cause to doubt you, that's my advice.'

So Tommy had killed Ronald Doheny, strangling him in a basement in Revere, and his sister had hated him for it, and Tommy had waited for the chance to avenge himself on Joey Tuna.

'Look, I never trusted him, Tommy,' said Dempsey. 'Him, and his stink, and the way he talked *at* you, not *with* you, like he always knew more than you did. If a truck had hit him, I'd have sent the driver a fruit basket. If he'd been electrocuted, I'd have written a thank-you note to the power company. But I didn't think that you'd kill him, Tommy, because they can't let that go. Now they'll keep coming after us until we're done. Because of it, we got no cards left to play.'

Tommy finished the cigarette and flicked it toward the road, watching it flare briefly before it exploded on the ground and faded to nothing.

'If you want to walk away, I understand,' he said. 'I won't blame you for it.'

'I don't want to walk away,' said Dempsey. 'But I don't want to die either.'

'So what's left?'

'You don't owe them, Tommy. You don't owe any of them.'

They looked at each other, and Dempsey was aware that, for the second time in recent days, he was discussing the possibility of a monumental act of betrayal, the very act that he had intimated might have led to Tommy's downfall. He tensed his abdomen, waiting to absorb the punch that might come, or the hand to the throat, or the gun beneath the chin and the oblivion that would follow. There had been times in the past weeks and months when he thought he might even have welcomed the peace that a bullet would bring. But Tommy didn't make a move, and he didn't look angry or even surprised. He even appeared to consider the possibility for a moment, then swat it away. For the first time, Dempsey truly understood that Tommy had resigned himself to what was to come. This garbage-strewn, weed-scarred parking lot was his Gethsemane. Only the thought of his niece was keeping him from facing his enemies directly and embracing their final judgment on him.

'I can't do that, Martin. You know I can't.' Gently, he laid a hand above Dempsey's heart and tapped his finger in time to its beats. 'And you can't do it either. If you did, I'd make sure that I lived long enough to kill you myself. We're not rats, Martin. Never that.'

Dempsey nodded sadly.

'You're right. I don't know what I was thinking. I'm frightened, I suppose.'

'You don't have to be frightened, Martin. We might get out of this yet. And if we don't, well, I'll be there with you at the end. You know that, don't you?'

His hand moved from Dempsey's breast to the back of his neck, his big palm cupping it fondly. There was no threat to it. It was a moment of contact between a father and a beloved, if sometimes troublesome, son, the older man letting the younger understand that he would guide him on the right path. Dempsey knew Tommy well, had learned to judge his moods and his silences, the cadences of his sentences and the meaning hidden in the pauses in his speech. He closed his eyes and smelled Tommy's breath on his face, and the sweat from the journey, and the smoke on his hair and his clothes. Dempsey thought of his own father. How long had it been since he'd seen him: six, seven years? They had never been close, and his mother's death had not brought them any closer. His father now lived somewhere outside Phoenix, in a house that he had bought with his second wife's insurance money. The old man had

307

outlived two of his women, and Dempsey believed that he might outlive one or two more. He was a hard man, but he drew women to him, drew them to him and then ground them down. Dempsey had never been to Phoenix. He wondered if he would ever make it now.

Tommy's hand lifted. He patted Dempsey on the back.

'Let's go inside. It's cold out here.'

'I was going to order a pizza. I haven't eaten since morning. You want something?'

'No, I'm good.'

'You should eat, Tommy. It's not good for you to be starving yourself. You'll need your strength. *We'll* need your strength.'

'You're right, Martin. Let me know when it comes. Maybe I'll grab a slice of yours.'

They walked back toward the motel. Ryan stood at the open door of his room. When he saw them coming, he went inside. Dempsey noticed how still the night was, how quiet. Their voices had probably carried back to Ryan. He was always curious, was Ryan. He was always listening. Who had said that to Dempsey once?

It came to him: Joey Tuna. Old Joey, who was trusted by everyone, or was said to be trusted by everyone, but trusted no one. Mr. Indispensable. Everybody's friend. He was gone now, but he'd have his revenge, even from beyond the grave. Men would kill them in his name, mourning him publicly even as they expressed private relief at his passing, because a man who is everybody's friend really has no friends at all.

'How long will we stay here, Tommy?'

Dempsey asked as the two men parted.

'Not long,' said Tommy. 'We'll wait, and then we'll move.'

'What are we waiting for?'

'A call. Just a call.'

Tommy went into his room, closing the door behind him, and Dempsey joined Ryan. He was now lying on one of the beds, flicking through the channels on the TV. The room was cleaner than Dempsey had expected. Everything looked worn, but he'd stayed in chain-hotel rooms that were worse. It was as if the office and the woman were a test, and the room the reward for passing it successfully, for not being taken in by appearances.

Ryan didn't speak. Dempsey thought he might have been sulking.

'I'm ordering,' said Dempsey. 'You hungry?'

Ryan shook his head. He'd found the same sitcom that the woman in the office had been watching. These shows were on some kind of perpetual loop, a domestic hell soundtracked by canned laughter. Dempsey had no time for any of them.

The phone in the room allowed local calls only, free of charge. Dempsey ordered a sixteen-inch margarita pizza, convinced that, once the food came, Ryan and Tommy would eat their share. But when it arrived Ryan was already asleep, and Tommy's room was dark. Dempsey knocked softly at the door, but there was no reply. He ate alone, the sitcom playing silently on the TV, lost in the pointlessness of it all. When he had eaten his fill, he slipped from the room and walked to the nearby bar. It was not dissimilar to the motel: unprepossessing from the outside but simple and cozy within. There was a pool table to the right of the door, and a CD jukebox to the left was playing *Waiting for Columbus*. All the tables were unoccupied, but three men and a woman were seated at the bar. The woman had a hand on the thighs of the men at either side of her, and the third man's knee was held between her legs. She smiled at Dempsey as he entered, as if inviting him to find a way to join in, and he smiled back before taking a seat as far away from the group as possible, with a pillar blocking their view of him. The bartender told him that he would be closing up soon, but nobody seemed in any hurry to get going, and the lovers had an assortment of liquor and beer racked up, the bottles still fresh from the cooler.

'Just one for the road,' he said. He put a ten and a five on the bar, ordered a boilermaker, and told the bartender to keep the change for his trouble. When the bartender went to the well, Dempsey stopped him and told him to make it with Jack's from the call.

'Don't make much difference if you're dropping it in a beer,' said the bartender.

'It does to me.'

'It's your money.'

'Sorry that it's coming out of your tip.'

'Don't be. It's my bar.'

He was in his sixties. Twin scars ran the length of both arms from the elbows to the wrists. He saw Dempsey looking at them and said, 'Motorcycle.'

'I figured unsuccessful suicide, but I'll buy the bike story.'

The bartender chuckled. It sounded like mud bubbling up from a hot pool.

'You staying at the motel?'

'That's right.'

'You meet Brenda?'

The question brought a burst of laughter from the group at the other end of the bar.

'I don't know. What does she look like?'

'Old gal in the office. Glasses. Big, big woman.'

'Yeah, I met her. She said you had pickles, but that I shouldn't eat them.'

This brought more chuckles from the bartender, and more gales of laughter from the lovers.

'Ayuh, pickles,' said the bartender, and wiped a tear of mirth from his eyes. 'That Brenda.'

With that, he left Dempsey to his drink. Dempsey couldn't see any pickles. It troubled him only slightly. 'Old Folks Boogie' was followed by 'Time Loves a Hero.' The bartender talked to the group at the bar. They ordered more drinks, and he served them, even though they had plenty still left from the earlier rounds, his warning about the imminence of closure seemingly forgotten. They sent up another boilermaker to Dempsey, and he made the obligatory polite conversation with them by stretching his head around the pillar, but they could tell that he wanted to be left to himself, and they were having too good a time to resent him for it. 'Mercenary Territory' came on, and

Lowell George sang about being qualmless and sinking, and the second boilermaker tasted bitter to Dempsey, although he had seen the shot being poured and knew that there was nothing wrong with it. He went to the restroom. When he came back, Ryan was standing at the bar. He was tense, and that tension had communicated itself to the rest of those present, because the level of conversation had dropped, and the woman was no longer as intimate with the men as she had been. Dempsey could see the shape of the gun beneath Ryan's shirt. He didn't know if the others had noticed it. Stupid. Stupid, stupid, stupid.

'Take a seat,' said Dempsey. 'I'll buy you a drink.' He called to the bartender. 'We good for one more for my friend?'

The bartender glanced pointedly at his watch but didn't refuse the order. Ryan pulled up a stool, but he didn't look at Dempsey. He just stared straight ahead.

'What are you doing?' said Ryan.

'What does it look like I'm doing? I'm having a drink.'

'I woke up and you weren't there.'

'What are we, married?'

He sipped his drink, trying to look unconcerned, but his hand trembled.

'You take your phones with you?'

'No, I left them in the room. What's it to you?'

The bartender arrived with another boilermaker, and Dempsey put a fifty on the bar and told him to buy everyone a round, and one for himself. The bartender just took the payment for Ryan's drink and returned Dempsey's change.

'I'm closing the register now,' he said.

'We won't be here long,' said Dempsey.

'Sometimes the cops come by,' said the bartender, and Dempsey knew that he had seen Ryan's gun.

'I understand,' said Dempsey. 'Thanks for letting us know.'

The bartender drifted away.

Ryan didn't mix the shot but drank it separately from the beer.

'Did you use the phone here?' he asked.

'What's wrong with you? What kind of question is that?'

Ryan's back was ramrod straight. He still hadn't looked at Dempsey.

'I asked you a question. Did you use the phone?'

'No, I didn't use the phone. You want to check with the bartender? Why don't you dust it for fingerprints? Jesus, Frankie, what's the problem?'

Some of the pressure eased from Ryan, and Dempsey realized that Ryan wasn't angry, he was scared. Dempsey could feel him trembling as he laid a hand on his arm and said, 'Talk to me.'

'I thought you'd run out on me,' said Ryan. 'I thought you'd sold us out.'

'What? How could you think that? I've never given you cause to think that way.'

'I heard you talking to Tommy. I didn't hear all of it, just some of it. You were talking about a rat, and how Joey Tuna didn't like having me around. It was like you didn't trust me, like you

313

didn't think I was sound.'

How had their conversation carried so far? Dempsey wondered. How much had Ryan heard in recent times?

'I know you're sound, Frankie. You've always been a stand-up guy. I know we've had our differences, but I've never doubted you.'

'I wasn't the rat, Martin. I swear it.'

'I never believed you were. Look, I don't even know if there was a rat. I was just thinking out loud.'

Now Ryan turned to him. He was like a child, thought Dempsey, a child with a gun who dreamed of killing other children.

'Can I ask you something, Martin, without you getting angry?'

'Sure you can.'

'And you can't take it personal, and you can't lie.'

'I promise you, I won't.'

'Were you the one who talked to Oweny and Joey Tuna?'

The enormity of the question nearly floored Dempsey. He couldn't even begin to conceive of how Ryan had found the balls to ask it. Ryan was asking him if he had ratted them out to Oweny and Joey. And if he said 'Yes', what then? Was Ryan going to pull out a gun and kill him? What was the kid thinking?

But Dempsey knew what Ryan was thinking. He knew because he was under the same pressures, and had made the same connections. By killing Joey, Tommy had killed them all. None of them would be allowed to walk away if they stuck together, but one of them might live a little longer if he sold them out to Oweny and the rest. All it would take was a phone call, and when the time came, and the motel doors were kicked in, and the guns roared and the blood flowed, they might remember that you were the guy who gave up Tommy Morris, and maybe they would stick to the deal they had promised you.

Maybe.

'No, Frankie, I never talked to them. My mother's gone, but I swear it on my father's life, and on my own. I never gave them anything.'

Ryan looked deep into his eyes, then turned away again.

'I believe you,' he said. 'I'd know if you were lying.'

Dempsey realized that he had been holding his glass too tightly, ready to use it on Ryan if it seemed that his fears were about to get the better of him.

'I had to ask,' said Ryan. Even though he thought Dempsey was an animal, Ryan knew that he represented the best hope of survival for Tommy and himself, because the men who were coming for them would be worse even than Dempsey. What mattered was only that Dempsey was sound.

'Finish your drink,' said Dempsey, and the two men sat together in silence until the lights dimmed, and the bar emptied, and the bartender disappeared, and there was only themselves and Lowell George singing 'Willin',' all of them out on the road late, all of them waiting for a sign to move on.

The traffic was sparse when at last they left the bar. They paid it no heed, and so neither of them noticed the car parked in the shadows across the street, or the occupants of the vehicle: a couple in their twenties, the horse-faced woman in the driver's seat no longer frightened and weeping as she had seemed in the Wanderer, her male companion beside her dressed in khakis and a polo shirt, not a single hair on his head out of place, each of them expressionlessly watching the progress of the two men.

23

Randall woke again to the silence of the house. He was worried. He didn't understand. The girl had still not returned. Where was she? He listened, half expecting to hear the sound of the television from downstairs. She wasn't supposed to watch it after ten p.m., but sometimes she did, and unless he was in a bad mood he would not fight her over it. But there was no noise, only the sound of his own breathing in the room.

There were times when he would play music late at night: Schumann, Tchaikovsky, Chopin. He had a collection of vinyl, and a good record player. He believed that classical music in particular sounded better on vinyl: warmer, more human. He had always wanted to be a pianist, but the handful of lessons he had taken since his release had revealed to him his singular lack of talent and application. He could have persisted, he supposed, but to what end? He could never approach even an iota of the genius of Ashkenazy or Zimerman, the great interpreter of Chopin, better even than Rubinstein. So he contented himself with admiring the greatness of others, and the girl was permitted to listen too, if she chose. Mostly, though, she tended to slip away. She resented his indulgences, resented anything that gave him peace or pleasure. Yet he forgave her her moods, because she was at once so young and so old.

Where was she? He wanted to know. This was not how it was supposed to end between them.

The girl had first appeared to him as he sat in one of the holding cells at the station house. They had isolated him from the other prisoners for his own security. The next day he was to be transported to juvie, and would remain there until his trial. Bail would not be applied for. The nature of the crime forbade it, but it was felt that the boys would probably be safer away from their homes anyway. Although Selina Day's killers had not been identified, even the birds in the trees called their names. One of Selina's aunts was interviewed on television, and said that she could find no forgiveness in her heart for those who had taken her niece from the world, children though they were themselves. When asked if she spoke for all of Selina's family, she replied tartly that she spoke for 'all good people.'

Selina's mother made no comment on the apprehension of her daughter's killers. It would not bring her little girl back, and the ages of the boys involved had only added to the horror of what had been done. The media was discouraged from approaching her as the black community closed protectively around the Day family, and thus there were no cameras to witness a woman of middle age approach the Day house and knock on the door; nor were there microphones to pick up her words as she introduced herself as the mother of William Lagenheimer. No reporter waited, pen in hand, to record his impressions of the scene as Selina Day's mother reached out to the older woman and slowly, softly embraced her, children now lost to both, the pair united in grief.

After the initial shock of discovery and confession, the boy had accepted his situation with equanimity, even stoicism. Later, the psychologists and the social workers would express surprise at that fact, and would make assumptions about his character based on it, but they were wrong in all that they thought. Just as he would later feel no sadness at coming to terms with his limitations as a pianist, and would refuse to rail at the Fates for not gifting him the talents that he desired, so too he found a strength within himself following the girl's death. Regret, he now knew, was a useless emotion, the poor cousin of guilt. As a boy, he would not have been able to couch his view in those terms, yet he had instinctively understood it to be true. If he was sorry for what they had done to the girl, it was only because of all that had resulted from it.

The cell was very warm, and the bed was hard. A drunk nearby had shouted at him until one of the policemen told him to shut up. The policeman had then checked on the boy. They had taken away his shoelaces and his belt. He didn't know why, not then. The policeman asked the boy if he was okay, and he replied that, yes, he was. He requested some water, and it was brought to him in a paper cup. After that he was left alone, and the cells stayed quiet.

He had been trying to sleep, his head turned to the wall, when he smelled her. He knew it was she because something of her odor was still with him. He'd tried washing it from his hands, but it had lingered: cheap drugstore perfume, sickly and cloying. It had prevented him from eating the prison food, because that smelled of her too. With her dying, she had polluted him.

Now the smell was stronger, more pungent, and he felt a hand upon his back, pushing at him, demanding his attention. He didn't want to look, though. To look would be to acknowledge the reality of her presence, to give her power over him, and he didn't want that, so he closed his eyes tightly and pretended to be asleep, hoping she would go away.

But she didn't. Instead, her fingers probed at him. She touched his eyes, and his ears, then stroked his cheek before forcing his lips apart. He tried to keep his teeth together, but his gorge was rising and he gagged. Now her hand was deep in his mouth, her fingertips on his tongue. He bit down on them, but the grip on his tongue grew stronger, and he was choking on his own vomit and the sweet-sour stink of her. With one hand buried in his hair, and the other holding his tongue, she made him face her, made him look upon what they had wrought.

She never spoke. She could not, for during the assault she had bitten off most of her own tongue.

He stared into her eyes, and she entered him, just as her attackers had once hoped to enter her. In that moment he was lost to her. She released her hold upon him, and kissed him, and he tasted the blood. A great lethargy came over him, and he fell into a deep sleep. When he woke she was gone, but she returned that night, and the next, and every night after. His only respite from her was during the hearing itself, and he came to welcome the tedium of it, the arguments and counterarguments, the testimony of experts, the milk and sandwiches and cookies that they gave him for lunch. His only wish was that his parents had not been there. They gave him no comfort, for he felt their shame at what their son had become.

In the evenings he would be returned to his new cell at juvie. They were called 'rooms,' but it was still a cell. A room you could leave when you chose to do so; a cell you could not. Sometimes, she would already be waiting for him there. He would smell her as he approached the cell, and his footsteps would slow, forcing the guard to steer him on, one hand on his arm, the other at his back. At other times, she would come only when dark had fallen, and he would wonder where she had been. They would not let him speak to his co-accused, so he could not ask him if the girl appeared to him as well, if she divided her time between them like a sluttish girlfriend who could not decide her favorite among her suitors. But, no, how could she be with them both? She spent every night with him. Whenever he woke, she was there. She was always there.

When he was almost eighteen they moved him to another facility, and she followed him. For a time, they made him share a cell, but that arrangement didn't last long. His cellmate was older than him by ten years and smelled of sour milk. One of his eyes was smaller than the other, and his eyelashes were crusted with hardened mucus. He had twisted fingernails. They reminded the boy of thorns. He did not speak, not ever. Nor, it seemed, did he sleep, for as the boy tossed and turned he could see the silhouette of his cellmate's head hanging over the edge of the bunk above, watching him.

On the third night, as he lay sleeping, the boy was attacked. He knew what the older man wanted, and tried to fight him off. Eventually his screams brought a guard, and the next day he was moved to another cell in a different wing while his cellmate went to solitary confinement. The girl consoled the boy. She held him in the dark. Nobody was supposed to hurt him.

Nobody, except her.

Three days later, his tormentor committed suicide in solitary by opening an artery in his left arm, tearing apart his flesh with a rusty nail in order to let the blood flow.

The girl had smelled different that night when she came to the boy.

She had smelled of sour milk.

He never mentioned her to the psychiatrists or the guards or to anyone else. She was not to be spoken of. He was hers, and she was his. He feared her, but he thought that he might almost have loved her too.

Now, years later, in another room, in another state, he wished for her to come, to confirm that it was over at last. As if she had responded to his wish, he suddenly smelled her scent. He rolled over in bed and caught sight of her, squatting in the shadows, watching him. The shock of it caused him to cry out. She rarely did that these days. If she entered his room at night she would crawl in beside him, working her way up under the covers from the base of the bed; or, if she was in a temper, she would pull the bedclothes from him or scratch at the window with her finger-nails, preventing him from sleeping. Otherwise, she kept to her own places, and the basement in particular.

But she'd been different since the detective came to visit, and he felt certain that her absence was linked to him. Then again, he couldn't remember the last time he'd entertained someone in the house. Randall's behavior did not strike anyone in Pastor's Bay as odd. The farther north one traveled in the state, the more likely one was to encounter families or individuals who didn't want to be disturbed, who liked to keep themselves to themselves. Maine was a state of scattered houses, scattered towns, scattered people. If you wanted folk living so close they could hear you scratch, there were big cities that would suit you better. If you wanted to scratch in peace, then Maine was the place. Even his local clients rarely ventured beyond the hall when they stopped by to drop off papers or clear up some item of business. Out of politeness he would usually offer coffee, or ask them to take a seat, but they rarely took up the invitation, and when they did the girl showed little interest in them. In her way, she was as solitary a soul as he was. They were twin dark stars, bound together by the gravitational pull of the past.

Nevertheless, Randall was not a hermit. He

attended meetings of the town council, and took care of its accounts gratis. He assisted at charity events, went out with his shovel in winter to clear paths for the older folk, and had even, very briefly, dated a divorcée who moved to Pastor's Bay from Quebec to paint landscapes, and who volunteered at the library. Their halting relationship had occasioned some gossip in the town, not least because it had generally been assumed that Randall Haight was gay. The fact that he wasn't disappointed those who thought that having a gay accountant, even a closeted one, added some much needed color to the social makeup of Pastor's Bay, and strenuous efforts were made to find someone else who might be gay in order to make up for the perceived imbalance.

The relationship hadn't ended badly as such. There had been no big argument, no accusations of one party misleading the other. Randall had simply stopped calling, and then had left town for a couple of weeks in his car without informing the woman of where he was going, or when he might be back. By the time he returned the woman had packed up her belongings and was preparing to move away, having decided that she could paint just as well in a place where there were more than two bars, and more than two eligible men. She had liked Randall, though. She told her friends that she couldn't understand why he'd suddenly gone cold on her.

But the girl knew why Randall had stopped calling her. The girl had drawn him a picture. She'd used a lot of red, and she'd left a rusty nail with it, just in case Randall was a little slow on the uptake. Randall was hers, and hers alone. They had been together for so long that she would not countenance the possibility of another person coming between them. Similarly, Randall had experienced an acute sense of betrayal on the two occasions that he had slept with the woman from Quebec in her messy bedroom, surrounded by half-finished canvases, the smell of paint and spirits making his head spin. Even as he moved with her, her face buried against his chest, he had found himself seeking a hint of the girl's familiar bloody, perfumed aroma, and when he closed his eyes and tried to lose himself in the act it was her face that he saw.

He sat up in bed. The clock read 4:13 a.m..

'Where have you been?' he said, but she did not, could not, answer. She simply remained where she was, lodged in the corner, her hands clasped in her lap.

'You want me to read to you?'

She shook her head.

'I've got a real busy day tomorrow,' he told her. 'I'll need a clear head. I've got to get some rest, and you know I can't sleep with you watching me.'

The girl stood and walked to the bed. Her lips moved, and the ruin of her tongue flicked like a snake head in the pit of her mouth. She was talking to him, but he couldn't follow the shapes that her mouth formed. He thought that there was a kind of tenderness to the way she was staring at him. She had never looked at him that way before, and he saw her pity for him. She

325

reached out and laid her hand on his cheek. He shivered at her touch.

'What is it?' he said. 'What do you want?'

And then she smiled, and it stilled his heart. In all their years together, she had never smiled at him. The fear of her that was always with him, but that he tried to hide from himself and from her, welled up. Her touch was so cold that it burned his skin, spreading from his face like poison seeping through his veins until every inch of him felt as though it were being consumed by a cold fire.

She took her hand away, and walked from the room. He tried to follow her, but his limbs would not respond. He sank back on the pillow, and sleep took him instantly. When he woke the next morning, his left cheek was sore and red, and the girl was gone from his house forever.

24

The third anonymous text was waiting for me when I turned on my cell phone first thing that morning. It read:

CHIEF ALLAN THE PEDOFILE IS
GETTING ANXIOUS.
HE MISSES HIS COOZE.

I stared at the message. It didn't take long to pinpoint what it was about it, apart from its contents, that bothered me. It was the spelling. 'Pedophile' was still misspelled, just as the word 'preys' had previously been misused. This time, it was the word 'anxious' that stood out, but only because it was spelled correctly. Perhaps I was trying to see a pattern where there wasn't one, but it struck me that 'anxious' was a difficult word to spell. Someone who genuinely had difficulty with the word 'pedophile,' and who couldn't make the distinction between 'prays' and 'preys,' would quite possibly misspell 'anxious' as well, or simply avoid using the word entirely. It raised the possibility that a smart individual was playing dumb in order to cast aspersions on Kurt Allan's reputation, but to what end?

As it happened, Allan himself was standing near Aimee's office building, drinking coffee and smoking a roll-up behind a tree, when I pulled into the lot before noon. His uniform shirt was sharply ironed, and his shoes were freshly shined, which made the sight of the roll-up more incongruous. I acknowledged him with a nod as I approached the door, but wasn't going to speak to him until he raised a hand and asked if I had a minute.

'Your mysterious client isn't here yet,' he said. 'In fact, you and I are the first to arrive, Ms. Price excepted.'

He opened his tobacco pack and offered me one of the premade roll-ups inside.

'You smoke?'

'No.'

'You ever smoke?'

'Couple as a teenager. I never saw the point. I preferred to spend my money on beer, when I could get it.'

'I wish I'd been that smart,' he said. 'I've tried quitting, but there's nothing like that first one in the morning with a cup of coffee, except maybe the second.'

Despite his lean, muscular build, there was no glow of good health about Allan. He had a shaving rash on his neck, and bags under his eyes. Seen up close, his mustache was ragged and poorly trimmed. A missing-child case will wear a man down, I thought, but a guilty conscience would have a similar effect. Fairly or unfairly, I knew that I was now seeing Allan's character refracted through the prism of the anonymous messages, but I had already taken steps to investigate the substance of the secret allegations being made against him.

'Was there something in particular you wanted to discuss, Chief?' I said. 'I'd like some time to consult with Ms. Price before our client arrives.'

'Sure, I understand. I just wanted to apologize for the way you were treated at the station. I think we started off on the wrong foot, and it just got worse from there on. We could have — *I* could have — been more civil. I hope you realize that we all just want to find Anna Kore.'

He sounded sincere. He looked sincere. Maybe he even was sincere, although one thing didn't necessarily follow from the other.

'I've been treated worse,' I said.

'Pat Shaye told me that you had some trouble with your car. He said that he helped you out. I was glad to hear it.'

Allan seemed anxious to ingratiate himself with me. I couldn't understand why. Then it came.

'You seen the newspapers this morning?'

I had. There had been some criticism in the Portland and Bangor papers of the handling of the investigation so far, with particular emphasis on the response of the Pastor's Bay Police Department when it had first been alerted to Anna's disappearance, as well as a perception that the authorities were not briefing reporters sufficiently on what progress, if any, was being made. It was mainly reporters blowing off steam, inspired in part by the closed nature of the community in Pastor's Bay, but Allan's response to the criticisms as reported in the articles made him sound defensive, and by pointing out that the Criminal Investigation Division was in

329

charge of the investigation he seemed to be trying to pass responsibility for any earlier failings on to someone else. It wasn't Allan's fault that Anna Kore was still missing, but people don't like it when young girls are abducted, and it was only natural that the blame game would start to be played. Allan needed a break, and he was hoping that Aimee and I might be able to provide it.

'It's frustration,' I said. 'Everybody wants a happy ending, but they're sensing that it's not going to come in this case. Don't take it personally.'

'But it is personal,' said Allan. 'I know Anna Kore. I know her mother.'

'You know them well?' I asked. I was careful to make the inquiry sound as casual as possible, but Allan still seemed to detect an undertone that he didn't like. I could see his testing of the question reflected on his face. He considered it the way a man might hold a piece of food in his mouth before swallowing, uncertain if it tasted right.

'It's a small town,' he said. 'Part of my job is to know its people.'

I dropped the subject of how well he might have known the Kore family. There was no percentage in pursuing it further for now.

'It'll hit the town hard if the girl isn't found,' I said.

'Worse than if she turns up dead?'

'Maybe.'

'You serious?'

'If her body is found there can be a burial, a process of mourning, and there will be a chance of finding the person responsible, because with a body comes evidence. If she stays missing her fate will haunt the town, and her mother will never have a peaceful night's sleep again.'

'You're talking about closure?'

'No. It doesn't exist.'

For a moment, I thought that he was about to disagree, but I watched him reconsider, although there was no way to tell if he did so because of his own experience of loss and pain or out of his knowledge of mine.

'I get it,' he said. 'It's better to know than not to know?'

'I'd want to know.'

Allan said only 'Yeah,' and then was quiet for a time.

'How long have you been chief of police?' I asked.

'Chief?' He picked a speck of tobacco from his lip and stared at it as though it had a deeper meaning in the context of his existence. 'You had it right the first time we met. I share space with the town's garbage truck and what we like to think of as our fire department. If there was a fire, I'd rather take my chances with spit and a blanket.'

He dropped what was left of his cigarette into the bottom of his coffee cup, where it hissed like a snake giving warning.

'I've been 'chief' for five years. My wife — my ex-wife — was looking to move out of Boston. She had asthma, and the doctors told her that the city air wasn't good for her. She'd grown up by the Maryland shore, and I was raised in the

Michigan boonies, so we kind of drew a line north from one place, and east from the other, and this is where they intersected. That's what we tell people anyway: The truth isn't as romantic. We weren't getting along in Boston, I saw the job in Pastor's Bay advertised, and took it in the hope that putting the city behind us might help. It didn't. Now it fills the hours, and pays my alimony.'

'How long have you been divorced?'

'Just over a year, but we were apart for almost another year before that.'

I waited to see if he'd add anything, but he didn't.

'Kids?'

'No, no kids.'

'I guess that makes it easier.'

'Some.'

A black SUV paused across from the entrance to the lot, waiting for a break in the traffic. Engel was sitting in the passenger seat, with a female agent driving. Almost simultaneously, Gordon Walsh arrived with his partner, Soames.

'Looks like the gang's all here,' said Allan. 'We're just waiting for the special guest.'

I excused myself and went in to confirm that Aimee was ready. An Olympus digital recorder was set up in the conference room, connected to a pair of external mikes. Aimee had agreed that the interview could be recorded, as long as it was made clear at the start that her client had voluntarily agreed to cooperate. She had also let it be known that she would stop the interview if she believed that her client was being badgered, or if any attempt was being made to link him, directly or indirectly, with Anna Kore's disappearance. This was an interview, not an interrogation. Aimee was wearing a black pant suit over a plain white blouse. Her dress was serious, her face was serious, and her mood was serious. At times like these, I was reminded of how good a lawyer she really was.

I closed the door behind me to ensure that we weren't overheard.

'I received another text from Chief Allan's admirer,' I said.

'Interesting timing. Can I see it?'

I handed her my cell phone.

' "Cooze," ' she said. 'I hate that word. Any thoughts on how this fits in?'

'Randall Haight is taunted about Selina Day, and now someone is bad-mouthing Kurt Allan. Makes you wonder how many potential blackmailers there might be in one small town.'

'You think it's the same person?'

'Possibly.'

'And if they were right about Randall — '

' — then there might also be some truth in what's being said about Allan.'

'We can't just sit him down and ask him if he's a pedophile,' said Aimee. 'It wouldn't be polite. We could let Walsh know, or Engel.'

'We could, but what would be the fun in that?'

'You have a strange idea of fun. Since the first option isn't a runner, and you don't seem keen on the second, what's left?'

'You don't want to know,' I said.

'Really?' She searched my face. 'Okay, you're

right: I don't. I really, really don't.'

The receptionist called through to let us know that Engel and company were in the lobby. We left the conference room, Aimee to greet the main players and show them through, and I to wait outside for Randall Haight. While I was there, I sent an e-mail from my phone. There was no message, and it went to a temporary Yahoo address.

Ten minutes later, Angel and Louis were breaking into Chief Allan's home, and LoJacking his truck.

* * *

Randall Haight arrived dressed just as one might have expected a small town accountant attending an unpleasant appointment to dress. He wore a blue suit undecided as to whether it was navy or not, and that even Men's Wearhouse might have frowned upon as too conservatively cut; a white shirt that overhung his belt, as though he were slowly deflating; and a blue-and-gray striped tie with a meaningless crest just below the knot. He was perspiring, and clearly unhappy. As he lingered by his car, the driver's door still open beside him, he seemed inclined to leap back in and make a break for the Canadian border. I could understand his reluctance to continue, and not simply because he was about to expose something hidden and shameful about himself to the hostile gaze of other men. Haight's prior experience with the law had been so traumatic, and had altered his life so radically, that here, in this leaf-strewn parking lot, he must have been reliving those earlier encounters. He was once again the boy in trouble, the child with blood on his hands.

I walked over to him.

'How are you holding up, Randall?'

'Not so good. I can't stop my hands from shaking, and I have a pain in the pit of my stomach. I shouldn't have come. I should never have agreed to this.' His anxiety dipped into anger, and his voice rose. 'I came to Ms. Price because I needed help. You and she were supposed to help me, and now I'm in worse trouble than before. I mean, you were supposed to be on my side!'

The trembling in his hands spread to the rest of his body. He was like an upright spring, vibrating with fear and anger. Above his head, a raven settled on a branch. It opened its beak and emitted a single mocking caw, as though chiding the man below for his weakness.

It would do Haight no good to enter that interview room in his current state. I didn't know how he might react if they began to question him harshly, as I had no doubt they would, despite Aimee's injunctions against doing so. She would try to stop the interview if they went too far, and she might even succeed, but the inevitable result would be that they would leave wondering if Randall Haight had anything else to hide. We should have coached him, and Aimee had acknowledged as much when she told me that he had at last agreed to talk with the police, but Haight had clammed up immediately after, and declined to consult further with her. Aimee had expressed her concern that, despite his promises, he might not show up for the interview at all. It was an achievement that he had made it this far. Now he just had to be calmed down a little.

'Let's take a walk,' I said. 'We'll get some air.'

He thrust his hands deep into his pockets and together we walked along Park Street.

'You should remember something, Randall. You haven't done anything wrong here. In fact, you're a victim in this. Someone is tormenting you about your past, but whatever you may have done as a child, you've paid the price for it. You made the amends that the law required of you, and you've tried to be the best man that you can be since then. That's all any of us can do. Aimee and I are not going to let you be railroaded in there, but you can help yourself by looking upon the interview as a way of gaining an advantage. Once you tell the police what's been happening to you, it will be in their interests as much as yours to find whoever is responsible, because they'll make some of the connections that I did. They'll wonder if the individual who is bothering you is also involved in the disappearance of Anna Kore. They'll take those envelopes, and those photos, and that disc, and they'll analyze them in a detail that's beyond my capacities. In the meantime, Aimee and I are still going to be working for you, because just as there are steps the police can take that I can't, so too there are things I can do that they, for various reasons, cannot. All you have to do is go in there and tell the truth.'

Haight kicked at a fallen acorn, and missed. He sighed, as if that somehow represented the story of his life.

'It'll get out, though, won't it? It's not a secret as soon as more than one person knows it.' He sounded like a little boy.

'It may get out, eventually. When that happens, we'll help you with it. It won't be easy in the immediate aftermath, but I think you may be surprised at how many friends you have in Pastor's Bay. Do you go to church?'

'Not regularly. Baptist when I do.'

'If your past does start to come out, then that's the place where you can own up to it publicly. I don't mean this in a cynical way — well, not entirely — but nothing makes a congregation happier than a sinner who acknowledges his failings and asks for forgiveness. You'll have to rebuild your reputation, and your place in the community may change, but you'll still have a place. In the meantime, we'll have people looking out for you, just in case.'

A school bus went by, loaded down with little kids on an outing. Two of them waved to us. I waved back, and the whole bus joined in. As they disappeared toward the highway, Haight said, 'I still don't have an alibi for the time of Anna Kore's disappearance.'

'Randall, half of Pastor's Bay doesn't have an alibi for the time of her disappearance. You've been watching too many old reruns of *Columbo*. I'm not going to lie to you: Once you've told the police about yourself, they're inevitably going to take a closer look at you. We'll make sure they're discreet about it, but their interest won't necessarily be a negative development, because somewhere in your recent past is a moment of intersection between you and the person who has been sending these messages. That person's position of power over you is about to come under serious threat. I'd say that, within twenty-four hours, he or she is going to start panicking.'

'Does that mean they might throw everything out there and expose me?'

'The opposite, I think. They'll retreat for a time, and perhaps try to cover their tracks, but in doing so they'll draw more attention to themselves.'

'You sound pretty certain of that.'

I sounded more certain than I actually was about most of what I had told Haight, but my sole purpose that morning was to ensure that he presented himself in the most positive light to the law-enforcement personnel in the meeting room. But about the psychology of Haight's stalker — and he *was* being stalked, in a most insidious way — I believed that I was right. Part of the pleasure in tormenting an individual in the way that Haight was being goaded lies in isolating him, particularly when there is the potential for blackmail. Stalkers like watching their victims squirm. Even Internet stalkers, who may be geographically separated from their victims, get pleasure from the reaction they provoke, the anger, the desperation and, ultimately, the pleading.

And that was when it struck me, and its impact was so forceful that I stopped in my tracks. I had been so distracted by other details — Anna Kore, the messages about Chief Allan, the connection to Tommy Morris down in Boston — that I had failed to make one very simple leap: Where did the pleasure in tormenting Randall Haight lie? He did most of his work from home, and made trips to clients only when necessary. He had almost no social life that I could discern, but what public interaction he did have revolved entirely around Pastor's Bay.

I was suddenly certain that whoever was taunting Randall Haight lived or worked in Pastor's Bay.

'What is it?' said Randall.

'Nothing,' I said. 'Just a thought. We should be getting back now.'

He nodded, resigned, but he was less troubled than he had been, and I thought that we might just get through this and come out ahead. He didn't stop to gather himself one final time as we entered the building, but held himself upright and walked, calmly and confidently, toward the meeting room, there to face his past, and alter his future.

25

Dempsey drove through the environs of Pastor's Bay. He had a map on the passenger seat of the car, but he rarely consulted it. He had already examined the area on Google and felt sure of where he was going. Dempsey had a prodigious memory for photographs, figures, and the minutest detail of conversations. He rarely let it show, though, for he had spent too long surrounded by men who might find such a talent troubling enough to seek its annihilation.

He and Ryan had woken that morning to find Tommy gone from his room, and the car absent from the lot. Dempsey had scribbled a note informing Tommy that they had left to seek out breakfast, and slipped it under his door. The massive lipidic woman was gone from reception, replaced by a sinewy string bean of a man with dazzlingly bright false teeth who informed them of the presence of a diner about a quarter of a mile west of the motel. Some of the clouds had cleared to leave swatches of blue sky, but it still felt unseasonably cold and there was a wind that blew straight into their faces as they walked. They took a corner booth in the diner, and Ryan ordered the biggest breakfast on the menu, while Dempsey stuck with coffee and a bagel. He'd never been much for eating first thing in the morning, and his stomach didn't feel right. He read the house newspaper while Ryan ate, but it was out of Bangor and contained nothing of relevance to them. The papers were full of the midterm elections; Dempsey had almost forgotten that they were happening, so lost was he in their own difficulties. He couldn't recall the last time he'd voted. He felt guilty about it. It seemed to him another aspect of his abandonment of control, of being subject to the plans and motivations of others. He made a promise to himself to start voting again if he lived. It seemed a modest, attainable ambition in the long term. Voting, that was, not living. For now, staying alive was strictly a day-to-day business.

Ryan excused himself and headed to the men's room. A police patrol car cruised by, but Dempsey didn't turn his head to follow its progress. He took in the other customers in the diner. They were mostly older people, and the waitress seemed to know them all by name. Dempsey reckoned that Ryan was the youngest person in the place by at least a decade or more. He closed his eyes and thought about how good it would be just to sit here for a couple of hours surrounded by friends, with no obligations for the day other than to shoot the breeze and plan for the next meal. He didn't have to imagine what it would be like to be old. He already felt old, and mortality seemed closer to him than it might have to even the most elderly of the diner's aging patrons.

When he opened his eyes again, Tommy Morris was standing before him.

'You done?' said Tommy.

'Pretty much. You want something?'

'No, I'm good.'

Dempsey called for the check as Ryan appeared from the men's room, and the waitress had it on the table before Ryan had crossed the room.

'What do I owe?' said Ryan.

'I got you covered,' said Dempsey. He took cash from his pocket and started counting bills. He was running seriously low.

'Nah,' said Ryan. 'I got this one.'

'You sure?'

'Yeah. Makes us even for last night.'

Tommy looked at him curiously.

'We went out for a drink,' said Ryan. He looked embarrassed. Dempsey thought he was probably wondering if they should have asked Tommy to join them while simultaneously being grateful that they hadn't, given the tone of some of the previous night's conversation.

'Good for you,' said Tommy. His head was bobbing slightly, and he was running his right thumb along the pads of his fingers, over and over. Dempsey thought of it as one of Tommy's tells, the signs that he had a job in mind, that he was ready to roll. There was a light in his eyes that hadn't been there for a while.

The car was parked behind the diner. Tommy had led them to it, spinning the keys around his right index finger, whistling to himself.

'You get that call you were expecting?' said Dempsey.

'No, not yet,' said Tommy. 'It'll come, though. We got work to do until then.'

'What kind of work?' said Dempsey.

342

'We have to boost a car,' said Tommy.

Which was how Dempsey came to be driving a tan Impala out of Pastor's Bay and toward the sea. He passed Valerie Kore's house but didn't even glance in its direction. There was a black Chevy Suburban in the drive alongside an ancient green Toyota Tacoma, and a Sheriff's Department cruiser was parked on the road. In the rearview, he saw the deputy turn to his in-car laptop. The cops probably ran the plate of every car that passed as a matter of routine. Dempsey wasn't concerned. This one wouldn't even be on the system for another hour or more.

He turned south where the road met the ocean, and followed the coast for a time. There was no beach to be seen, just black rocks like broken, rotted teeth against which gray waves broke. Dempsey could not understand why someone would choose to live in a coastal town with no sand upon which to walk, and no beauty upon which to gaze. Here nature was a hostile force at war with itself. The wind twisted the growth of trees, and the sea ate away at the land. As he drove, Dempsey found himself wishing for the security of the city. In this place, he felt exposed in body and soul.

The turnoff was little more than a dirt track. He put the sea behind him and followed the trail through a patch of woodland that brought the car to within sight of the Kore house. He hit the trunk release, and by the time he'd killed the engine and got out Tommy was stretching his back by the side of the road.

'Comfortable?' asked Dempsey. They had

figured that one man alone in a car would attract less attention than two.

'I'll live.'

Dempsey had Tommy's piece in his hand. He offered it to him, and after a moment's pause Tommy accepted it. Together they watched the back of the house from the woods but could see no sign of a further police presence. Still, Tommy had figured that there would be at least one cop inside with her.

'You sure you want to do this?' said Dempsey.

'I have to talk to her,' said Tommy, and Dempsey again saw in him the peculiar combination of fatalism and hope that afflicted those who knew their time was drawing to a close and wanted to settle their affairs before it was too late. His niece's disappearance, appalling though it was, had given Tommy an excuse to reach out to his estranged sister, to do this one last thing for her.

'Then let's go talk,' said Dempsey.

He was about to move when Tommy's hand gripped his elbow. Immediately Dempsey looked around to see who was approaching, but there was no sign of movement.

'What is it?'

Tommy seemed to be struggling to speak. His eyes were fixed on Dempsey's face. Eventually he said, 'Thank you.'

'For what?'

'For standing by me.'

'We'll figure out a way, Tommy. We'll make it right.'

'No,' said Tommy. 'No, we won't. When the

344

time comes, you try to stay alive. You take Francis, and whatever money is left, and you hide yourselves away. Maybe they'll be content with my head. If they give me a chance, I'll tell them that you're no threat to them. No revenge, Martin. Understand?'

Dempsey nodded. 'I understand, Tommy.'

The grip on his arm tightened once, and then was released.

'We'll talk no more about it,' said Tommy.

Using the trees as cover, and sprinting across the patches of open ground, they came to the backyard. As they drew nearer the house, Dempsey saw a woman pass by the kitchen window. Her reddish-brown hair was pulled back severely from her face and tied tightly with a scrunchie. She was filling a coffeepot with water.

Leaving Tommy against the north wall, Dempsey checked out as much of the single-story dwelling as he could without exposing himself to the deputy on the road. There were three bedrooms: one with a queen bed and woman's clothing scattered on the chairs and floor; the second a smaller room with a double bed and walls decorated with posters of bands whose names and faces were largely unfamiliar to Dempsey; and a third room with a single bed surrounded by assorted boxes and cases. Beside it was a small window of frosted glass: the bathroom.

On the other side, a door from the kitchen led into a big living room that ran most of the width of the house. A man in a golf shirt and chinos sat at a cheap desk reading a paperback novel.

Dempsey looked around for monitoring or recording equipment but didn't see any. Dempsey waited, and a second man appeared. He wore black pants, and a long-sleeved blue shirt. Both men wore Glock 22s at their waists.

Not cops: FBI.

Eventually, Valerie Kore entered the room and handed each man a cup of coffee. They thanked her, and she left. He saw her step into the hallway. She didn't come back.

Dempsey returned to Tommy.

'Two feds watching the phone in the living room.'

'Feds? You sure?'

'They're wearing Glocks. Standard issue for federal agents.'

'Fuck.'

'You want to back off?'

'We've come this far.'

Tommy tried the kitchen door. It opened silently, and he and Dempsey moved into the house. Dempsey counted down from three with his fingers, and they burst into the living room. One of the agents was so shocked that he spilled his coffee on himself and swore, but he and his colleague raised their hands without even being told.

'Tommy Morris,' said the one in the golf shirt. 'You gotta be kidding me.'

Tommy told them to shut up and get down on the floor. He kept them covered while Dempsey pulled their hands behind their backs and cuffed them with plastic ties he'd picked up at Home Depot. They heard the sound of a toilet flushing.

346

Tommy took the door, and when his sister entered the room he put his hand over her mouth. At the sight of the agents on the floor she began to struggle, but Tommy pressed the barrel of his weapon against her cheek and she grew still. Slowly, he turned her around. She recognized him, and tried to pull away.

'Valerie, I just want to talk,' he said, his hand still covering her mouth. 'I can help you find Anna.'

And, instantly, the fight left her body.

'I'm going to take my hand away, okay?'

She nodded, and Dempsey got a good look at her for the first time. She had naturally pale features sprinkled with a dusting of freckles, and large brown eyes. He'd heard that she used to be a looker, especially with a little makeup, but now her eyes were sunk deep into her skull with gray-black bags beneath them, and spots had broken out on her skin. She had probably been prescribed sedatives and sleeping pills, but his guess was that she wasn't taking them. She'd hate lying awake at night, but would fear sleep more. Awake she might still be of some use to her daughter, while to embrace temporary oblivion was to be selfish. What if those who had her daughter called? What if she was sleeping, and somehow the chance to get Anna back safely was missed?

'Why did you come here?' she said. 'I have enough troubles.'

'I told you, I want to help. Come on, let's go to another room where we can talk in private.'

She led him to one of the bedrooms, and soon

Dempsey could hear the low murmur of their voices. He drifted toward the window, where he could keep an eye on the front of the house. The deputy hadn't moved from his cruiser, and no more cars passed.

One of the agents spoke to Dempsey.

'You made me burn my balls,' he said.

'That's sad. Maybe they'll swell up to the size of a regular set.'

The agent sighed into the carpet.

'I don't know who's crazier,' he said, 'you or Morris.'

'Me,' said Dempsey. 'Definitely me.'

* * *

Valerie sat on her daughter's bed. Tommy leaned against the wall, taking in the pictures on the walls and the photographs of the niece he hadn't seen in so very long.

'How did you find me?' said Valerie. 'You see me on the TV?'

'I knew before that,' Tommy replied. 'I've known where you were for a long time.'

'The FBI said this might be something to do with you. Is that true?'

'No.'

'How can you be sure?'

'Because I asked.'

Even after so many years, she remembered that tone.

'Did you ask Joey Toomey?' she said.

'We talked.'

'The FBI thinks you killed him.'

348

'I thought just what you did: that Anna's disappearance might have been a way to get at me. I had to be sure that it wasn't.'

'Did killing him make you certain?'

'No. Killing him just made me feel better.'

There was disgust on her face, but it was mingled with another response. Perhaps, Tommy thought, she still has some of the old blood in her.

'They say you're in trouble.'

'Who says?'

'The FBI. They say that Oweny Farrell has put a price on your head.'

'Oweny Farrell couldn't afford to pay for one hair,' he said, and the bravado sounded hollow even to him.

'Why did you hide from me?' he asked. 'Why did you run from your own family?'

She looked at him with bewilderment.

'Are you crazy? Are you out of your fucking mind?'

'Don't talk to me that way.'

'What way should I talk to the man who killed the father of my little girl?'

'I didn't know,' said Tommy. 'I swear I didn't know.'

'You didn't know what? That he was her father, or that he was to be killed? What didn't you know? Tell me. Which was it?'

He didn't answer.

'You didn't *know*.' She spat the last word. 'I don't believe you. I didn't believe you then, and I still don't.'

Tommy was forced to turn away from the fury in her eyes.

'You should have come back,' he said. 'If you'd come back and let me look after you, then maybe this — '

She raised an index finger to him, the nail ragged and bitten.

'Don't say it. Don't you dare say that. I swear, I'll blind you with these nails if you try to play that game with me.'

Tommy stayed silent.

'I'm sorry,' he said at last. 'You're right. That was wrong.'

She didn't reply.

'You and Anna are all the family I have left. I — '

She interrupted him. He didn't like it. She'd been away from men for too long, he thought. She'd forgotten her manners.

'We're not your family, Tommy. That ended when you put Ronnie in the ground. Anna has no memory of her early life, thank God, and I haven't told her anything to change that. As far as she's concerned she has no uncles, no cousins, nothing. She just accepts that's the way things are for her.'

Tommy let it go.

'None of this will bring her back,' he said.

Suddenly Valerie started to cry. It surprised her almost as much as it disturbed Tommy. She didn't think that she had any tears left.

He came to her, and stroked her hair, and she allowed him to press her face to his belly.

'Tell me,' he said. 'Tell me everything that you told them.'

Dempsey was still waiting by the window when Tommy returned.

'Finished?' Dempsey said.

'Finished.'

Tommy squatted in front of the agents. From his pocket he took a roll of duct tape.

'Sorry about this, boys,' he said. 'No hard feelings.'

'Come in, Tommy,' said the one in the golf shirt. 'Come in and talk to us. We're your best chance now.'

'I hope that's not true,' said Tommy. 'If it is, I'm in worse trouble than I thought.'

He wrapped the tape around their mouths and their legs. He had similarly restrained his sister, although he had left her mouth free, and her nail scissors were within reach. She had promised to give them as much time as she could before freeing herself and the agents.

'Did you learn anything?' asked Dempsey, as they returned.

'It was enough to see her, and for her to know that I'm on her side. I want to do this for her. I want to find my niece. I have to try to make things right, Martin, before the end.'

Dempsey said nothing, because there was nothing to say.

They called Ryan from the road, and dumped the car at a strip mall. They'd boosted it from outside the Colonial movie theater in Belfast after watching the couple pay for a matinee show and give their tickets to the usher. Their movie would probably have finished by now, and they'd have noticed that their car was missing. Ryan picked them up, and they returned to the motel. Tommy was more upbeat than he'd been in a while. Dempsey saw some of his old dynamism returning, and believed Tommy might have been reinvigorated by the meeting with his sister.

He was only partly right. Tommy Morris's mood had been improved by seeing Valerie after all this time, but he was also anticipating the possibility of a more direct contribution to the search for his niece.

Tommy Morris was about to be given a name.

26

Randall Haight and I stood at the door to the meeting room. From inside we could hear the sound of men's voices, and I thought I recognized Gordon Walsh's dulcet tones.

'Are you ready for this, Randall?' I asked.

'Yes, thank you.'

I opened the door with my left hand, and patted Haight on the shoulder with my right, although it was as much a means of giving him an extra push over the threshold if required as it was a gesture of reassurance.

Chief Allan gave a muffled grunt as Haight entered the meeting room, but it was the only sound that anyone made. Haight took a seat beside Aimee on one side of the table, facing Allan, Gordon Walsh, and Soames. Engel and his fellow agent had taken two seats by the window, slightly apart from the main group. I sat against the wall and listened.

Walsh made the introductions for his side, and slid a recording device closer to Haight, who gave his name for the record. There were notebooks open and ready. Once Haight had settled into his chair, Aimee asked him to tell everyone, in his own words and in his own time, why he was there.

He began haltingly, but as he went on he grew a little more confident, and stumbled less. He kept his hands clasped in front of him,

353

untangling his fingers only to take an occasional sip of water. His story began with the circumstances surrounding the death of Selina Day, his sentencing and imprisonment, and his eventual move to Pastor's Bay. There was nothing in it that I hadn't already heard, and he was interrupted only twice, once by Walsh and once by Allan, to clear up minor points. He then described receiving the succession of missives that had led him to this room. When he had finished, Aimee produced a number of sealed plastic bags, each containing an envelope and its contents, and handed them over to Walsh.

Only Engel appeared disengaged from what we had heard. I could see him zoning out shortly after Haight started speaking. This was of no use to Engel. His interest didn't lie in an old killing far from the Northeast. It didn't even lie in the safe return of Anna Kore. Engel wanted Tommy Morris, and Randall Haight's disclosures would bring that consummation no closer.

Walsh asked if he and his colleagues could be excused in order to consult for a time, but Aimee offered instead to take Haight and me into her office until they were ready to resume. Haight went to the restroom, and while he was gone Aimee raised an eyebrow at me and said, 'Well?'

'He was as good as could be expected, and they let him talk. The next part will be more difficult for him.'

'I know.'

Despite all her warnings, Aimee knew that we would have to expose Haight to a certain amount of aggressive questioning. It was like cleansing a

354

wound: It was better to get it done all at once than in small painful increments.

Haight returned.

'How did I do?' he asked.

'You did fine, Randall,' said Aimee. 'We both thought so.'

He was relieved, and not only because we felt that the first part of the interview had gone well. He had something of the spiritual lightness of a penitent who has recently unburdened himself of his sins and been absolved. He had told his story and no one had reacted with obvious disgust or anger. He was not cuffed, and he had not been pilloried. He had confronted that which he most feared, and he had survived thus far.

'The FBI man, Mr. Engel, was in the restroom when I went in,' said Haight.

'Did he speak to you?' I asked.

'No, he just nodded. I couldn't help noticing that he didn't seem very interested in what I was saying.' Haight sounded mildly offended.

'Maybe you weren't what he was expecting,' said Aimee.

'But what was he expecting?' asked Haight, and I raised my hand gently at Aimee in warning. This was not an area that we needed to explore with the client; not yet, not until the next stage of the interview process had been concluded, but Haight wasn't a fool. He sensed that there was a disparity between what we knew and what he was being told.

We were saved by a knock on the door. Aimee's assistant stuck his head in to say that they were ready for us.

'We'll talk about it later,' I told Haight. 'I promise that it doesn't involve you, and it won't affect anything that's said in the next room, or any question that is put to you. When we're done, we'll take time to go over any other relevant details, okay?'

Haight had little choice but to agree. He had come this far, and although he could have sat in Aimee's office and refused to come out until we'd told him everything, including the truth about UFOs and who had killed Kennedy, he didn't, largely because Aimee and I kept him moving, and by the time we were back in the meeting room it was too late for him to do anything but sit back down in his chair and wait for the questions to come.

Walsh handled the next stage. He was careful, and consistent, and studiedly neutral at the start. He went back over Haight's story, asking many of the same questions that Aimee and I had asked of him. He clarified Haight's movements in the years since his release and touched on the subject of Lonny Midas.

'You have no knowledge of Lonny Midas's current whereabouts?' said Walsh.

'He's not called that anymore,' said Haight. 'Lonny Midas doesn't exist, just like William Lagenheimer doesn't exist. They gave both of us new identities so that we couldn't contact each other even if we wanted to.'

'So you have no reason to think that Lonny Midas might have found you?'

'None.'

'Were you frightened of him, Mr. Haight?'

'A little.'

'Are you still frightened of him now?'

Haight began tugging at a loose piece of fingernail. I could see him doing it from where I sat. He pulled so hard that I saw him wince at the pain he was inflicting on himself.

'William Lagenheimer was,' said Haight, 'but Randall Haight isn't. Do you understand the distinction, Detective? That's why I didn't want to come here today. I wanted to stay hidden. Nobody could find me as long as I stayed hidden.'

'But someone *has* found you, Mr. Haight. Someone knows who you are. The damage has been done now.'

'Yes. Yes, I suppose you're right.'

'Do you have any idea who this person might be?'

'No.'

'Could it be Lonny Midas?'

Haight just shook his head, but his reply didn't match the movement. 'Lonny always bore grudges,' he said. 'Lonny never forgave anyone who did him a bad turn.'

'And he bears a grudge against William Lagenheimer, because William told the cops what was done to Selina Day?'

'I think Lonny probably hates William. He probably hates him more now than he did on the day that he told. Lonny was a brooder.'

'Could Lonny have taken Anna Kore to frame you?'

'Yes,' said Haight softly. 'That's the kind of thing Lonny would do.'

Walsh let the subject go. He moved on to

357

routine questions, most little more than clarifications. Haight answered them easily, and I felt him start to relax again. He grew more loquacious in his replies, giving Walsh more than was necessary to answer the questions. Walsh even cracked a small joke, something about accountancy training and jailhouse lawyers, and Haight smiled in return. Everybody was getting along just dandily. I caught Aimee's eye and shook my head, and she interrupted Walsh's next question.

'I'm sorry, Detective, I just need a quick moment with my client.'

Walsh wasn't happy about it, but he couldn't object. Instead he contented himself with giving me the hard stare. I knew what he'd been doing and now he'd been caught. This was a version of 'good cop-bad cop' with Walsh about to slip from the first role into the second.

Aimee murmured in Haight's ear. As she spoke to him, he glanced at Walsh, and his face assumed an expression of hurt. When the interview resumed, he was noticeably more restrained in his mode of answering.

'Tell me about Anna Kore,' said Walsh. 'Did you know her?'

'No, I didn't.'

'But you'd seen her around town? After all, Pastor's Bay is a small place. Everybody knows everybody, right?'

'I guess I'd seen her around.'

'Did you know her by name?'

'No, I'd never spoken to her.'

'That wasn't what I asked. Did you know her by name?'

'Well, sure. As you said, Pastor's Bay is a small town.'

'So you did know her?'

Haight was flustered. 'Yes. Well, no, not in the way you mean.'

'What way do I mean?'

Aimee intervened.

'Detective, let me remind you that this is not an interrogation. Mr. Haight is here of his own free will. He has provided information that may prove to be of assistance in your investigation, and he is himself the victim of a particularly insidious form of intimidation. Let's not add to it, okay.'

Walsh raised his hands in mock surrender and resumed his questioning.

'Had you met Anna Kore's mother?' he asked.

'Yes. She came to a couple of meetings of the town council earlier this year. She wanted to talk about trees.'

'Trees?'

'The trees growing on Bay Road. There was a storm, and some pretty big branches came down. She was concerned about the safety of her daughter and her property.'

'That sounds like a pretty minor matter.'

'Not if you're hit by a falling tree,' said Haight, not unreasonably.

'What I mean is that I'm surprised you remember it so clearly,' said Walsh. 'There must be a lot of business discussed at these meetings and yet you have no trouble recalling Valerie Kore's concerns.'

But Haight was on familiar ground here. 'I'm

359

an accountant: I spend my life remembering small details. I don't attend every meeting of the town council because it isn't necessary for me to do so, but I can certainly give you chapter and verse on any issue that has relevance to the town's budget: sanitation, tree pruning, fence painting, the replacement of appliances, of vehicles. So, yes, I remember Valerie Kore's point, but I remember also that Chief Allan had spoken just before her on the subject of acquiring a used Crown Victoria to supplement his motor pool, and at the same meeting Vernon Tuttle wanted to know why his store had been cited for littering when he'd been asking for six months that a permanent trash can be placed on his stretch of Main Street.'

Chief Allan shifted in his seat. So far he had said nothing since we resumed, and he didn't look as if he was anxious to involve himself now, but by speaking about him Haight had given him little choice.

'You know, that's true, Detective,' he said. 'Mr. Haight has a hell of a memory for detail.'

Walsh let it go. He returned to Haight's knowledge of the Kore family, but didn't get much return on his buck. When Haight told him that he had no alibi for the day of Anna's disappearance, Walsh perked up some. He was about to pursue the matter further when help came from an unlikely source. Once again Allan moved in his chair, this time with obvious unease. Even Walsh noticed, and looked at him in irritation. Allan indicated that he wanted to speak to him in private and the two policemen consulted quietly for a moment. When they returned to the table Walsh informed us that he was finished with his questions, unless anyone else had something to add. Even Engel appeared surprised enough to rouse himself briefly from his torpor, but said nothing.

We all stood. Walsh gave Aimee a receipt for the sealed bags containing the envelopes, and told Haight that he might need a more detailed statement about them in the coming days. While they spoke, I followed Allan outside, where he was fumbling for one of his cigarettes.

'Can I ask what that was about?' I said.

'Randall Haight has an alibi for the day that Anna Kore disappeared,' he replied. '*I'm* his alibi. I dropped by his place around three that day to deliver some quotes for the vehicle purchase that he mentioned. He was asleep on his couch with a blanket over him, so I decided not to disturb him. I went back shortly before the call came in about Anna Kore and he was still there. He hadn't even moved. I met him on the street the next day and he had a nose like Rudolph's. He didn't take Anna. We would just have been wast ing our time in there at the end.'

'Thank you,' I said.

'You don't have to thank me. It was the truth.'

'Do you have any opinion on the rest of what he said?'

'Nope.' He lit the cigarette and drew long, holding the smoke deep inside, savoring it. 'Why? You expect me to say that he doesn't look like the type, that you never can tell? I'm just surprised he managed to keep it quiet for so long. Hard to do in this day and age. Somebody always finds out.'

'Somebody has found out.'

'You get anywhere on that?'

'No, not yet.'

'I guess Walsh will have those envelopes examined, just in case there's a connection to Anna. Between the state police and the feds we've got twenty-four-hour turnaround on any DNA, so we'll know soon enough if there's a trace. We'll also have to get those records in North Dakota unsealed.'

'Can you do that?'

'Sure. That might take a couple of days, but once the formal request for assistance is made they'll eventually have to share whatever they have with us.'

'Including Lonny Midas's new identity?'

'I guess so.'

I was curious to find out if Lonny Midas had also been targeted. If so, I might yet be proved wrong in my belief that Randall Haight's tormentor lived in or close to Pastor's Bay.

'In the meantime, we'd like to keep what he told you confidential,' I said.

'We'll do our best. We wouldn't want people getting some fool ideas into their heads about him.'

He leaned back against the wall and pressed a thumb and forefinger into the bridge of his nose.

'I need to rest up,' he said. 'I haven't had more than a couple of hours' sleep a night since Anna went missing. I'm going to take a day off tomorrow to pay my bills and recharge my batteries. I'll still be on call, but it'll be a respite.'

I left him to finish his cigarette in peace. After all, there were plenty of other people that I could bother, among them Engel, who was waiting for his ride by the front door.

'Your lack of interest in the proceedings was noted, Special Agent Engel,' I said. 'Maybe you were hoping I was going to bring in Whitey Bulger himself.'

He was clearly debating whether talking with me was better than getting wet. He seemed to decide that it was, although not by much.

'That's an interesting client you have, Mr. Parker. He's just not that interesting to me.'

'Because he wasn't going to jump for a five-K motion?'

A 'five-K motion' referred to section 5K1.1 of the sentencing guidelines, under which a prosecutor could argue for a term shorter than the advised sentence for an offense in return for 'substantial assistance cooperation' from the defendant. It was a snitch's charter, but it was a popular weapon for the prosecution during organized-crime trials, as they so often depended on statements from mobsters who had turned on their own. Engel had been hoping the surprise guest might be someone with a connection to Tommy Morris that could be exploited. He had been disappointed.

'The only person your client could rat on is himself, and he's done that,' said Engel.

'That's kind of why I was anxious to get your attention,' I said. 'If word of what he said here today leaks, he could be at risk.'

'Because angry, frightened people don't tend to look too closely at the fine print, right? Because one child killer is as good as the next? I told you, we don't have any interest in him, but you know it'll get out. The state police are going to have to investigate his story, and Allan will be drawn in. There'll be calls, paperwork. I hope you've prepared him for the worst. His name is about to become lower than dirt in Pastor's Bay.'

'It wasn't just the locals I was concerned about.'

Engel's SUV pulled up alongside us. The driver looked quizzically at Engel, who started to move. I put a hand up to stop him.

'What do you think you're doing?' he said.

'My question exactly.'

'You'll have to forgive me. I'm not psychic, so I have no idea what you're talking about. Now put your hand down or I'll have you arrested.'

'No, you won't. You've taken the opportunity presented by a young girl's disappearance to lure a dangerous man north in the hope that you can corner him and persuade him to turn federal witness. You have only a passing interest in the safety of Anna Kore, or of anyone else. All that matters to you is getting Tommy Morris in a room and cutting a deal, and you'll let him run loose until then.'

'Mr. Parker, you have no idea what you're talking about.'

He pushed my hand away. Simultaneously, his cell phone began to ring, along with the cell phone of the agent in the car. Engel answered the call as he was getting into the vehicle, and his usually impassive features flooded with surprise. All I heard were the words 'He what?' as the door closed and the SUV sped away.

I checked my phone. There was an e-mail from the Yahoo address. It consisted solely of a smiley icon. The job at Allan's house had been done. I cleared the screen just as Gordon Walsh came up beside me and tapped me hard on the shoulder. Soames lurked behind him, his mouth set in a thin, unimpressed line like that of a Sunday-school teacher faced with the town drunk.

'You and I are going to have a talk later, clear?' said Walsh.

'Clear. I'll even pay for the drinks. Just as long as you don't bring your friend along. I don't think he's a fun guy.'

Soames scowled at me. Then again, he scowled at everyone. It was less a mode of intimidation than an ongoing disability.

Before either of them could say anything else, a monster truck pulled into the lot, dwarfing every other vehicle parked nearby. A massive bass was pumping so many decibels that the ground vibrated. Since the truck was too big to fit into any of the available spaces, the driver just parked it facing the building and killed the engine.

The driver's and passenger's doors opened, and virtually identical men who appeared to have been constructed entirely from flesh-colored cinder blocks stepped from the truck and dropped awkwardly to the ground. They had dressed for maximum shock and awe: blue polyester big-man pants, dark-blue sport shirts so tight they'd have to be cut out of them later, and matching gold neck chains that could have anchored a ship. Even Soames stopped scowling for a moment as his bottom jaw dropped. Tony and Paulie Fulci in all their heavily medicated glory were indeed a sight to behold. Walsh, by contrast, seemed more amused than impressed.

'It's the Fabulous Unfurry Freak Brothers,' he said. 'What happened, the circus leave town without you?'

'Detective Walsh,' said Paulie, assuming an air of wounded dignity. 'It's very nice to make your acquaintance again.'

Tony and Paulie knew most of the senior cops in the state, either personally or by reputation. The knowledge was reciprocated, and not just in this state either.

'What about you, Tony?' said Walsh. 'You happy to see me again?'

'No,' said Tony, who lacked his brother's finely honed diplomatic skills.

Walsh turned to me. 'Let me guess: These knuckleheads are working for you.'

'Knuckleheads Inc., that's us,' I said.

'Well, keep them on their leash, and don't let them break anything — furniture, buildings, people. They're also convicted felons, so if I hear that they're carrying even a water pistol I'll put them behind bars.'

'What about a bow?' said Paulie.

'Are you trying to be funny?'

'No, we got bows. For hunting. We got licenses too.'

Tony nodded solemnly in agreement. 'We got them with us.'

'The licenses or the bows?' asked Walsh, drawn in despite himself.

'Both,' confirmed Tony. 'And arrows.'

Walsh regarded them both carefully. Where the Fulcis were concerned, it often wasn't entirely clear when they were joking. Louis had once commented that he wasn't sure if they were deadpan or brain-dead.

'Jesus,' said Walsh. 'Bows and arrows. Well, remember: The sharp end points *away* from your face. Although feel free to practice the other way if the mood takes you.'

He and Soames returned to their car. The Fulcis watched them go.

'I lied,' said Paulie. 'It wasn't nice to make his acquaintance again.'

'Same,' said Tony. 'Except without the lying.'

27

Randall Haight didn't respond well to the news that Anna Kore's uncle was a Boston mobster who was being hunted by his own people and the FBI, and who would almost certainly attempt to involve himself in the search for his missing niece. He knew that he was at risk from Tommy Morris if word got out about his past. It wouldn't matter to Morris that Haight had been questioned and effectively cleared by the police of any involvement in his niece's disappearance. He was a child killer, and Morris would instinctively assume that he knew more than he had revealed.

Briefly, Haight fired Aimee and, by extension, me. He reconsidered when he realized that, if he was in trouble now, he'd be in more trouble without us. I also introduced him to the Fulcis, which simultaneously reassured and unsettled him, in the same way the Duke of Wellington was said to have noted of his soldiers that, while he was uncertain of their possible effect on the enemy, by God, they frightened him. Then again, Wellington had also called his own men 'the scum of the earth', which the Fulcis were not. They had their own code of honor, particularly when it came to women. Insults centering on mothers did not sit well with the Fulcis. I was pretty sure that there were other aspects of behavior about which they might have set concepts of honor, but I couldn't think of any offhand.

Haight was reluctant to have the Fulcis stay at his home unless it became absolutely necessary, and it was true that the sight of their monster truck parked on his property might attract attention to him. In addition, it was unclear what the result of his discussions with the police might be. I was sure that Walsh and Allan would let us know if there was any indication that Haight's story was about to become public knowledge, and it was in their interests as much as ours to keep it quiet. The last thing they needed was misguided media speculation about a possible suspect, which would further strain their manpower. Nevertheless, I would have preferred it if Haight had acceded to our request to let the Fulcis bed down in his house, but the more we pressed him, the less willing he was to consider the possibility. The concession we reached was that the Fulcis would become his shadows if we learned that the facts of Haight's past could no longer remain hidden. Depending upon the situation, they could either plant themselves on Haight's property like the trunks of trees or they could move him to safety. I had already made arrangements for him to be quietly placed at the Colony near Sebago Lake if necessary. The Colony was a retreat house for troubled men, often those suffering from addiction or other social difficulties. The company might not be to Haight's taste, but those involved in the Colony's running would make no judgment upon him, and they were very, very discreet.

After a little more sulking, and some calming words from Aimee and me, Haight returned to Pastor's Bay. I gave him a half hour start, then followed him north.

Angel and Louis had checked into an inn called the Blithe Spirit, about four miles from Pastor's Bay. It was run by an elderly couple named the Harveys, whose first question to them was 'Are you gay?'

'Would that be a problem?' said Louis.

'Oh no,' said Mrs. Harvey, who was bent almost double by arthritis but moved surprisingly fast, like a hare with a minor disability. 'We like gay people. They're very tidy.'

Her husband nodded along enthusiastically, although his smile had apparently faltered as he tried to balance their firmly held belief in the neatness of all gay people with Angel's presence on their property. They had provided Angel and Louis with a large room on the second floor overlooking the neat garden at the rear of the house. The Harveys had only two rooms available to rent, and the other was unoccupied for now. According to Angel, the decor erred on the side of chintzy but was otherwise perfectly acceptable.

'So, tell me about Kurt Allan,' I said, as we sat in the living room of the inn, its picture window looking out on a small pond and a glade of black ash trees that had lost most of their leaves. The Harveys had provided a pot of tea, served on a silver tray alongside china cups and the kind of dainty cookies that small girls fed to dolls at parties.

'If he is a pedophile, he's hiding it well,' said

370

Angel. 'I went through his computer files, his library, even his attic. There was one skin mag, but it was standard stuff. Same with the porn websites that he's accessed. His e-mail is so dull that I almost dozed off reading it. He has a landline, but it doesn't look like he uses it much; there was dust on the phone. On most levels, he looks clean.'

He let that last statement hang.

'Meaning?'

'He makes a base salary of fifty thousand dollars. Over the last year, he's managed to supplement that through overtime, but it's only brought him up by another five grand. He's eating alimony payments of a thousand a month, although it looks like he agreed to them and didn't contest the figure.'

A thousand a month was a lot on a salary of 50K. That pretty much constituted a punitive payment.

'Any indication of why he agreed?'

'He has a file of correspondence from the divorce, but it very carefully avoids mentioning specific details. Stated grounds were 'irreconcilable marital differences'.'

''Irreconcilable marital differences' is a catchall,' I said. 'It can cover anything from bank robbery to whistling 'Dixie' during sex. They didn't want the real reason for the divorce to be made known in the filing.'

'There were a couple of references to the 'troubling nature' of Allan's behavior in the letters from his ex-wife's attorney to his attorney, but that was it.'

'Where is she now?'

'The alimony payments are made to a bank in Seattle, which is about as far away from her ex-husband as she can get without moving to Russia. There's no evidence in the house that Allan and his wife have stayed in touch.'

'So Chief Allan is living on mac and cheese in order to buy his wife's silence?'

'You'd have thought,' said Angel. 'He has twenty-three hundred dollars in his checking account, and is making minimum payments to his 401(K). But until last year he was paying a lot of bills in cash, and even on a quick run-through it's clear that his outgoings and income don't balance. The disparity isn't huge, but it's there.'

'How big is the disparity?'

'Uh, five hundred a month, sometimes more. I'd guess that, until a couple of months ago, he had money coming in on the side, enough to take the sting off his alimony, but that's now been cut off. Could be bribes, or maybe he just picked up some other work along the way: security, escorting businessmen to the bank, collecting bottles for the fifteen-cent deposit. It's not a lot of cash, but it was there, and it was regular.'

'You tag his truck?'

'Yeah, behind his rear fender. It's small, with a limited power supply. We could have run it off his battery, but that truck is a piece of shit. Any trouble under the hood and a large device would be spotted before the engine cooled. We'll get a couple of days out of it, max, then we'll have to change it.'

'He's taking time off tomorrow. If he's doing something he shouldn't be doing, then he won't be looking to the Pastor's Bay PD for his ride. It's best if I keep my distance, so you stay with him. If he does anything interesting, let me know and I can come take a look.'

We drank some more tea, and I gave them the summarized version of all that had happened at Aimee's office.

'If the cops have it in hand, seems like you're out of a job,' said Louis.

'I wasn't exactly cracking the case wide open before they got to it,' I admitted. 'But I'm curious about Lonny Midas.'

Haight had implied once again that Midas might hold a grudge against him for admitting to the police what they had done to Selina Day. I still believed that Haight was holding back on aspects of his history, including the precise extent of his role in her death. After all, he had been there right until the final act, and he could have backed out at any time. He might have been in thrall to Midas, as he claimed, but he had also confessed to a degree of sexual interest in the girl. Nevertheless, Midas had to be seen as the instigator of the assault. Again, I had only Haight's word on how troubled Midas might have been in his youth, but if he was capable of targeting a girl and dragging her into a barn then he was already manifesting an aberrant sexuality. Haight had received counseling and therapy while in custody, so it was probable that Lonny Midas had too. The unsealing of the records would provide some insight into both of them, as well as the degree to which Midas blamed his friend for confessing their crime to the police. Also, if the cops were given Midas's new identity they could begin to trace his movements and find out if he had made his way to this state.

But if Midas was involved he probably wasn't acting alone. He couldn't risk being seen by Haight, assuming he hadn't made some dramatic alteration to his appearance, so he'd need somebody close to Pastor's Bay who would be able to report back on how Haight was reacting. All of these strands connected back to a killing three decades before in a small North Dakota town.

'Have you ever been to North Dakota?' I asked Louis.

'Yep. Second-coldest state in the Union, after Alaska. You know what's the third coldest?'

'Let me guess: Maine.'

'Give that man mittens.'

'Have you been to Alaska?'

'Yep.'

'Well, go you. You're collecting the set.'

There was a soft knock on the door, and Mrs. Harvey padded in to take away the tray.

'Hello,' she said. 'Are you gay too?'

'No,' I said, 'not yet.'

'Oh.' She tried to hide her disappointment, then brightened. 'Well, you never know,' she concluded, and patted me on the shoulder before picking up the tray and disappearing.

'Tolerant,' I said.

'Accepting,' said Louis.

'Senile,' said Angel.

28

The rest of the day was a dead loss. My ISP seemed to have gone into meltdown, and I was reduced to working off the middling signal in a coffee shop, which was useless for the kind of searches I needed to do. The only interesting piece of information came from Aimee Price who, through various gossip channels, had found out why R. Dean Bailey, the scourge of gays, immigrants, the unemployed, the impoverished, and other dangerous threats to right-wing hegemony in North Dakota, had agreed to support Judge Bowens's proposal to provide Lonny Midas and William Lagenheimer with new identities upon their release. It appeared that Bailey didn't care much for colored folk either, and took the view that Selina Day, in a phrase beloved of barroom misogynists everywhere, had probably been 'asking for it' by going into that barn with two white boys. He was, though, torn between appearing to be tough on crime and not enraging the black community — especially one that might have links, however slight, to terrorists — and not condemning to a lifetime behind bars two white kids whose hormones, in his view, had just got the better of them. So Judge Bowens had played Bailey while promising him quiet support for any future political ambitions he might manifest, support that subsequently turned out to be closer to absolute silence. In order to facilitate the creation of the new identities, Bowens had contacted like-minded judicial figures in other states and, without going into too many details about Lagenheimer and Midas, had arranged a complex series of prisoner transfers between states on various political and compassionate grounds, like a huckster mixing the cards in a game of 'Find the Lady.'

Night fell, and it came time to meet Walsh. He had left a message on my phone requesting my presence at Ed's Ville, a dive bar northwest of Camden on Route 52, so named because the rear half of a '58 Coupe de Ville was embedded in its side wall. This might have been considered a little tasteless given the number of alcohol-related accidents that had been ascribed to overimbibing at Ed's, but most people preferred to look upon it as a token of black humor, just as no local ever referred to the bar by its proper name; to those in the vicinity of Camden it was universally known as 'Dead-ville.' It served good beer and better food, but it wasn't particularly a cop bar, which was probably why Walsh had chosen it for our meeting.

The man himself was already mostly done with a Belfast Bay Lobster Ale when I arrived. Actually, strike that: From the glaze in his eyes he'd left the first one behind some time ago, and looked halfway to a good drunk. He had taken a booth and was stretched out along one side, the top button of his shirt open and his tie at half mast. His enormous feet overhung the edge, crossed at the ankles. They looked like a pair of midget canoes.

'You're late,' he said.

376

'Are we dating? If I'd known, I'd have made more of an effort.'

'I wouldn't date you if we were in jail, although I'd farm you out for cigarettes. Sit down. You're intimidating me with your sobriety.'

I slipped in across from him, but I kept my jacket on and my shirt buttoned.

'Hard day at the office?' I asked.

'You should know. You contributed to it.'

'It's a no-win situation with you. I was damned when I wasn't giving up my client, and now I'm damned because I did.'

'Your client's a piece of shit.'

'No, my client *was* a piece of shit when he was fourteen. Now he's a small-town accountant who just wants to get on with his life.'

'Unlike the girl he killed. How's her life coming along? Oh, wait, she doesn't have one, because she's dead.'

'Are we going to do this? Because if we are, I have some catching up to do before I can come over all boozily self-righteous.'

'You don't need booze to be self-righteous. I bet you came out of the womb all holier than thou. The midwife should have slapped you harder, then put you up for adoption with religious zealots.'

The waitress came over, but she did so hesitantly. It was clear that we weren't yet having a good time, and she was uncertain if more alcohol was likely to remedy that situation.

'He'll have what I'm having,' said Walsh. 'And I'll have what I'm having too.'

He laughed. The waitress didn't laugh back.

'It's okay,' said Walsh. 'I'm a police officer.' He fumbled in his jacket for his shield and showed it to her. 'See, I'm a cop. They only give these to detectives.'

'That's great,' she said. 'I feel safer already. Would you like to see some menus?'

'No,' said Walsh.

'Yes,' I said. 'He needs to eat. Why don't you just bring us the biggest burgers you have?'

'Are you a cop too?' she asked.

'No, he's a crusader,' said Walsh. 'He's the white knight.'

'Apparently I'm the white knight,' I said. 'You can take your time with the beers.'

She left us, relieved to be doing so. Walsh sighed and put his shield away. 'My wife doesn't like me talking to waitresses.'

'I imagine waitresses don't like you talking to waitresses either.'

'She thinks every woman wants me as much as she does.'

Either Walsh was ignoring me or he was just so lost in thoughts of wives and waitresses that my presence had ceased to register for a time.

'Give me her number and I'll set her mind at rest,' I said.

'She's great. You'd like her. She wouldn't like you, but you'd like her.'

He drained the last of his beer and set the glass down on the table so heavily that it was a miracle one or both didn't break.

'So why the buzz, Detective?' I asked.

He closed his eyes for a few seconds, and when they opened again I could see that the

378

glaze had lifted and his eyes were clear. He wasn't drunk; he just wanted to be very, very badly, and he was tired enough that another couple of beers would make it happen.

'You know how much closer we are to finding Anna Kore than we were when we started?' he asked. 'Nowhere. We're nowhere near finding her. Nobody saw anything. The parking lot at that little mall she disappeared from doesn't have cameras. We came up with a list of vehicles that were parked there at the time but it's only partial. Of the ten that we've tracked down, eight were driven by women, and two by elderly men. They're all clean, but we're going to go back over them again tomorrow in case we missed something. That's what we're reduced to: raking over dead leads.'

'What about the father?'

'Alekos? We tracked him down today. He's been living in a Buddhist retreat in Oregon for the last four years. Doesn't read the papers, doesn't watch TV, doesn't use the Internet. The feds interviewed him and believe he's clean. He was even allowed to speak to Valerie Kore on the phone this afternoon. He's out of the frame for this.'

'You still have Randall Haight,' I said. 'You have the envelopes, and his story.'

'Allan took Haight's prints this afternoon. We'll use them for elimination purposes. There are prints on some of the photographs, but I'll bet they're Haight's. The photographs them-selves are at least second-generation, so whoever sent them probably didn't take them. We'll analyze the glue on the envelope in the hope of finding saliva traces, and we may get epithelial cells from the paper and the interior. It could be we'll get lucky with a hair or an eyelash, but unless the DNA is in the system it'll only be useful in the event that we pick up a suspect. The address labels were machine-printed, so hand-writing analysis is out. For now, that glass is half empty, my friend, and that's even assuming whoever has it in for your client is the same person who took Anna Kore.'

'What about Lonny Midas?'

'The mysterious vanishing accomplice? We've already been in touch with North Dakota, and they're going to release copies of the records. They'll be with us by Monday.'

I wondered if I could persuade Walsh to let me take a look at them.

'I can hear your thoughts,' said Walsh. 'The answer is 'no.' No, you can't take a look at the records.'

'That's impressive. You should work the boardwalks. Have they kept track of Midas and Haight since their release?'

'All we know for now is that Haight stayed in touch for a while, but Midas didn't. The details will have to wait until we get the records.'

'So they don't know where Midas is?'

'Indications are that they have no idea.'

The beers came. I sipped mine slowly, and Walsh did the same with his. The drunk show was over for a while.

'The only bright spot in the day,' said Walsh, 'was Tommy Morris. And, yes, initially I was as surprised by the mention of his name as you are now.'

'The feds got him?'

'No, he got them. You're going to love this. Tommy Morris, along with his right-hand man, a reputed boom-boom guy named Martin Dempsey, walked into the Kore house and held two agents at gunpoint while a sheriff's deputy counted clouds outside. Tommy wanted to talk to his sister, so what's a guy to do?'

It was routine in a missing-child case to have two officers or sometimes, if the FBI became involved, two agents staying with the family at all times. Mostly this was to offer support and help, but it also enabled the investigators to take a closer look at the dynamics of the family. Since Valerie Kore was Tommy Morris's sister, that made her family dynamics particularly interesting.

'Were they Engel's agents?'

'Yeah. They're supposed to be liaising with the feds' own Child Abduction Response Team, but there hasn't been much liaising to do. In the end, they're there primarily because of Tommy Morris and not Anna Kore.'

'Did Valerie Kore say what passed between her and her brother?'

'Just that Tommy was concerned for his niece's safety and wanted to know what progress was being made. She didn't have much to tell him. He tied her up, more for appearance's sake than anything else, left the agents bound and gagged on the floor, then disappeared back down his rabbit hole. The car they used was stolen from a movie theater and later dumped at a strip mall, but the woman behind the counter of a knitting store saw Tommy and Dempsey being picked up. The pickup vehicle turned out to be stolen too, and we still haven't tracked it down. We figure they left that somewhere as well, and are now on to the day's third ride.'

'Facing down two feds — that's impressive.'

'Engel didn't think so. The two agents are halfway to Boise by now. A career in tracking potato smugglers beckons for them. On a more serious note, the news from Boston is that five of Oweny Farrell's boys have dropped off the radar. Three of them are big hitters, and the other two are gifted novices. Engel is hoarse from screaming, and Pastor's Bay is starting to feel like Tombstone on the night before the big gunfight.'

'Engel is a curious man,' I said. 'He's taking a big risk using the Kore case as bait to land Tommy Morris.'

'As today's events demonstrated.'

'But Engel isn't stupid.'

'No, he isn't.'

Walsh was watching me, waiting to see where my train of thought might lead. Either he knew something more than I did about Engel's game or he had come to the same conclusion that I was approaching.

'A stupid man would let Tommy Morris run wild and hope that good luck or common sense prevailed,' I continued. 'A smart man would make it look that way.'

Walsh still said nothing, but his left eyebrow

rose encouragingly, and when I spoke again I received a short, ironic round of applause from him.

'He has a lead on Tommy Morris,' I said. 'Somebody is talking to the FBI.'

29

The night sky was clear when Walsh and I at last left the bar. He had not commented further on my belief that Engel was being fed information from Boston, either from someone within Tommy Morris's increasingly dwindling circle or from someone close to those who wanted him dead, and I knew better than to press him on the matter. Instead we had returned to the subject of Anna Kore, and I came to understand that Walsh, who had no children of his own, had adopted her disappearance as his personal cause and was becoming increasingly unhappy with Engel's mercenary attitude toward her fate. When he had earlier baited me for being a crusader and a white knight, he was describing himself as much as he was taunting me.

He asked me what I was going to do now that Randall Haight had 'unburdened himself of his past.' I told him that I didn't believe Haight's burdens could so easily be put aside.

'He's angry,' I said.

'Why?'

'Because he believes that he has been defined by a single bad act, and he can't escape that definition.'

'But nobody knew what he'd done until he came to you and Aimee Price.'

'He knew. He's a mass of contradictions, a muddle of identities. The only thing he can be sure of about himself is that he was there when Selina Day died, and even then he disputes the extent of his involvement.'

'He's part of a social experiment,' said Walsh. 'Except nobody kept a close watch on the test subjects once they were released into the wild.'

I had found instances of other similar efforts, but not many. The schoolboy killers of the toddler James Bulger, in England, in 1993 had been given new identities upon their release, although one of them, Jon Venables, had since been sentenced to two years for possession of child pornography and was back in jail. His accomplice in the killing, Robert Thompson, had apparently remained out of trouble. The media were forbidden to reveal details of the men's new identities. It seemed that Judge Bowens had been ahead of his time in anticipating some of the problems that Lonny Midas and William Lagenheimer might face upon their release. Unfortunately, he hadn't factored in the psychological difficulties of adjusting to a new identity, particularly after the commission of such a crime against a child while still children themselves.

'You seem very interested in Lonny Midas,' I said.

'You and I, we've been doing this for a long time,' said Walsh. 'Put a man behind bars with a grudge to nurse, and maybe he'll find a way to get his revenge once he's released. As soon as we receive those records from North Dakota we'll know more about Midas, and then we can bring him in or cross him off the list. I'm not going to leave Valerie Kore twisting in the wind for years, not if I can help it. I want her daughter found, preferably alive. But there's something hinky about this whole deal, and what Haight had to say today just confirmed it. We're all being played here, not just Randall Haight.'

After that, he'd called for the check, although he made me cover it. Now the November darkness stretched above us, punctured by the light of dead stars. My grandfather knew a little about the night sky, and had tried to pass on that knowledge to me. From memory, I could find Aquarius and Pegasus, Pisces and Cetus, with Jupiter at their center. Soon Venus would become visible below the waning crescent moon low in the east-southeastern sky. As the month went on, it would grow both smaller and brighter, decreasing in distance even as it drew closer to the sun. The New England astronomers had promised that two meteor showers would become visible that month: the Taurids from Comet Encke, and the Lenoids from Comet Tempel-Tuttle. The Taurids would be brighter, the Leonids more plentiful. Those who witnessed them would be reminded of the ceaseless, rapid orbit of the Earth around the sun, of our planet's motion through space, and, if they were wise enough, of their own inconsequentiality. Walsh stared up at the night sky, wavering against its immensity. The intoxication that he had wished for earlier had not become a reality, but 36 hours without sleep had worn him down, and I was resigned to an argument over his car keys.

'She's like one of those stars,' he said.

386

'Who is? Your wife?'

'No, not her. That's not what I meant. Anna Kore's like one of those stars. She's lost out there, and we don't know if she's alive or dead. We just have to hope that her light keeps shining until we can get to her.'

'You need to go home, Walsh. You want me to drive you?'

'Too far to drive. I'll sleep in my car. Anyway, even if I was desperate I wouldn't want you to drive me. I don't want to be collateral damage when fate eventually catches up with you.'

'You know, you're a poetic near-drunk. I like that about you.'

'And you're not all bad. I'm sorry for what I said about your little girl back in Pastor's Bay. That wasn't right. That was — I don't know what it was. It was desperation talking.'

'I didn't take it personally.'

He swayed with exhaustion. If he toppled, it would be like a building falling.

'Anna Kore is dead,' he said.

'We don't know that. If you start thinking that way, it will determine how you approach the investigation. You know that. Believing that she could still be alive is the spur.'

'The three-hour rule, man. If they're not found — '

'I know the rule,' I said. 'We live for the exceptions.'

'We've put her mother on television. We've made the appeals. If it's a freak, he'd release her, or kill her. He hasn't released her, therefore . . . '

He raised his hands, then let them fall

impotently by his sides.

'I don't know what we're missing,' he continued. 'Later, you figure it out, like that guy in *South Park*, fucking Captain Hindsight, and you think, yeah, that was it. You either catch it in time, and you're the hero, or you spot it later, the big clue that should have been picked up but you only figure it out when everyone's looking for someone to blame and the mist has cleared. Then, if you're smart, you stay quiet. If you're dumb and idealistic, you confess, and you get told to stay quiet. The end result is the same — a dead child — but if you open box one then nobody's pension is put at risk.'

'I'm driving you home,' I said, taking his arm. 'Come on.'

'Get your hands off me! I don't want to go home. My wife hates it when I come home drunk. No, she hates it when I come home *maudlin* drunk. Nobody likes a whiner.'

The main door to the bar opened, and our waitress came out. She had her car keys in her hand and was shrugging on her coat. She saw both of us, thought about continuing on her way and minding her own business, then reconsidered and came over to ask if everything was okay. Her name, I recalled from the check, was Tina.

'We're good,' said Walsh. 'I just need to find my car. First rule of drinking and driving: Always remember where you parked.'

'Don't worry,' I reassured her. 'He's not driving anywhere. I'm going to put him in my car and take him to a motel.'

'Are we dating?' asked Walsh, throwing my line

388

back at me. ''Cause I don't remember asking you out. Go drive yourself, asshole.'

Tina stood in front of him, her hands on her hips. It clearly wasn't the first time she'd dealt with a difficult customer, and she had no fear of Walsh or me.

'Listen, mister,' she said. 'I served you tonight, and I kept serving you because I thought you'd be smarter than the other jerks who drink until their eyeballs float, because you had a badge. We don't allow people to sleep in the lot, and right now you couldn't drive a nail into butter. You listen to your friend and let him take you somewhere to sleep it off.'

'He's not my friend.' He tried to sound affronted but just came off sulky.

'Compared to me, he's Jesus himself,' said Tina. 'Quit acting like a child and do as you're told.'

Walsh swayed some more, and eyeballed Tina.

'You're mean,' he said.

'I've been on my feet for seven hours, I got a second job that starts at nine in the morning, and I have an eight-month-old baby at home who's set to start crying in three hours' time. If you don't get right with the Lord, I'm going to knock you to the ground and feed your nuts to squirrels, you understand?'

She had a way about her. It wasn't exactly tough love, but it was tough something.

Walsh was suitably chastened. 'I understand, ma'am.'

'You see a ring on this finger? Am I fifty? Do I look like a 'ma'am' to you?'

389

'No, ma'am — miss.'

'You know, sometimes I hate this job,' she said. 'Give me a hand with him.'

With her on one side and me on the other, we guided Walsh to my car and laid him on the backseat. He mumbled an apology, told Tina that she was better than any man deserved, then promptly fell asleep.

'He's had a bad week,' I said.

'I know that. I heard you talking about that missing girl. You going to look after him?'

'I'll see that he gets a bed for the night.'

'You'd better. And you'd better help him find that girl too.'

She spun on her heel and stomped to her car. I followed her lights for a time along a road overhung by bare trees, and her presence gave me consolation until she turned west and was lost to me. From the seat behind, I heard Walsh whisper, 'I'm sorry,' and I did not know to whom he was speaking.

★　★　★

Randall Haight was still wearing the same clothes that he had worn during his interview with the police that morning. Beside him was a bottle of scotch that a client had given to him as a Christmas gift four years earlier, and which had not been opened until that evening. Randall did not drink very much at the best of times, and preferred wine when he did. Even then, he tended to limit himself to one or two glasses. The girl did not like him to drink more than that.

But the girl was gone.

He was lost in his own house without her. She had been with him for so long that he had grown accustomed to her presence. His fear of her had become a facet of his existence. In its way, it had provided him with an outlet, a focus for other, more abstract concerns: his dread of exposure, of being returned to prison, of the unraveling of the web of half-truths in which he had secured his personality. Without her, he was too much alone with himself.

But he was also afraid of allowing himself to countenance that her torment of him might now be at an end. Perhaps even entities like her grew tired of their games. He could not bring himself to call her a ghost, for he did not believe in ghosts, a peculiar exercise in logic that even Randall admitted was unlikely to bear the weight of close intellectual scrutiny, but which nonetheless permitted him to regard her as a peculiar manifestation of primal energy, a version of the same energy that had fed the fatal attack on her all those decades ago. He knew there were professionals who, had he admitted to them that the specter of a dead girl shared his house, would have fallen back on Psychology 101 and interrogated him about his feelings of guilt and regret. Randall would then have been forced to lie to them, just as he had lied throughout his period of incarceration, and in the years that followed his release. Randall was a good liar, which made him a better actor. He could feign a whole range of emotions — repentance, humility, even love — to the extent that he was

391

no longer always able to distinguish the counterfeit feeling from the genuine, even as he expressed it.

He was sure of the veracity of one emotional response as he sat in his favorite chair: He was furious. He was furious at the lawyer, and at the private detective. He was furious at his forced exposure, and that the potential danger posed by Anna Kore's mobster uncle had been kept from him. He was furious at whoever was responsible for taunting him about his past. He was furious at the town of Pastor's Bay for failing to shield him from the vile regard of an enemy.

And he was furious at the girl: furious at her for haunting him for so long, and now for leaving him.

He drank some more of the whisky. He wasn't enjoying it but he felt that it was more appropriate to his mood than wine. His stomach growled. He had not eaten in many hours, but he wanted liquor more than food. He would suffer for it in the morning.

Randall reached for the phone and dialed the lawyer's number. He had been reconsidering his relationship with her all day, debating the consequences of his actions back and forth, and the booze had tipped the balance. Time was running out. He knew that. Soon he would be forced to shed his current identity and find another. The presence of the lawyer and the detective in his life would only make that more difficult. He left a message informing her that he would no longer require her services, or those of the detective. Neither would he be needing the dubious protective presence of the two idiots who were supposed to shield him if the necessity arose, assuming they could get their fat asses in gear in time. He was coldly polite as he thanked the lawyer for all that she had done for him, requested that a final bill be sent to him at her convenience, and hung up the phone with a sense of empowerment. He had started withdrawing all of his money from his accounts as soon as the taunting messages began to arrive, and he now had $15,000 in cash on hand. It wasn't much, but it was a start. The house he would just have to abandon for now. He'd figure out what to do with it later. He'd have to inform Chief Allan that he was leaving, just so he was all square with the law. He and Allan had always got along well in a cordial, professional way. He'd tell Allan that he was frightened and wanted to keep some distance from Pastor's Bay until the Kore case was concluded, if it ever was. He might even spend a couple of nights in a nice inn before quietly heading elsewhere: Canada, perhaps. This time, he'd try losing himself in a big city.

The knock on the back door startled him so much that he tipped over the side table, and the bottle of whisky began to empty itself on the rug. He picked it up before it could do too much damage, then screwed on the cap and held the bottle by the neck, brandishing it like a club.

The knock came again.

'Who's there?' he called, but there was no reply. He went into the kitchen. There was a glass panel on the locked door, but he could see nobody outside, and the motion sensor that turned on the night light above the door had not been activated. He wished that he had a gun, but the nature of the gun laws meant that it wasn't possible for him to acquire one without complications, and he had never had a reason to seek out an illegal weapon. He put down the bottle and took a carving knife from the rack. He glanced out the kitchen window and saw, on the back lawn, the figure of the girl. She cast no shadow, despite the light from the waning crescent moon, for she was barely more than a shadow herself. She raised her right hand and beckoned to him with her index finger, and he was about to open the door when another figure caught his attention.

There was a man standing behind her, between the twin willows at the end of his garden. Their almost bare branches hung so low that their shape and his became one, so that he seemed a construct of bark and twigs and brown, dying leaves. The man did not move and Randall could not see his face, but Randall still knew who he was. After all, they had both had a hand in the death of Selina Day.

Randall backed away from the door. The girl could no longer be seen on the lawn, and now the knocking came once more.

Tap-tap-tap.

She was at the door once again. Come out. Come out, come out, because time is pressing, and a friend has arrived, just as you always knew that he would. You can't hide from him, just as you can't hide from me. Running won't help, not

394

now. The end is approaching, the reckoning.

Tap-tap-tap.

Come out. Don't make us come in there to get you.

Tap-tap-TAP.

He retreated to the living room, and watched the figure of the man appear against the glass, the girl beside him, and the doorknob turning — once, twice — but still the motion-activated light did not come on. Randall picked up the phone and tried to call the police, but there was only an empty, whooshing noise from the receiver, like a fierce wind blowing across barren peaks. This was not the sound of a dead line. The phone was still connected, except now it was connected to someplace else, somewhere deep and dark and very far away.

The shapes of the man and the girl disappeared. The line cleared. The voice of the emergency operator asked him what service he required, but he did not answer. After a couple of seconds he dropped the phone back into its cradle and slowly sank to the floor. The girl could have come in. She didn't need doors or windows. Why didn't she enter?

The answer was that the girl had a new friend, a special friend.

And Randall saw, in the night sky, the flickering of long-dead stars.

IV

We're stitching up
all your fancy mistakes.

We're stitching up
your mother's face.

We're going to stitch you a new one.

We're going to take our time.

from *The Dead Girls Speak in Unison*
by Danielle Pafunda

30

I didn't need a reminder about the necessity of following Allan that day, but in case I did there was another text message waiting for me when I woke. It read:

CHIEF ALLAN THE PEDOFILE IS A
HORNY DOG TODAY.

I could taste beer at the back of my throat, and although I had slept straight through the night I did not feel rested. For a long time after the deaths of Susan and Jennifer I had not touched alcohol. I had never been an alcoholic, but I had been guilty of abusing alcohol, and I had been drinking on the night that they died. Such associations are not easily set aside. Now I drank the occasional beer or glass of wine, but my taste for either in any great quantity had largely vanished. Walsh had far outstripped my intake the night before, but I had still drunk more than I was used to and my head and liver were making their objections known.

I checked in with Angel and Louis, but Allan's vehicle had not yet left his property. The tracking device on Allan's truck was based on one that had previously been attached to my own car. The vehicle's movements were mapped on a computer utilizing the same technology that provided coordinates to drivers using GPS units. The advantage was that the trackers didn't need to maintain visual contact with the target vehicle all the time, but in our case this advantage was diminished slightly by the necessity of finding out not only where Allan was going but whom he was seeing.

But for the early part of the morning Allan did nothing interesting. He didn't appear until shortly before eight, and then only to produce a chainsaw and trim some trees in his yard. He worked until noon, reducing the cuttings to firewood and piling them to dry. Angel watched him from the woods nearby, chilly and bored. In an ideal world we'd have monitored Allan's cell phone too, but that was a complex business and assumed that, if he was doing something wrong, he'd be dumb enough to make calls related to it on his cell phone of record. If the day's surveillance revealed nothing then it was among the other options that we could look at, but I was hoping it wouldn't be necessary. If the anonymous messages had any truth to them, then any liaisons that Allan conducted were likely to be personal and not electronic. Eventually, freshly showered and wearing clean clothes, Allan got into his truck and made his way into Pastor's Bay, and the pursuit of him began in earnest.

★ ★ ★

While Angel rolled up the sheet of plastic on which he had been lying, wondering how his life had come to this moment, and Louis tracked

400

Allan's progress from the warmth of his car nearby, I dealt with Aimee Price, who had called to tell me about the message from Randall Haight that had been left on her answering machine. I dropped in at her office on my way to Pastor's Bay: If and when Allan met his 'cooze' I wanted to be close by. There were no muffins and coffee that morning. Aimee was preparing for Marie Borden's bail hearing, Marie Borden being the woman who had objected with a hammer to her husband's ongoing physical abuse.

'Borden?' I said. 'That's her name? Lucky it wasn't her mother she laid out.'

'You think you're the first person who's cracked that joke?'

'Probably not. What about Randall Haight?'

'He's no longer my problem,' she said. 'Either he's looking for new legal representation or he's going to be alone when he sits for a polygraph.'

'Assuming he's willing to take the test.'

'And that there's any point to it in the first place. The state's polygraph experts are good, but they don't like firing questions into the dark. It's hard to see how the polygraph will help, apart from going some way toward conclusively eliminating him as a suspect, assuming any doubts remain after Chief Allan's contribution yesterday. It looks like Randall caught a break with that. Two cheers for him.'

'You don't sound too sorry to have lost a client,' I said.

'I don't know how much more we could have done for him,' she said. 'Being in charge of a protection detail while juggling my moral and legal obligations is not why I spent all those years in law school. Besides, I didn't like him, although I hid my feelings better than you did. He gave me the creeps. Bill me for your time and I'll take care of it.'

'That's kind of why I'm here.'

'Are you upping your rate? We had an agreement.'

'You just assumed that we did. My rates weren't specified on that contract you had me sign. For a lawyer, you're a very trusting person.'

'You're a secret moralist, but you wear a cynic's overcoat well. I know that I'm going to be sorry for letting you keep talking, but go on. I'm listening.'

'I know I'm off the job, but I need a little indulgence. Expenses only: mine, and Angel and Louis's.'

'Yours I can afford. I'm not sure about theirs.'

'We'll keep them reasonable.'

'For how long?'

'A couple of days.'

'And I would be doing this why?'

'Because you're curious about what Randall Haight has kept hidden from us, and what Kurt Allan does in his spare time, and because somewhere in this mess may be the answer to the question of Anna Kore's disappearance.'

'You could just hand over what you know to the police.'

'I could, but all I have is a couple of anonymous texts about Allan and my own insatiable curiosity about the details of other people's lives. Anyhow, it's more interesting this way, and more satisfying.'

'I'll give you two days. And I want receipts. And nothing over five hundred dollars without prior approval. And if anybody asks, or you get caught doing something you shouldn't, I'll deny any knowledge of this conversation.'

'And if we find anything useful to the cops?'

'You can tell them I guided your every move with a firm but gentle hand.'

'You make it sound dirty.'

'It is,' she concluded. 'And not in a good way.'

I drove on to Pastor's Bay, making some calls along the way. According to Haight, Lonny Midas had one older brother, Jerry, but I had been able to find no trace of a Jerry Midas in Drake Creek or its vicinity. Neither could I find a Social Security number linked with a Jerry Midas and originating in North Dakota. It was a long shot, especially as it was Sunday, but I made a call to the sheriff's department in Drake Creek. After a delay during which I listened to the same couple of bars of Pachelbel's 'Canon' played over and over on what sounded like a child's xylophone, I was put through to Sheriff Douglas Peck. A Sheriff Douglas Peck had been named in some of the newspaper articles following Selina Day's killing. Three decades later, he had either started out young or law enforcement in the county was a family business.

'Can I help you, sir?' he said.

'My name is Charlie Parker,' I said. 'I'm a private detective up here in Maine.'

'Congratulations.' He didn't say anything

more, which suggested that Sheriff Peck was a man with a sense of humor, albeit a sarcastic one.

'You wouldn't be the same Douglas Peck who worked the Selina Day killing?'

'I'm Douglas Peck the third. My father was Douglas Peck the second, and he was sheriff at that time. My grandfather was plain old Douglas Peck, and he was never a sheriff anytime or anywhere. If this is about the Day murder, then I can't tell you more than what you can find on the Internet.'

'You can't, or you won't?'

'Both.'

'Perhaps I could talk to your father?'

'Not unless you got access to one of them mediums. He's been dead these past five years.'

'I'm sorry to hear that.'

'You didn't know him, so you can't be sorry. Now, are we done here? I don't want to be rude, but just because I don't want it to rain doesn't mean that I won't get wet if I step outside, if you catch my drift.'

I wasn't sure that I did. 'I've been working for a man your father might have known as William Lagenheimer.'

'Hold on a minute,' said Peck. I heard the phone being put down, and then much of the background noise was muted as a door was closed.

'Run that by me again,' he said.

'I've been working for William Lagenheimer, although he goes by another name now.'

'Are you going to tell me in what capacity

you're working for him, or do I have to guess?'

'He was receiving unwanted messages in the mail from somebody who had learned about his past and his previous identity. He wanted me to find out who was responsible.'

'And did you?'

'No. He has since dispensed with my services.'

'Not surprising if you couldn't help him.'

'I try not to take these things personally. I also try not to let them get in the way of pursuing my inquiries.'

'Why? You a charitable man? You must be if you like working for nothing.'

'I just don't like loose ends. I also don't like it that a fourteen-year-old girl has gone missing up here, and from the same town in which Lagenheimer now lives.'

'You think he had something to do with it?'

'He has an alibi. I think he's in the clear. It's Lonny Midas that I'm curious about.'

'And where are the police in all this?'

'A request has gone to the North Dakota Attorney General's Office requesting the information contained in the sealed records pertaining to the imprisonment and subsequent release of Lonny Midas and William Lagenheimer.'

'So? The AG will oblige by releasing the information, but as you're not a law-enforcement officer you have no right to it. Will that be all?'

'Jerry Midas,' I said.

'What about him?'

'You can't tell me anything about Lonny Midas, but you can tell me how to get in touch with his brother.'

'And why would I do that, assuming I knew anything about him in the first place?'

'Because there's a girl missing, and I want her found as much as the cops do. Look up my name, Sheriff Peck. If you need someone to vouch for me, try Detective Gordon Walsh of the Maine State Police. If you have a pen, I'll give you his number.'

I wasn't sure that Walsh would vouch for me, but I figured he owed me for the night before. Even if he didn't feel any obligation, my interest in Jerry Midas might pique his own interest and I could possibly browbeat him into sharing whatever he discovered.

'Let me have it,' said Peck.

I gave him Walsh's number and my own.

'Leave it with me,' he said. 'I'll get back to you.'

An hour later I was back in Pastor's Bay, standing in Hallowed Grounds while the same tattooed barista worked behind the counter, although this time he was wearing a faded Ramones T-shirt and the music playing was a cover version of the Carpenters' 'Goodbye to Love' by American Music Club. I had that tribute album. Hell, I think I even had the original album somewhere.

'Morning, snitch,' I said. 'I saw an old lady jaywalking earlier. I didn't get her name, but she can't have got far. Maybe you can call someone and have her picked up.'

He tugged at the massive hole in his left ear created by a circular piercing through the lobe. I could have put my finger through it. It was a tempting image.

'You get a good look at her?' he replied. 'We've got a lot of old ladies here. I wouldn't want to be responsible for a miscarriage of justice.'

'A rat with a conscience. I may yet find it in my heart to forgive you.'

'Hey, no hard feelings, man. I was just doing what was right.'

'Yeah, you and Joe McCarthy both. It's okay. In your position, I might even have done the same. To make up for my discomfort, you can brew me some fresh coffee. That pot smells like you're stripping bones in it.'

He grinned and gave me the finger: customer service the Maine way.

'The name is Danny, by the way.'

'Charlie Parker. Don't think this makes us friends.'

I leafed through some of the paperbacks on the shelf. A sign described them as 'Gently Used,' but there were retired hookers who'd been used more gently than these books. Some of them were old enough to have Caxton's thumbprints on them.

The front door opened, and Mrs. Shaye entered, her son Patrick ambling amiably behind her. They looked as if they'd dressed for church.

'Danny, do you have that order of subs ready?'

'Sure, Mrs. Shaye. I'll just be a second.'

'And we'll need two iced coffees, and as many of those doughnuts as you can fit in a bag.'

Danny set the coffeepot to fill, and sprinted off to do Mrs. Shaye's bidding.

'I'm the spare pair of hands,' Pat said. 'She made me clean them too.' He showed them to me as proof.

'They're spotless. In parts.'

'Don't talk to strange men, Pat,' said Mrs. Shaye. 'Mr. Parker, will you be joining us for lunch?' But she said it with a wry smile.

'I hope not, Mrs. Shaye. All out of cookies?'

'I'm working such hours now that I don't have time to bake them. It's good news for Danny here. You know that this is his business? Before him, we had to make do with takeouts from the store.'

I raised an eyebrow at Danny, who had just reappeared with a tray of Saran-wrapped subs, and was looking for a bag for the doughnuts.

'And there he was, telling me that the management didn't like him to play depressing music.'

'The management doesn't,' said Danny. 'The fan does, but the manager wants to stay in business.'

Mrs. Shaye handed the tray of subs to Pat, added a half dozen bottles of iced tea to the pile, signed for everything, and took the bag of dough-nuts herself. I held the door open for them.

'Bye, now, Mr. Parker,' she said. 'Stay out of trouble.'

'Good advice,' said Pat.

I went to the window to watch the world, and I witnessed a peculiar moment. A group of young girls were hanging out near the grocery store. They were probably about fourteen or fifteen years old, and well on the way to becoming striking young women. Unfortunately, they hadn't reached that stage yet, so I tried to find some-where else to look.

Chief Allan didn't seem to have such qualms. He was sitting in his truck on the other side of the street, sipping a soda and taking in the girls' bodies. One of them had bought a magazine, and they were huddled around it, giggling and pointing. They didn't notice Allan, but Mrs. Shaye did. I could see her clock him, and the direction of his gaze. As Mrs. Shaye and her son crossed the road, she rousted the girls.

'Hey, you kids, be about your business. You're like a brood of hens blocking the path.'

The girls headed east up Main Street. Allan started his truck and moved off. Mrs. Shaye held open the door of the municipal building for her son, her head flicking to follow Allan's progress before she followed her son inside.

And I wondered how good Mrs. Shaye's spelling was.

★ ★ ★

Walsh called me while I was finishing my coffee.

'I'm your referee now?' he said. 'What are you doing, giving my name out to hick sheriffs as your go-to guy?'

'I hope you said nice things about me.'

'I just got the message. I haven't called him back.'

'I know there's a 'yet' missing from that sentence. You haven't called him back yet.'

'I may not call him back ever.'

'And after all I've done for you. How's your head?'

'Surprisingly clear and obligation-free. I don't

409

recall everything about last night, but I do remember telling you that I wasn't going to let you see those sealed records, and now you go trying your luck with North Dakota. You just don't know when to quit.'

'I'm interested in Lonny Midas's brother. I didn't think the sealed records were relevant in his case.'

'You're looking for the brother because you believe that he might know where Lonny is. Lonny Midas is the subject of those sealed records.'

'Come on, Walsh, I just want to talk to the brother. If he blows me off, then we'll have whatever is in the records to go on.'

'*I* will have whatever is in the records. You will have nothing.'

I ignored him. 'And if his brother does know something I'll share it with you and you'll be ahead. So either you win or you stay as you were, but you're not going to lose on the deal. Come on, make the call.'

There was silence on the other end of the line.

'Did a waitress threaten me last night?' he asked.

'She promised to feed your nuts to a squirrel if you continued to annoy her,' I said.

'I thought that was what she said.'

'She also told us to find Anna Kore.'

'I seem to remember that too,' said Walsh. 'Shit.' He thought for a moment. 'Engel says you got one favor coming to you for the Randall Haight thing, but this can't be it. It's too close. We have feelers out for Jerry Midas too, and I don't want you getting in the way. You let this one drop. Understood?'

'Yeah, I understand.' And I did: There would be no call back from Sheriff Peck.

'Okay,' said Walsh. 'Thanks again for the ride last night.'

'*De nada.*'

'Right. *Más tarde.*'

He hung up. There was free wireless access in the coffee shop, so I opened up my laptop and went through my copies of the newspaper reports of the Selina Day killing. The *Beacon & Explainer* was still going strong. I found its number and got through to the editor, a man named Everett Danning IV. Like law enforcement, the *Beacon-Advertiser* turned out to be a family business as well, but Danning was a little more co-operative than the sheriff. He wasn't able to tell me a great deal, but he confirmed that Lonny Midas did indeed have an older brother named Jerry, except that wasn't quite his given name.

'He was baptized Nahum Jeremiah Midas, after the prophets,' said Danning. 'That's what you get for having a Bible-thumper for a father. His younger brother got off easier, mainly because even old Eric Midas wasn't blind to the fights his firstborn got into over his name. He gave Lonny his own father's name, Leonard, and saved the Biblical stuff for the kid's middle name, Amos. Don't ask me how 'Leonard' became 'Lonny' instead of 'Lenny,' although I think it was because there were two other Leonards in his school, and they all had to be

411

differentiated somehow. Jerry Midas ditched 'Nahum' pretty early on, or tried to. He was a couple of years ahead of me in school, but that name stuck for a long time.'

'Does Jerry Midas still live in Drake Creek?'

'No, there are no Midases left here now.'

'Any idea where he might have gone?'

'None.'

I thanked him. In return, I gave him a little of the background to what was happening, but I tried to keep it as vague as possible, telling him only that the former William Lagenheimer now lived in Maine. I did promise him that, if it became possible to reveal more at some point in the future, I would.

Five minutes later, thanks to the wonders of Google, I had found Jerry Midas.

31

It turned out that Jerry Midas had always had an artistic bent. He had been sketching since he was a boy and had adapted his talents to book illustration, graphic design, and, for the past two decades, computer games, providing initial portraits and backdrops for companies that prided themselves on the depth and beauty of their virtual worlds. He was known to those who called upon his skills simply as N. J. M., for that was how he signed his work, or otherwise as 'Nate.' All this he told me when I finally tracked him down in San Mateo, California, having first had to persuade his wife to let me speak to him. His voice sounded hoarse down the line, as though speaking might be painful for him.

'Throat cancer,' he said. 'I'm in remission, but it's a bitch. Know what? I never smoked. Don't even drink much. I always tell people that, because they make judgments, you know?'

'I'll try not to keep you talking for too long.'

'Well, that's kind of you, but there was a time when I was worried I might never talk again. I don't take the facility for granted. My wife says you're a private investigator, and you want to talk to me about my brother?'

'That's right.'

'Why?'

'Until recently, I was working on behalf of William Lagenheimer.'

From the other end of the line came an expectoration of disgust.

'Now there's a name from the past. Little William. Lonny told me that he hated being called Billy, always insisted on William. Don't know why, just the way it was. Naturally, everyone called him Billy, just to watch him burn.' He wheezed, and his breath seemed to catch in his throat. 'Dammit.'

'Lagenheimer is living under a new identity in the state of Maine. A girl has gone missing here.' It was more than I wanted to reveal about Haight, but I had little choice.

'I've read about it, I think. Anna — something.'

'Anna Kore.'

'Unusual name. Ironic, even.'

'Why is that?'

'It's a Greek dialectical variation on the name 'Persephone.' Persephone was the daughter of Zeus and Demeter who was abducted by Hades to the Underworld. Benefits of an amateur classical education, you might say. And where does Lonny fit into this? They trying to pin the girl's disappearance on him?'

'When the girl disappeared, Lagenheimer had the same concern for himself that you just expressed for your brother. He believed his past might lead to him being suspected of a crime that he did not commit, so he came clean to the police about his past, which meant telling them about Lonny as well. If they haven't already been in touch with you, they soon will be.'

'But you found me first.'

'It's what I do.'

'Maybe the police should use you to help them find that girl.'

'It's an unofficial inquiry, but to the same ends.'

'If you're asking me where Lonny is, I don't know. I haven't heard from him in many years, not since shortly after his release, and that was just one call to let me know that he was alive and out. He used to write me from his first prison, and I wrote back occasionally, and sent him a card at Christmas, but we were never close. We got on okay, but there was a big gap in age between us.'

'You didn't feel protective of him as his older brother?'

'Protective of Lonny? Lonny didn't need protection. Other people needed protection from Lonny. He was a wild one. But when he killed that girl . . . '

He paused. I waited.

'He marked us all, you know? Our family name became associated with that crime. That's why I tried to reduce it to a single letter. I suppose that for all these years I've been hiding from my family, from myself, maybe even from Lonny too.'

'But your parents stayed in Drake Creek?'

'My father was a deluded zealot, and my mother lived in his shadow. Lonny's sin was a cross that my father could bear, and he forced my mother to share the burden of it. I think he even found a way to blame her for it. He was a God-fearing man, so the fault must have been in her *ab ovo*, from the egg. He wore her down, but she never complained. Her heart had already been broken by Lonny. I was long gone by then, though, and didn't care much for going back, although I made a couple of trips for my mother's sake. Drake Creek wasn't a big place, and I didn't like to hear people whispering behind my back as I walked down the street. Even if Lonny hadn't done what he did, I still wouldn't have wanted to live there. It had a small-town mentality in the worst possible way.'

'Was there a lot of animosity toward your family as a result of Selina Day's murder?'

'Some. The colored folk put the windows of our house in I don't know how many times, but eventually that stopped. Would have been worse if she was a white girl. Don't get me wrong: I'm no racist, but that's just the truth of it. What bothered people more was that they'd interfered with her before she died. They didn't like that. Even if they'd raped her and left her, people would have dismissed it as boys getting out of hand, but they didn't care for the combination of killing and sexual assault. That's how I read it, anyway, but my take on it is pretty poisonous. My take on William Lagenheimer too.'

'Why is that?'

'Because everybody blamed Lonny for what happened, as though he was the only one who was there. Even at the trial he was portrayed as the bad boy who led innocent little Billy astray, but it was more complicated than that. Lonny and Billy, they set each other off, you understand? It was like each of them had a part

416

missing, and the other fit it perfectly. They were the bow and the arrow, the bullet and the gun. Without one, the other was pretty much useless. I don't believe Lonny would have gone after that girl had he been alone, nor Billy. But Billy Lagenheimer was worse than Lonny in some ways. Lonny was all up front. You looked at him, and you knew that he was trouble. Billy, he kept it hidden. He was insidious. If you crossed Lonny, then he'd call you on it. He gave his beatings, but he took them too. Billy, though, he was the kind who'd come up on you from behind and slip the knife into your back, then twist it just to be sure. He was a self-righteous little prick, but there was real harm in him. He had a way of goading my brother, pushing him, daring him. If Lonny killed that girl like they say he did, if he put his hand over her mouth and suffocated her, then Billy Lagenheimer was behind him, screaming him on. He wouldn't have tried to stop him, not the way he claimed that he did. It took two of them to kill her, doesn't matter whose hand felt her final breath.'

As I listened to him, I was reminded of Randall Haight telling his story, first to Aimee, then to both of us, and finally to the unsmiling agents and detectives in Aimee's conference room. Each time the telling had been similar, practiced. But as Jerry Midas spoke, pain both physical and emotional in his voice, I recognized the sincerity of true insight. He had held these thoughts in his head for so many years, but rarely had he spoken them aloud: to a therapist, perhaps, or to his wife when the memories came and his mood sank, but not to a total stranger. Later, he would perhaps wonder if he should have been so open, and the police, when they came to him, might get a different version of the story as a result. Still truthful, but less revealing.

'And you haven't heard from Lonny since his release?'

'No. Wait, that's not true. He called me after he was released, but we didn't talk long. I told him to come down and see me sometime, but he never did. That was the last contact I had with him. I don't even know what name he's living under.'

'And your parents?'

'My father died halfway through Lonny's time in prison. Heart attack. Passed away behind the wheel of his car on his way to church. My mother died a couple of years before Lonny was due to be released. She used to take the Greyhound bus to visit him once a month before they moved him to Washington.'

'Washington?'

'Yeah, the Washington Corrections Center in Mason County. He was there for a while, and then I lost track of him when they moved him again.'

'Under his own name?'

'Yes, as far as I can recall. After that, old Bowens's bleeding-heart scheme must have kicked in, because I lost track of him, and my mother was dead by then. She was old, and tired. I know that Billy's momma eventually sold her house in Drake Creek so that she could be with him when he was released. I only heard rumors, but Mrs. Lagenheimer's life stopped when Billy was jailed. She kept talking about him as her little boy, even when he was a grown man. It was like she'd put his childhood on hiatus, and they could pick up on it again as soon as he was released.'

This was interesting.

'Do you know where she moved?'

'She tried to keep it quiet, but mail had to be forwarded, and you couldn't fart in your own bed in Drake Creek without half the town complaining about the smell. She went to New Hampshire somewhere.'

Berlin, or its vicinity, I thought. That was Randall Haight's last place of imprisonment. It was New Hampshire's newest prison, opened in 2000 for medium-minimum security prisoners: the ideal place in which to conclude the experiment, the journey that had led William Lagenheimer to become Randall Haight.

I thanked Jerry Midas for his help, even as I wished that I could have seen him in person. Only one detail of his story did not ring true. He had spoken so passionately about his brother that I was not sure I believed him when he said he had received no word from Lonny since his release, a single telephone call aside. Jerry was the only blood left to Lonny, and Lonny had reached out to him upon his release. He was family, and Jerry had given no indication of a falling-out between them, the natural distance between them excepted. Would a man who had been in prison for the best part of twenty years, and whose first instinct was to call his brother, not try to reestablish their relationship? Similarly, would an older brother who seemed to know his younger sibling so well not attempt to remain in touch with him?

But Midas had more to say, as though he had picked up on my doubts. 'What my brother and Billy did was a terrible thing, Mr. Parker, and they'll have to live with it for the rest of their lives, but that doesn't mean they don't deserve a chance to be better men. I'd like to know that Lonny's okay, and if you find out where he is you could tell him that I was asking after him, but if he's started again somewhere new, then I wish him only good luck. He was a boy when he committed his crime. He's a man now, and I hope he's a good one.'

'I hope so too, Mr. Midas.'

'And Billy? How's he doing? I know that Lonny blamed him for blabbing to the cops, and maybe my opinion of him is biased because of that. Billy never was very strong, not like Lonny. He got bullied a lot in school. Lonny looked out for him, I think. Without Lonny beside him, Billy wasn't the same kid. But I guess Billy wasn't all bad for Lonny either. These things even out in the end, I suppose.'

'Why was William bullied?' I asked.

'He was slow. No, that wasn't it. He was really smart, but he had some disorder. He had to work really hard in school to understand words and numbers. They'd get mixed up in his head. What's he doing now?'

'He's an accountant,' I said, the words

tumbling out of my mouth before I realized that I'd said them.

'An accountant?' said Midas. 'Well, isn't that something? I guess people do change, because Billy Lagenheimer never could add for shit.'

32

Louis and Angel were growing impatient. Tailing people wasn't what they were good at. They preferred a more confrontational aspect to their work. They were particularly frustrated by Allan, who appeared to be intent only on performing the kind of mundane tasks that might be expected of someone who had been working long hours without a break, and now had to catch up on the basics of maintaining his household. Allan visited a bank in Rockport, and a hardware store. He stopped at a sub shop for a sandwich, then stocked up on cheap household items and cheaper food at a bargain store as Angel disconsolately trailed him around. So bored was Angel that it took him a minute to notice that Allan had stopped in the diaper aisle and was adding a jumbo pack to the canned foods and chicken pieces already in his cart, followed by the kind of baby food that came from Asia and needed to be checked for formaldehyde and broken glass before it could be fed to a child.

Angel abandoned his basket of obscurely branded cookies and close-to-expiration coffee, and returned to the car. Louis was trying to calm himself by listening to more Arvo Pärt, which Angel muted as soon as he closed the door behind him. Angel had decided that his first act upon ascending to the throne of world domination would be to turn America's nuclear arsenal on Estonia unless it handed Arvo Pärt over to him.

'You turned off Pärt,' said Louis.

'How can you tell? Anyway, forget that. Take a look.'

Allan was emerging from the store, his cart loaded with bags.

'Guess what he has in the bags?' said Angel.

'Cheap shit.'

'Cheap baby shit.'

Louis roused himself to a point just past indifference.

'Really?'

'Exciting, huh? That's what people in the trade call a 'clue.''

'Let me jump ahead of you, Sherlock. You're thinking that he doesn't have a kid.'

'That we know of.'

'I'm thinking that he has a sister.'

'That we don't know of.'

'Exactly. And maybe she has a kid.'

Some of Angel's enthusiasm dissipated, but he recovered enough to bet Louis a dollar that Allan didn't have a sister. Louis took the bet, and raised Angel ten that this was as eventful as the day was going to get. As it happened, Louis would be eleven dollars down by the day's end.

Allan drove to a wood-sided apartment building on the northern outskirts of Lincoln-ville. There were three cars in its lot, none of them less than a decade old. A drape moved at a first floor window as Allan pulled in. Moments later, a girl appeared at the door. She was very thin, and wore a pink oversized man's shirt and dark blue jeans. Her hair was black and hung loose, partly obscuring her delicate features but failing to hide how young she was. Her feet were bare, and she had a cigarette in her right hand. Allan removed most of the shopping bags from the trunk of his car and brought them with him as he went to greet her. She rose onto the tips of her toes to kiss him, her arms curling around his neck, her mouth wide open as she pressed herself against him. Angel and Louis watched them from a block away through a gap between two of the neighboring houses.

'His sister,' said Angel.

'They're very close,' said Louis. 'Call Parker.'

★   ★   ★

The building was owned and managed by a company called Ascent Property Services, Inc. One of the cars, a 1997 Subaru, was registered to a Mary Ellen Schrock. Mary Ellen Schrock was nineteen years and ten months old. A further search revealed that Mary Ellen Schrock had given birth to a baby girl, Summer Marilyn Schrock, thirteen months earlier. Mary Ellen Schrock had declined to name the father on the birth certificate. I told Angel and Louis all of this as I sat in the backseat of their car, watching the property.

'What's the age of consent here?' asked Angel.

'Sixteen, but it's sexual abuse of a minor if she's under eighteen and the offender is over twenty-one.'

'Which makes it legal between them.'

'Legal when the child was conceived, and just barely,' I said. 'But there's no way of knowing when Allan started seeing her.'

'Assuming he's the father.'

'Which we're assuming,' I said.

'Because he is,' said Angel.

Allan had told me that he'd been divorced for a year, but the marriage had ended sometime before. Perhaps his wife had found out about his affair, or Allan had felt the need to confess to her after the girl became pregnant. He was a smalltown police chief, bringing in enough to keep himself and his wife but not in anything approaching luxury. There would be no way to hide any payments that he needed to make to the mother of his child, and it didn't look as if she was living with her parents, which meant he would have been under pressure to provide for her and the baby. Confess or get found out: It wasn't much of a choice. His wife, either out of pity or a desire to rid herself of her errant husband as quickly as possible, had allowed her silence to be bought, leaving Allan with an illegitimate child, the child's dependent mother, and a job that paid barely enough to keep his head above water. But if anybody found out about the child, and particularly about the youth of the mother, Allan would be out of a job, and would be facing awkward questions about the girl's age at the commencement of the relationship. Even if it had started when she was over eighteen, or he could persuade her to say that it had, his reputation would be destroyed, whether or not there was a moral turpitude clause in his contract with the Pastor's Bay Police Department.

But somebody had found out about his young girlfriend, and after what I had witnessed outside the Hallowed Grounds coffee shop that morning I was prepared to guess who that might be. It would be hard to hide secrets from Mrs. Shaye, who struck me as a woman who knew the value of storing up hidden knowledge in a small town. She would want to safeguard her own job, and turning whistle-blower on her employer over a personal matter would almost certainly result in his successor's finding an excuse to dispense with her services as soon as it was possible to do so without leaving the department open to a legal challenge. After all, nobody likes a rat. Better, then, to feed the information anonymously when the opportunity arose. The disappearance of Anna Kore had provided both that opportunity and the impetus to tell. The fact that Kurt Allan had a young girlfriend didn't necessarily mean that he was a pedophile. Neither did it mean that he was connected to whatever had happened to Anna, but it didn't look good.

'What do we do now?' asked Angel.

But I was distracted. Working from my cell phone's Internet connection, I was trying to trace William Lagenheimer's mother in Berlin, New Hampshire. Jerry Midas had said that Mrs. Lagenheimer had bought, not rented, a property in New Hampshire, and I assumed that property would have been near the correctional facility in

Berlin. The Coos County Register of Deeds was based in Lancashire, New Hampshire, but did not accept online or telephone requests. Searches had to be done in person, and that wouldn't be possible until the registry opened on Monday morning. I made a call to the home of a realtor I knew down in Dover, and asked him to do an owner's search for Marybeth Lagenheimer in New Hampshire, but probably in the vicinity of Berlin. The realtor said he'd get back to me in a few minutes.

'Hey. Again, what do we do now?' said Angel.

'Did you get pictures of him with the girl?'

'What are we, idiots? Of course we did.'

'Then stay with him when he leaves. Whatever he has or hasn't done, I think his time as chief is about to come to an end. Once he's safely tucked up at home, we can talk about e-mailing the photographs to Gordon Walsh at Maine CID.' I gave them Walsh's e-mail address from memory, just in case it became necessary to alert him sooner. 'Once you're done with Allan, I want you to keep an eye on Randall Haight.'

My phone beeped. The realtor had come through. I now had an address for an M. Lagenheimer in Gorham, New Hampshire, on the edge of the White Mountain National Forest. There was no phone number connected with the property.

'I have to go,' I told them. 'I'll be back in four or five hours. Remember: Allan first, then Haight.'

'You think Haight could be in trouble?'

'Not just that — I think he could be about to run.'

33

It was a three-hour drive to Gorham, but I did it in closer to two-and-a-half, slowing only as I passed through the towns. For the most part I encountered little traffic once I left Gray behind and went west on Route 26. The big rigs hauling logs on Sunday were heading south, and even the larger standard trucks were gone entirely once I passed South Paris.

Although its setting in the Washington Valley was dramatic, nobody was going to mistake the town of Gorham for anywhere excessively pretty. It functioned as a northern gateway to the White Mountains, so in fall it made its money from hunters, in winter from snowmobilers and winter-sports enthusiasts, and in summer from the rafting and hiking crowd, and those with camps in the woods. It had a couple of decent restaurants, some diners and pizzerias, and a clump of chain fast-food joints at its northern end, where the road continued to Berlin and the prison from which Randall Haight had emerged. In this part of the world, though, it was pronounced *Ber*-lin, not Ber-*lin*, a blue-collar town with a strong French influence, despite its name. The paper mills had once made this part of the state stink pretty badly, just as they once had the town of Lincoln in Maine, which was still routinely referred to as 'Stinkin' Lincoln,' but the big Berlin pulp mill had been demolished in 2007, striking a serious blow to the local economy. Without the Northern State Correctional Facility, the town would have been swaying on its feet and waiting for the referee to stop the fight. Instead, the economics of punishment had saved Berlin and its environs. A prison might have been bad for the soul of a town, but it represented salvation for its finances.

Marybeth Wilson Lagenheimer had purchased a house on Little Pond Lane, a mile or two north of town and within easy reach of the prison by car. An online search indicated that all taxes had been paid to date, and there were no outstanding liens on the property. Just as there was no phone number linked to the address on Little Pond Lane, so too none of the online databases to which I had access listed a cell phone number billed to that address. The utility companies appeared to have no involvement with the property. There were no gas, oil, or electricity accounts. Mrs. Lagenheimer did not have a credit card, and her bank account appeared to be dormant, yet her tax obligations to the town were being met. I could find no death certificate on record for a Marybeth Wilson Lagenheimer. I tried Marybeth Wilson and Marybeth Lagenheimer and got some results on the former, but the ones that fell into the relevant post-2000 period were both in their thirties when they died, which ruled them out. It seemed that Randall Haight's mother was quite the recluse. Maybe she was living off the grid, holed up in Gorham with a generator, a shotgun, and a grudge against the United Nations.

Randall Haight had said that he was no longer in touch with his mother. The dynamics of families never ceased to surprise me, but it struck me as odd that a woman who was so devoted to her son that she would move halfway across the country just to be near him could, in her old age, be cut off by that same son. It wasn't impossible, though, and if Jerry Midas was right then Marybeth Lagenheimer had been damaged in unquantifiable ways by her son's crime and his subsequent incarceration. If she really had tried to pick up their relationship once again at the point at which it had been sundered, with her as the mother and her son as a little boy, then that son, now a man, might well have found her presence stifling to the point of intolerability.

But there was another possible explanation for Mrs. Lagenheimer's silence. Dyscalculia: that was the name for the condition Jerry Midas had described, a less well-known form of dyslexia linked to numbers. There were strategies to cope with it, and it was possible that someone could develop them given time and encouragement, even within the prison system, but to hone them to the extent that one could then go on to make a living through one's ability with numbers seemed unlikely. As I drove west, a picture began to emerge.

The clearer skies of recent days were now under siege from masses of dark cloud as I headed north out of Gorham. There was a storm front heading down from the north, and flooding had been forecast for low-lying areas. I touched base with Louis and Angel, but Allan had not yet left his girlfriend's house. *Chief Allan is a horny dog.* It was an odd turn of phrase. Each time I considered it I heard a woman's voice speaking, and I thought of Mrs. Shaye scattering young girls like pigeons, and the look she had cast in the direction of her employer. But 'cooze'? Would a woman like Mrs. Shaye use that word?

Somewhere out there, too, was Tommy Morris, with Engel circling him but not approaching, waiting for him to make his next move. They should have been tearing Maine apart to find him after that stunt he'd pulled at his sister's house, but they were not. In fact, word of what had occurred had not even made it to the media. It might simply have been Engel trying to save the Bureau's blushes, and for that he could hardly be blamed, but it fitted in with a larger pattern of concealment and gamesmanship that had underpinned all of Engel's actions so far.

And behind it all, like the marks on a wall where a picture had once hung, or the clean space on a dusty shelf, the evidence of absence, was the fact of Anna Kore's disappearance. Allan's relationship with an unusually young woman, Haight's mess of truths, half-truths and possibly outright lies, Engel's desire to entrap Tommy Morris, and Morris's efforts to escape his enemies and perhaps redeem himself by acting on his sister's behalf, all were as nothing compared with the fate of the lost girl. I saw Gordon Walsh framed against the dark and the stars, and I heard him say again that he thought Anna Kore was dead. He might have wished to

431

believe otherwise, but the tenor of his investigation was predicated on the likelihood that she was already the victim of a homicide. He found it difficult to hold two opposing possibilities in his head — one of life, the other of death. The odds favored death, and a shallow grave in the woods. The wardens had been searching with that in mind, and they knew how important it was that the girl's resting place was found before the snows came. Winter would alter the landscape and hide forever any trace of digging and concealment, but this was a huge state and they could not search every inch of it. If Anna Kore's body had been removed any distance at all from Pastor's Bay, it might never be found.

But I wanted her to be alive. I needed her to be alive. I did not want to have to tell my daughter that a young girl had been dragged into the underworld, either vanished forever with no trace of her to be found, or with something of her returned to this world, ruined and decayed and without its soul.

According to my *New Hampshire Atlas Gazetteer*, Little Pond Lane lay off Jimtown Road, right at the edge of Moose Brook State Park. The light was already fading as I found the turn, due in part to the waning of the day but also because of the gathering clouds. There were only two houses on the dead end, one lit and one unlit. The darker house was at the termination of the lane, where the road bled out into forest. It was a manufactured home painted gray and white, with an A-frame roof and a screened front porch. The yard was thick with fallen leaves from

432

the mature trees that surrounded the property. At the back of the house, a shallow slope led down to what I assumed was Little Pond itself, which didn't exceed the expectations raised by its name. It was about fifty feet in circumference, and coated with a pale scum.

I knocked on the porch door for form's sake, but there was no reply. It opened to the touch, but the front door itself was locked, as was the back, and the windows were sealed. Still, it doesn't take much to break into a trailer home; one shattered frame of glass later, I was inside. Apart from some cheap furniture and a couple of polyester rugs, the house was entirely empty. I could find no clothing, no pictures, no indication that anyone lived there. A thin layer of dust coated everything, but it was the accumulation of a couple of months, not years. The bathroom was clean and the mattresses in the two bedrooms were stripped of sheets and pillows, the bed linen neatly folded and placed back in their original zippered packing to save them from damp, the pillows and comforters tied up in big plastic bags from Walmart. There were no personal papers, no photographs, no books. All the drawers and closets were empty.

I went back outside. The dying sun, mostly obscured by clouds, gave a faint yellow tinge to the filth on the pond. I walked around the property, finding nothing untoward apart from the remains of a couple of broken cinder blocks that had accumulated a coating of mold, leaves, and cobwebs. I moved one of the shards and watched insects scurry in alarm across bare earth. I looked back at the house. I could see no cinder blocks, and there was no evidence of any kind of construction nearby, not even a barbecue pit.

I headed down to the other house on the lane. This one was a permanent dwelling, and well maintained, although winter blooms, a child's bicycle, and a battered basketball hoop indicated that this was still a family home. I knocked on the door and a woman opened it. She was plain-looking, and in her early thirties. There was a paring knife in her hand. A boy of two or three peered around her legs, chewing on a piece of raw carrot. I showed her my ID, and explained that I was looking for the owners of the house at the end of the lane.

'Oh, we never got to know them,' she said. 'They'd moved out by the time we moved in. We never met them but once.'

'Do you remember anything about them?'

'Nah. The woman was old. I think her name was Beth or something. Her son lived with her. He was kind of shy. We introduced ourselves after we bought the house, but we couldn't move in for a while. This place had been empty for a couple of years, and it needed a lot of work done to it. My husband did most of it. He knew the old lady to say hi to while he was fixing things up, but he had to stop for winter, and when he got back to work they were gone.'

'How long ago was this?'

'Well, we've been here more than ten years, and that was right at the start.'

'Who looks after the house now?'

'A relative. I think he said he was a cousin, or a nephew. The old lady, Beth, she found the cold too much, he said, and moved down to Florida. Tampa, I think. He comes by a couple of times a year. Sometimes he stays for a night, because we see a lamp burning — there's no power to the house — but he keeps himself to himself. We don't mind. It's not unusual up here.'

'A relative? Not her son.'

'No, he looks like him. He wears his hair the same way, and the same kind of glasses, but it's not him. I have a good memory for faces. Names not so much, but faces I never forget.'

I thanked her and was about to leave when I saw a pile of threaded rods lying by the garage door. They varied in length from three to six feet.

'My husband's in construction,' she explained, then added, 'He'll be back soon,' just in case I had any bad intentions in mind.

'I know this sounds weird,' I said, 'but would you mind if I borrowed one of those rods for a few minutes? I'll bring it back.'

She looked puzzled. 'What will you be using it for?'

'I want to test the ground.'

She looked even more puzzled, but agreed. I picked up a rod that was about four feet long and headed back to the first house. There had been a lot of rain, and the ground was relatively soft so close to the pond, but it was still an effort to force the rod down. Starting at the pile of broken blocks I began to work my way out, probing as deeply as I could at the ground, trying to stick to grids of about two square feet. I'd been working at it for only five minutes when the rain came, and for another five minutes or so when a truck pulled into the yard. Stenciled on the side was the name 'Ron Carroll — Independent Contractor.' A big man in tan work boots, old jeans, and a red windbreaker stepped from the truck.

'How you doing?' he said. 'Mind if I ask what you're at?'

'Mr. Carroll?' I said, trying to buy myself some more time as I continued to probe at the dirt. There was rain dripping down my back, and my clothes were already pasted to my skin, but I wasn't about to stop, not unless someone forced me.

'That's right.'

'I think I met your wife.'

'I think you did. She said you were a detective, and you told her something about wanting to test the ground.'

'That's right. I — '

The rod struck something hard. I pulled it out, shifted position, and inserted it again.

'Do you have another of these rods in the back of your truck?' I asked. The wind must have been gusting at forty miles an hour, and I was starting to shiver. The big nor'easter that had been forecast might ultimately present as snow on the mountains, and when the weaker trees fell they would bring power lines down with them, but here it was falling as icy water. Tonight the cops would be tied up with accidents and power failures. In a way, it was all to the good if I was right about what I believed was buried beneath my feet.

'What have you found?' asked Carroll.

'Broken cinder blocks.'

'Why would somebody bury cinder blocks?'

He was beside me now, his shoulders hunched against the rain. I pulled out the rod and moved it a foot to the right. This time it encountered no obstacle. I moved it two feet to the left. It went in eighteen inches before hitting stone.

'To keep something from being dug up by animals,' I said. 'You remember Mrs. Lagenheimer? Your wife knew her as Beth.'

'Yeah, the woman who used to live here with her son. She moved out years ago.'

I leaned on the rod. My back ached from pushing, and my hands were raw.

'No,' I said, 'I don't think she ever left.'

* * *

It didn't take us long, working together and using the rest of the rods from Carroll's truck, to mark out the boundaries of what I believed was a grave. The rough rectangle was six feet in length and about two in width. When we were done, I gave Carroll one of my cards and told him that I'd be back as soon as I could.

'Shouldn't we call the cops?' he said.

'They're not going to come out tonight,' I said, 'not in weather like this. Even if they do, they won't be able to make a start on a dig until it gets light again. And, you know, it may just be a pile of broken blocks.'

'Yeah.' Carroll didn't sound as if he believed that was the case. I could barely hear him above the sound of the wind and the beating of the rain.

'Look, I'll call them from the road, okay?' I said in an effort to mollify him. He was a big man, and I didn't want him to try to stop me leaving. He wouldn't succeed, but if things got physical one or both of us would get hurt.

'I don't get why you can't just call them now,' said Carroll. 'And maybe you should stick around, you know? Doesn't seem proper for you to just leave if you're right about there being a body buried here.'

Bodies, I thought, but I didn't say that.

'You have my card,' I said. 'Whoever, or whatever, is down there isn't going anywhere.' Then I told him the truth, or something of it. 'And I think I know who did this, and I want to see his face when I tell him I've been here.'

Carroll searched for the lie, the rain streaming from our faces, and didn't find it.

'I don't hear from them in an hour, then I'll call them myself,' he said.

I thanked him. At his invitation, I followed him back to his house in my car and he gave me a towel with which to dry myself, and a flask of coffee to warm me on the journey. I called Randall Haight from the road. He answered on the second ring.

'Mr. Haight, it's Charlie Parker.'

He didn't sound happy to hear from me. I didn't care.

'What's this about, Mr. Parker? You're no longer working on my behalf.'

438

'Tommy Morris,' I lied. 'We think he's going to make his move soon.'

'Am I in danger?'

'I don't know, but I'd like to get you out of there. I want you to pack some clothes, then sit tight until I get to you, okay?'

'Yes, absolutely,' he said, the fact that he had fired me now conveniently set aside. 'How long will it take?'

He was scared, and he wasn't pretending.

'Not long,' I said. 'Not long at all.'

You have to be careful what lies you tell. You have to be careful in case your lies are heard, and the gods of the underworld mock you by turning them to truths.

34

I was half an hour from Pastor's Bay when Angel called.

'Allan is on the move again.'

'Going home?'

'Kinda. He came part of the way, then stopped at a gas station and made a call. Now he's sitting in his truck smoking a cigarette, and not in a relaxed way. He's making me nervous, he's wound so tight. Why does someone with a cell use a pay phone?'

'Because he doesn't want anyone to have a record of the call.'

'Exactly.'

'Keep a note of the time of the call, but stay with him.'

'You sure? What about Haight?'

'He's not going to run out before I get there. He thinks I'm coming to protect him.'

'And you aren't?'

'I just want to talk to him. I'll do it at gunpoint if I have to, but it may not come to that.'

I was close now, and I was starting to understand something of the nature of the man who called himself Randall Haight. I believed that Marybeth Lagenheimer, Randall Haight's mother, was buried on her property near Gorham, New Hampshire. What I didn't know was if she was alone down there, but I was guessing that she had some company in the

440

grave. The man who occupied the neat, anonymous house with the ugly paintings on the wall had put her there. He had graduated from the killing of a child to the murder of an adult. He had piled lie upon lie, identity upon identity, creating a series of new selves without cracking or revealing the truth about his imposture, and only the intervention of an outside force, an anonymous tormentor, had finally threatened his existence. He was a killer who had taken the lives of at least two people, their deaths separated by decades but connected by the blood that flowed from the first killing to the next.

Yet Randall Haight, or the man who claimed to be Randall Haight, still had an alibi for the time of Anna Kore's disappearance courtesy of Chief Kurt Allan, who was himself apparently a predatory male with a taste for younger women. If they were working together, it made sense for Allan to have provided Haight with an alibi. If they weren't, I had simply exchanged the mystery of Anna Kore's fate, for which I didn't have an answer, for another mystery, one for which I thought I did have a solution.

The road was dark and empty as I drove. Rain had fallen here too, but the storm from the north had been at its strongest over New Hampshire and large parts of Vermont. Coastal Maine, by comparison, had barely been touched. Lights burned in Pastor's Bay, and through the window of the police department I could see figures moving. The State Police Winnebago was still in the lot, but its windows were dark. There was no sign of the big SUVs beloved of Engel and his agents.

Randall Haight had drawn the drapes at his living-room window, but a sliver of light was visible through the gap. I peered in and saw him sitting at the kitchen table with his back to me. Three cardboard storage boxes were piled one on top of another on the floor beside him.

I rang the front doorbell. My gun was by my side, but I kept my body turned from the door so that it was not visible.

'Who is it?' said Haight. 'Who's there?'

He was calling from inside the living room. I could hear the fear in his voice. I wondered if he had a gun.

'It's Charlie Parker, Mr. Haight.'

Footsteps approached the door, and I heard the security chain being removed. When he opened the door his hands were empty, and there were two suitcases in the hallway.

'I see you're planning a trip,' I said.

'Even before you called, I felt that it would be safer for me if I left town for a while. I planned to inform the police tomorrow morning. I've made a reservation at a hotel at Bar Harbor. I printed off a copy of the reservation confirmation for the authorities.'

He saw the gun in my hand.

'Am I in danger, Mr. Parker?'

'No, Lonny.' I raised the gun and pointed it at him. 'But am I?'

Lonny Midas didn't react. He didn't become fearful or angry. He merely looked confused. In truth, I don't think even he knew who he was anymore, not for sure.

'You'd better come in,' he said. 'I don't think

we have much time.'

He backed up. I entered the house and pushed the door closed behind me.

'Why do you say that?'

'It's a sign. Your coming here, it's a sign. Soon the others will come too, and then it will all be over. It's already started.'

'What others, Lonny?'

He just shook his head. His eyes were glassy, and his smile was that of a man who has glimpsed the guillotine from the window of his cell and feels the first touch of the madness that will cloud his fear and make the end easier to bear. He retreated into the living room, his hands held away from his sides, the palms upturned. His shirt was clean and neatly pressed, his tie a pale pink. I could see that he was not armed, but I put him against the wall and frisked him anyway, just to be sure. He did not object. He said only 'Have you seen her?'

'Who? Anna Kore?'

I stepped away from him and he turned slowly around.

'She likes you,' he went on, as though I had not spoken. 'I knew it from the first time you came here. Then she came to me one last time and I thought that I understood. Did she go to you? Is that why she left me?'

'I don't know what you're talking about, Lonny.'

'I think you do. Not Anna. It was never about Anna. I'm talking about Selina Day. Will you tell her that I'm sorry?'

'I think you need to sit down,' I said, and he

443

understood that he would receive no confirmation of his beliefs or his fears from me.

'Never mind,' he said. 'I'll tell her myself, when she comes.'

★   ★   ★

He thought that he had always intended to kill William Lagenheimer. He'd given himself other reasons for finding him, but secretly he knew how any meeting between them would conclude. It had all been William's fault: the years in jail, the pain inflicted upon him by others, the haunting by Selina Day that would, in time, become something else, something more complex and ineffable, although that would only be revealed to others later upon the discovery of his diary. All of it was William's fault because he was weak and couldn't keep his mouth shut. They had been friends, William and Lonny, and friends were supposed to look out for each other. Friends didn't tell. They kept their secrets. He'd warned William about that, just before they closed in on Selina Day and began putting their hands on her body.

'You mustn't tell, William. Whatever happens, you mustn't tell.' Sometimes he would annoy William by calling him Billy, but not this time. It was too serious for that. They were about to do something Very Bad.

'I won't tell,' said William, and Lonny had wanted to believe him. He had wanted to believe him so badly that he swallowed his doubts and ignored the way William's eyes couldn't quite meet his. His mouth was dry and the blood was pounding in his head. He could almost feel the girl beneath him, the warmth of her, the smell of her. He needed William there to help him, to make it happen.

They'd both wanted to do it. Of course, that wasn't the way William told it once they'd made him cry by telling him that they'd lock him away from his mommy for years and years, lock him away and put him in with the big men, and you didn't want to know what the big men would do to you. *Remember what you wanted to do to Selina Day, Billy? Well, they'll do that to you, except it'll hurt more. They'll do it over and over until the pain gets so bad that you'll want to die. You'll call for your mommy, but she won't be there to help you. Right now, we're the only ones who can help you, Billy, so you'd better start telling us the truth, because not far from here your friend Lonny is being offered the same deal, and the first one who comes clean wins the teddy bear. He gets looked after, and there'll be doctors who will try to help him be a better person, and the big men won't get to lay their hands on him. The other one, the one who doesn't talk in time, he'll get thrown to the wolves. That's the deal. That's the way these things work. So you'd better start talking before your friend does.*

Except Lonny wouldn't talk. Lonny would never tell. He kept his arms folded and he didn't cry, not even when one of the policemen hit him so hard across the back of the head that his vision went funny and he bit the inside of his

445

cheek and had to spit the blood from his mouth. Every time they asked him why he'd killed the girl he just shook his head, and the only words he spoke were to tell them that he hadn't done anything at all, that he didn't know what they were talking about. And even as he spoke he knew they were asking William the same questions in another room, and he prayed and prayed that William would be strong just this once, that he'd remain true to his promise and keep their secret. He refused to countenance any other possibility, as though by sheer force of will he could hold William together just as he was holding himself together.

But William had broken, and that was why they blamed Lonny for everything that happened. Poor little William Lagenheimer was led astray by the bad boy. William was really sorry for his part in what had happened to Selina Day; he'd tried to make Lonny stop, but Lonny was too strong for him.

But William didn't tell the police that he'd touched the girl too, and that when she started bucking and kicking it had been he who pinned her legs so she couldn't throw Lonny off. Oh, he'd been crying when he did it, but Lonny didn't have to tell him to hold her down. He just knew. Still, it had been Lonny who suffocated her, and it was Lonny who was portrayed as the leader, the instigator, the 'alpha' as one of the psychiatrists termed him, and so it was that the big man got to play with Lonny, just as they'd promised, although he didn't get to play with him for long. The girl had seen to that.

It hadn't been difficult to find out where William was staying after his release. After all, his mother didn't try too hard to hide her tracks. She always had been a dumb bitch, doting on her little boy. All she cared about was looking after him again: cooking for him, washing his clothes, ensuring that he had a clean bed and a safe place to stay once they let him out. She trusted people to send on her mail to a post-office box in Berlin, as though ten miles between the box and her home would make any difference, and she'd never considered how she might be in danger of undoing all the good work that had been put into giving the boys new identities. Even the Negroes no longer spoke of the killing of Selina Day, or of what they were going to do to the two boys who murdered her. She was gone to a better place, and forgotten by most.

Except that part of Selina Day had stayed — the angry part, the vengeful part — and she wouldn't let Lonny forget her. It was she who had whispered to Lonny that there was unfinished business with his old friend, and maybe he ought to look him up once he was a free man again. So Lonny had made some calls, including one to his brother, Jerry, and Jerry told him what he knew about Mrs. Lagenheimer, because Jerry had been forced to make trips to Drake Creek to settle their mother's affairs, and people had talked, the way people will talk. Lonny didn't tell Jerry what he was planning to do, and he didn't know if Jerry suspected anything. If he did, Jerry was too smart to ask.

They never spoke again, but that was Lonny's decision. It was easier that way.

Both he and William had been released within a couple of months of each other — William first, Lonny later — and Lonny had been worried that William and his mother might already have moved on by the time he got to New Hampshire, but William was in the throes of a deep depression, and the medication prescribed to combat it meant that he was even less resistant to his mother's suffocating love than he might otherwise have been. Lonny had found William walking in the woods near the shitty little trailer home that his mother had bought — *bought!* She was so dumb that she hadn't even rented, as if a guy being released from jail in a strange state would want to stay living within a few miles of his final prison. But William was too battered and acquiescent to strike out for himself when he was released, and had they been left to their own devices they might have remained there on a dirt road beside a stinking pond until one or both of them passed away.

So there was William, his hands in his pockets, his whole body bent slightly after years of trying to deflect the attention of predatory men by making himself smaller and less obvious. Lonny approached him from behind when William stopped to stare at his reflection in that scummy pond, so that Lonny's own reflection gradually appeared next to William's. Their time behind bars had accentuated rather than diluted the similarities that had always existed between them. They were both carrying jail weight from bad food, and their faces were prematurely aged and weathered. Lonny stood straighter than William, though, and his hair was lighter and longer. In addition, William now wore spectacles, the cheap metal frames making him appear at once sadder and more vulnerable.

For a moment William just stared at the two reflections, as though uncertain whether he was seeing a manifestation of a real being or a wraith conjured up by his own damaged mind. Then the figure said his name, and William heard it spoken and knew that what he was seeing was real. He turned around slowly, and instantly they were fourteen again, with William taking the subordinate role, except this time there was an added sense of resignation to his posture and speech. Like Lonny, he had always known that they would meet again. Perhaps that was why he hadn't objected to his mother's preparations, and hadn't tried to move far from the prison. He was waiting, waiting for Lonny to come.

'How you doing, Lonny?' he asked.

'I'm okay, William. You?'

'Okay, I guess. When did you get out?'

'A couple of weeks back. It's good to be free again, right?'

'Uh-huh.'

William blinked, and pushed his spectacles farther up his nose, although it didn't seem to Lonny that they'd dropped since they'd begun talking. Maybe it was a nervous tic. His tongue licked at the little scar on the left side of his upper lip. Lonny noted its presence. William hadn't been marked in that way when Lonny knew him as a boy.

'How'd you find me?' asked William.

'Your momma. Her mail. It wasn't hard.'

'It's nice here,' said William. 'Peaceful. You want to go inside, have a soda or something?'

'You got anything stronger?'

'No. I'm on medication. I'm not supposed to drink alcohol. It doesn't matter so much. I tried it when I got out but I didn't like the taste.'

'Could be you just tried the wrong kind.'

'It was whisky,' William said. 'I don't remember the name. I went to a bar. I thought that was what you were supposed to do, you know, when you got out. That's what everyone else talked about doing.'

He sounds so young, Lonny thought. It's like he froze mentally at fourteen, so that his body grew older while his consciousness stayed the same.

'That's what I did,' said Lonny. 'I thought it tasted good. Got me some pussy too.'

William blushed. 'Gosh, Lonny,' he said. 'Gosh.'

You child, thought Lonny. You weak little boy.

'What are they calling you now, William?'

'Randall. Randall Haight. I don't know why they chose that name. They just did. And you?'

'Daniel Ross. I don't know why they chose that either.'

'It's an okay name.'

'Yes, it is. Let's go inside, 'Randall.' It's cold.'

Side by side, they walked back to the house.

'My momma's out,' said William. 'She plays

bingo at the American Legion every Friday. Before that, she has dinner at a restaurant and reads her magazines. I went with her a couple of times, but I think she preferred being alone.' The house came into view. 'I heard that your momma and poppa died,' said William. 'I'm sorry.'

'Yeah. Well, you know.'

Lonny trailed off. He didn't want to talk about that. They were gone, and that was the end of it.

The inside of the house smelled of damp clothes and bad cooking. William took two cans of soda from the refrigerator, but Lonny had already found a bottle of vodka in one of the kitchen closets.

'Thought you said you didn't have anything stronger?'

'That's momma's!' said William. He sounded scandalized.

'She won't mind,' said Lonny.

'She will. It's hers. She'll know someone has been supping from it.'

'She won't, William. Trust me. I'll make it right with her.'

'No, you can't be here when she gets back. She won't like it.'

'Why is that?'

William clammed up. This wasn't a subject that he wanted to explore.

'Because I'm the bad one, right? Because I made her little boy do a bad thing?'

William remained silent, but Lonny knew that it was true.

'I know that's what she thinks,' continued Lonny. 'I know, because that's what everyone thinks.'

He found two glasses, poured a generous measure of vodka into each, then added Coke from one of the cans. He handed a glass to William.

'Take it.'

'I don't want it.'

'Take it, William, and drink it. Trust me. It'll make things easier in the long run.'

William took the glass. He sipped at the drink, but didn't like the taste. He started to cry.

'Drink it, William.'

'I'm sorry, Lonny,' said William. 'I'm so sorry.'

Lonny forced the glass back to his mouth and made him drink. When the glass was empty, he refilled it.

'More.'

'I don't want any more.'

'Just do it. For me.'

He clinked his own glass against William's in a toast, then drank long. Already, William looked a little woozy. He held the glass in two hands and drank. This time he didn't struggle so much with the liquor, but he was still crying. There was snot dripping from his nose, and a string of spittle linked his mouth to the glass.

'You weren't supposed to tell,' said Lonny. 'You were never supposed to tell.'

William just stared at the floor, his body jerking with the force of his sobs.

Lonny put his glass in the sink. He didn't want to make a mess. A mess would make it more likely that he'd be caught. He took the rope from the pocket of his coat. He'd told himself that he was only going to use it to scare William, or tie him up if he had to, but it was a lie, just one of many lies he would be forced to tell, and to live.

'I'm sorry, Lonny,' William repeated, but his voice was different now. The sobbing suddenly ceased. 'But you should be sorry too for what we did to Selina Day.'

He swallowed the last of the vodka and Coke, then turned and knelt on the floor, his back to Lonny. Lonny couldn't move. He had expected arguments, or excuses, but not this: not this abject surrender.

'Don't hurt my momma,' said William. 'She's a nice lady.'

It was those words that broke the spell on Lonny and set in motion all that was to follow. He flipped the rope over William's neck, put his knee against his back, and slowly strangled him. And when William's mother came home he did the same to her.

On that night William Lagenheimer ceased to exist, but Randall Haight did not.

★　★　★

At the kitchen table, the man who had once been Lonny Midas, then briefly Daniel Ross, and finally Randall Haight, pushed his spectacles farther up the bridge of his nose. He still didn't need them, and the lenses were just clear glass, but they were a part of who he was, even down to that little tic. He'd seen William do it, and he'd absorbed it. After all, he hadn't had a whole lot to work with, so he'd taken whatever of Randall Haight that he could. The scar he'd

453

created with a razor, and it had hurt like a bitch. The rest he'd made up himself.

'They blamed Lonny for everything,' he said. 'William was innocent, Lonny was guilty. Becoming William seemed the perfect solution.'

'Where's Anna Kore, Lonny?'

'I told you already: I don't know. Selina didn't know either. If she was dead, Selina would have told me. She might even have brought her along to show me. The dead know the dead. But, dead or alive, I didn't have anything to do with her disappearance.'

I heard a voice say, 'I don't believe you,' but it wasn't my own. I tried to move, but I was too slow. I caught a glimpse of three men as I rose, and then there was a shocking pain in my head as the first blow connected. Others followed, but after the first three or four I ceased to feel anything at all.

35

Kurt Allan pulled up a short distance from the entrance to the department building, and killed his engine. The department's Explorer was parked up, which meant that Ken Foster, Allan's senior officer, was inside. Knowing Foster, he probably already had a cup of coffee in his hand, and was scavenging for sweet foods. Allan was right. When he entered, Foster's large ass was facing the door as he poked around in the closet beneath the coffee machine.

'Quiet night?' said Allan.

'Hungry night,' said Foster's voice from inside the closet. 'And the staties have cleaned us out. I think they even ate the bugs.'

'Why didn't you pack a sandwich?'

'I did pack a sandwich. Then I left the sandwich on the kitchen table.'

Allan liked Foster. Hell, Allan had hired him, so he supposed that he must have known what he was doing. Foster wasn't about to solve a great mystery anytime soon, but his heart was in the right place and he managed to combine an inability to take shit from anyone with a gentle hand, which was no mean trick. The big man emerged from his foraging and took a seat behind the empty reception area.

'You're out late,' he said.

'I find it hard to relax lately.'

'Yeah, me too.' Foster toyed with his coffee

cup, and watched Allan take some papers from his in-box. 'Detective Walsh left those,' he said.

It was the report on the analysis of the envelopes sent to Randall Haight. From what Allan could tell, it contained nothing of note: no hairs, saliva, or DNA. There was something about organic matter, but it was complicated and he was too distracted to take it all in. If it had been important, someone would have called him.

'Anything?' asked Foster.

'Nothing.'

'Chief, you think she's still alive?'

It was the first time Foster had asked him that question. Allan knew that it had been on his mind, because it was on everyone's mind. He'd found Mrs. Shaye looking up newspaper reports on the Internet of girls who'd been missing for years and years before they turned up, like that girl in the basement in Austria, or the kid who'd been found living in a makeshift home of tents and sheds at the back of her abductors' property. They were the exceptions, though, and what they went through during the period of their captivity didn't bear thinking about. Too often, snatched girls turned up dead, and that was only if their captors were careless, or unlucky, or just didn't give a rat's ass either way if they left trace evidence or not. The smart ones made sure that their victims were never discovered.

'She's still alive,' said Allan. 'She's still alive until we find out otherwise. Look, why don't you go get something to eat? Buddy's is still serving food, right?'

'Yeah, bar snacks.'

'Go eat. I'll take care of things here.'

'You sure?'

'I don't have anything better to do. At least I won't be worrying about your delicate constitution.'

Foster didn't argue. Allan watched him drive away. When he was sure that Foster was safely gone, Allan checked the time once more. His cell phone rang twice, stopped, then rang twice again. The number, in each case, was blocked.

Allan sat back in his chair. It had begun.

★　★　★

Angel and Louis watched the station house from the shadows off Main. Both were uneasy about Allan but uncertain of how to act beyond simply staying with him. If Allan did have Anna Kore, then she wasn't on his property. Similarly, a search of his girlfriend's apartment while Allan bought her and the kid an ice-cream down the street had revealed no trace of her, which meant that if Allan was involved in her disappearance Anna was either being looked after by another party or she was dead. Randall Haight might have provided an answer to that question by now, but there had been no word from Parker, and when they tried his phone it had simply rung out.

'What do you think?' said Angel.

'I think Allan's staying in there until fat boy comes back,' said Louis.

'We have him tagged.'

'Yes, we do.'

'So if he moves, we'll know where he went.'

'That we will.'

'Wouldn't hurt to swing by Randall Haight's place, just to make sure all is copacetic.'

'Wouldn't hurt at all.'

Louis started the car, and made a U-turn so that they wouldn't have to enter the main street. They headed east. About half a mile from Randall Haight's house, they saw night hunters heading into the woods. Three of the five men had shotguns in their hands. It was not an uncommon sight during hunting season.

Except it was Sunday, and hunting was illegal in the state of Maine on Sundays.

* * *

I never lost consciousness entirely. I was aware of the sound of fists slapping flesh, and I heard snatches of questions and fragments of answers. At some point I managed to turn my head, but my vision was blurred and I could barely make out Lonny Midas's form in the chair. I could see the blood, though, for his face and shirt were stained red.

Eventually I was lifted to my feet. I struggled to stand. The pain in my head was ferocious, and I felt dizzy and nauseated. I seemed to be deaf in my right ear. I was allowed to fall back to the floor. Somebody grabbed my legs and began dragging me. My head banged against the kitchen step, and then there was wet grass under my back, and stars peered coldly through the gaps in the clouds. The grass turned to dirt and leaves, and the sky was fractured by the branches of bare trees. The cold and damp of the night air cleared some of the fog from my mind. I lay on my side and watched what was about to occur, powerless to prevent it.

Lonny Midas was on his knees in the clearing. His face was ruined. I wasn't even sure that he could see anymore. A long thread of viscous blood hung from his mouth, and his breath whistled through the mess of his nose.

Two men stood over him, one young and redheaded, the second older, with long dark hair. To one side, a third man in his sixties watched them. He was bald, and heavyset. I thought he might be Tommy Morris, for I had seen pictures of his younger self in the documents sent from my Boston source.

'Ask him again,' said the oldest of the three.

'He doesn't know anything, Tommy,' said the dark-haired man.

'Martin, I told you to ask him again.'

The one named Martin leaned over to talk to Lonny Midas.

'He just wants to know where the girl is. Tell him, and we'll let you go.'

Lonny shook his head, but said nothing.

'We're losing him,' said Martin, but Morris didn't reply.

Martin tried again. 'If you know where she is, just nod. We'll clean you up, and we'll go and get her. It'll be for the best.'

But Lonny just shook his head again.

'I swear, Tommy, he doesn't know. If he knew, he'd have told us by now. I couldn't stand up to the punishment he's taken.'

'What about him?' said Tommy, pointing at me. 'You didn't ask him what he knows.'

'He's a private detective, Tommy,' said Martin. 'He doesn't have your niece.'

'Maybe he knows where she is.'

There was something robotic in the way Tommy Morris was speaking. Looking back, I believe he could think only of Anna Kore, for she was all that he had to keep himself moving forward.

'Tommy,' said Martin, and he spoke as gently as he could, 'if he knew where she was he'd have told the cops. I've heard of this guy. He doesn't screw around.'

The redheaded man had drawn his gun. He was pointing it at the back of Lonny Midas's head.

'Frankie,' said Martin. 'What are you doing?'

'He killed a little girl,' said Frankie, and a kind of sob caught in his throat. 'What kind of man does that?'

'It was a long time ago,' said Martin. 'He did it when he was a kid himself.'

'It doesn't matter,' said Frankie. 'None of it matters. I just want it to end.'

'He's right,' said Morris. 'Kill him. Kill them both.'

Martin took a gun from his coat. He looked at it for a moment, contemplating what was ahead, then pointed it at the one called Frankie.

'Put the gun down, Francis.'

'What?'

'Put it down. Slowly.'

460

'He's a child killer! He's a piece of garbage. Nobody's going to miss him. Nobody!'

Martin shifted position slightly, so that both Frankie and Tommy Morris were under his gun.

'What's this about, Martin?' said Tommy.

'It's over, Tommy, that's what this is about. I'm a federal agent.'

Tommy didn't react at first. Slowly, a smile spread across his face.

'No, you're not.'

'Francis, I mean it: You put the gun down. Tommy, you keep your hands where I can see them.'

'You're not a federal agent, Martin. You're one of us. You've drunk with us, you've beaten men down with us. You've even killed for us.'

'I never killed for you, Tommy. Those people you sent me after, they disappeared, but not the way you thought. Even the Napiers are under federal protection now.'

'The panty hose,' said Frankie. He spoke as if remembering a dream. 'Mrs. Napier. I thought you raped her, but she wasn't wearing any panty hose when we went into the house, and later there was a panty hose on the floor. You never touched her. It was all a set-up.'

'I'm not a rapist, Francis, and I'm not a killer either, but I'm giving you one last warning. Put — '

But Frankie wasn't listening. He raised his gun from Lonny's head, and Martin shot him twice in the upper body.

'Ah, Jesus,' said Tommy, and then there were men moving in the shadows behind him, hunters

461

in shades of gray, and I thought: This is wrong.

The forest exploded with gunfire. There were shots from behind me, shots from right and left. I ran for cover, staggering like a drunk. A bullet blew splinters and bark from a tree close to my head, and I hit the ground. I thought that I heard someone run through the bushes nearby, but I couldn't see him clearly. I had no gun, and could see no way of acquiring one. I found the cover of a big tree and picked up a fallen branch. It was better than nothing, but only barely. After what seemed like too long a time, the shooting ceased, and I heard a familiar voice call my name.

'It's done,' said Angel. 'It's done.'

★ ★ ★

With the first shot, Lonny had hit the ground. He had learned in prison that when trouble started it was best to keep your head down, or else somebody would beat it down for you. As the shooting continued, he had crawled through the dirt and fallen leaves like the wounded beast that he was until he slipped into a depression in the earth. His eyes were almost swollen shut, but he could see and, more important, hear well enough to take himself away from the conflict. There were men in camouflage clothing, and they had fired first. Then a black man and a smaller white man had appeared from the woods, shooting as they came, and three of the hunters had fallen beneath their guns. That was when Lonny ran. He had no idea who was shooting at whom, or why. All he knew was

462

that he had been standing at the precipice, facing the void, and now he had been offered the chance of living. When he was sure that he was unobserved, he made his break from the woods.

The night gave him cover as he ran, and the sounds of gunfire receded. He realized that he was heading east, away from his home and toward the main road. He needed help; the men had hurt him badly. After the initial burst of adrenaline that had taken him away from them he had slowed down, and he was now aware of the intense pain in his face and in his belly. They had broken something, maybe a rib or two. There was an ache in his innards. Somehow he managed to keep moving, but he felt his strength ebbing, and he forced himself to walk more carefully. He feared that, if he fell, he would never rise again.

He came to the road, and turned left, heading for the town. There were other houses nearby. His nearest neighbors, the Rowleys, always kept a light burning at night, and he could almost see it through the trees. He stumbled on, his right arm stretched across his body as he tried to hold himself together physically and mentally. He heard a vehicle approaching, and in his confused state he struggled to discern the direction from which it was coming. If it was coming from behind, then it might be the men who had tortured him arriving to finish the job they had started. If it came from town, it might be someone who could help him. The pain inside was growing worse. It wasn't just his ribs that were busted. The men had burst something soft and vital in there, and the stuff of it was spilling out.

Headlights illuminated the trees ahead of him, and he began to weep with relief: The vehicle had come from Pastor's Bay. He waved his left hand to flag it down as it came around the bend, and it slowed in response. Lonny moved to the side of the road as it pulled up alongside him, and he recognized the driver before the window rolled down.

'Oh, thank God,' said Lonny. 'Thank God it's you.'

The night air shimmered, the atoms forming themselves into the shapes of a girl and a man. They were holding hands, Selina Day's left hand clasped tightly in William Lagenheimer's right. Selina extended her right hand, inviting Lonny to join them. He didn't want to go with her. He knew where she wanted to take him. They were leaving this earth, all three of them together.

He was about to utter his final words when Chief Allan shot him in the chest.

⋆   ⋆   ⋆

The man named Frankie was not yet dead. He lay on the ground, the life bubbling redly from him. The other one, Martin, knelt beside him, gently stroking his head as the last breaths forced themselves from Frankie's body, and his mouth opened as he tried to speak of what he was seeing, and his eyes grew wide with the wonder of it before the life left them forever.

Tommy Morris was slumped at the base of a

464

tree, one cheek lying against the bark, the other shattered by one of the bullets that had killed him. Three men lay dead nearby, their hunting clothes stained dark by blood and shadows. A fourth had been shot in the guts and the legs. He would live if help got to him in time. The fifth man had fled the fighting, and Angel and Louis had let him go.

Martin was injured. His left arm hung uselessly at his side, the radius and ulna shattered by shotgun pellets. He did not weep over the body of the young man that he had killed, although his face was a mask of grief. He got to his feet, and looked for the first time at Angel and Louis.

'They're with me,' I said.

'There'll be questions to answer,' said Martin.

'Not by them,' I said.

'Then tell them to get out of here. That's all I owe them.'

Without another word, Angel and Louis left us. My vision was still blurred at the edges, but my balance was improving. The pain in my ear was no longer as severe, and I could almost stand without swaying.

'Which one of you hit me?' I asked.

'We all did,' he said.

'You worked Lonny Midas over pretty good as well.'

'I did what I had to do. And I thought his name was Randall Haight.'

'Randall Haight's dead. A man named Lonny Midas killed him and took his place.'

'Why?'

'Because he didn't want to be who he was anymore. Because he didn't *know* who he was anymore.'

'They'll find him,' he said, then corrected himself. 'We'll find him.'

'Assuming he lives long enough after that beating.'

'I did what I had to do,' Martin repeated.

'For what? Because you thought he had the girl, or just because Tommy Morris told you to do it?'

He thought about the question. His eyes were dull. 'I don't know.'

'Is Martin even your real name?'

'Does it matter?'

I watched him take a cell phone from his pocket and start to dial.

'I'm going to look for Lonny,' I said.

'No, you stay here.'

'Go to hell,' I said, and started to walk away.

'I told you to stay here,' said Martin, and his tone made me turn back. The cell phone was now in his left hand, held awkwardly because of the pain, and a gun had taken its place in his right.

'You've spent too long in the darkness, Martin,' I said.

The gun wavered, then fell.

'My name's not Martin,' he said.

'I don't care,' I replied, and I left him to the shadows.

★ ★ ★

466

I found Lonny Midas lying in a ditch by the side of the road. His was the second body that I found. The first was that of the hunter who had run. He lay only a few feet from Midas, just beyond the tree line. Lonny had been shot through the heart at close range, the hunter in the chest and head. Not far from the hunter's body lay a cheap, matte-finish, carbon-steel Colt Commander. The hunter's own pistol was still in his hand.

I sat down with my back against rough bark and waited with them until the lights came from the south.

V

In the worst of all men there is a little bit of good that can destroy them.

William Rose (1914–1987)

36

I spent a long night at the Pastor's Bay Police Department. The local doctor, an elderly gentleman who looked as if he'd graduated from medical school with Hippocrates himself, took a quick look at me and decided that I was suffering from a burst eardrum and a mild concussion. I might have disputed the use of the word 'mild,' but it didn't seem worth the effort. I was advised not to sleep for a while, but as there were lots of questions being asked, and only a limited number of living people available to answer them, sleep wasn't really an option. So night became morning, and still the questions came. To some I had answers, and to others I had none.

Sometimes I just lied.

At first light, the New Hampshire state police started digging in the garden of Randall Haight's former residence, alerted by a call from Carroll, the details of which were confirmed by me while I tried to deal with inquiries about an entirely different set of corpses. It didn't take them long to reach the blocks. Beneath them were Randall Haight and his mother. Decomposition of the bodies in the cool, damp soil had been slowed by saponification. When they were revealed, the Haights' remains were coated in a waxy adipocere formed from the bodies' proteins and fats. They resembled insects frozen in their pupal stage.

Then the records arrived from North Dakota,

471

and it was remarked how alike William Lagenheimer and Lonnie Midas had been, even as boys.

I never learned the real name of the FBI man who had been known as Martin Dempsey to Tommy Morris and his associates. Within hours, he was gone from Pastor's Bay, and in the reports that followed he would be referred to only as an 'undercover operative.' He left me with more lies to tell. I told Walsh that I did not know the identities of the two men who had intervened to save Dempsey from Oweny Farrell's men. In the confusion of all that had occurred, and all that was still happening, I don't think he cared. It might also have been the case that Engel, who drifted in to listen for a time then drifted out again, knew or suspected the answer to the question already, and took the view that the truth would only complicate an already troublesome situation. Dempsey was alive only because of Louis's and Angel's intervention, and the one thing that could have made Engel's life worse at that moment was the presence of a dead FBI man in Pastor's Bay.

Finally, a temporary halt was called to the questions. The doctor came back and examined me again. He gave me some more painkillers and told me that it was probably okay for me to sleep now. I told him that I was going to sleep anyway, whether he thought it was advisable or not, because I couldn't stay awake any longer, and if I never woke up again I wouldn't be sorry. If Engel hadn't followed him into the room, I'd have curled up on the floor right there and then with my jacket for a pillow. Instead, I drew on the last of my energy to keep my head clear.

Engel bore the weary expression of a man who had held on to his stocks for a little too long, and had watched them plummet just as he had hoped to cash them in. All that he had left was junk. Tommy Morris was dead, and all his knowledge had died with him. Engel's undercover man was out of the game, and was a prime candidate for an extended period of therapy. If my head hadn't been aching so badly I might almost have felt sorry for Engel, but, as it was, his undercover agent was one of the reasons that my head was aching to begin with. Since he was no longer around to blame, I was happy to let Engel carry the can.

'Hell of a mess to clean up,' I said.

'I've had a lot of practice,' he replied, then added, 'You're lucky to be alive.'

'I've had a lot of practice too.'

Engel took a notebook from his pocket and opened it to a blank page. He laid a gold fountain pen beside it.

'I've finished the initial debriefing of Martin Dempsey,' he said.

'I hope you took his gun away. I don't think he's too sure about where it should be pointed.'

'He's been deep for a long time. To be good at it, you have to subsume your old self in a new identity. It can be hard to restore it again, but I'm confident that he will.'

'Is that part of your speech for the press conference? It sounds trite enough.'

'You could always sue the federal government

for the injuries you've received.'

'I'll add them to the list,' I said. 'The FBI already owes me a family.'

In what probably passed for a gesture of contrition, Engel closed his notebook without having written a word.

'Six men died in that initial confrontation: five at the scene, and one more on his way to the hospital. Francis Ryan was killed by Dempsey before the real shooting began, and Dempsey says that he also fatally wounded one of his attackers. You didn't have a weapon. Tommy Morris died at the hands of Farrell's killers. That leaves three men unaccounted for. Dempsey says that he didn't see anyone else clearly, but he was aware of figures in the forest who might have taken down the remaining shooters. You have anything to add to that?'

'Nothing except my grateful thanks to those involved.'

'I figured you'd say that. You tell your hired gunmen to stay out of the state for a time. I'd also advise them against visiting bars in Dorchester, Somerville, and Charlestown. You never know how word spreads in these cases.'

'Which raises an interesting question,' I said. 'How did Tommy Morris find out about Randall Haight, or Lonny Midas as we now know him? Somebody leaked the substance of the interview with him, otherwise Morris and your confused operative wouldn't have ended up pummeling him in a chair. Were you responsible? Was it a calculated gamble to make Tommy trust Dempsey more?'

'It wasn't us,' said Engel.

'You're sure?'

'I have no reason to lie to you. The operation is ended.'

'That's not good enough. Somebody in that room told. Either deliberately or inadvertently, the information about Randall Haight's confession was leaked to Morris. I didn't do it. Aimee didn't do it. That makes it someone on your side: one of the cops or agents in that room, or someone else who was subsequently made aware of what had been said.'

'Well, the answer to that question may emerge in the next stage of the investigation, namely: Who killed Midas and the last gunman? They were both shot with the same weapon, left at the scene. It was an unregistered firearm, but we're going to run ballistics matches on it. I have to ask: Were your dubious angels responsible?'

'No.'

'They wouldn't lie to you?'

'No, they wouldn't. They also prefer not to leave guns lying around. They're evidence, whatever way you look at it.'

'Maybe Farrell sent a backup, just to be sure,' said Engel. 'We'll ask around. For now, an operation that started half a decade ago is nothing but dust: years of effort for no result. Maybe if you weren't such a lone wolf we could have got to Lonny Midas in time to use him as bait. We could have been waiting for Morris when he came.'

'You're forgetting that you had an agent in place all the time. It seems kind of harsh to put the blame on my shoulders when all Dempsey had to do was pick up a phone.'

'Morris kept him out of the loop on this, right until the end.'

'Maybe he didn't trust him so much after all.'

'We'll never know.'

'Right. And Anna Kore is still missing. You forgot to mention her, but then she was never a major concern of yours, was she?'

'We're going to search Randall Haight's property — my mistake, *Lonnie Midas's* property, given what we've now learned about him. It's possible that he might have had an accomplice. Right now, it's the best lead we have.'

'Allan gave him an alibi,' I said.

'I know that. Do you have any reason to doubt it?'

I took out my cell phone, opened the message folder, and showed him the anonymous missives about Chief Allan. He read through them, then handed the phone back to me.

'Why didn't you mention this before?'

'I tend to be careful about potential slanders. I prefer to look into the possible truth of them before I go disseminating their substance.'

'And what did you discover?'

'Chief Allan has a girlfriend in Lincolnville. She's young, and she has a child. If Allan is the father, then she was either barely legal when she became pregnant, or not legal at all if he was having sex with her for any length of time before she conceived.'

'When did you discover this?'

476

'Just yesterday, but then it was a day of discoveries for all of us.'

'You have a name for the girl?'

I gave it to him, along with the address of the apartment building and the number of her car's license plate.

'And your thinking is that Chief Allan is a man with a taste for young women, in a town where another young woman has gone missing?'

'That's the thinking of whoever has been sending these messages.'

'You're just full of surprises, aren't you? We'll talk with Allan. We'll get a warrant to search his house as well.'

'She's not at his house,' I said.

Engel raised a quizzical eyebrow.

'Dubious angels,' I explained. 'If Allan does have her, then she's someplace else.'

Engel thought for a moment.

'All right. Anything else, while you're unburdening yourself of secrets?'

'One more thing: Allan made a call from a pay phone at the gas station on Main in Lincolnville at 8:34 p.m. yesterday.'

'Just before a lot of men with guns descended on Pastor's Bay,' said Engel.

'It would be interesting to know who he called.'

'Wouldn't it? You know, you might have made a good cop if you'd stuck with it, if you'd had the self-discipline and the ability to tame your ego. Instead you're a mercenary who withholds information and makes bad judgment calls.'

A horse-faced woman wearing a blue FBI

windbreaker entered the room, a younger, preppy-looking guy hovering behind her with a gun at his waist. Engel nodded at them and stood. His mouth formed a moue as he looked down on me.

'You should leave while you still can, Mr. Parker, before somebody takes it into his mind to put you under arrest. You didn't behave well here. None of us did, but you in particular have done nothing to enhance your reputation.'

I didn't argue with him.

37

Chief Allan couldn't be found. His cell phone rang out, and there was nobody home when Engel, accompanied by Gordon Walsh and two state troopers, paid a call to his house. His truck wasn't in the drive either, so his license-plate details and a description of his vehicle were passed to both local and state forces, as well as to police in the contiguous states, the border patrol, and Canadian law enforcement. Walsh visited the apartment building in Lincolnville with a female state trooper named Abelena Forbes, and Mary Ellen Schrock admitted that she had been seeing Allan, but told Walsh and Forbes first that she was eighteen then, on reflection, seventeen when their sexual relationship began. Forbes asked her if she was sure of this, and she said that she was, but both Forbes and Walsh believed that she still was lying. But the girl stuck to her story: Allan had pulled over a car in which she was a passenger, and the driver, a twenty-two-year-old friend of Schrock's, was found to be marginally over the limit. He was let off with a warning by Allan, who offered to drive Schrock home, although she could not recall the date of the alleged incident. Their relationship had begun a week later. When they asked her if she was aware of any similar relationships in which Allan might have been involved, either now or in the past, she grew agitated and said that she was not. This they also believed to be a lie. When they asked her if Allan had ever mentioned Anna Kore to her, she told them to leave.

At the door, Forbes told her to find someone to look after her child, because when they came back with an arrest warrant they'd be taking her to Gray for questioning. It was Walsh who played good cop, figuring that Schrock was a young woman who responded better to male authority figures, particularly older males. He told her that they didn't want her to get into any trouble but they needed to talk to Allan, and if she had heard from him then she ought to tell them. He reminded her that there was a girl missing, a girl who might at this very moment be suffering grave torments, who was probably very frightened and at risk of death. All they were asking for was any help that she could offer.

Schrock began to cry. She was, in the end, little more than a child herself. She told them that Allan sometimes used her cell phone when he visited, both to make and to receive calls, but deleted the numbers before he gave the phone back to her. Schrock did not have online access to her account, as she simply topped up her phone credit when necessary. Walsh sought and received permission to access her call records from her service provider when she told him that Allan had used her phone the day before. Walsh made them coffee in the kitchen while Forbes called Engel about the cell phone records on the grounds that the feds could retrieve the relevant information faster than anyone else could. While they sat on the uncomfortable furniture, drinking cheap coffee and looking at the bare walls of Schrock's dingy, dark apartment, the baby began to cry, and wouldn't stop until Walsh took a turn with it, whereupon it promptly fell asleep in his arms.

At that point, Schrock admitted that she had first had intercourse with Kurt Allan when she was fifteen.

★ ★ ★

Both of the numbers called by Allan, and from which he had received calls, were traced to throwaway phones bought in Massachusetts and Rhode Island, as was the final call made from the gas station the previous night. The cell phones in question, though, had not been thrown away. One was found in the pocket of Tommy Morris, and the other in the car used by the hunters to drive to Pastor's Bay. Allan had not only sold out the man he believed to be Randall Haight; he had also sold out Tommy Morris to his enemies. The apartment building in Lincolnville had previously been owned by a shelf operation in Boston, UIPC Strategies, Inc., and looked after by a property-management company based in Belfast. While the Belfast company still maintained the property, they informed the state police that the building in question had been sold three months earlier by a Boston bank when the company of ownership had defaulted on its loan. That company, UIPC, had been a front for Tommy Morris's property investments. The trail became clearer: Allan had been one of Morris's

481

tame cops in Boston and had kept up the connection after moving to Maine, keeping an eye on Morris's estranged sister while feeding him information that might be of use to him and facilitating the movement of drugs, weapons, and other contraband when required. In fact, it seemed likely that Morris had pointed Allan toward the job in Pastor's Bay in the first place. In return, Morris paid him a retainer, and eventually gave his girlfriend and his child a place to live. But as Morris's problems had mounted so Allan's cash supply had been cut off, and his new family was no longer able to live free, or at a reduced rent, on Morris's dime. The disappearance of Anna Kore had provided Allan with an opportunity to make some money off Tommy Morris's scalp, and so he had lured him to Pastor's Bay, baited his trap with Randall Haight, and then informed Oweny Farrell's crew of where Morris could be found.

A subpoena was immediately sought for access to Allan's own cell phone records. The previous night, shortly after nine p.m., he had received a call to his cell phone from a previously unknown number. Foster, the Pastor's Bay officer who had officially been on duty that night, confirmed that when he returned to the station at 9:10 p.m., Allan was gone. The phone used to make the call to Allan had not been found, but through a process of triangulation the source of the call was narrowed down to the woods near Lonny Midas's home. Attempts to trace Allan by 'pinging' his cell phone proved fruitless, just as they had for Anna Kore's phone. If Allan was still in possession of his cell phone, he had switched it off and removed the battery.

★ ★ ★

Allan's truck wasn't found by the state police or the feds but by a sixteen-year-old boy and his fifteen-year-old girlfriend who had driven to a coastal lookout called Freyer's Point in order to watch the sun set and enjoy a little quality time together. They spotted a vehicle in the woods as they approached the lookout, and not caring to engage in acts of intimacy when someone might be watching, decided to turn back and find somewhere more private. The boy saw that the driver's door was open. Concerned, he went to take a look, and thought that he recognized Chief Allan's truck. Rumors had already begun to spread around Pastor's Bay that the chief was missing, so the boy called 911. The state police and the feds descended and found two cell phones in the glove compartment: Allan's own, and the one that had been used to call him from the woods. To the police and the FBI, it seemed that Allan had fled. It was only when $10,000 in twenties and fifties was found hidden beneath the spare tire that they began to reconsider their assessment.

Alongside the money and the phones, tied up in a blue plastic bag and freshly laundered, were Anna Kore's blouse, skirt, and underwear.

38

I missed the furor caused by the discovery of Allan's truck. Once Engel and Walsh had consented to let me leave the station house, although not the environs of Pastor's Bay, I went to the disturbingly low-key bed-and-breakfast inn off Main Street operated by the twin sisters of uncertain age, and asked for a room. I was in no state to drive. My perforated eardrum was still causing me pain, although the feelings of nausea and vertigo had almost gone, but I was exhausted and my head ached. When I arrived at the door of the B and B, my clothes caked with dried mud, I expected to be told to find a tolerant motel or sleep in my car. Instead, the sisters, who answered the door together dressed in identical pale-blue dresses, showed me to their largest room 'because it has a bath.' They pointed out the robe in the closet and told me to leave my dirty clothes in a bag outside my door. They asked if I wanted something to eat, or a pot of coffee, but all I wanted to do was sleep. Their kindnesses were offered in an unsmiling, matter-of-fact way that made them all the more affecting.

I slept from noon until after four. When I woke, there were three messages on my phone. I hadn't even heard it ring. One was from Angel, pointing out in the most discreet way, without mentioning any names, that they hadn't been able to remove the tracking device from Allan's car before leaving town, and maybe I might like to see about rectifying the problem. He also advised me to check my email.

The second message had been left by Denny Kraus's attorney, informing me that the judge had just decided that Denny was mentally incompetent to stand trial, based on Denny's proposed solution to the whole problem of the killing of Philip Espvall.

'Look,' Denny had apparently told the judge that morning, his face a picture of reasonableness, 'I'll just get another dog . . . '

The third message, which reduced some of the benefits that my rest had brought, came from Gordon Walsh, ordering me to return his call as soon as I received his message, or face the direst consequences. He hadn't left me much choice, so I dialed his number and let his wrath wash over me. In between calling me every kind of asshole under the sun, he let me know about the interview with Allan's girlfriend and told me that Allan's truck had been found, along with a sum of money and clothing similar to that worn by Anna Kore when she disappeared. The tentative assumption the cops were now operating under was that, in addition to double-crossing Tommy Morris by selling him out to his enemies, Allan had also provided a false alibi for Midas. Both men had colluded in the abduction of Anna Kore, and Allan was now a suspect in Midas's murder, killing him in order to cover his tracks when Tommy Morris failed to do the job for him, then killing Oweny Farrell's last surviving

485

gunman as well just to be sure. The truck was already being forensically examined, which meant that, if the job was done well, the tracker would be found, and whatever trouble I'd been in up to now would be as nothing compared with what would follow. A fingertip search of both the Midas and Allan properties was also under way.

Walsh then called me an asshole some more, and informed me that Mrs. Shaye had admitted to sending the series of anonymous text messages about Allan to my phone. She told the cops that she'd known about Allan's relationship with Schrock for some time, based on conversations that she'd overheard between Allan and his then wife, and subsequently between Allan and the girl. While she said that she hadn't necessarily connected Allan to Anna Kore's disappearance, she still didn't feel that he was a suitable person to be involved in such an investigation or, indeed, to be the chief of police. My arrival had given her the opportunity to alert someone to her boss's indiscretions, and she had taken it. She apologized for any trouble she'd caused, and for not being more open in her approach. She had tendered her resignation from the department but it had been declined, at least while the investigation into Anna's fate continued.

Walsh then called me an asshole one last time, just in case I hadn't been listening closely, and warned me that I still wasn't to leave Pastor's Bay until he'd had an opportunity to call me an asshole some more in person, and maybe see about having my license permanently rescinded this time.

'Asshole,' he said, in conclusion, before hanging up. Even after the substance of the preceding conversation, he managed to make it sound fresh.

★ ★ ★

There was a basket outside my bedroom door. My clothes, now cleaned and folded, were inside, along with two fresh scones wrapped in a napkin. I showered again, and ate one of the scones while I dressed. I turned on my laptop, but the Internet service for the B and B was password-protected. There was nobody around when I went downstairs, so I left a note to say that I wasn't checking out yet, and used the second key on my door fob to lock the front door behind me.

The news trucks were back with a vengeance on Main Street, and not just the locals either, while the parking lot of the municipal building was jammed with official vehicles. Danny was still behind the counter at Hallowed Grounds. He was playing the last Roxy Music CD, so he should have been wearing a tuxedo with his bow tie undone instead of a T-shirt featuring the original cover of Ray Bradbury's *Fahrenheit 451*.

'You don't look so good,' he said.

'In this case, appearances don't deceive,' I replied. 'Mind if I check my e-mail?'

'Go ahead,' he said. 'I'm about to close up, but you take your time. I've got a lot of stuff to do first, so I'll be here for a while.'

I took a seat at a corner table. Without asking, Danny brought me coffee.

'On the house,' he said. 'Hear you were involved in what went down last night.'

'That's right.'

'Still no sign of Anna Kore?'

'Not that I know of.'

'They're saying Chief Allan might have taken her.'

'That on the news?'

'I don't watch the news, but if people are talking about it then it soon will be.'

He locked the front door, turned the sign to CLOSED, and started cleaning up behind the counter. I checked the local news sites and found Allan's photo on all of them. He was now officially a suspect in Anna Kore's disappearance, but speculation abounded that he might have committed suicide, or made it appear that he had done so.

I logged in to my e-mail account. There was a Yahoo message with Angel's distinctive '777' tag on the temporary address. It contained a new cell phone number, along with the words 'necessary evil.' I called it from my own cell. I wasn't worried about the number being traced back to Angel and Louis. That cell phone would be in pieces by the end of the day.

'You get the tag from the truck?' he asked.

'Have you seen the news?'

'That's what concerns us. Pity. It was a nice piece of equipment. We'll erase everything, clear the tracks.'

'Send the record of Allan's journeys to me first,' I said.

The GPS program automatically recorded the

route taken by the trace vehicle. It also allowed for timings to be retained, so that it was possible to figure out how long the subject had spent in any given location.

'If your laptop is subpoenaed, it'll be an admission of guilt. Without it, you have deniability.'

'Send it anyway,' I said. 'I lost deniability a long time ago.'

After about fifteen minutes, the record from the tag came through as a series of maps. Angel had separated each journey Allan had taken into a series of files, with the dates and timings recorded beneath. The trips themselves appeared as red lines on the maps.

If nothing else, the trip record confirmed that Allan had killed Lonny Midas and the unknown gunman. It showed him leaving the Pastor's Bay Police Department at 9:08 p.m. and traveling to the spot at which the bodies had later been found before heading back to the outskirts of town, where he waited for the alarm to be raised.

Allan's final trip, taken shortly before eleven a.m. that day, followed a route from the municipal building in Pastor's Bay and west out of town, but Allan's home lay south, across the causeway. According to the timings, his truck had remained at a point on Red Leaf Road for two hours before continuing southwest to its final resting place at Freyer's Point.

I opened the white pages and did a reverse address search for Red Leaf Road. It came up with three names. Two of them I didn't recognize; one of them I did. I clicked on the name, noted the number of the house, and did a Google map search for the address. When I had it, I compared its location on Google to the point on the map where Allan's truck had stopped for an hour.

They were the same.

Allan's last trip had included a stop at the home of Ruth and Patrick Shaye.

39

The Shaye house was set back from Red Leaf Road behind a line of maturing silver birches, now denuded by the fall winds. It was a large, three-story dwelling, and had been freshly painted with off-white paint, probably during the summer. There were planter boxes on the sills of the upper and lower windows filled with hardy green shrubs, and the garden had been planted with winter flowers and perennials: cardinal flowers and larkspur, comfrey and obedient plants. The lawn grass bore signs of patching, although the old and new growths would soon be indistinguishable, and the boundaries of the beds were marked with house bricks painted white. Fresh gravel had been laid on the drive. It was all very neat and clean, the kind of house that forces its neighbors to step up to the plate and not allow their own properties to fall into neglect.

Before leaving Pastor's Bay, I had checked to see if Mrs. Shaye and her son were still at the municipal building. They were: Patrick I could see in the parking lot, and Mrs. Shaye was working behind the main desk. I called Walsh along the way, but his phone rang a couple of times and then went to voice mail. I figured he'd rejected the call when he saw the number. I left a message telling him what I knew — that Allan had stopped off at the Shaye house before vanishing — then turned my phone to silent. It didn't necessarily mean much when I heard myself speak aloud what I knew for Walsh's benefit. There were lots of reasons that Allan might have visited the Shaye house. After all that had taken place the night before, there had probably been a certain amount for everyone to discuss.

But two hours was a long time, especially when there were so many bodies on their way to the M.E.'s office in Augusta.

I parked my car on the road beneath the trees instead of driving directly onto the property. There was no response from the house when I entered the empty front yard, the gravel crunching loudly under my feet. I didn't ring the doorbell but took a narrow path to the left that cut between a high green hedge and the side of the house. There were two windows in that wall, one at the living room and the other at the kitchen, but I could see nobody inside, and a red door blocked access from the path to the rear of the property. It was closed but not locked. I turned the handle and it opened easily.

The back yard bore no resemblance to the front. Here there was no grass; the area around the kitchen door was roughly paved with heavy concrete slabs upon which sat two iron lawn chairs and an iron table, the dark gray of the metal showing through the yellowing paint work. Beyond was an area of pitted dirt in which pools of dirty rainwater glistened, the oil on their surface like a series of polluted rainbows. Two cars and a truck stood in varying stages of cannibalization beneath the bowed roof of a long

492

single-story garage. The contagion of filth and neglect had even infected the back of the house itself, which had not been painted when the front and sides were tackled, and from which white flakes peeled like bad skin. The windows were all masked with drapes, except at the kitchen, where the sink was stacked high with dirty crockery. A network of washing lines ran across the yard, and from them hung drying sheets, carefully positioned so that there was no danger of the sheets dragging along the filthy ground beneath. They swayed gently in the breeze. I tried the kitchen door, but it did not open. All seemed quiet within, yet I found myself reluctant to make any unnecessary sound, as though, like a character in some old fairy tale, I might wake a slumbering presence by my incaution.

I walked to the garage, avoiding the puddles along the way. It effectively formed the back wall of the property. The thick hedge at either side of the yard came to an end where the garage began, and tendrils of it had already begun to seek purchase on the walls. The two cars inside were relatively new, or at least I could see how they might yield parts of value, but the truck was a wreck. Its windshield was gone and its side windows were broken. The hood was raised, most of the exposed engine was rusted, and most of what wasn't rusted was absent entirely. The truck had a dented cap back, and was parked so that the rear was flush with the garage wall.

And yet its tires were inflated, and there were marks on the concrete where it had recently been moved.

The garage might once have been used to house animals, for the three vehicles were separated by wooden walls, although the pens looked too wide even for cattle. I searched for indications on the back wall where pens had been removed to create the wider spaces, but could find none. I slid along the side of the truck, my jacket catching on rusted metal and splintered wood. Even before I reached the back wall, I could see that it was newer than the rest of the building. At some point it had been repaired or replaced. I went back outside and tried to gauge the distance between the inner wall and the outer walls. The angle made it hard to judge, but it seemed to me that they didn't quite match. There was a space behind the new wall. It was narrow, probably barely wide enough for a man to turn around inside, but it was there.

I took a closer look at the truck and saw that the hand brake had been set. I was opening the door to release it when something pink caught my eye on the floor behind the front left wheel. It was a small piece of fiberglass insulation batt, used between interior walls and floors for noise control and to prevent heat from escaping. I took my little Maglite from my pocket and shined it on the floor, and then inside the cap. There were more of the batts here, still in their packaging, and all with a high R-value indicating their resistance to heat flow. The higher the R-value, the greater the insulating power, and this stuff had an R-value in the thirties, almost as high as one could go.

I released the hand brake and pushed the

truck forward. It was heavy, but it moved easily on its tires. When I had pushed it about six feet, I reapplied the brake and returned to the back wall. A painted square steel door, three feet to the side, had been expertly fitted into the brickwork at the point where the back of the truck had met the wall, its lines almost as difficult to distinguish as the separation between the old and new grass on the front lawn. A smaller panel was inset midway down the left side of the door. It lifted up to reveal a handle. There was no key. There didn't have to be. After all, who was going to move a dilapidated truck in a run-down shed for no good reason?

The first thing I saw when I opened the door was a ladder. It lay against the interior wall, and beside it was a trapdoor, similar in size to the first, but this time set into the ground. It was secured, but only with a heavy lock and hasp. Beyond it I could see a pair of small air vents. A larger vent in the roof let in sunlight and air.

'Hello?' I said. 'Can anybody hear me?'

After a couple of seconds, a girl's voice sounded faintly beneath my feet.

'I can hear you. Please help me! Please!'

I knelt beside the first vent. 'Anna?'

'Yes, I'm Anna! I'm Anna!'

'My name's Charlie Parker. I'm a private detective. I'm going to get you out, okay?'

'Okay. Don't leave me. Please don't leave me.'

'I won't, but I have to find something to break the lock. I'm not going to go without you, I promise. I just need a minute.'

'Hurry, just hurry!'

I went back into the garage and found a crowbar, then set to work on the lock. It took a couple of minutes, but eventually it broke and I opened the trapdoor.

The cell was about six feet deep and roughly square. Anna Kore was chained to the eastern wall. There was clear plastic sheeting on the ground beneath her, and a slop bucket in the corner. She wore sneakers, oversized jeans, and a man's sweater, and had wrapped her upper body in a blanket to ward off the cold and damp, despite the layers of insulation that had been laid into the walls and on the ground under the sheeting. She had a small battery-powered lamp for illumination, and there were magazines and paperback books scattered around her. She raised her arms to me.

'Get me out!'

I turned to get the ladder, and heard a sound from outside. It was a vehicle approaching, and then the engine died and all was quiet again.

'What is it?' called the girl. 'Why aren't you coming to get me?'

I went back to the edge of the trapdoor. 'Anna, you have to stay quiet. I think they're here.'

She gave out a little mew of fear. 'No, don't go. Get the ladder. It will only take a minute. Please! If you go, you won't come back, and I'll be left here.'

I couldn't stay. They were coming. As I moved away, Anna Kore began screaming, the noise carrying up from below and echoing off the walls, and I did something that broke my heart: I closed the trapdoor upon her. Her cries grew muffled, and when I climbed back into the garage I could not hear them at all. The breeze had picked up, and the sheets billowed and snapped, obscuring my view of the yard beyond. I had hoped that the return of either Mrs. Shaye or her son was a coincidence, but as I was climbing through the connecting door I spotted the little wireless sensor beside the lower hinge. I had broken the circuit by opening the door. It had probably sent a message to one or both of their cell phones, and so they had known that someone was on their property.

I had just reached the hood of the truck when the first shot came, blowing a hole through one of the sheets and blasting the wall to my left with shotgun pellets. The second shot struck the hood and knocked away the supporting rod. I saw a figure in overalls moving between the sheets, and caught a glimpse of Pat Shaye's face as he pumped the shotgun and took aim for a third time. I threw myself to the ground and started shooting.

The bullet took Shaye in the right thigh. He stumbled into one of the sheets, and I saw the form of his body pressed against it. I fired again, and this time a roseate stain bloomed against the white. The third shot brought him to his knees and he dragged the sheet down with him, gathering it around him like a shroud as he fell. The shotgun lay in a puddle beside him as he struggled weakly against the material, the blood and oily water spreading across the whiteness of it.

I heard a woman scream. Mrs. Shaye appeared

from the side of the house, and then was lost to me in the billowing of the sheets. Like a movie projected with damaged frames, I saw her move through flickers of white from the corner to the center of the yard, pause for a second as she took in the sight of her son wriggling in his cocoon, then — another white flash, another moment lost — make for the shotgun. I gave her no warning. The bullet struck the house behind her, but when I tried to fire again the gun jammed, and she was almost at the shotgun. I was already looking for cover when Gordon Walsh appeared from the side of the house, his gun raised.

'Police!' he said. 'Put your hands in the air.'

Mrs. Shaye stopped in her tracks. She raised her hands and fell to her knees, but she no longer had any interest in the weapon. She simply inched her way across the yard on her knees until she reached her dying son, and she wrapped her arms around him as he shuddered against her in his death throes. Walsh did not try to stop her.

Only when her son ceased to move did she start to cry.

★   ★   ★

While Walsh kept an eye on Mrs. Shaye, I raised the trapdoor and let down the ladder into the cell. Mrs. Shaye had confirmed with a nod that both she and her son had keys to all the locks, and I used her set to free Anna from her chain. She climbed from the hole and emerged blinking into the fading light, then sprang at Mrs. Shaye.

Her left hand tore a clump of hair from the older woman's head, and her right raked four parallel cuts down her right cheek before Walsh and I could drag her off. I led Anna into the yard, and her eyes found the shrouded form of Patrick Shaye.

'Is he dead?' she said.

'Yes.'

Anna said something else to me, but I could not understand her words.

'What did you say?'

'Don't leave her down there,' she repeated. 'The other girl. Please don't leave her down there.'

'What other girl?' I said

'She's in the hole,' said Anna. 'I saw her bones.'

And still Mrs. Shaye said nothing, and silent she would remain until they came to take her away.

40

All that we subsequently learned was pieced together from what Anna Kore told us, itself a product of overheard words, snatched sentences, and the words of Pat Shaye when he came to her at night, whispering to her as he touched her. He had taken her in the parking lot, a crime of opportunity made easier by her familiarity with him, but his mother had provided him with an alibi when the police questioned everyone. She had been angry with him, though, Anna had said. They had kept her in the house that first night, and she had heard them arguing.

'You don't shit on your own doorstep,' Mrs. Shaye had told her son. 'There'll be questions. They'll be looking for her.'

But Pat had been overcome with desire because the other girl had died. Anna didn't know her name, or where she'd come from, but they'd had her for a while: a year, she thought, maybe a little more. That was how they worked, how *it* worked, because Pat Shaye had needs. Pat Shaye liked little girls, and his mother had come up with a solution: You don't molest lots of girls, because that's how you get caught. Instead you just take one, and you use her until she's too old for your tastes, and then you find another.

And the other girl, the one who has grown too old? Well, you do with her what you do with anything that's too old and needs to be replaced.

500

You throw it away, or you bury it.

Except the girl had died before her time. Anna didn't know how, or why. Mrs. Shaye had told her son to give it a rest for a while, to use porn, whatever it took. She was worried about creating a pattern, leaving a trail that could be followed. That was why they always kept the girls for so long.

But Pat had seen Anna Kore, and desire had become action.

Such needs he had, such needs.

He'd tried to rape her that first night, but she'd fought and fought. She'd fought so hard that she'd hurt him, and hurt him badly. Her mother had taught her how to do it, because her mother had lived around violent men. She'd told her daughter that, if it ever came down to it, she had to be as cruel and merciless as she could imagine. The eyes were best, her mother had said. Aim to blind. But Anna couldn't get close to Pat's eyes, so she'd gone for the next best thing. She'd gripped and twisted his testicles, digging her nails into them, and she'd injured him down there, leaving him screaming in agony. His mother had been forced to help him from the room, and Anna's punishment was to be put in the hole, down where the dead girl lay. It hadn't been used in a while, and the insulation was bad, but they wanted her to know that she'd done wrong, and doing wrong brought consequences. So Pat Shaye had repaired the insulation, and while he worked he told her of all the things that he was going to do to her once he had recovered, of how he was going to rape her for days once the pain went away, maybe even rape her to death and then find another girl, because there would always be other girls.

But then something had happened. When Pat came down to feed her on that last day he was worried, but he still found it in himself to torment her just a little.

'You were almost rescued, honeybunch,' he said. 'The chief came, and I found him snooping. If I hadn't returned in time, well, who knows? You might have been out of here. So close, uh, honeybunch? So close. Then again, the chief, he might have joined in, because he likes them young. Still, we'll never know.'

Then he'd touched himself while he stood over her.

'Almost healed now,' he said. 'Another day and I'll be as good as new, and then we can get to know each other better. It won't be for long, though. You've become a liability, so I'll have to make it special while it lasts.'

And what had led Allan to the Shaye house? Crumbs of evidence. Literally that: crumbs. There had been traces of cookie crumbs in two of the envelopes sent to Randall Haight, and lodged in the glue on the flaps. The last page of the report, which Allan had probably read only long after the previous night's killing was done, had suggested cookies or stale cake as a possible source of the organic matter found in the envelope. No hairs, no skin cells, no saliva, no DNA: Pat Shaye had just been a greedy boy nibbling on his mother's cookies while he worked. Allan hadn't come to the Shaye house in

502

search of Anna Kore, although he might have been hoping that whoever was sending pictures of naked children and barn doors to Randall Haight might also be responsible for Anna's abduction. Perhaps also his hunch about the crumbs might have caused long-buried suspicions about Pat Shaye to find concrete form, for on some level they shared the same tastes. So he had gone to the Shaye house, and being a clever man he might have looked at the abandoned truck, at the inflated tires and the marks beside them, and begun to wonder.

That was where Pat Shaye had found him, and he buried his remains in a shallow grave.

The final piece of the puzzle came later, once the investigation into the Shayes began in earnest. The Shayes, it emerged, were nomads of a kind. They had tended not to stay in any one place for longer than three or four years, perhaps to make it difficult to connect the disappearances of young women to them, avoiding the necessity of taking two girls from one particular geographic area. Sometimes they changed their names, Mrs. Shaye using her maiden name of Handley, or Patrick using his middle name of David. They even had different Social Security numbers to go with their various identities, numbers that would now have to be tracked down in case it was not only young girls that the Shayes had killed over the years in order to protect themselves. Then they had arrived in Pastor's Bay and found that its remoteness suited them, as long as they were prepared to hunt farther afield for their prey. One of Mrs. Shaye's previous jobs, under the name of Ruthie Handley, had involved showing houses for realtors on a freelance basis, among them the realtor who had sold a home to William Lagenheimer's mother. Her son had even helped to repair a crack in the siding before the sale went through, and Mrs. Shaye and Mrs. Lagenheimer had got to talking, and, well, some small secrets were shared, because Mrs. Lagenheimer was very lonely, and very sad, and very delusional.

So it was that, some years later, when a man calling himself Randall Haight moved to Pastor's Bay, the Shayes had been very curious indeed. They had watched him, and they had followed him, and Pat Shaye had visited the empty house in Gorham where his mother had once sat with Mrs. Lagenheimer. They had filed away all that they knew about Randall Haight until it might become convenient to use it against him. At first, they had considered blackmail, because who knew when they might need a little extra money? But when Pat Shaye's desires became too much for him, and he dragged down into his personal Hades young Anna Kore — a local girl, not a stray or a runaway but someone who was going to be missed — his mother came up with a much better use for the man who claimed to be Randall Haight, and what she knew about Chief Allan's tastes helped to muddy the waters too. Anything, anything at all, to ensure that her son, her beloved son with his unusual needs, remained above suspicion.

The fingertip search of Lonny Midas's house also turned up one envelope that had not been handed over to Aimee Price. The postmark identified it as the final communication sent to him, dated only three days earlier and delivered the day before he died. It had probably been intended to make him run at last, and draw the police after him. It was found hidden behind a panel in his closet along with bank statements, share certificates, the money that Lonny had gathered to help him disappear, and a thick journal filled with tiny, near-indecipherable script: Lonny Midas's testimony, his private attempt to hold on to his identity and his sanity. Later, when the journal's contents were examined, it would be concluded that he had failed on both counts. After all, he was a man who had believed himself to be haunted by the ghost of the girl who had died at his hands. What else could he be, but mad?

The last envelope Lonny had received contained a photograph of the house in Gorham, and a newspaper cutting about the Selina Day case, along with a printed note. The note read:

'RANDALL HAIGHT' IS TELLING LIES.
WHO ARE YOU?

VI

For the soul is dead that slumbers . . .
Dust thou art, to dust returnest,
Was not spoken of the soul.

From 'A Psalm to Life'
by Henry Wadsworth Longfellow

IV

41

I left Pastor's Bay with my license intact, barely, but not my reputation. Engel watched me go. He was holding something in his right hand as I pulled away: the tracking device from Allan's truck. I had confessed to planting it. I didn't know if Engel believed me. In the end, it didn't matter. It was just one more weight on the scales that seemed to be tipping against me.

Anna Kore lived, but it is possible that she might have been found earlier if it had not been for my arrogance, if I had spoken out sooner. It was Louis who pointed out later that, similarly, had I not acted as I did then she might not have been found at all, or not alive. But I still felt hollow when Valerie Kore thanked me, and kissed my cheek. I tried to apologize, to say that I was sorry, but she shook her head, and touched her finger to my lip, and silenced me.

'She's back,' she whispered. 'That's all that matters. The rest will heal. I will make her well again.'

Here is a truth, a truth by which to live: there is hope. There is always hope. If we choose to abandon it, our souls will turn to ash and blow away.

But the soul can burn and not be damned.

The soul can burn with a bright fire and never turn to ash.

* * *

Above Pastor's Bay six ravens flew low, barely rising over the skeletal trees. High in the clear blue sky the last geese were heading south, but the ravens moved north toward forests and mountains, toward ice and snow. They flew fast and sure into the coming dark, that they might tell the waiting wolf of all they had seen.

Acknowledgements

A number of people gave help, advice, and assistance in the writing of this book. Without their kindness and generosity, it would be a poorer offering. My thanks to Lieutenant Brian T. McDonough, commanding officer of Unit I of the Maine State Police's Criminal Investigation Division, who took the time to explain the work of his unit and, in particular, its handling of juvenile abductions; John Purcell of the law firm of Purcell, Krug & Haller in Harrisburg, Pennsylvania, who was kind enough to ensure that the legal aspects of this story erred on the side of factual wherever possible; Shane Phalen, for ensuring that Parker's methods bear some small resemblance to those of a practicing private investigator; to Vladimir Doudka and Mark Dunne for translation assistance; Ben Alfiero and all at the wonderful Harbor Fish Market in Portland, Maine (www.harborfish.com), who put white flesh on the bones of Joey Tuna; and to my fellow author, and friend, Chris Mooney (www.chrismooneybooks.com), who shared with me his library and his knowledge of Boston. He is a fine writer, and a finer friend. I am deeply indebted to them all, and any mistakes are my own, as indeed are any opinions expressed.

I am immensely grateful to Dr. Danielle Pafunda for permission to quote extracts from her haunting verse project, 'The Dead Girls Speak in Unison' a work in progress. It's unusual, and humbling, to encounter work in another medium that not only resonates so deeply with one's own, but does so with such economy and beauty. *The Brothers Bulger* by Howie Carr (Grand Central Publishing, 2006) was hugely helpful in providing a backdrop for the activities of Tommy Morris and his associates. Incidentally, as I write, Whitey Bulger has just been apprehended after sixteen years on the run, bringing to an end that particular chapter of Boston's criminal history.

As always, this book was considerably improved by the input of my editors, Sue Fletcher at Hodder & Stoughton and Emily Bestler at Atria Books. To them, and to all at both houses who have supported my work for so long, my love and thanks. Thanks, too, to my beloved agent Darley Anderson and all those who work with him. They have found homes for my odd books, and I would not be publishing without them. Meanwhile, Clair Lamb, Madeira James and Jayne Doherty maintain a close watch on www.johnconnellybooks.com, and keep me from making too much of a fool of myself, for which I am very grateful.

Finally, much love to Jennie, Cameron, and Alistair.

THE WHISPERERS

John Connolly

The border between Maine and Canada is porous. Anything can be smuggled across it: drugs, cash, weapons, people. Now a group of disenchanted former soldiers has begun its own smuggling operation, and what is being moved is infinitely stranger and more terrifying than anyone can imagine. Anyone, that is, except private detective Charlie Parker, who has his own intimate knowledge of the darkness in men's hearts. But the soldiers' actions have attracted the attention of the reclusive Herod, a man with a taste for the strange. And where Herod goes, so too does the shadowy figure that he calls the Captain. To defeat them, Parker must form an uneasy alliance with a man he fears more than any other, the killer known as the Collector . . .

THE GATES

John Connolly

Samuel Johnson has a number of problems: his dad cares more about his car than his family; his mother is lonely, and only Samuel's dog, Boswell, truly understands him. Oh, and as if things couldn't get any worse, Samuel's neighbours, led by the villainous Mrs Abernathy, are trying to open the gates of hell. It's up to Samuel to stop them, except nobody will believe him, and time is running out . . . Now the fate of humanity lies in the hands of one small boy, an even smaller dog, and a very unlucky demon named Nurd . . .

THE LOVERS

John Connolly

When Charlie Parker was still a boy, his father, an NYPD cop, killed a young couple. A boy and a girl barely older than his son. Then took his own life. There was no explanation for his actions . . . Stripped of his private investigator's license, and watched by the police, Parker is working in a Portland bar and staying out of trouble. But in the background, he is working on his most personal case yet, an investigation into his own origins and the circumstances surrounding the death of his father, Will. It is an investigation that will reveal a life haunted by lies, his father's betrayal, and by two figures in the shadows, with only one purpose: to bring an end to Charlie Parker's existence.

THE REAPERS

John Connolly

They are the reapers. The elite among killers. Men so terrifying that their names are mentioned only in whispers. The assassin Louis is one of them. But now Louis, and his partner, Angel, are themselves targets. And there is no shortage of suspects. A wealthy recluse sends them north to a town that no longer exists on any map. A town ruled by a man with very personal reasons for wanting Louis' blood spilt. There they find themselves trapped, isolated, and at the mercy of a killer feared above all others: the assassin of assassins, Bliss. There's only one man who can help. Charlie Parker.

THE UNQUIET

John Connolly

Daniel Clay, psychologist, has been missing for years following revelations about harm done to the children in his care. His daughter Rebecca believes that he is dead. But someone who does not believe that he is dead is the revenger Merrick, a father and a killer. He harasses Rebecca, obsessed with discovering the truth about his own daughter's disappearance. Rebecca hires private detective Charlie Parker to make Merrick go away — but he will not be stopped. And there are other forces at work here. Someone is funding Merrick's hunt, a ghost from Parker's past. And Merrick's actions have drawn others from the shadows, half-glimpsed figures intent upon their own form of revenge, pale wraiths drifting through the ranks of the unquiet dead. The Hollow Men have come . . .